Adventures of a Big Girl in a Flat City

Yulia Pylyavskaya

SilverWood

Published in 2021 by SilverWood Books

SilverWood Books Ltd
14 Small Street, Bristol, BS1 1DE, United Kingdom
www.silverwoodbooks.co.uk

ISBN 978-1-80042-131-8 (paperback)
ISBN 978-1-80042-132-5 (ebook)

British Library Cataloguing in Publication Data
A CIP catalogue record for this book is
available from the British Library

Page design and typesetting by SilverWood Books

YULIA PYLYAVSKAYA was born in Kazakhstan, brought up in Ukraine and moved to London in 1999. In London, Yulia discovered that women were treated like normal people with driving skills and not like home pets who are best quiet.

When Yulia was a child, she got bullied by her classmate and repeatedly received threats in writing that she will be caught one day and a champagne (or cava) bottle will be inserted into her vagina. Then someone kind will jump on her stomach to make sure it's nicely crushed inside her. To everyone's relief none of those threats took place. After writing this book Yulia managed to overcome the trauma that those threats created, although she still keeps those letters for sweet memories.

Her novel *Adventures of a Big Girl in a Flat City* has been published in three languages: Russian, Ukrainian and English. Yulia is the director of the Creative Writing company Andprose Ltd, head of the juries and a main organiser of the annual international literary bilingual story contest, Bez Mezh, established in 2017. It was created and sponsored by her to support Russian and Ukrainian speaking authors all over the world. She is also author of the Wine and Prose tasting nights, information on which was published in *El Periodico* newspaper and the book *Barcelona Out* by Ana Sanchez.

Yulia lives in Sant Cugat dels Valles, Catalunya, raises her 12-year-old son, teaches creative writing and takes her stand-up comedy classes seriously.

@FindYourFunnyStandUpComedyCourses
@yuliapylyavskaya
www.andprose.com

facebook.com/Adventures of a Big Girl in a Flat City
facebook.com/YuliaPylyavskaya

Prologue

In a town called Kholmysty, near Kiev, roguls, businessmen, athletes and chavs are the only ones who own mobile phones. Which is why I'm in a reddish-yellow telephone booth, all the glass missing, the walls scratched with words beginning with "f" and "c" and the ceiling jammed with greying, stale chewing gum. The year is 1999.

The receiver of the phone is connected to a frozen, rigid wire. It looks like melted dark chocolate that has cooled and solidified in the frost. The chavs were probably bored.

My hands shake as I dial his number. Need a drink. I sniffle and hold myself upright.

He answers almost immediately: "Hello."

"Stapler?" I say.

His name is Ostap. I call him Stapler because he holds his girls down.

"I'm leaving for England. Genuinely and for real." I sniff. "Come out and say goodbye?" I look down at my bare legs, half blue from the November wind.

Just call and I'll come. Do something, stop me, forgive me, fuck me in a way that will never make me want to leave. I could be your bride; I'll birth your kids. My legs are freezing!

"You're talking bull," he answers in Ukrainian.

Regardless of me talking Russian to him.

If you ever want to remind someone that you aren't on the same wavelength, talk in a different language. Stick a knife in their ear.

"I'm gonna shoot off now," the phone adds.

My head starts spinning, as if the booth has been whirled up by a tornado out of the blue.

"My brides are waiting." Then silence.

I understand: his brides are no brides, just girls, and one is probably 'in a relationship' with him. Well, for tonight, anyway. And they most probably get together for a 'double date', probably at green-eyed looker Rudi's. His pad is usually free (parents in the countryside, even though it's November outside and there's no need to dig up potatoes). If he is with Rudi, they get beautiful 'brides' tonight. Need to breathe to let air into my lungs. Can't breathe.

"Stapler, I'm really going... On Wednesday. I already have a ticket for the coach."

His lip chomping becomes louder, as if I've said something sour. He will remain silent for a while, so I understand that I'm the fool, I'm talking bull, that he's gonna shoot off now, and that his wives are waiting.

In the ninth grade Stapler had read Mao Zedong and informed his friends and relatives that he didn't say anything twice. But I'm not talking bull!

I give up and slam the receiver down. A sign of weakness, according to Mao Zedong. The receiver flies off the wire and dangles, so twisted by the chavs that it can't stay on. Did they do pull-ups on it or something?

I pick up the receiver and smash it against the dial. Whose fault is it then? Anger chokes me.

Crying doesn't work. Breathing works. Deeply.

I am Osha, by the way. I am twenty-one. It's far too obvious now that Stapler doesn't love me and my life sucks because of it.

Dialling Ally.

"I'm gonna buy and down a bottle of cognac myself and smash the phone booth into pieces," I say.

"I'm...already...near the phone booth," Ally grunts.

I can picture her attempting to pull up her skirt with one hand. She must be in her tights now, but no make-up. In Kholmysty, no respectable woman leaves her house without make-up. Even to take the rubbish out.

"Magic hat is on," Ally continues, "and I'll only be able to take it off in five minutes...with the help of the cab driver." She pauses, pulling her coat on presumably. "Ten minutes, max," she adds. "Wait, don't drink... Don't move. I'm coming now."

In five minutes, the cab will drop her at the local square, the Parapet.

Yep, a cab. Very cheap here in Kholmysty. Less than a quid to any point.

In the Parapet square, chavs and roguls are stretching their consonants, chattering away on their mobile phones. I buy a bottle of cognac and a pack of light Trussardi. One thing about this town – chavs smoke Marlboro, and the misfits smoke Trussardi. Known to the masses as "trousers".

I shuffle off to the side where Ally and I always chill on our favourite purple bench. Once, between 2 and 3am, we nabbed some paint from an unlocked minibus and painted that bench. Even chavs don't dare to stick gum on the seat. They assume somebody might have our back. Let them think that. I light up. The first drag induces a nasty weakness, Ally's favourite state for some reason. The dumbing of the soul…now feels lighter. Getting drunk today. "We are not girly girls," Ally loves saying. We don't yak about guys. I don't know who Ally is seeing, but do know that there is someone. She doesn't know who I'm with and that's not even difficult. That evening I almost tell her everything about Stapler, which would have shown weakness one time too many. Instead we take to doing our favourite thing, observing chavs and roguls hanging around Parapet square.

I have explained the difference between chavs and roguls to Ally. Ally came from Kazakhstan three years ago. She doesn't know: chavs talk in Ukrussian and pretend to be businessmen.

Businessmen wear jackets the colour of a lilac peony blossoming in May. Roguls talk in Russiainian and pretend to be athletes. Athletes wear Nike and Adidas.

A classic example of a chav using his special businessman's moves at his best: in May-peony-coloured blazer, standing in a club next to a huge speaker, which is making the shop across the road vibrate. The speaker is blaring out the song about short skirts. He shouts into his mobile phone, the size of a boom box: "Ehhhhhhhh. Listen, mate, leave it out, I toldja I'm busy! Bee! Zee!"

After which, having forgotten to press "end call", he resumes raving to the short skirts song with some girl whose eyes swell with pride followed by a somewhat tragic smile, as if she is saying goodbye to Leonardo DiCaprio in the ocean to the melody of "I Will Always Love You".

Roguls wear tracksuits from "Nuke" and "Odidos", bought at six in the morning from the Asians at a market in Troyeshina. Rogul, as well as chav, does need an audience, bless them both. A rogul is less picky with it, though. He can survive without the whole disco staring at him. Therefore, grannies on benches will do excellently.

'Special Effects' of a good rogul: leave the porch, take out a pack of Marlboro Lights from left tracky pocket. Light a cigarette and put the packet back in the same left tracky pocket. Take out a huge mobile phone from the right pocket. Forgetting to press 'dial', let out a consonant-filled garble through gritted teeth.

It's important to stretch the consonants, and not the vowels, as chavs stretch those. Maybe this gives more rigour? Ally and I haven't decided.

The chavs and the roguls perhaps think we are slaughtering pigs, and they are probably asking themselves why we are screeching every time we laugh, bending down on our knees as if looking for mushrooms. But we aren't looking for mushrooms and we aren't slaughtering pigs. We are spinning theories about chavs and roguls and not talking about Stapler.

A decent amount of cognac is consumed that evening, but despite my best efforts, I remain sober like a frog on a drizzly April morning. At two in the morning I walk home with a bottle of beer. Past my door, to his – a habit developed over the last five years. We live on the same block on Friendship of Nations Street; number nineteen. My heels clatter on the wet concrete.

Then I see this: his light, the only one on, on the ninth floor. On the first floor is Maryam Shmulevna's, our instructor for the basket-weaving club in the House of Culture of Karpenko-Kary, probably brewing valerian in her fight against insomnia. Cognac, Maryam Shmulevna, cognac.

I move over to the middle of the yard and stand under a street lamp. He'll see me more easily that way; smoking on the balcony or randomly glancing out the window. He'll notice me, come down and take me by the hand – won't pick me up though. He wasn't the best at press-ups at school.

Silently we will walk back to his. In the lift, we will tightly embrace. Then will laugh at ourselves because we're both idiots.

We will make love till the morning and then I won't want to go to England for anything. How can I, if he proposes to me in the morning, and after marriage we'll want a kid? Or we'll leave together. We'll decide. Also, we'll finally start to speak because we'll have a future.

Two silhouettes appear on the balcony – a man's and a woman's. The man's – tall and thin, with Stapler's fringe. The woman's with a ponytail. The two silhouettes then join together in the face region. Having had enough of joining together in the face region, they slip away from the balcony. The lights go out in every room one by one.

A desire to smash this bottle in my hand against the pavement looms over me, so sick and so sad, but my limbs don't listen and just hang side by side like a decoration at Christmas, which I, most likely, will celebrate in a different kind of country.

No point in drinking any more. For the whole evening I couldn't get drunk and the flashing images of Stapler with his wives – kissing each other all over in all kinds of places in silent passion up on the ninth floor, where the bed is creaking (hope it snaps in half) and no one else is in and the silhouettes don't bother stopping till they've been on the armchair, the table, the sofa, the floor, leaning with one leg on the counter, next to the clever book *Mao Zedong Teachings*. I will definitely, one hundred per cent, not be able to relax and sleep tonight. No snow or rain, to decorate with romance, this pain. A mean November night.

A whole block of flats, curtains drawn, asleep. Behind me, near the boiler house, a rusty carousel peers from beneath a naked weeping willow. No more breathless whispering and kissing here. Just a setting… After gently placing my full bottle on the carousel, I drag myself home.

Fear of the sleepless night makes each step feel like cotton. I shuffle home, short steps like the exhausted Asian student who passes me, probably off to the market to flog stuff. The tears that night don't flow.

The next morning. Richie the cat snoozes on my pillow, resembling a white, smooth-combed rabbit hat. Me – the polar opposite: shaggy, unwashed and sleepless. Dressed in my PJs with a lump in my throat and a feeling of filth in my soul, I take out some drawing paper from the narrow hanging wardrobe and start to draw… A girl crying, in her pupils the silhouettes of two figures on an illuminated balcony.

I like the drawing. I wonder what floor I'll live on in London. Imagining a view from the twenty-sixth. The Thames in the midst of sky scrapers. I'm on a balcony, smiling onto London's sunshine, behind me a room with a wide bed, a big TV and a wardrobe so huge there's a special compartment for shoes. A shower and a toilet are mandatory. A big white satellite dish is attached to the balcony. In Kiev all the new-builds are plastered with these satellite dishes, like a space station at a UFO summit. The dish catches all the channels in the world so *Melrose Place* is on repeat. Beautiful! I'll colour in the picture after breakfast.

On the day of my wedding to a rich philosophical Englishman, I'll post it (the picture) to Stapler.

Preferably, the Englishman will be a singer like John Lennon.

So, while I'm in the registry office, Stapler will see the black silhouettes in the pupils of the girl and realise that I love him for real. Stapler will come bursting in shouting "I love you!", breaking up the ceremony. I will toss startled John Lennon and his gold-plated fountain pen to one side. An ink droplet will fall right on the dotted line but it won't matter as I'll throw myself onto Stapler's neck and marry him right there in the registry office.

Could kill for two fried eggs. Meandering to the kitchen.

Or maybe it'll be different. I'll come back in a year. And find out from Tolik Pushka in the queue at the bakery that Stapler's getting married. To a boring lady with a potato nose and a huge soul, who consumed too much salo that winter. On the morning of his wedding day, I'll anonymously send him the picture; the earlier the better so that he receives it before anything official happens. He will, of course, realise that he has been a doofus (finally!), break up with his Potato Nose bride (she could be a Cherry Nose, but he'll leave her more quickly if she's a Potato One) and will marry me on that same day. I'll make sure to fast the day before. Or not— wait, what is this yellow water soaking the tearful girl's face, whose eyes reflect windows with black silhouettes? The sharp tang of cat urine hits the nose. Dreams of England and the picture of a happy marriage with Stapler thrash and flutter out of my head like a flock of pigeons.

Richie, you dog. What kind of cat wees on the table! I throw an old towel on the picture, and it slowly starts to soak up the pee. Losing patience, I start to rub the paper lightly with a towel. Eventually, the paper rolls into little grey sausages. The picture's ruined. The spark is gone. Richie, you broke my life. I shuffle back to bed and once again I feel like an exhausted Asian trader. Swaddled in a blanket, as if I have the flu, I bury my face in my pillow, and finally start to cry. Loud, like a drawn-out sad Romani song.

I won't say a thing to Crip. Schizophrenics can be cunning; he'll rig the coach or steal my passport.

On the bus I will have time to reflect on all of my flaws and faults. No Crips, no Staplers, and no Vicks. Just find a good one. So that he'll take care of me, like Crip, when sober; a true friend, like Vick, and loves me with fantasy like You-Know-Who.

With Crip we'll do this: in the letter I'll explain everything, and Ally will personally hand it to him after my departure. Or else there'll be a coach explosion.

I write a long letter to Crip, full of snot and rhetorical questions. I reread it. Why did I use the name 'Sunshine' for a person who threw bottles at me, nailed me under the table with size-eleven boots so recklessly that he shattered my nose while doing it? Maybe Vick knows? He was the one suggesting I forgive and acknowledge the 'higher love' in this event.

I make three obvious conclusions:

1. I will try to answer all these questions on the coach.
2. Mao Zedong wouldn't sit within a mile of me to brush his teeth.
3. I'm writing crappy farewell letters to aggressive schizophrenics.

In the evening, on the way to the tea hut, I give in and once again ring Ostap. Good old sign of weakness. A sign of strength, I presume, is to never tell anyone anything. Just send people with a neutral tone to different places.

To one place, mostly, maximum three.

Once again, he (Stapler) picks up the phone after the second ring. Is he on duty or something?

"Off to England tomorrow. Chick-chick, black coffin is already on your road!" I say. Silence. Demonstrative sign of strength. "You wanna see the ticket?" I ask.

"Well, toodles!" he says after a silence, as if squeezing out some tooth-paste from a half-used tube. Could have just hung up the phone.

"You don't want to say goodbye properly?" I tightly bite my lip.

"Why? For what?"

"You don't want to say goodbye properly?" I forcefully bite my lip.

"For wha'? Why?"

I want to answer: to get wasted and fuck properly for the last time. That's for wha' an' why. As by the looks of it, there's no point in getting hopes up for the wedding and two nice kids, first a boy, then a girl.

"Well, if you end up changing your mind, come to the tea hut," I say.

"End up changin' my mind? For wha'?"

I'm silent. I drop the phone. For that, Ostap! For! That!

Yes, I'm weak. I don't actually know who Mao Zedong is, to be honest. I just remember our philosophy class teacher quoting him: "To have faith is to trust yourself to the river. When swimming across the river, do not think you will sink. If you think – you will sink, if you don't – you won't."

Would be good to translate and learn it by heart before leaving.

"Get up, you alky!" Mum's ringing voice crashes into my sleeping brain.

The first question pops into my head: "Where did you get so wasted last night?"

It's a request for the password to my computer, the answer to which I happened to have forgotten.

My mental process tries to boot up, like the oldest version of Windows we had in IT class in '94.

Why do I need to get up? Trying to rack my brains.

Vick's sad puppy eyes flash. Ally's sobbing as she falls into the snow.

Lots of people, lots of toasts, wishing me a 'good journey'. The tea hut's dim light…we were washing down our vodka with tea. A full house, a sad full house, like a funeral.

I smile. The smile turns out pretty sour, as only the mandatory facial muscles are involved.

Poor Ally. She flopped into my porch and burst into tears. I felt like I was watching a silent film – Ally seen in the entrance through a door slightly ajar. It was pitch black in the entrance hall – the chavs smashed all the light bulbs. It felt like I was watching her from a coffin. This is probably how the dead would observe their mourners if they had an open casket and could see. I wanted to go back to her, hug her, cry with her, but I couldn't. I was deceased… Otherwise we'd be wailing till dawn. Vick was there somewhere… and so I left to go home.

"So, you getting up, no?" Mum interrupts my fantasy about the parallel world.

She uses the word 'no' like an interrogative and adds it to all questions and statements. This word substitutes her favourite "Am I right or am I right?" She also likes "Let's say".

"Get dressed and go eat your breakfast, time to leave soon. Dad's already gone to get the car."

Which means: no need to rush, I have exactly fifty-seven minutes – shower, get dressed, breakfast. We have different perceptions of time.

Mum was once late to her maths class as a kid; this traumatised her forever. Children's minds are not strong, as it happens. Now she has a small heart attack at 6.15am, every time we are expecting guests to arrive at 5.30pm. I usually ignore her calls to capture Zimny Palace at such an early hour, quietly sleeping and getting ready to greet guests exactly an hour and twenty-seven minutes in advance, that is, from 4.03pm. Deep clean of the house and serving of the table, plus two salads – Russian salad and dressed herring. Rational idiotism? Rational idiotism. And who do I take after? Hmm.

I get to the kitchen on autopilot. Sit down, eat buckwheat with cutlets. Listen to Mum's resonant voice as she asks: "So how was your farewell party?"

"Touching," I reply, swallowing the buckwheat. "One hundred and fifty-nine people turned up."

"One hundred and fifty-nine?" Mum freezes, kettle in hand on her way to the hob. Small droplets on the floor.

I'm laughing. Buckwheat falls out of my mouth.

"Mum. Always falling for the same jokes. One hundred and fifty-seven, five hundred and thirty-four. There were lots, Mum. Lots of people turned up."

"Your silly jokes... Let's say I never will understand them." She crashes the kettle on the hob as if it's made of cast-iron.

Actually, all of Mum's actions are noisy, as though she's a blacksmith. Whether she's opening a cupboard, washing up pots and pans, closing a door. Don't even get me started on her ready, steady cook attempts or her search for the front door keys. Everything is clapping, jingling and splatting on the floor so much you want to run away from home.

Maybe it's because of this that whenever I leave, I do so quietly, tightly and carefully shutting the door behind me. Much as I would love to slam it shut.

"They came, they drank, they left," I continue. "Tasha got wasted again."

I lift up my index finger like I'm sharing ancient wisdom: "If Tasha has a red and unwelcoming face, she is already wasted."

"That's horrible." Once again Mum doesn't react to the joke.

"For the last time, we took her home, we stood her up at her front door according to old Iraqi tradition, rang the doorbell and ran."

Mum shakes her head. Tut-tut-tut. Good thing she isn't asking about this Iraqi tradition. Would have to explain, fourth time round, that it's a joke from my friends in stand-up comedy.

"Vick danced with me sadly all night," I continue.

"Was the Question Mark there, no?" Mum asks.

The "Question Mark" refers to Ostap.

I shake my head side to side. Chewing and looking out of the window, as if I am a cow outside trailing its herd and as if I wonder: how am I gonna catch up with you guys? All I need is a tail to get rid of the flies to match my expression.

I can't look Mum in the eye. Why does she always sit opposite me, looking straight through me?

"Mmm, yeah," says Mum, not moving her neatly folded arms, like a schoolgirl. Smiling and looking straight through me. Why does she always look through me? Maybe she's cross-eyed?

I shrug my shoulders.

"Uh well, makes it easier to leave, no?" she says.

I take a deep breath. "Five years I love him, and with absolutely no point whatsoever," I say.

The front door slams.

"Ahoy, Paint Brushes! The car's ready." It is obvious at once what sells most in Dad's stationery shop.

We're on the platform at Moscovsky Coach Station.

"Take the blue bag with you on the bus. There's food in there," Mum says.

I lift my head to the sky and slowly let out the letter "O" into the cold air. "O-okayyyy."

People shuffle around their suitcases. It's cold. A woman comes round with two big brown bags and asks in Ukrainian: "Would you know if this is the coach to London?"

"Yeah, this is the one," Mum answers in Ukrainian. She is the most willing to speak Ukrainian out of the whole family. I only speak Ukrainian with Ostap.

Mum looks on with interest at the middle-aged woman with a worried look on her face, and a colourful headscarf. "Are you going to London too, zhinochko?" Mum asks. "Zhinochko" is Ukrainian for "dear lady".

"Nee... I just wanna send over with the driver some things for my son. He's in London, calls me and goes: 'Mamo! I gots everything, but ain't got no Ukrainisky khlib, salo and vareniki!'"

We all chuckle lazily. I bet this is something I will miss too. Ukrainian bread, pork fat and dumplings are my favourite food too. Everyone's favourite, in fact.

I look at the two brown bags, each the size of an old Soviet colour television, and try to imagine just how much salo, Ukrainsky khlib and vareniki fitted into them. Maybe there's some borsch too?

"Well, we can send you things like this as well, no?" says Mum.

"No," I answer with enthusiasm.

Like a ship from overseas arriving at the island of Buyan (my favourite island from Pushkin's fairy tale), smooth and stately, the coach arrives, engulfing us with its fragrant smell of foreign smoke, then pulls to a halt.

The doors and sunroofs open. People place their things and take their seats while I entertain myself with the dialogue nearby:

"Mickey, over here! There's space!"

And after two seconds: "*What* the hell did you stuff in there, Mickey! Are you planning to open a library over there or something?"

"Eh? Wha'du' suggest then, working like a wanker as a kitchen porter twenty-four seven?" well-read Mickey answers. I totally agree with him; besides the idea of opening a library sounds good too. And then he adds:

"Told my sister, give me something, anything, magazines or sumfink... So, the silly cow stuffs it wiv Chekhovs and Bulgakovs!"

So, no point in counting on Mickey's support then when opening a library. Nevertheless, he knows the names of some books.

The coach has six people in it. The rest of the crowd, like the woman with the worried look, rush to speak with the driver and shove their money at him. The driver seems sensitive and respectful – receiving the notes, he squints like Ded Moroz, or 'Santa Claus' I should start saying, shouldn't I? Without looking at the people, he just nods where to put their bags presumably filled with Ukrainian bread, salo and dumplings.

Dad places my suitcase in the luggage hatch. I jump on the coach, throwing my bag with food into an empty seat, along with my new edition of *Analysis of the Aura. Book Two*, given to me yesterday by Pashya as a valuable gift for the road. "Anal Ices of Zaura." I laugh for the umpteenth time and jump back out to my parents.

"When you get to London, ring me straight away. I'll be worrying. They must have phone booths, no?" says Mum.

"Mamo, don't worry. Everything will be all right. I can cook borsch, remember."

"Oh, you know so much, don't you?" Mum says firmly. And I accept that I don't know a lot of things about this life, compared to her.

The engine of the coach gives a big roar. I tightly embrace my parents, who smell of muscat perfume and L&M Red cigarettes.

"Maybe I'll come home after a week. We can laugh our faces off." I swallow a lump in my throat.

"You have a return ticket. If anything happens – back on the coach straight home," Dad picks up, and I can see that he successfully swallows a lump in his throat too.

"Well, go then," Mum says softly, and I understand that she can't swallow the lump in hers.

She makes the sign of the cross over me, as I try not to smile sceptically. I want to say "love you", but end up muttering some gibberish, smiling awkwardly.

I board the bus with seven passengers including me. It's warm and cosy; I sit in the soft seat by the window.

"Your destiny awaits you in London. Your destiny is connected to the number seven." More mumbo-jumbo from Pashya.

Under my window Dad forces a smile. Mum looks straight through the window, straight through me. I'm guessing that she is praying. Usually in these situations, I turn back to glance behind me, as if there is someone else she is looking at. Normally this makes her smile, but it doesn't work this time.

The coach makes a move. I breathe a sigh of relief. I hate farewells. I don't want to cry. From the window I can see how Mum has buried her face in Dad's chest. Dad hugs her close. Looking at the static figures: he's in a black jacket, she's in a red coat, behind them the hustle and bustle of Moscovsky Station. The coach turns onto the main road and drives off.

The sun rises over a frosty Kiev. A normal, working day is about to begin. People will be doing their usual Wednesday routines. Stapler's going to uni, his first lesson is English. Ally's going to work, hungover from the night before as usual, but this time with puffy eyes from crying too.

Vick will be bunking off today, smoking half a packet before lunch, then he'll go to play snooker, drink a jug of beer, and slap the waitress's butt.

Me alone in my spaceship, flying through Kiev, further and further away. A long journey away from Kholmysty, the chavs, Kiev and my home, Ukraine.

I look on through the window as a new fairy tale trickles into my day.

"Any journey starts from the farewell," said Pashya last night. He is right on this one.

A familiar chill. I get a feeling like I'm about to be taken, not by those two slobbering Berkuts (about them later), but by my Stapler. Ally yesterday was declaring, with a fragile voice, that London will bring new friends, who will one day be seeing me off back to Ukraine. Now Ally, and Vick and Stapler, and Crep, all remain as characters from Kholmysty. Yesterday was the final episode.

I'm scared to breathe. Yuri Gararin, 1961, 12th April…and between the past and the future, is me, free falling. My head feels clear, floating away. This is probably how it feels after death. My friends and family will mourn me for a bit, and then life will flow on, as if I never was.

Forwards, to the Big Country, on the one-hundred-and-twenty-something floor, with a white satellite dish, porridge by the fireplace in the morning, and the new, real Crepovickostap.

To the Big Country, where it's not entirely clear if there are phone booths in the street, and if there are, whether they are scribbled with the "f" and "c" words, or not.

I close my eyes, and dive into my memories. Five years ago, eleventh grade…

PART ONE

How It All Began

CHAPTER ONE

Sitting on the Windowsill

"I like him over there. He's fit," Katka says while sitting beside me at the same desk. She snuffs through her nose, sounding like a baby elephant from one of those Soviet cartoons as she drops her head on my shoulder. Katka mainly speaks through her nose, and I think this is probably why she never gets a blocked nose.

We're in the eleventh grade in the last lesson of the second term. Tonight is the New Year's Eve party and we only want to speak about silly stuff.

I peel my eyes from the book on the table, checking out the boy in front, shuffling down the room – Ostap Sokira.

"Kapets," Katka adds her favourite word, eating him with her gaze. Kapets – means she is in awe of him. If Katka were British, she would say "oh man" instead but she is a Russian Uzbek who grew up in Ukraine like me.

I want to tell Katka that she has horrible taste but Ostap's sly look and innocent kid's smile are thrown in our direction and it disarms me.

Everybody calls him either Ostap or Stapler. Vick calls him Ostap Bender, as in the main character from *The Twelve Chairs*. *The Twelve Chairs* is a popular comedy by two Odessan authors, Ilf and Petrov. The story is about a picaro, a poor but smart half outsider chasing his fortune while wearing a scarf.

My Ostap wears glasses and no scarf. In any case he's got Ostap Bender's crafty gaze and resourceful mind like all rogues.

"I still love my Lobick." I sigh.

"Such a good faithful girl. Lobick is on the Carpathians right about now, and you're near Kiev. It's already been like half a year!" Katka moans, with long beautiful fingers scraping the paint off the desk.

"Time – ain't no drawback," I say. "Have you ever heard his Carpathian accent? And then, he kisses so…"

"Oh, stop bickering about your Carmanian accent." Katka flutters her blueberry eyes. "And I saw him borrowing twenty copecks from the team leader. Ostap is not that shallow."

"Why didn't I just give myself to him straight away?" I dreamily brush my cheek with my hand. "He would have already come after me with a marriage proposal. Where's the logic in moral preaching? Keep your virginity, like a fool…"

"Shhhh!" Katka hisses, staring at her desk as she peels the paint from it.

"If you don't have sex when it's on offer," I whisper, "then you have to suffer half a year with wet dreams and erotic visions."

Katka bursts out in a splutter. "I know one really effective method," she answers in a whisper, and grabbing her pen, she starts to draw a hedgehog on the back of her chemistry book. I put my head on her shoulder. "Oi boi…"

We're both now studying Katka's half-drawn hedgehog as if it is the method of curing a victim from flawed moral preaching or the tormenting of one's own erotic visions.

"You get into a hot bath," she whispers conspiratorially, "turn the tap all the way and put your most valued part under the stream of water! Kah-pets."

"Ooh, that's more like it. And what's next? 'Cos all you've been offering so far is some rogulish Ostaps and the like."

"Ostap is not a rogul!" She raises her voice to an urgent, hysterical whisper. "He speaks Russian better than Vick! And reads philosophy. You should chat to him."

Stapler is the teachers' pet and now Katka's too by the looks of things. He knows more than needed about any subject. The main thing is, he knows, that he knows more than needed about any subject. Also, he reads *Kobzar* (something like three hundred pages of Shakespeare's sonnets) off by heart and all of Taras Shevchenko's biography (the Shakespeare of Ukrainians), which initially helped him to enrol at the University of T. Shevchenko, the biggest and most influential university in Ukraine. Rumour has it that without ten thousand dollars you wouldn't be let past the gates. Whether the rumours are true, I don't know. I do know that for normal people it is much harder to get in than for those whose daddies wear peony-coloured blazers and Nike or Adidas tracksuits. Although maybe it is simply because their kids are substantially more gifted. That is also possible, right?

"Shh, come on, more about the stream of water," I say, flicking my fringe back.

"Katsapki, Katsapki," Vick interrupts with a wide smile, resembling Dr Livesey from the Soviet version of the *Treasure Island* movie. Look at him. It's impossible not to smile back.

"After school, you girls skip home, quickly change, and come to class for six with bottles and cakes."

"Ku-pets... We will of course be thur..." says Katka, plastering on a wide smile. "You go, we've gut sum-thing importunt tur discuss..."

"Abuut...chuuurmistry," I add.

"Abuut...wuter," adds Katka.

"Yeah but, maybe I can help you..." he says.

"Balls you will help me; you copy all my work!" Katka says.

"And mine," I say, widening my not-so-large eyes.

"OK, OK, I'm off; was happy to help. Hmm. Gm..." Vick backs away to his desk from our widened eyes and smiles.

Anyone speaking Russian in our school is a "katzap". A Ukrainian speaker is a "khokhol". The names come from historical dress. Back in the old days, Russian Cossacks had pointy beards like goats (katzaps) and Ukrainian Cossacks were famous for their shaven heads with a long patch of hair (khokhol) sticking out from the middle of the head. They are not offensive names. Back in Kazakhstan I was ckhokhlushka to all my relatives, and here, in Ukrainian class, I am katzapka to all my classmates. And Katka from Uzbekistan is "my partner in crime".

A year ago, we transferred from Russian class to Ukrainian. Well, I went from the big, undivided love for Keswick with his fair-haired fringe, who at graduation kissed me from head to toe in the next room and told me, dishevelled and with no clothes on, that he never did love me. Actually. How timely. Had he said that before the undressing and the kissing in different places the effect would have been totally different.

My fourteen-year-old girl's heart broke forever. Later at the party I smoked two cigarettes in a row, not inhaling, and decided to transfer to the Ukrainian class.

The Ukrainian language will help me to get into the University of Foreign Languages. Katka also wants to get in. After hearing all my theories over the summer about the urgency of learning Ukrainian, forgetting about her appeals that Russian classes were cooler, and that only roguls went to

Ukrainian classes, on the first day back, she ends up sitting next to me in Year 10B. For all our fellow classmates, we are katsapki. Especially for Vick.

'Least we're not roguls, Katka thinks.

In his family, Vick's mum is the only one who speaks Russian. The father refers to her lovingly as "katsapka".

At least not a rogul, I think.

I look out the window: it's snowing. It makes the night sparkly. In the classroom it's dark. Flashing music lights from a vibrating speaker, Dr Alban is loudly persuading us it's his life. On the tables there are outlines of cakes, extra-large cola bottles, jugs with diluted Yupi water. Katka and I jest, once again slurping on vodka from the bottle and drinking Coke from a plastic cup in the corner of the room. It's my twenty-fifth song, I'm soaking. Vick is dancing Katka into the circle; I use the moment and head to the teacher's desk for a break. To rest on the only windowsill without any coats on it.

Near the table it smells of oranges. Someone tall is sitting on the windowsill. I end up face to face with Ostap.

"Want an orange?" Ostap shouts over the Macarena and gives a cheeky smile.

"I want to sit." I end up between his knees, our noses almost touching. I notice that we both have long noses. On the other hand, he is so tall. He's sitting and I'm standing and our noses are on the same level. His expression has something of Lobick-the-Carpathian – it is a sly, cheeky look with a straight fringe.

He tightly embraces me with his long arms, seriously gazing at me as he peels an orange behind me slowly. "Let's stand like this," he offers.

And I obediently stand. Looking at his eyes. I hear people behind me dancing, throwing garlands around, going crazy, and we are just gazing at each other, and it smells of oranges.

I understand that looking at him with his dark brown, almost black eyes, like a cobra at a rabbit, could make anyone fall in love with him so much that there wouldn't be any Keswicks or Lobicks left in anyone's head, even with the strongest Carpathian accent.

He carefully bites on his orange, pulling me to him, and I feel the tenderness of the orange on my lips. My head is spinning and it's aromatic, and... The light turns on. The music stops.

24

Someone screams, "Vick, what have you turned the lights on for?!"

"It's over, children! Time to go home! Principal popped in and said to wrap it up." Vick sounds serious. This is why you shouldn't choose people like that as class reps. They'll split their forehead.

Katka drags me away from Ostap; she is whining that it's time to go. Everybody squints at the light, reluctantly getting dressed. Unwillingly, I put my coat on, deliberately flapping the sleeve in Katka's face. Katka shrugs it off and giggles sourly. She glances over at Ostap. He is hypnotising...me or Katka?

The whole class pours out into the courtyard.

Vick hangs onto the top step and shouts from there, "Children! Celebrating New Year at Tolly Pushka's hut, ya heard?"

I feel like rejoicing as if I've had an offer to play a lead in the most famous film in the world. I find Vick's dreary look pointed right at me. I'm ashamed of my joy, as I smile at him. Vick generously smiles back and starts to shout with a new-found strength. "Did you all get it? New Year's at Tolly Pushka's! Lads bring the booze; ladies bring the cakes."

"Kah-pets, let's all bring booze. What the hell's the point of cakes? We'll just be throwing them up afterwards," Katka responds.

Vick continues gladly shouting, "This time in favour of the booze, and not cakes," and I think, maybe me smiling at him is a bad idea. Bet he switched on the lights on purpose.

"And oranges," whispers Ostap, having suddenly appeared at my ear.

I smile and look through Vick. And he's probably asking himself if I am cross-eyed at this hour.

"I always wanted to know," he whispers, inhaling the scent of my hair. "Why are you called Osha?"

I smile and reply, "When I was small, I couldn't say the letter 'k'. I called the koshka" – cat – "'osh-a', so Mum and Dad called me that. And it stuck."

"Charming," he whispers, and I'm already swinging among the stars, clinging onto the hem of my skirt at the edge of the moon.

New Year's Eve at Tolly Pushka's is full of people. The clock strikes twelve. Shouts of "Happy New Year!", screams, laughter, clinking of glasses. I notice that Vick is creeping through the crowd towards me, like a bear through raspberry bushes, and I retreat to hide on the balcony with a half-finished glass.

The glass-paned balcony is fresh but not cold and quiet. Firecrackers, fireworks and singing can be heard. The door opens, and I close my eyes.

"My God, will he ever give me peace ever?"

I turn to the doors with an angry face. In one hand Ostap holds a glass, in the other – an orange. I drift into his mysterious smile, and for some reason shiver.

"Happy New Year, Stapler."

"Yeah, Year is New," he replies and stands his glass on the table.

"What?" I ask, lovingly smiling.

In return he grabs the glass from my hand and stands it next to his.

Then he firmly presses me to him. Brave, gentle, first kiss. Makes my heart soar, as if stepping onto the moon for the first time, and thereafter tumbling into the snow in a fur coat. Warm and terribly, terribly ticklish everywhere.

People leave and enter the balcony. Smoking. Clinking glasses. Telling not-so-funny jokes. Laughing. Joking about us.

"Stapler, Osha, you smoking? Maybe not, by the looks of it."

"Is it Stapler with Osha or Osha with Stapler?"

"You'll get a clearer picture from here."

We don't find it funny.

Dawn. Tolly delicately expels us from the balcony: "Of course, you can continue to freeze, but parents will soon come and make you warm up with Gorilka and a sing-along. And my parents love a sing-along."

At home, sleepy and happy, I write in my diary: *I met him. End of the era of Lobick. And not in the Carpathians. With pleasure I'll part with innocence. Not today, no. He-he. Happy New Year.* And then add: *Yes. The year is new.*

I thought that this was the only conversation we had this year. But I didn't note it down…

Chapter Two

Why Isn't He Calling?

I'm sure he'll call. Well, not the next day, but after a day he'll definitely call. What does it mean – waiting all day for a call in an era without mobile phones? It means you go to the toilet – leave the doors open. It means, when in the shower – keep your phone within hearing distance – on the floor in the bathroom. That is possible only if your dad is an electrician and has monopolised the supply of extension leads in the house.

First days of January. Parents are at friends'. I craftily refuse to go. What are all these Sokolenkos with Melnicks for, with their dull kids in younger grades?

Staying in an empty house calms me. No distractions from the waiting and nobody's watching now that I am worried and cannot eat. On the morning of the fourth of January, Vick is at mine.

"So, I owe you congratulations?" he says casually, vigorously gobbling a piece of Kyivsky tort (my favourite cake ever), and not taking his eye off the chubby TV host from the programme for teens, with his small microphone.

"With what?" I say and sip my tea.

"As always, with nuts." He turns to me and smiles toothily, crumbs falling out. I laugh in response.

"Oh, so you're not asking about the cake?" he says and I laugh not so enthusiastically this time. Vick tends to verbally masturbate his jokes. We have that in common, to be honest.

"Well, you know, you're soon marrying Bender, no?" he replies seriously and turns back to the TV. "As far as I'm aware, after spending the night with a man and leaving with him in the morning in an unknown direction, the man simply has to marry you. Or is it me supposed to babysit your kids?"

He puts down his plate with his half-eaten piece of cake, glances at my dumbfounded look and continues, wiping his hands on his jeans:

"What, are you not against giving birth to an illegitimate child?"

"The napkins on the table!" I interrupt.

"Well, your liberation, I never doubted." He reaches for a napkin on the coffee table.

"You're silly," I say. "We went to a familiar location, home. Pushka escorted us out. Were you watching or something?"

"Ended up near the entrance of Tolka's block of flats." Vick continues to rub his hands with the napkin.

"Hmyeah. Didn't freeze anything out near the entrance of Tolka's block of flats? Sherlock Holmes." I put my elbow on the arm of the couch and put my hand over my cheek.

"We went home. He went to his first door, and I, to my sixth. So, the babysitting services won't be required."

I glance over at him once again and fold my hands in my lap. "Is this your smart way of finding out whether we slept together or not?"

"You just went?" Vick narrows his bear eyes above his snub nose.

"We just went."

"You to yours, and he to his?"

"I to mine, and he, believe it or not, to his." I nod to him, as if grandmother to her seven-year-old grandson, revealing that sooner or later, caterpillars will turn into butterflies.

"And he didn't even walk you?" Vick continues squinting.

"And what's there to even walk, five doors?"

"Mmyeah. I would have walked."

"Listen, why are you hassling me. Just eat your cake."

I put my hand on my cheek again.

"Well, well, no offence, hun. Just concerned for a close friend."

I look at him with annoyance. "Vick, don't be jealous."

"Yeah, there is a little bit of that."

"Why?"

I shrug my shoulders, softening because he doesn't deny it. "If it wasn't for him, you and I still would be just friends. It is what it is. The relationship can be so good, though it is still only friendship. But lovers come and go; friends stay."

Vick pauses in silence. His face turns greyish, and you can hear him gritting his teeth. A habit of his, which I could never stand. "Well... I can still hope a bit?" he adds. "And anyway, Bender's arrogant. He'll hurt ya."

"Come on, I'm arrogant too."

"You're not arrogant. You are Osha."

On the 6th of January it is Christmas Eve in Ukraine. I call Katka: "Come on, let's go up the hills, do something."

Outside in the street I begin to feel free. Maybe, because there is no need to organise my life around a phone. Our town is called Kholmysty – "the town on the hills" translated from Ukrainian. It is a few high-rises between two hills, surrounded by a pine forest. Dad calls it "a piece of Alaska".

He worked in Alaska when I was in first grade and I used to really miss him. Writing letters every day. Afraid that an avalanche would swarm down on him or on the postman with this letter in his bag. I will not let my future husband work "in all sorts of Alaskas". Why traumatise a child?

Activities of Holmistians are simple: In summer they either leave for their dachas, summer homes outside the town or in the forest, for a special kind of barbeque called shashlick, or to the river Stugna, which is behind the paper factory, for sunbathing and boat rides. In the winter they can't go to any of these places; therefore the population walks across the town in all sorts of directions, hoping to bump into all sorts of Ostaps. The most popular walking place is the park called the Dubki, full of oak trees, and the Parapet.

We walk past the oaks, and heading towards us is a crowd of guys. Ostap's head rises above the crowd. By his head, we recognise our classmates. Next is a convoy on the go, like a lazy roll call: "Where you?"

"Walking."

"Well, walk."

I say: "Kinda reminds me of my favourite joke about Timur and his team and Red Riding Hood. You know?"

"No."

I am telling her a joke, in which Red Riding Hood walks in the forest, sees Timur and his team (characters from the childhood book by Arcadiy Gaydar, where a bunch of cute teenagers help old people incognito). Red Riding Hood sees the cute boys and in the hope of a group shag takes her knickers off and lies down on the ground. The team rush past her and she finds a note next to her basket: "Red Riding Hood, don't worry – the pies for

29

grandmother are delivered, pants are washed. Timur and his team."

While Katka is laughing, I continue talking, as I don't want her to say anything about what's just happened:

"You know, I found Timur very attractive, helping out all those old people and all. I've had the hots for him since I was eight. Without realising it, of course. Just had all sorts of hots in my body," I say to Katka. I don't want her to speak so I continue: "I even looked after a disabled person for a while with a group of eight-year-olds. Then I was expelled from the team under suspicion of shortchanging. They gave me fifty kopecks and sent for milk. I didn't give them twelve kopecks change. They thought I did it on purpose. I did, to be honest, as I assumed it was my pay for the work. My parents always let me keep the change. But in their eyes, I was a thief."

"Wait, hold on, I don't get it: is it over between you two?"

"Between me and the disabled person? It was half of my life ago, so yeah, I assume," I say.

"You know who I am talking about." Katka loses patience. "You and Ostap. You were slobbing each other all night. Remember? Five days ago. A long time, right?"

"Well, what do you suggest, Katka, to just jump into his arms then?" I try not to let the storm burst inside my head.

"I'd have jumped." Katka shrugs her shoulders. I get annoyed with myself, that shy insecure Katka would have jumped and outgoing no-limits me chickens out with some sad story from the past.

"No way, we haven't had enough between us to jump about. So, what, a kiss on New Year's Eve. Who doesn't have that?"

A high-pitched squeal in my head.

"Not bad," Katka notes. "After that inferno it wouldn't be easy for me to leave."

"Katka, for six days he didn't call. What's that mean?"

We boldly go in silence. The snow crunches under our boots. Frost.

"Well, is he hurt?"

"About what? That I clung to him on the balcony till the morning?" I say. Katka giggles.

"Yeah, kapets, you blazed it up."

We pass the school stadium.

"Why don't you ring him. What if he's hurting? Couldn't he have seen you with Vick?"

"No, and what does Vick have to do with it? Vick is my friend… I can't spend time with a friend?"

"Well, that's what you think. Although you're right as well. We'll see. Reckon he'll call soon."

On the 8th January, at eleven minutes past five the phone rings. I drop the potatoes I'm peeling and run to the hall for the phone. "Hello?"

Silence in reply. I can tell it's him. "Want some oranges?"

I exhale: "You?" I plonk down into a soft chair and close my eyes. As if by keeping them open I'll see my reflection in the glass cupboard doors and notice how stupid I look when blushing.

"Ninth floor, apartment seventy-eight," he says.

"Well, I need at least an hour to get ready…" Nobody is listening to me down the phone.

On the way to his I decide not to ask him why he didn't call for so long. What if it's a sign of weakness according to Mao Zedong? I don't know Mao Zedong well. And Katka told me that Ostap knows him very well.

First, his head needs to spin just as much when I ring him as when he rings me. I'm deliberately late by an hour and a half. Let him wait.

The door of seventy-eight is ajar. Come in, whoever you are, take whatever you want, I think. It's dark in the apartment. From the back room, through the closed door, psychedelic melodies can be heard of the Doors' song "The End".

Back then, I didn't know of this song, or this band. It's later on that I'll be mad for Jim Morrison as much as for Ostap. I'll translate all his lyrics into Russian, I won't miss a single article about him and I'll see his film fifteen times. Then a long time later, I'll find out that Ostap is paying attention to which song I'll come in to. He is guessing, maybe this is a sign that I am walking in on "The End". I am guessing, a sign of what?

Now, sitting on the bus, I understand that neither the nose, broken by Crip's size-eleven shoes, nor the launched-into-the-wall beer bottle that flew past my ear will bring as much pain as those figures on the balcony, who destroyed all hope. Hope that was born almost five years ago, then, stepping into his room to the music of that song. I also realise I have never loved Crip.

31

But back then I simply found Ostap's music encompassing, sucking me in.

I knock on the closed door. Nobody responds. Maybe he didn't wait for me and asked somebody else, I think. Rubbish. The front door would be closed.

I open the door. In the room, it is even darker than the hallway. Where is the window? All this, of course, really intrigues me, but seriously, where to go, and what and who is even here? I feel for the switch on the wall near the door. A small room appears, flickering in a dim red light. As though from a small candle in the basement. "Wow, how did he come up with that?"

An almost transparent red rubber Kewpie doll has been pulled over a normal light bulb, with its trousers down to its knees.

Peculiar, I think.

Ostap is lying on the bed against the wall, on his back, eyes closed.

He's asleep. He didn't wait. Should have come earlier.

I sit on the edge of the bed. The window is covered with lids from big cardboard boxes.

Dude doesn't like light. I smile. Mole.

On the walls, there are posters with photographs of Chinese women in bikinis. I find this pleasant. I don't have much of an opinion in my narrow eyes, with their Chinese cut. All five girls on the posters...not only the eyes but also the shape of the bodies, faces and lips are like mine. Hmm... In that case, it's not surprising that he likes me. I suddenly feel attractive. Very, very attractive and can't blame Vick for being so into me. Now let's work on this one.

I sit on the edge of the bed and study his sleeping face. Flat nose, prominent cheekbones. Smooth skin on his cheeks. Something jaunty about the corners of his large well-outlined mouth. He looks like a fourteen-year-old Damien from *Omen*. The object of my teenage obsession.

The red light works in his favour, I think. To draw him like this...

I gently touch his forehead with my fingertips. I trail it across the line of his nose with my ring finger, as if with a brush. The back of my hand touches his cheeks. I stroke his lips with my fingertips. His lips gently nip my fingers. "Not sleeping, then," I whisper.

He gently pulls me to him. His hands go around my face, hair, and then under my sweater. Gentle caresses switch to near love bites. I bite his neck and scratch his back, stroking his cheeks and gently kissing them. His tongue in my ear – I melt. He knows the trick of the teens at school discos during slow dances. The main thing here is not to accidentally peck. I gently grab his neck and pull his face to my lips.

I'm on my back with my bare flat stomach. Droplets of orange juice down my navel. He licks. I'm flying away. But I won't give in today. I won't let him take my trousers off.

A few hours later, charged with caresses, we listen to the howling of the Doors, and breathe as if we've just run a hundred-metre sprint. I give in to his attempts to take my top off (trousers stay on!) and do everything that Tasha has taught in such cases. In return, his eyes are clouded with delight. I gaze at the Kewpie on the ceiling and hear: "How many did you have before me?"

He also likes to count!

I draw attention to the formulation of his question: not whether I've had it with someone, but how many of them I've had.

"You're the seventh." I admit that I do keep count. "Well, up to the shoulders. Up to the waist, third. Below…nobody's been below. That makes you zero."

Why admit it? Hating myself right there. Now he'll definitely think I'm some romantic in-love fool!

"Hmm… Wow, I got the impression that Osha runs about nightclubs with chavs," he says doubtingly.

I smile. Well, I had created an impression about myself. That's because I walk around with a baseball cap, laugh out loud, and Tasha visits me and Katka at break. That's who goes to nightclubs and hangs with chavs. "I was once in a nightclub, two years ago. I got smoke in my eyes, and I choked on Tasha's homebrew moonshine."

We both laugh. Finally, I make him chuckle.

"I coughed so hard that my tears were like hail. And Keswick, Tasha's guy at the time, who I fell out of love with at this point, decided that I was desperate to be with him and that I actually went there because of him. This isn't true. But I don't go there anymore."

"He's a fool, Keswick," says Ostap. "We study together for CPC. He doesn't clean his ears."

"Nor his teeth either," I admit.

We laugh again.

"And how many have you had?"

"You're the third. Well, the first two were the childhood."

Third time lucky, hey. Nearly said it but bit my lip on time.

I am so excited that I don't have the strength to speak, just squeezing his hand. All that was before me, he called "childhood".

So that means we're grown up... And how did he learn these tricks? Wow. My boy, sucking orange juice from my belly button, please, anytime...

"It's past eleven. I've gotta go. At eleven I've got to be home," I say.

"Sleep here." Ostap hugs me to him, wrapping me up in a blanket.

"Mum will get angry. Won't let me out. Walk me? Please?"

Ostap only wraps himself tighter and, it seems to me, is already asleep.

I am lying there. Listening to the Doors. Gazing at the Kewpie. Realising that I'm not going to be walked.

"I would have walked," says Vick in my head. I free myself from Ostap's embrace, get dressed and leave.

I want to be angry with him, but the orange memories arouse butterflies in my stomach, and I fearlessly march with not one single lamp to guide me to my dark porch.

CHAPTER THREE

Red Kewpie, Chinese Girl and a Man in a Canvas Jacket

"Why are you always silent?" I ask him once, looking out from under the blanket at Kewpie.

"Always." Ostap smacks his lips, as if he feels a bad taste in his mouth. "Is a tasteless word."

I smile at his idea that words can have a taste. He adds after a pause:

"Words are mechanical waves. Speaking is to make mechanical waves."

I am silent for a long time.

I want to say something clever in response, and I open my mouth a few times in the expectation that this smart thing will fly out, but then I close it, as nothing is flying out. I look around at the room. On the table, a book: *The Teachings of Mao Zedong*.

It dawns on me: the Chinese culture craze is not limited to the choice of girls. Above the bed, on the ceiling, a new poster of a Chinese girl. Maybe it's my sick fantasies, but in the red light of the Kewpie the girl is the spitting image of me. Or Stapler is just teasing me. It's the same as if he came to mine and saw a photo of a nerd with specs and flat cheeks above the bed. Actually, why don't I hang one up? Myagkov, young Woody Allen lookalike, for example. Mum wouldn't understand. Listen, my parents are strict. No Kewpie on a lamp or a poster on the wall. Boring.

And then on the wall I see the earring with red stones hanging on the tiny nail, the one that I lost on the balcony on New Year's Eve.

"I lost one like that," I say.

"Are you sorry?" he asks.

I shrug my shoulders. He sees this as, "Yes, I'm sorry."

"Never have what you can't say goodbye to within thirty seconds," he says pointedly.

"Is that from some film or did Mao Zedong advise?" I say.

Ostap, after a pause, replies: "Mao Zedong advises: to learn."

Is this him saying that I should leave and not take his time away from learning? Is he going to study in the night? Or is it that I have to brilliantly parry with a response quote? For example: "Within thirty seconds, you can only have a wasp. And even then, only if you are a wasp." But I don't know if a quote exists that I can respond with and remain silent. And anyway, why is he being rude? Though I can guess why.

I want to talk about this with Ostap but I fear with each word my ratings will drop. This is the fourth meeting for the whole of winter, including February 23rd, Men's Day, last Friday. I dragged him to the basement on the way from school. I wanted to hear his moans. He moaned a bit and went home.

What a fool I am. What a fool for coming to him without an invitation. Despite all my efforts in bed, he isn't even in the right spirit. I get carried away by his kisses, and he gets blown away by his inflamed desire – I don't let him below the belt. Dodging his attempts to strip me is getting harder, more tempting.

Give in? Or maybe offer more of something? He'll be my first man. But he doesn't have to know about this. And why do I have to apologise for it? Why is he not apologising for the fact that in two months we've only met three times? Of which, one time was in the basement. And he doesn't explain. He doesn't like to speak.

So what if we see each other at school every day. I get it – exams are coming, we're finishing school, starting uni; you have to study but it's a real shame. We have to learn. And how did Mao Zedong advise to learn, if learning is what was thrice advised by Lenin? While Lenin was waving his arms with his advice, Mao soberly nodded his head at the side. And only Mao got into the shot. The Chinese channel translated Mao, as if Mao can advise to learn with his mouth closed. In Russian. It was Ostap who watched the wrong channel. You have to learn. You go yourself and learn.

I am so hurt; I want to leave. Not for Lenin, of course. And if he doesn't like to talk then I'll leave silently. I get out of bed. Dress in silence. Silently leave the room. Quietly and firmly shut the door behind me. Like a motor boat, I could have slashed along the shore, so that long after the waves would splash against the shore like broken latches.

Touching my way down the dark stairwell. No lamps in the porch either.

There is a hope that he would run after me. Say to me, that I am such a fool, that he loves me, and sex isn't everything, and he would wait and do all sorts of sweet utter nonsense. And he's not in the mood for it because... he's jealous about Vick, for example. And I'll say that's ridiculous. And giggle. He won't be jealous of Vick. Now, if it was green-eyed looker Rudi. What a neck chain he has. But those neck chains don't hang round just anyone, only special people.

It's always like this – right before Women's Day on 8th March, which is widely celebrated in our country by the boys giving presents to the girls. I'm left without a gift. It was like this with Keswick in the ninth grade: I gave him some boxers on 23rd February, and he left to stay with relatives on 8th March. In the eighth grade it was even worse – I gave Pogodkov some boxers, and he forgot it completely. At least last year I didn't give anybody any boxers and went home dreamily, bobbling from side to side and carrying two roses, one from Pogodkov and the other from Keswick. And then I even went to a camp in the Carpathians and fell in love with some Lobick with a Carpathian accent.

At least then I drank and had fun. Now everything is so serious; not only am I sober, but also I have something with Ostap. And what happened? Languid expectation. In the trousers! That's the whole point. You've got to take off the trousers. For this you need meetings. Lots, and often. And not once a month. And he doesn't walk me home. And then, where is my end pleasure? I want to receive it too. But I'm not receiving for some reason. As soon as Ostap gets his, he turns to the wall and falls asleep. Maybe he doesn't know how to give it. What are your hands for? There are ten fingers on each. I have counted. I got this at fourteen, actually. Maybe he's not comfy. And I'm stomping home. Without the end pleasure. Everything is comfy to me. Even now. Frost, snow crunching under my feet, my soul feels cold.

People walk past. Not comfortable... For the first time I'm returning home so early from his. Not used to seeing people. My dark staircase at home groans with its rusty door. There's also a lamp near the lift. An unshaven man in a canvas jacket with a red face is waiting for the lift.

Maybe walk? I think sluggishly. The lift opens. But who needs me? The man walks in.

I gallantly step behind him. He presses fourth floor. The doors close. The lift fills with alcohol fumes. I can't breathe, like a dolphin in a tank for goldfish. I examine my boots soaked in the snow. With my peripheral vision, I see that he is leaning towards me. I look up and stumble into his advancing look almost right at my nose and I scream with all my might. Right into his chin. At the same time the doors open on the fourth floor. The guy palms me in the face in fright and disappears.

In our block, the lamps for the lift aren't on every floor. There aren't any on my floor. With shaking hands, I press the button for the seventh floor. My shaking hands grope for the key and squeeze it hard, like they taught me at karate – so that I can drive the tip of it right into the eye or the forehead. And if the key gets stuck in the forehead or the eye, how will I get home? Thank God I don't need to plant or dig anything out.

My hands still shaking, I get the key into the lock. The flat is full of guests. Celebrating Mum's birthday, which was yesterday.

"Osha! Well, finally. For once in your life you'll socialise with your parents." Mum greets me on the way out of the kitchen with a misty Sovetskoye champagne bottle.

"The youth has arrived!" shouts Dad from the table. Before him is a plate of half-eaten Olivier salad and herringbones.

"Paint Brush, sit down! Why did Katerina let you go so early?"

"Yeah, today I decided not to stay too long. Guests at home, after all. And I'm hungry."

I look around the table piled high with food and settle on fried chicken. I always settle for it. If I talk about what happened in the lift just now, they won't let me go anywhere, plus it will spoil everybody's mood. I'll make up with him sometime and will want to return, but not now. Too scared right now.

CHAPTER FOUR

Pies From Pushi's Mum, Red Rose and Pink Bunny

Eighth of March. Dad greets me in the morning with tulips and cake. Then Vick calls: "I wish you to graduate school with an 'excellent' and hurry up and fall in love with me. It's too cold."

"Very noble wishes," I reply.

"Bender not called yet?" Vick asks. I cringe. He doesn't ask about Ostap for no reason.

"No. You're the first," I say, exhaling.

"I want to be first in everything," states Vick.

"Vick, what a piss-take. You are my first male friend, how is that for a title?"

"Crappy, if I'm being honest." He says his favourite phrase: "Will you go out with me?"

I hesitate. If I did, I'd miss Ostap's call. And if he doesn't call, I'd sit again at home and breathe into the phone. What if he left to go to his relatives...?

"I don't know yet. Mum is sending me to the shops to get eggs."

"Very well. Actually, if we can't go out, we will go shopping. I'll be there in ten minutes."

"But not for too long, I still have to..." Vick has already hung up. Why do guys do that when arranging a date?

Vick arrives with huge, most-expensive red chamomile lookalikes. Love Gerberas.

"Wow. My favourite!" I exclaim. "They're so expensive!"

Vick starts to resemble a melting chocolate teddy bear, whose eyes are about to start streaming.

On the way to the shops, he turns to the topic: "Went yesterday to Bender's. Saw a long red rose and a pink bunny. Thought it was for you. Bender denied it. Said Pushi's mum is baking pies. Pushi invited him."

I feel as if I've been dipped in water. Vick paces beside me, sniffing in the cold air joyfully. I want to hit him. So, no point living all day near the phone, while Ostap stuffs himself with pies from Pushi's mum.

No chance. Pushi, Tolly Pushka's cousin, I always thought was beautiful. Small, chiselled body, eyes with fluffy thick lashes, like an Indian actress. Her mouth decorated by bold plump lips, like in an advert for lipstick. Even near-sightedness: when she blinks, looks very cute. Quiet, feminine, will she cry or giggle? No one knows. Or maybe she'll sneeze.

It's all over.

He can go and kiss Pushi's ass and her mum's as much as he likes. In turn and all day. Now I get why he rings me once a month and not on the morning of National Women's Day, 8th March, when all men get in touch with their loved women. He loves her and uses me. Like I use Vick. For jealousy and self-esteem reasons.

Although I don't kiss Vick, especially not below the belt. And Vick doesn't leave me at midnight when I've already fallen asleep to the howling of the Doors.

Vick continues to blab about something and I understand that Ostap won't call today, and won't wish me anything nice, and generally doesn't love me.

I'm not small, not quiet or big-eyed. I actually run to his myself and I leave to go home myself; nobody walks me. He isn't worried at all that I could get attacked in the lift by unshaven drunks in canvas jackets.

Pushi – I reckon he definitely would have walked her home because she is small, quiet and big-eyed.

Lobster-eyed midget and a goody-goody Ms Quietness.

Only why the hell would he hang a Chinese girl on the wall? I should advise him to change it to an Indian girl, Indira Gandhi, for example.

I get home around evening time.

"Someone called you," says Mum from the kitchen. "Some polite class-mate, Ostap."

"Stapler called?" I exclaim, as if my favourite team just scored a goal.

"What is Stapler?" Mum says, peering at me. As if astounded, wondering since when did I become interested in football.

"Just a classmate," I say with an apologetic tone, as if Chelsea scored, while the whole family for the last one hundred and two generations had supported Manchester United.

"Some of our class are probably at his," I continue, making a huge effort to pull myself together. "I was looking for Katka today; maybe she's there. Here, let me ring."

And with a completely straight face, as if I'm selling train tickets to passengers, I walk over to the phone to dial.

Stapler picks up on the second ring.

"You rang?" I say.

"I," he answers.

"Well, what?" I say.

"At Rudi's. I give you ten minutes," he says.

Asking at least one question in front of Mum? No chance. "OK," I say. And hang up before he hangs up.

"Mum, I'm going to Rudi's. Whole class is there."

"Go on then." Mum spreads her hands helplessly. "Home by eleven."

"OK, but I'll be a bit late, today's celebration and all? Please?"

"Half an hour will be enough for you, no? Only let someone walk you home."

"You're my best mum in the world!" I jump in the air.

"Oh, whatever," she replies with a smile.

Overjoyed, I dash off, glancing at the mirror in the hallway, which reflects moist eyes and red gerbera in a vase.

I run to Rudi's. Where is my big rose and pink bunny? Why does Ostap eat pies at Pushi's mum's, and my mum only knows him as a polite classmate?

The door opens – Ostap. Behind him there is no light. This means, nobody is home at Rudi's, apart from Ostap. I understand that all my questions will have to wait till later.

Step towards. Kiss. Like falling into deep snow, wrapped up in a fur coat and sky filled with stars above. He clicks the lock behind me shut. My scarf falls on the floor. Then coat. My back against the cold wall. His hot mouth under my skirt. My quiet sigh. It's getting dark, in other words.

It's night outside. Festive shouts, laughter, screams of the town upon a hill have quietened. We are lying there, where we met. In the hallway. Can feel my head against one of Rudi's dad's boots. In the depths of the hall, the

41

electronic clock in the darkness shows eleven twenty-three. Time to get dressed, go home and ruin the vibe.

"I'm gonna go," I say. My voice sounds lifeless.

"Let's sleep like this."

I shake my head. "I can't."

He sighs. Gets up off the floor. Pulls his jeans on. Turns the TV on in the hall. The blue flickering of the screen lights up the vase of flowers on the table in front of it. A rose. Under the rose, a bunny.

Oh, Pushi didn't accept the gift? Vick-in-my-head points out.

Get the hell out of here. This is my bunny, I reply.

Ostap is shuffling towards me with the gifts. "Happy 8th March."

I smile. And here is the answer to all my questions. "Thank you," I say softly.

"Wow...the scent!" I bury my nose in the flower. "Walk me home?" I look at him pleadingly.

"Yeah?"

"Yes."

"Stay?"

"I can't. Mum won't get it."

"Oh no. Well, let's go." He sighs.

CHAPTER FIVE

Wrong Answer

The spring arrives in April, the real spring, with green leaves, nightingales and forest freshness. I go out to the balcony. See him. Smile dreamily. For it to be like this every day... He's off somewhere with Rudi. In a light-coloured coat. At that same second the phone rings. I don't run. It's like I'm seeing them off. Only on the tenth ring, when the silhouettes of Ostap and Rudi have disappeared into the greening oaks, do I pick up the phone.

"Itty cat, how are you?" Vick says in his deep voice. "Are you feeling the spring?"

"Don't call me a cat. It's like a brother flirting with his sister." I wince. "You guessed right. And what are you feeling over there?"

"Still all the same. Played tennis with Ostap and Rudi. They went to drink beer but I thought I'd give you a call. You want a beer?"

"I don't like beer." My mood is ruined. Ostap doesn't want to call me for a beer but Vick does. And who out of those two loves me more? Three guesses. And you can even guess that Vick isn't an idiot: while Ostap is drinking, the evening with me is guaranteed...

"Well, who won the tennis?" I ask, deflated.

"Aghh it was a draw! Bender was full of beans today, no way of beating him. Definitely ate lots of pies at Pushi's. What does she put in them? Maybe I should get a recipe. You could bake me some too? Eh?"

"L... Let's talk later. Mum's calling me from the kitchen to peel potatoes," I say in a hurry. I want to put the phone down immediately. I want to never hear Vick's voice ever again, informing me of Ostap's tasting menus at Pushi's house.

"So, can you come out or not?"

"I can't. We have guests today," I lie, hang up and start crying uncontrollably, sobbing so much that if my parents were in their room, and not at Aunt Valya's, they wouldn't be able to tell if I was laughing or crying.

Again pies, Pushi, Mum... If I'd had a tennis racket at that very moment

I would have first mutilated Pushi and her beautiful lips and eyelashes so much that her lips would be on her eyelashes and eyes covered in red lipstick. And Ostap would get it right on his important parts. And then on his brazen face so that his glasses cracked and one lens fell behind his ear.

I wipe the tears, pulling over my coat, spraying myself with perfume, and fly out of the stuffy flat into the evening spring.

I walk. Walking helps. Why do I always forget that walking saves me from sadness? Sadness turns into anger. I want to carry on crying but the anger and fresh air make me unable to throw it out, out of my head forever. He is trash. I hate him. I am tired of him. I am no longer paying attention to him. Solidly and firmly. And, by the way, it's time to fast. No food, only water. One week left till Easter. It will help to be indifferent. He'll see an indifference and won't understand. And I'll be indifferent and thin. This thought calms me down. That's it. No cheeky smiles, no jokes, no attention. I quit. Only water.

CHAPTER SIX

The Result of Fasting

"...flat stomach and hard cherries. How can anyone sit on a chair with a thin ass? I don't understand," I whisper to Katka.

"Only water?" exclaims Katka to the whole class.

"Stop shouting," I groan in my favourite stand-up comedian Zadornov's voice.

"Or shall we go and tell the principal. We can put an ad in the local *Pioneer's Truth* in big red letters and run into each class at lunch break."

Katka laughs.

"Olga Smekhova," says the historian Ivan Vasilyevich. "Firstly, take that bottle of beer off the desk, and secondly, give out the workbooks."

"That's not beer, Ivan Vasilyevich, it's water. She's drinking water for the fifth day. She'll be kapets without water."

Hissing at Katka is useless. She doesn't get that she's uncovered the secret of my indifference... Anyway, if she had read Paul Bragg's *The Miracle of Fasting*, she would understand that such things should be kept secret. Armed with a silent smile as if quietly mad, under shocked exclamations of classmates, I take the stack of workbooks and hand them out.

"Valovoy, Dziuba, Tkachuk, Sokira..."

"...my God, so thin," I hear from his desk as I put his notebook in front of his face.

"Katerina Marchenko, Vysochenko Andrey..."

Ignore. Ignore. Great opportunity to ignore. I've waited for this moment for five hungry days. The moment when he would speak to me, and I would ignore him. Generally, it's not difficult. The body only uses energy for walking and smiling. But for extra head turns in different directions it doesn't use anything. That's why men like women who look sick. They do not spill any willingness on the activity; they're indifferent to it all. More chances that she'll be yours. These are the thoughts during fasting. Paul Bragg would envy me.

Most importantly, he's noticed that I've lost weight and I'm in a short skirt and nylon tights.

CHAPTER SEVEN

Katka's Love

Easter passes. April ends. The school year is coming to an end. Ostap does not call. I cackle with Vick and Katka almost every lesson. I finished fasting with bread and sausages on Easter day, and was puking it all up into Auntie Olina's toilet. I am happy with my appearance. Confident, machined, glowing. That's how I see myself in the mirror every morning. I imagine that Ostap is looking at the glow in my eyes and suffering because of his eating pies at Pushi's mum's. But after school, I come home and sadly scribble in the diary about how passionately I love him, and he isn't even batting an eyelid. Am I really so terrible and unattractive that it's impossible to love me even after six days of fasting?

I'll soon find out the answer to my questions. The Last Call school celebration is coming soon, which is also Ostap's birthday.

I'm waiting for it, like Richie waits until his hake is cooked in the blue pot. Like a mother, fertilising her harvest throughout April, waiting for strawberry season. Like frogs waiting for the ice to melt, to indulge in ribbiting.

I am waiting for an opportunity to accidentally, not on purpose, but accidentally, bump into him on the way to the toilet, and he just comes out fastening his belt. Just to think of a possible romance – to celebrate his birthday, instantly make up and together as a pair, me and him, the next day show up at the Last Bell.

And then I can also accidentally drop into the conversation: "In winter I loved oranges so much, and now I'm so put off by them…must be out of season." And then still peel an orange and loudly laugh at Vick's joke.

Also, I strengthen the friendship with Vick. I hope he tells Ostap about me. I also hope that nobody finds out about my hopes. And if Ostap doesn't feel indifferent to me, then he will definitely feel jealous. And then, I can talk with Vick about anything – the arrow on my tights, bags under my eyes – he doesn't mind my mechanical waves.

And Katka, it has to be said, becomes more interesting. She willingly throws herself into discussions about why it isn't working out with Ostap.

"I'm sure it's not because of Pushi," Katka enlightens me on the phone. "They have a friendship like you and Vick. There's nothing more there."

I nod gratefully into the phone and think: though Katka is a bit of a dork, she feels me on a different kind of level.

On that day, the eve of Ostap's birthday, we trudge home from school. The yearly exam in biology and tomorrow's day have squeezed out all the juices from within, plus I am really hungry and can barely drag my feet. Katka, on the other hand, is just glowing. Her radiance is so unlike her. I say to her: "You haven't fallen in love, have you? Eyes like the suns."

"Really?" Katka purrs. I've guessed right, hitting the nail on the head.

"Or the new jacket and pearl earrings just really suit you?" I add.

"It's strange that you ask that," Katka begins through her nose. "But that's exactly what happened to me."

"Wow! Wow! Wow! Tell me, tell me!" I babble in Vick's manner and run forwards, blocking the road.

"I really rarely ask. Always blabbing about Ostap this, Ostap that. Bet you're tired as hell of it!" I carefully take a step back.

"Hm... Well, it's complicated... I actually wanted to tell you about this a while back, but just haven't got around to... It's a long story, and Mum has made amazing stewed potatoes. Eat at mine and I'll tell you?"

Katka knows I love to eat, and stands out with her hospitality.

"Of-by no means-course, let's go," I say briskly, walking next to her again, taking her hand.

"I'm hungry, as always, as you know me."

"I don't know where to start," says Katka to the plate of potatoes.

"Smells so yummy! Your mum is just a culinary genius." I put the spoon of aromatic clear broth to my lips.

"Ah, come on, your mum cooks great too." Katka nervously smiles and starts tapping her fingernails on the table.

"Well, start from the beginning. Where you saw each other, how you met, kissed, didn't kiss. I want to know everything." I am wriggling on the chair in anticipation like before my favourite TV series.

"Hmm. We kissed." Katka smiles slyly.

"It started so fast. Actually, it all started from the kiss. He just threw me on my shoulder blades! Kapets. Lifted my sweater. I couldn't get this out of my head for a long time, and realised I was in love."

"Oh, I know what you mean," I say longingly. "See, mine's also from a first kiss... Well, go on, carry on, when was it?"

"Back in February," she says.

My February just sweeps past me. All I have got with Ostap in February is ten minutes of his sighs in the basement. Not much, better than nothing though.

"I just needed a book on the history of Ukraine," Katka continues. "Only Ostap had it... So, I called him."

"Ostap?!" I am delighted. If Ostap is involved then I must know who it is. Rudi? Now that would be awesome! But I don't interrupt.

"Yeah," she continues. "He says, 'Come and get it then.' So I went."

Definitely Rudi, I think. Well, who else could she have met near Ostap's place? Not Vick or Tolly Pushka. I mean I hope not.

"So, I got there...we yakked for a while. About you, about Vick, Pushi..."

"Yakked?" I am stunned. "I can't squeeze a word out of him! Listen, Katka, you have a talent. In February? Why were you quiet? Did he speak about me?"

Katka looks at me like a kitten who's eaten half of a giant sausage.

"Nothing good, by the looks of things," I say quietly and put my spoon on the plate.

"To be honest, I mostly talked. And he just threw me down on my shoulder blades..."

At this moment everything becomes clear. I shouldn't have eaten the potatoes. What shall I do with them? Next, like often shown in films, Katka is talking to me through sound-proof glass, and in front of my eyes she is falling on her shoulder blades a thousand times, while Ostap lifts her sweater and glares at her big boobs with a maniac's arousal. I try not to look. Why does he throw her down with such fury?

He'll give her a bump. They are falling on the floor, right? Or will she be standing while chatting with him for eighty hours about me, Pushi and

Vick, before he jumps on her like a tarantula. On the bed, must be on the bed. Then it wouldn't have hurt at all…

"Did he put a pillow under your head?"

"What?"

I get up from the table and uncertainly walk towards the door. The main thing is not to puke out the potatoes on Katka's polished floor. On the other hand, that is exactly what needs to be done. I still want to clarify whether it's on the floor or the bed. I stop in doubt. I walk to the door once more. We're always on the bed. Only once in the corridor on the floor.

"Itty, don't go…" Katka rushes forwards. She is crying. Katka the nerdy dork is crying. For the first time.

"If you go, I'll do something to myself…"

"Do it." I shrug. "Get out of my way."

I look into her eyes. I want to hit her really hard. Katka pulls away from the door and from my gaze. I pick up my shoes and walk out barefoot. She stands at the doorway. I put my shoes on. A burning desire to give her one on the ear with my heel. Shame I don't wear heels. After an eternity the lift comes. Breaks the awful silence, as if family members from every apartment have gone to war, so nobody can speak, or laugh… I get into the lift. Katka, along with the doors, goes up.

I want to scream, cry, kick the doors of the lift, but none of this even thinks of escaping out, just lying at the bottom of my stomach with the two spoonfuls of potatoes.

I frantically run home. Wind in my eyes. Lump in my throat. Hard to breathe. Eyes water from the wind, but I don't cry. I run across the road, through the market, up the stairs to the seventh floor. In the hallway I crash into Mum, who is calmly combing her hair.

"Jeeze, Osha, you scared me, has something happened?" she says.

In response, I breathe, sporadically.

"Osha, what's up with you?"

I lean against the closed doors, cover my face and howl into my palms…

CHAPTER EIGHT

The Sweetness of Saying "No"

I'm drawing a caricature of the maths teacher on the table.

"Osha! Are you gonna come to my birthday today?" I hear Ostap's happy voice behind me.

It's break time. Sveta, Juka and Rudi on the third desk near the window surround Ostap. They are having a lively discussion about how much vodka is needed for the evening and who's coming. Katka, behind our desk, is intensely outlining the title of her chemistry book. Next to her is an empty space. My bag is next to Vick's on the second desk.

On the birthday the whole class gets together. This is tradition. So, am I going to Ostap's birthday party? Hearing the question, I feel many things in several seconds before I turn my head in his direction. Tickles in my tummy. If I didn't know about "shoulder blades", I would rejoice from the bottom of my heart and utter a quiet "Yes". Ostap would smugly turn to Sveta, Juka and Rudi, and say something like: "Less' get 'nother bottle of vodka. Or better, two."

Do I have a right to be mad at him because of the shoulder blades? What if Katka and Pushi also got a rose on 8th March? I want to give him the loudest "no" he's ever heard. In front of everybody. It would hurt him. Even if he doesn't love me. I turn my head ever so slightly towards him and say quietly, "No, I won't be coming," and turn back to finish drawing the maths teacher's potato nose. I manage to catch a glimpse of a smile and a glistening in his glasses.

Behind me, a silence reigns. I turn around sharply this time. Like a U-turn. Bravely look Ostap in his eyes, raising my eyebrows, as if I'm surprised myself that I just said such a thing. Ostap badly hides his discouragement and double-blinks.

"Come on," he says, in the tone in which people usually say "yeah, right".

I smile, like my dad smiled to my question when I was six: "When you were in Alaska did you live in a wooden hut or in an iced one?"

I turn back to my desk.

"Ah, why?" he asks behind my back, half as quiet, as if my favourite dog has died, and I don't want to talk. Ostap likes to start his answers with "Ah". And I notice it just now, five months after the first kiss. We do have a super-close relationship, no doubt about that. I put on a fatherly facial expression and reply:

"Ah...tonight I'm reading about the history of the Ukraine. We've only got one book for the whole class, you see. Got it from Katka just yesterday. The Katka with the lovely boobs, you know."

Drawing the teacher's profile, I can feel the fire of stares into my back. Cheeks and eyes are burning. Only the board can see that my lips are shut tight, like Nan's purse one day before her pension.

The caricature turns out perfectly, with a brutally underlined schnozzle, round beer belly and eyes filled with hatred. Why did I do her like that? My favourite teacher.

I think even now that when I turned away, I missed the most important thing his face was showing at that moment.

"Well done," whispers Vick, at hand.

"Yeah, I'm a good drawer," I whisper in reply.

"Osha!" I hear Katka's voice. I've already left the schoolyard, walking past the greenhouse.

"Wait!"

Not stopping, I attentively take a look at the dusty windows of the greenhouse and its missing glass panes. I don't want to talk to her; I want to throw that pot of tradescantia that stands on the windowsill. She catches up with me. She walks silently next to me. And I think that's exactly how she appeared in my life. First of September two years ago she walked next to me and decided for both of us that we would be friends.

"You not going to Ostap's birthday?" she asks through her nose and this time it really annoys me. Why does she have to talk as if she's got a runny nose or is crying? All the time.

"I am sure you heard everything," I say.

"I'm not going either if you're not going," she says quickly.

I shrug my shoulders and say: "Oh, I would go if I were you. He'll get drunk, lay you on your shoulder blades again, then it'll be another four months to remember. It will last you all the way till October, think about it."

"Itty, listen. Wait!"

She pulls me by the sleeve and starts speaking monotonously, as if she is in church and reading a piece from the Bible. Quite scary actually. "You left yesterday, and I poisoned myself with Dimedrol. My mum pumped me back to life. She came home from work and I was in the bathroom unconscious," she continues.

I stop. Then I shout: "What, are you stupid? Why? Are you OK?"

I want to hurl the tradescantia at her even more.

"What was I supposed to do?" she cries back.

"Hang yourself, at least!" I tease her.

She mewls with Piglet's voice whose balloon has just burst.

"You'll never forgive me, and Ostap doesn't love me. I hate myself. But I really fell in love. I can't do anything about it," she exclaims. "Kapets!" She finishes with a howl, which brings out all the hopelessness of her situation.

I look at her fingers, hiding her wet face. I just want to spit at her, and now is the right time, as I wouldn't even get her in the face but in her fingers, and then to rush home quickly to eat Mum's borsch. But I start to feel bad leaving her near this dusty, windowless greenhouse, alone with unreturned love and betrayal.

I hug her and say into her hair: "You're such a fool. And why did you appear in my life? Fuck knows."

"I'm sorry," she whispers into my shoulder, and I wince as if her words smell of mouldy cheese. Yep, just like Stapler would do. Cynical fucker.

"Oh, what else am I supposed to do with you?" I sigh. "Just don't hang yourself any more, please, in the bathroom before your mum's arrival from work because of some rubbish. According to my dad, do you know how many other Ostaps there will be in our lives?"

"Let's never fall out over guys again." Her voice goes back to normal.

"Let's at least never lie again for four months in a row, so I don't blab about the heavenly taste of his saliva, and you don't bite your toe in jealousy."

Katka is giggling. Me too. And we go home together.

*

53

The lock is jammed, and the phone rings. Finally, sorting the lock, I fly into the hall and grab the phone, slamming the door so hard that the windows shake. People throw themselves at the phone like this usually when they show hope that Ostap is ringing and you can refuse him again. "Hello," I exhale into the phone.

"I understand that it makes no sense to persuade you," says the familiar seductive voice.

"It makes no sense." I sit down in the chair, savouring each word, as my left knee shudders. Mechanical waves have to be used sparingly. "You understand correctly, young man."

We're silent. I take note that I'm not at all eager to fill the silence with chatter.

"And...if I say 'please'?" he says.

I like this game.

"Ah, won't work," I answer.

"Katka is despicable. She could have waited till after my birthday..."

"And you talk crap. Happy birthday, crap talker." I hang up.

Is he not a bastard? Accusing Katka of telling me about the shoulder blades. If she hadn't told me, it would have been so good. You can floor and kiss anybody's boobs you want, as long as no one says anything. Ugly. Although I agree about Katka. Probably told me on purpose before his birthday, so that me and Ostap wouldn't kiss on the balcony all night, while she smoked on that same balcony. But I did well. Resolute tone, sharp words.

I put on Queen's "Barcelona". Sing. Dance. Vigorously waving my arms around. Sometimes my legs. I'm spinning around. I hit the chandelier, and it's jumping on a thin wire. Don't care.

Another hour passes. Zhuka rings.

"I was asked to get you to come today to Ostap's. They're saying you didn't work anything out. Forgive him, it's his birthday. Katka isn't going either 'cos of you. Without you all it won't be the same."

And that's really good that without us it won't be the same, I think, filing my nails.

I say out loud: "I'm not stopping her though."

"She said if you go then she will go, otherwise not."

"Zhuka, hun, it's impossible. I only got the book yesterday."

"What the...you fell out over a book?"

"Ah, yeah. I just don't get how you can keep it for four whole months. If Katka hadn't given it to me yesterday, I would have gone in to the exam unprepared..."

"Yeah..." Zhuka sounds puzzled.

"Yep, yep," I reply.

"I don't think I get any of this," says Zhuka.

"That's because the person that asked you to call me doesn't like sharing information."

I don't dare find out from Zhuka who asked her to ring me. If it was Katka, then that's low. Which means she still wants to go to the birthday party of a person whom she's in love with while still being my friend. Now Ostap will definitely have to choose who to kiss on the balcony and who to throw on her shoulder blades under the table. Ugh. I feel a hatred for Katka. Should have thought about it sooner. I would have never let my bra be pulled off by the person whom my friend has been yakking about for the last four months. Stuff her. I'm not even sorry. I'll just use her to my advantage, like she does with me. And now I don't have to laugh at her dumb jokes or listen to how nasal she is. Hell, yeah.

If it's Ostap, then let him know that I'm a tough nut to crack. To refuse him is a greater pleasure than to melt into his arms. That's for sure!

I go out onto the balcony. Spring. Birds. The smell of acacia. Boys walk with girls, crackling sunflower seeds, from the market to the Parapet through Dubki, local oak trees park, and to the school stadium. The last day of school is over. Only the Last Call party is left. My first love story ends in bruises. Good thing I didn't let him...you know.

There, on the other side of the Dubki, Katka suffers from undivided love. Five blocks away, Ostap suffers from his lies. He'll get drunk today.

I stand on the balcony and feel a sense of pride, because I allowed myself to say no, and a sense of loneliness because it's the time to enjoy the end of the school year and the whole school era in general, drinking vodka, dancing till you drop, kissing in corners, and I'm proud and lonely, like a scarecrow in the middle of a sugar beet field. And in front of me is the longest night of my life.

I decide to study English for two hours, then go running for an hour, then by nine o'clock get into the bath, and then fall straight into bed.

CHAPTER NINE

Last Call

The next day is the Last Call celebration. I turn up washed, ironed and sober.

"Split into pairs. Lad, lass, lad, lass," says Vera Viktorovna, our class teacher, pronouncing her "s" with a local accent, in a "sh" way. We call her Vishvish. Ostap appears next to me, grumpy, furrowed and dog-tired. Probably wants to be a pair.

"Well, well," I say brashly. "How was the birthday?"

"You shoulda come and had a look yerself."

"Yeah, not possible. I couldn't tear myself away from the book. Powerful thing, turns out. Start reading, and fall straight on the floor, right on the shoulder blades, and can't stop. Just read and read. Oh, Vick! I thought you swapped me over for Pushi or Katka."

"No way! What, am I a dumb ass or somethink?" responds Vick with his rich bass voice, offering me his arm.

"That's my boy." I smile and take Vick's arm.

"Hurry, Stapler!" I say over my shoulder to Ostap. "Pushi and Katka will get picked and you'll have Vishvish to go out into the line with."

Ostap pours his chocolate, piercing gaze over me, glasses flashing. With a smile plastered on my face, I suddenly feel as if a fork has been dug inside my stomach, feeling sorry that I didn't turn up yesterday. I follow Vick into the line, getting tangled in thoughts about how wonderful life would be if I didn't love Ostap but loved Vick instead. We would probably get married this very day, not even waiting for the end of exams, then ending up God knows where with God knows how many kids.

"So? How was the birthday?" I ask Vick.

"Everyone got drunk. Especially Bender's dad."

"Well, that's not surprising," I say. We both know that Ostap does not like his father, because he's a womaniser and a drunk. In fact, absolutely not like Ostap himself. Nu-uh. Never.

Vick continues: "His dad said a toast, even wished him to have a chick who would a) cook well, b) get laid well, and c) only and exclusively to him."

"Wow," I say, completely nonplussed.

"Yeah." Vick pursed his lips.

"What was characteristic about Bender's reaction to 'get laid and cook' was his wandering smile, but when he heard the 'only and exclusively to him' part, the smile on his face kinda…fell off."

"Two times two makes four" starts playing. The song that we went out to form our first line to, ten whole years ago. We march ceremonially. Graduates' faces show sadness, some holding back their tears. I dance and pretend to play along with a trumpet and guitar, which amuses Vick and me. We try to hold back our bursts of laughter, while walking in silence with our classmates and teachers. Behind us Katka walks with Rudi. Behind them, Ostap and Pushi.

I try to guess how many women Ostap's dad can lay and cook for. And I doubt that it would be only one. Because it's no secret that he has at least three lovers.

We stop and turn to face the middle, where the main ceremony takes place.

"Olga Smekhova." I hear the whisper of our biology teacher. "Too much laughing and distracting others."

I quieten down and lean onto Vick. No longer worrying that Ostap may take it the wrong way.

"Smekha Olgova," I whisper to Vick over my shoulder.

"Too much distring and laughacting others.'

"Gosh, Osha, when did you get so vulgar?" Vick mutters.

"Dear Year 'leven!" yells the principal into the microphone, forgetting the letter "E". The microphone beeps, piercing our eardrums. The principal nervously looks at the deputy in a red suit. The deputy rushes to the podium, shifts something and then nods to the principal. A pause.

"Dear dearlevenyear!" says Vick, pronouncing the letter "E" in the principal's style.

I barely contain a spurt of laughter again. Tears coming out of my eyes.

"Dear-Class-Year-of-the-classleven!" says Rudi, standing behind Katka.

The four of us are dying from laughter. I furtively glance at Ostap. He instantly shifts his gaze from me to the principal.

Yup! Gotcha! He stands next to Rudi. Some eleventh graders they are…
One shags Petrova on Saturdays, who is two years older, and the other throws
eleventh graders onto their shoulder blades, as if they are trees… I stealthily
survey him. A white shirt, two buttons undone at the top. Fringe falls straight
onto his wide forehead, which everyone thinks is smart. Lips chapped and
red. I feel a greedy desire to sink my teeth into those lips and rip his shirt
apart. Buttons flying in every direction. Backhand him on his cheeks from
an animalistic jealousy, biting his neck, shoulders, scratching his back. I turn
to look at Katka giggling next to me. I hate her. I'll get with him, and she
will hear in full detail how many times he came, and whether he moaned or
groaned. I feel awkward. I turn my gaze to look at the principal. If Ostap is
going to be mine, I tell myself, as an adult tells a child not to crush snails,
then only if he loves me… And if he loves me, I'll be the happiest person in
the world and will feel sorry for Katka. But he doesn't love me, he and Katka
kissed, so I hate them, although he definitely doesn't love Katka, she doesn't
understand jokes and is very nasal. In general, it's clear I have a high opinion
of myself.

And the principal is still speaking, loudly mispronouncing his Russian
words in Ukrainian style.

CHAPTER TEN

Beginning of the End of a Little Girl

Friday. Slogging. Nerves. Sometimes tears. Finally, the last maths exam is done. After a lot of melon vodka by the name of Stopka we are at Tolly Pushka's house. Ostap appears nearby. A soft gaze.

"Do you have a cig?" I ask. First attempt to speak since the day of the form line.

"Yeah…let's go have a smoke, babe," he says and gently touches my shoulder.

The word "babe" has a magical effect on me. I obediently head to the balcony. Katka's voice behind: "You peeps smoking? I'm coming with you."

I sigh and roll my eyes. Again, she's on my case. Next time I'll go to the balcony unnoticed.

The situation turns. Everyone is grimacing about something. I find him looking at me, and head out to the balcony. Ostap instantly appears. I look at him. In silence. Without hate. His glance is brave and honest. Mine is observing. Everything inside squirms. I don't know how it would have ended up, but behind Ostap, the door creaks ajar. Katka's nasal voice: "Do you have a cigarette?"

Behind Katka, Vick's voice is heard:

"Rudi is so lucky. While we're out here smoking, he's munching all the crab sticks!"

"Well, I'm coming with you as well." Rudi is heard behind Vick. Ostap heads away from the door, and the whole gang, one by one, spills onto the balcony.

"Used to be like…" continues Rudi, handing out lighters and cigarettes at all angles. He himself holds a white pen, clasped between two fingers, sucking on it like a cigarette. "Lads go out to smoke, and I stay to chat up all the lasses. Now all the lasses smoke as well, so I'mma chase straight after them."

I laugh and light up from Vick. I'm surprised and elated that we've been interrupted. Telling myself off for softening to Ostap. Why did I invite him to the balcony with my gaze? Why did I look at him without hatred?

Under no circumstances, in any case, am I to be left alone with him, looking at him without hatred! I haven't forgiven him for anything. Again, the same five months will repeat themselves from the beginning. Stormy kisses on the balcony, and then waiting for his call for months on end. I stub out the butt. Crawling between people's backs, I climb inside. Get to the front door, put my shoes on and leave Tolly's flat. Just like at Katka's before, run down the stairs home. It's only 4pm. I'll hide at home, study English, and then I'll go running.

From the drunken vodka, smoked cigarettes, my heart begins beating faster. I slow down my pace. Not going to go running, already drunk vodka. I stop on the second floor, sit down and put my head in my hands. The idea of quietly disappearing and hastily studying English with perseverance for the remaining five hours begins to lose its originality. What the hell am I supposed to do now? Why do I have to fight my feelings? Why can't I love a normal person, one that won't cheat on me with my girlfriends? Why do I feel sick from one kiss with Vick? He's not a bad guy. Broad shoulders. Tall. Hairy though, and snub-nosed. But big lips. Almost like Marlon Brando in his youth. If I go tell him, he'll get so happy. But Ostap wouldn't get happy. Firstly, I'll go buy some cigarettes and a lighter, so as not to ask shifty characters with their sad insolence. And I'm not his "babe"!

With a pack of Marlboro Lights and a lighter in my pocket, I jump into Tolly Pushka's flat and, at the door, announce:

"Vick, I was going out to get some cigs, and thought…" I stop at the door shaking off my shoes. "You're a spitting image of Marlon Brando in his younger years."

Vick laughs, badly hiding his shyness. Ostap sits on the sofa, striking his lighter. Nodding his head at the same lighter in agreement, smirking. And I'm thinking, that after such a valuable observation, I doubt he will want to retire with me alone to the balcony.

"You should walk Katka home instead. I've literally got two steps to my door," I say to everybody and head in the direction of my block.

"Osha, do you want to end up like last time?" Vick shouts in my direction.

"What was it last time?" I ask. Why did he have to word it like that? Now Ostap is going to think that there was some kind of last time between Vick and me. I want Vick to walk Katka with the others, stopping Katka from enjoying Ostap's company. Vick wants to weave himself around me so that he can stand in the lift for two minutes and once again realise that there won't be anything between us.

"I meant like last winter, when that man was latching onto you in the lift!" shouts Vick to my tracks. Now Ostap is going to think there was a last time that I told Vick about, and not him.

"God, well, how long ago was that?" I take two steps towards mine and stop.

"Stand here. If I don't come out in two minutes screaming 'Murder!', that means that the man is busy. Peeling potatoes or getting ready for exams."

Vick wants to say something else, but I'm running. Maybe now Ostap will ask, and Vick will tell him all about the man in the lift in winter, and Ostap will feel guilty that he never did walk me home. But he won't ask. And Vick won't tell him.

CHAPTER ELEVEN

End of the End of a Little Girl

The next morning, on the Friday, I'm having breakfast in front of the TV. The phone rings.

"Let's go camping." Ostap's voice sounds lively. New. I finish chewing my sausage into the phone, and say:

"Your voice, it's as if you were thinking all night about this ingenious suggestion."

In reply Ostap is…laughing. Laughing?

"Maybe," he says, which completely puts me into a dead end.

I get a sneaking suspicion that he really was thinking about it all night.

"I could go camping." I liven up and stretch over for my cup of coffee.

"Overnight," he adds.

"Don't have a tent," I say, sipping.

"I do. A three-room one."

His multi-purpose tone begins to tire me out. But I do believe in the three-person tent; you never know what his dad brought back from his trip to Egypt twenty years ago.

I grow suspicious: a farmer's brain, and he ventures to Egypt. Maybe he's in the KGB? "Wow…" I play along. "Ah, who's going?"

"Whole class," he replies.

"Whole class? When did everyone manage to plan this? It's 11am."

"Phone's been blowing up since nine," he says. And adds conspiratorially: "Getting together at mine in an hour."

"Well, I'm going to ask then." I put the phone down and conclude Ostap can be…fun, I would even say. Hm… And he's declared his next chess move…check. Next, I'm covered by an indescribable happiness: a three-bedroom tent! Overnight! What am I supposed to take? Got to call Vick. I'll pull over three pairs of jeans, so he doesn't take them off! Hm, Vick doesn't pick up. What if Mum doesn't let me go? She'll see my helpless excitement…

Mum lets me off. I promised that on Sunday by 11pm I'd be home. She helps me to cook some food. I'll take a kilo of potatoes, seven boiled eggs, a chunk of salo in a bag, a quarter of a bread bun, a bunch of radishes, a knife, and salt. My bag is near the doorway.

Shower. Make-up. I collect my stuff. Knickers. Knickers again and again. Better even, four pairs. Better with knickers and without happenings than with happenings and only one pair of knickers. In that case better without any knickers at all.

Ten to twelve. Better to be a little late. At least by five minutes. On the other hand – the whole class is going. Bad to keep everyone waiting. And don't really want to hang out at home for any extra time. What if Mum changes her mind or tells me to change into something else. I leave the house, unaware that I will return home a different person.

Sunday. Eleven o'clock in the evening. Back. Good thing that parents are asleep and won't see my face. That's where all is written. I haven't slept for two nights, and my face is glowing a wild blue. I swim into my room. Like the Apostle Peter on water... Got to hide myself under the covers, or else I could get nicked. Can't be having such happy eyes from a lack of sleep. No, we did sleep once on Saturday, from six in the morning till midday. In his three-room tent. It was hard to tell whether it was am or pm; that's why everything seemed like a two-day night. And everything is written. I brush my teeth and see his hot chocolate eyes in the mirror. Put on my nighty and feel his silk hands on my shoulders. Under the duvet, on the pillow I breathe in the aroma of his skin and hair. I want to kiss, caress, embrace all these blankets and pillows. Butterflies in my stomach fly around without perching. Come on, butterflies, stay. Once again, like a film, this short, long, two-day three-room important night flies around in my memory. I close my eyes and am taken away to the beginning of the camping trip.

I walk up to his door. Just like for the first time in winter, the door is open. Not a soul in his flat. Where is everyone? Quiet. I lock the door shut. Walk to his room. It's pitch black. Turn on the light on the right-hand side. The Kewpie intimately glows red. I make my way to the table on the opposite side of the room, where the window is patched up with cardboard. I sit on the chair. I understand everything. There is no trip with the whole class. This is shown by the absence of pre-outing mess in the kitchen and the imposingly stretched-out Ostap on the bed in darkness. Jim Morrison purring quietly in the background is also showing this. I want to jump onto Ostap and wildly love him. Why do I always want to jump on him? Maybe I was a monkey in my past life? And he – a tree. I smile. To deafen my own "want", I hit the switch on the table lamp, and clearly announce: "I want to speak and vodka."

He, as if some sort of accordion, folds into a lotus pose. He asks solicitously, like a doctor asking a mental patient: "Will champagnske work?"

I nod quickly and sit opposite him in the same pose. He pulls out a bottle of champagnske from under his bed without looking up. Opens it. I don't blink and don't cover my ears as the bottle pops.

He pours the glasses, which are already standing on the stool next to the bed, like a table of pills at the bedside for the ill.

I excitedly take the glass, asking: "What do you want from me?"

"To have champagnske." He shrugs his shoulders.

"I haven't been faffing round with you for almost a month now," I lie.

"That's a pity," he says. Lying?

"And you're at it again… Stapler, listen to me." I inhale air into my lungs. Am I really about to say what I'm about to say?

"I'm going to ask you something very seriously now."

Ostap receives my nerves. He stands the glass back on the stool, folds his hands, as if to pray, presses his face onto them and looks at me.

"Please, leave me alone," I say theatrically.

I'm silent. We're both silent.

I continue loudly: "I can no longer stand any Katkas, who dart back and forth for textbooks, like mimsy were the borogoves[1], no more Pushis, whose mums cook awesome pies, for whom you went like a fox into a chicken farm…"

I don't see a guilty smile in reply and am taken aback for a moment. Ostap doesn't move a single muscle in his face. In general, maybe it's uncomfortable for him to react because his chin is clamped between his fingers.

"And why do they have to be my friends?" I continue. "I'm happy for you! You're popular; girls are throwing their pies, their bras, rare textbooks at

---

[1]   The line from the Jabberwocky poem, *Through the Looking-Glass, and What Alice Found There*

you. Good one, carry on. But I'm not playing these games anymore." I make an effective pause and regain my breath.

"I can't." I shrug.

"I won't." I exhale heavily for even more effect.

"So, let's drink to that."

With a sense of relief, I lean over with my glass of champagne to his on the stool. Ostap doesn't move.

I shrug my shoulders and down mine in one. Bubbles in my nose, my ears. I begin to feel light and almost indifferent, that he doesn't love me. I'm ready to accept it with a smile. I've said my piece. Yeah! Ostap slowly takes his glass, looks at it and is silent.

"I knew you'd be silent. That's fine. I've said what I wanted to. And now I want to leave."

I try to pull my legs apart from my pose. To jump from the bed, and to disappear, like a doe from the edge of a thicket, but my legs are numb.

"And I want a toast," he utters.

"Wow, it speaks." I stop untwisting my legs. "The achievements of technology these days." I stretch my legs forwards. The tips of my toes touch his knees.

"Go on," I say more quietly, careful not to scare away the warmth that his knees are sending to me.

"Also wanted to start with a conversation."

Start, I note to myself. I personally want to finish. Will there really be an offer? The butterflies startle again. Maybe I should drink something from the insects? A bark of oak or some shell of walnut balsam. Spray some anti-moth. I lean over for another sip of champagnske, to quench the awoken instinct of a monkey.

"Honestly, I'm kinda shocked by your speech, ma'am," he says in Russian. Underlining his disposition to me.

It's easy to imagine with how much pleasure I catch these notes. They appear extremely rarely. And when they do appear, I realise without any disgust that I feel like a dog who has pleased its owner. Strange, because I always thought that love should be equal. But I am in the middle of realising that his every word, intonation, gaze, decides my mood.

And sitting on the bus, leaving my love in another country, the reason for breaking up becomes clear to me: the war of two kinds of love. One is big, like an elephant – the love for Ostap. And the second, small like an ant – the love for myself. This same ant, in the span of five years, fought for space, which was taken over by the elephant. I realise here, on the bus, that the ant is growing. But back to our conversation.

"Firstly," Ostap continues his correct Russian speech. "Vick is always around you."

"And what's he to—"

"No…" Ostap takes his index fingers from his chin. "…interrupting. Please."

I once again fall humbly silent.

"I'm upset that you let him be around."

I nod discreetly as a sign of understanding.

"On the third day after New Year's Night…"

I smile, touched. He remembers New Year's Night. So, it exists! So, my world in which there is a New Year's Night exists. The one in which looking at the love bite on his neck makes your insides rip apart from the flood of memories, but all you can do is dreamily smile and make it look as if you're listening to the teacher… My God, how much I love him. Can hardly breathe at times.

"I was coming back from the village, from grandma's and uncle's," Ostap continues.

"Cherishing the thought: I'm going to ring Koshka[2] so we can both listen to the Doors." Ostap takes a pause, from which I understand that I am Koshka, and now he's going to tell me why he didn't ring after New Year's Night.

"I saw how Vick was swerving through to yours. That evening I listened to the Doors and ate oranges alone."

He fell silent, and I looked, my eyes full of regret, as if I had done a do-do on the mat, and because of this they took my bone, on which there was still meat.

---

[2]   Kitty (trans. from Russian)

"Every holiday, 23rd February, 8th March, I knew that he had been to yours or was coming over. Pushi and Katka were only to make you feel the same pain..."

I want to throw my arms around his neck and lick him until he heals. Till he completely forgives and forgets that pain. Because I know how much it hurts, and don't want him to feel it. But I am quiet and drink my champagnske. Let him speak out.

"I go to Vick's the next day with some booze, deliberately. I ask him: 'Is there something between you and Itty?' He replies: 'There is hope.' So you gave him this hope. Right?"

"Can I speak yet?" I ask him huskily.

"Not yet." He continues: "So, from this I become all melancholy, and Katka comes to hand. I don't want to be a cigarette in a packet next to any Vicks, Keswicks, and whomever else you manage to kiss. And who knows what else you did to them before me..."

In Ostap's room, which is illuminated with his desk lamp and red Kewpie, where his walls and even his ceiling are plastered with posters of Chinese girls, the purring of the Doors is interrupted by a sharp slap!

"I didn't do anything to anyone!" I shout, clearly remembering our interaction in the cellar in February. I try to jump from the bed and run, this time forever, when all of a sudden, Ostap's long arms grab me and put me on the bed. We breathe unevenly onto each other's faces. Tears appear. I look through them into his eyes. They're full of gratitude and hell knows what else; that touches the bottom of my soul. I'm lying on my shoulder blades. I can't forget Katka. I hold back my desire to rip his shirt: "We haven't finished."

"So, let's finish." His voice is calm, his cheek burns. I feel calm under his gaze, like a snake being charmed under the magic sounds of a pipe. A boa. He gets off me reluctantly, and we take to the starting position. He – into the lotus; me – legs forwards.

"I'm sorry. I didn't mean to offend you, ma'am."

I nod, and think to myself, you did.

"I'm really glad if it's like this," he continues. "If it is not at the highest level of experience, I dare to suggest that you might actually have feel—"

"I'm going to choke you if you utter even another letter on the subject," I hiss.

Ostap smiles widely, just like Vick. His hands are on his lap now. And doesn't say anything else, just swaying lightly, like a rocking horse. I drill him with my gaze.

"So, what's the toast to?" I ask.

Ostap looks at me, at his untouched glass of champagnske, fills mine up and says:

"To the slap."

I don't move. He dries up completely.

"I understand that you're finished, young man?"

"Yes." He puts the glass on the stool. I can reply now. And I say:

"So. Vick is my friend, just like he is yours. Yes, he rings me, comes round, knows my mum, but as a friend should. What's stopping you from doing the same? You have friendships with mums of all these Pushis. And if you don't like my mum that much, don't be friends with her. But why throw Katka on her shoulder blades, when she comes round to yours for a textbook?"

We both fall silent.

"So stupid," I declare out loud.

"Don't think so," he says.

"Can I just ask one thing about Katka?"

He raises his eyebrow.

"What did she say to you to make you jump on her like a panther on a squirrel, which made her fall in love with you so hard?"

Ostap is silent. He won't answer.

"I'll say this," he begins.

He will answer! I strain my ears.

"She said all this rubbish about you and Vick being an ideal couple. So, there I decided was the right moment to shut her mouth and win my bet with Rudi. This was when you both first came to our class…"

I am not surprised. I knew it – a sporting interest: who will show the other their breasts first.

"Well, you won then," I say. "Rudi hasn't seen Katka's or mine. I hope you bet something clever?"

"On a bottle of beer." Ostap shrugs his shoulders.

A sip of champagnske. A feeling of incompleteness. I look at the mark from the slap on his face. Good work. To sink into his lips…too early.

"I want to smoke," I declare. "A break."

I go out of the dark room onto the balcony. The same one on which I'll see the figures, four years later. The light of the early evening cuts into my eyes. What time is it…must be around 5pm?

In the isolated room, with its wallpaper and newspapers, not for the first time I forget there is another reality outside of Ostap's. Laughing couples lightly walk around the lake, through the oaks around the Parapet, chewing on semechki. The noise of the carousel, on which two drunken men are riding, never kids. The moisture of the wood, the smell of blooming cherries, the croaking of frogs. The second day of summer is on the streets, the last day of exams has been left far behind back in early June, and now the youth wander the streets in the evening and exam takers don't hate them anymore.

A week today is our graduation ball. Silk dresses, mostly beige, blue and pink, but you can find wine-red, and dark blue; jackets with all kinds of peony shades, and only Rudi's is dark green; teachers with curls all over their heads, and armfuls of flowers.

But all this is after, in the next life, a week from now. And right now, I'm standing on the balcony of the ninth floor, smoking and feeling stupid and happy, like a newborn piglet. Ostap is jealous. There's no need to be, but it feels good. Let's face it, hehe. My face has an asexual, piggy unattractive smile. I resist the urge to softly grunt. My head is filled with out-of-place phrases from my favourite film. For example, this one: "Well, that means he does actually thisandthat me."

The door behind me creaks. A lighter strikes.

"Alright here on the rock," he says.

He speaks in Ukrainian.

He's like this now – soft, defenceless and happy. Probably also realised that I thisandthat him so like this and like that and like this and…

"Yeah, it's a good place this one…" I nod.

We smoke. Just like Richie the cat with his nose right up to the window, trying to catch the air of the fresh dusk.

"Kinda dark for 5pm. It's gonna rain," he purrs. He switches to Russian. Shy.

A dense purple cloud hastily pulls the sky and leaves a thin bright violet strip on the horizon.

"Heavy cloud," I say. And at that same moment, on our ninth-floor ledge, just like on all the other ledges, huge raindrops start to fall, almost as if they're soap bubbles.

"Bang-bang-bang," the rain drums. The youth scatters to their houses, under the carousel, or into the Kidev, a Georgian restaurant. You can drink cognac there, dry up and eat hot khinkali. Loud cheerful shrieks and bass-tone voices "ahhing" can be heard. The fine bright slit in the horizon disappears. The thick line of rain shields us from the trickling problems of Holmistiy. And we will never know where the youth scattered to in the end – under the carousel or into the restaurant.

Ostap's hands tightly entwine me; he presses his cheek firmly close to mine.

"I don't want to argue anymore," he says quietly. In Ukrainian. I turn to him. Lean onto the wall of the balcony. His hands fold behind my back.

"Why did you call me to the tent? And not Katka or Pushi?" I ask.

His eyes glisten, and the thin dimple from the edge of his nose to the corner of his mouth makes him look shy.

"Why do all the girls in my room look like you?" he asks softly.

I knew that they looked like me!

My face stays serious, but soft.

"Because you're not Pushi or Katka. You're Koshka. And you're mine. Yes?" he finishes with a whisper.

I can no longer stand his gaze and nod several times to his chest, bare, under two buttons. Not knowing where to put my eyes, so as not to scare him with my happiness, I count his moles, which are arranged in a row under his collarbone. Seven moles, similar to the tail of a comet. The first is the largest, the last barely visible.

"I want to get wet," I whisper to the moles.

I pull off my shirt, under which is a violet swimsuit providently pulled over me for the camping trip. I lean over the balcony railing. Drenched with rain, as if from a wooden bucket. From the rainy shower I return back into shelter, to a sweet kiss. Raindrops from my hair onto his cheeks, his moles. And we don't think about Pushi or Katka or Vick that night and the next nights. One by one things drop from us. The swimsuit, the T-shirt. Then his trousers on the floor are joined for the first time ever by my jeans. A whole eternity passes before we are on the bed. He freezes for a long while, looking inquisitively at my eyes. As if my eyes promised him something back on the balcony. His sweat drops onto my forehead.

"Are you mine?" he whispers.

"Yeah," I answer, whispering back.

And this time we are taken away for real.

I wake up. The electronic clock on the stereo glows two zero three. Ostap sits still on the chair, looking at me attentively. Taras Shevchenko would have sat like this, writing his poetry about the thirteenth year passing by.

Here he is, for the first time. In response, I confusedly stare at him and decide that something has happened. Maybe we forgot to close the balcony, and then it got wet from the rain and I...? Fell off. I don't hurry to ask. It feels nice that he's looking at me. Deeply, attentively. As if my face has a difficult equation scratched onto it from a Skanavi textbook.

"Let's go for a walk," he says in the tone of our maths teacher, when announcing a correct answer.

It's moist, dark, warm on the street. Soundless. Nobody. We walk in silence.

"Do you regret it?" he asks.

I walk next to him. Squeezing his hand. Silent. What do I say? It's magical. Indescribable. I'm in a fairy tale. Mechanical waves. And do a ballet pas. Shoot, forgot my tutu. Or joke with him that the first time with him is much better than, for example, it would be with our bold historian Ivan Vasilyevich, if I'd gone for that?

I run forwards and bury myself into my newly loved place, into his moles. He tightly embraces me. And we stand like this for a long time. In the middle of an empty night-wet street, under the blooming apple trees. Steam from the asphalt. And cars not driving past us.

PART TWO

Little Girl In The Hilly Capital

A Conversation With Denis, Who Doesn't Like Deodorants

My favourite chocolate bar falls on my lap. Like a piece of badly glued paper, I tear my glance away from the window. Lift my head.

"This is for you," says a well-built guy with grey eyes. *He smiles with pushed-forwards teeth, which remind me both of a donkey and the detective from the cartoon* The Bremen Town Musicians. *His appearance says he's about thirty... five. He looks grown up.*

Good thing you explained who the chocolate's for, I think, and smile.

"My favourite," *I say out loud.*

"He's hitting on you," *Richie would have said with boredom, if he were sprawled out next to me.*

"My name is Denis. Where are you from?" *he asks, sitting next to me.*

Help! He sat next to me. That's exactly why I don't like these kinds of guys. Give me a treat and go away. But no, he has to get an interview for that.

"Olga. From near Kiev. I doubt you know the town. It's called Kholmysty," *I throw over my shoulder, frowning.*

The main thing is not to start being witty with him, because then he won't ever leave.

Well, why is he not saying anything, just sitting there and stinking? Let's ask him something, let him jibber-jabber quickly and then back to his seat.

"And you?" *I ask.*

"And I," *the guy shakes his head in a devil-may-care kind of way, as if to say, yep...that's me...surprising you right now:* "I'm from Odessa."

Tedious type. I really don't care where he is from.

I stare out of the window. Rustling the unopened chocolate bar in my hand.

"Were those your parents seeing you off?" *asks Denis, not shying away at all. Probably thinks that I'm just nervous and that I've got nothing better to say. And he's going to save the day with his question.*

No. My classmates Tanya and Vanya, I almost blurt out. Maybe I should give him back the chocolate? He still won't go away. But will just keep asking me if I respect him or not.

Instead of all this, I nod.

"And how did they let their daughter go so far?" he asks. I notice that his "s's" all sound more like "sh", like that man from Odessa who presents the comedy show. I want to say: "Lishten, mate, pleash leave. Can't you tell I'm bishy, looking out the window?"

But I reluctantly shrug my shoulders, as if I don't know how I got so lucky, but still cherishing the moment when he'll finally leave to look out of his own window, and not mine.

"Are you the only one in your family or do you have brothersh, shistersh, so there's someone to look after?"

"The only one," I exhale.

"And why are you going to England?" Denis asks.

Yep, he's got a whole goody bag of shiny questions. Lay them all out before the road. Annoying! And I've still got a day and a half with him on this coach. I present to myself the idea of pretending to fall asleep.

"Did you by any chance arrange this trip through Lena?" Denis asks another passing question. He moves awkwardly, which emits another gush of cat-piss-like-sweat smell.

"Yeah, why?" Hearing a familiar name, I once again turn to him and lean on the window. Got to maintain some sort of space, mate, eshpeshially if deodorants aren't an option.

"I'm meant to be getting picked up by Michael Vishkvarka," says Denis.

"Me too." I'm disappointed. But his underarms are shut, so at least I can breathe. Please don't move, please don't move!

"So, we can find him together! Class!" exclaims Denis and he raises his hands, as if it's New Year's tomorrow. I am about to cry as I contemplate the hours of time ahead of me enduring stinky gases that actually bite your eyes.

"Do you know English? My English is shit, to be hornest."

To be hornest… Hey Vick, I think.

"Ten years in school, four in college. Let's see, what have I learned," I say.

"And me only in school, but I don't remember nothing. Well you rest up; eat your chocolate, we'll chat later."

I breathe a sigh of relief. I'm happy for Denis that he has found himself *a translator and immediately freed me from his questions. If I didn't know English, he'd have kept annoying me. It's fine; a pair of strong hands will come in handy.*

And the next moment, as if there never was a fair-haired guy called Denis, I return to my memories.

So, what happened, if Pushi, Katka and Vick all sank into the background?

CHAPTER ONE

When We Got Enrolled

Graduation. Love on the desk in an empty classroom. Love next to the greenhouse behind the bushes where I shrug my shoulders to the dusty vases with tradescantia. The dress hides what the bushes don't. But nobody walks past. The murmur of the vodka-candy evening in its motley dresses and peony jackets gathering in the auditorium. Soon the kaleidoscope of lovemaking changes to greeting the sunset near the river.

We're on a boat on the shore of Stugna. The lads throw their once-starched, ironed, and now wet and stained shirts, jackets and trousers off and are launching themselves off the boat into the water. The girls scream and whoop and drink for every guy that jumps.

Ostap jumps. Screams. Whooping.

"For Ostap!" shouts Juka.

"For Ostap!" we scream.

Silence. We drink.

"You know," Katka puts an empty glass next to her bare, neat knee, "I still like him."

I shrug my shoulders. Me too. Therefore, no chance.

"You know, it reminds me of that scene from that comic TV show Yeralash," I say. "When this boy is eating an orange, and the other says: 'Now, if I had an orange, I'd definitely share it with you.' To which the first boy replies, 'Yeah, it's a shame you don't have an orange,' and smiles smugly."

In response, Katka smiles, but sourly. Not a funny scene for her, I understand. "And do you have one?" she asks, watching the wet Ostap climbing up the steps to the deck.

Water is dripping from him; he's fresh-faced, mischievous and in general nice to look at. I pour some vodka into my cup, then into hers.

"I do have an orange." I look her in the eye, leaning over with her cup. It's better to chop the dog from its tail straight away, than piece by piece. "And the orange is mine, Katka."

Katka looks through me, glass-eyed.

"For Rudi!" Zhuka shouts again. We didn't notice how Rudi had dived in the water too.

I'm hooting and whooping. Drinking. Katka doesn't move and looks through me, still the same. Did she swallow potassium cyanide or something? I put a hand on her shoulder and say, like a witch uttering a scary tale about toil and trouble: "There's a whole sack of pears in the shed, just lying there. Look at Rudi, for example."

Katka widens her eyes and looks at Rudi. We both do.

"He's a beauty, not just a guy. Probably does a hundred push-ups a day, a chain with a cross on his chest like an athlete. Black wet hair, cheeky eyes and a shameless glare! This one can do you so well, he'll wipe your memory for a week," I say, surprising myself.

Katka raises her eyebrows. As if what I said about Ostap is nonsense compared to what I just revealed about Rudi.

Katka and I don't talk about Ostap anymore. My mornings and days are filled with preparation for the entry exams to the University of Foreign Languages, and evenings with the smell of oranges. That summer, we peak to such highs, that Katka's and Vick's woes are no longer visible. And the altitude of the wave, either the size of a mountain or a haystack, makes no difference to me. As long as it is high. Once in the middle of July, I hear:

"Tomorrow I'm getting ready for an exam. I'll call you myself."

Tomorrow goes by very broken, and I am itching to go to his, even for an hour! At the same time, Ostap's voice: "Stupid!"

On the day of enrolment Ostap's phone is silent. The scariest thoughts creep into my fallen-in-love head. He doesn't love me; he's bored of me. Or no: he doesn't want me anymore. Pain. I'm convinced of this till exactly 9pm, when at 9pm, the doorbell rings. Ostap stands at the doorway, with a strong smell of something alcoholic. His eyes from underneath his glasses bobble with happiness. Later we are up in the woods, on his grey jacket. His hot body is on me. We selfishly breathe in the pine air. Up above is a jolly moon, which gallops atop a pine tree.

Then I listen open-mouthed, to how the Shevchenko Uni committee was put in a difficult position, listening to an applicant who calmly recited *Kobzar* for the last twenty minutes. By the evening Ostap's surname is gleaming on the list of the accepted. That's how you can save yourself ten thousand dollars.

I don't tell Ostap that tomorrow I've got my entry exam. Afraid that he'll send me home to study. At five in the evening, the next day, I walk to his in a smart shirt, with an empty plastic bottle and an offer to go to the brook for some water.

Near the brook, on the sandy edge, are shaggy bullrushes and his most violent orgasm in the world. I whisper: "And also: I got enrolled!" He tightly squeezes me to him, and we sit like this for a long time. I am on him, with his lowered trousers on the wet sand, frogs in the plants croaking with envy, and the rippling of the brook emanating from the distance.

Now we'll study in Kiev and live in Kiev too, probably. We'll visit each other; go to all sorts of cafes, theatres, boozing with new student friends.

What is rushing around in his head, I don't know. I only know that there, under the rippling of the brook, we sit and dream. And the frogs in the bullrushes still croak.

CHAPTER TWO

Baba Masha or Miss Marple

First of September. The students of Kholmysty march in unison to the 'school' bus stop, getting on the bus and leaving to study in Kiev at their new universities. I also march to the stop. Apart from the intention of learning and not bunking any lectures, so that I'll become "At least some sort of human being" in the words of Mum, I plan to rent a room in Kiev. Doesn't matter what kind. As long as it's far away from my parents. As long as it's closer to Ostap. Katka is properly lucky. She is given shared halls. I am getting ready to go over to hers after lessons.

After the set formalities, and our introductory lecture to English, I walk up to reception. A middle-aged woman with violet lips hands me over a magazine for ten minutes, as there is a queue. Flicking through the pages, behind me, are two student girls with pigtails.

"Start reading from the end, not from the beginning," says the violet lips strictly. "Those ads are two years old."

"Ah, oh yeah," I grumble.

The students with pigtails giggle at my completely reddened ears.

Barely making out the handwriting, I read: "For rent, five minutes' walk from uni, on the Grand Vasilkovskaya, one hundred and fifty karbovantsiv a month."

One hundred and fifty karbovantsiv a month!

That's one pound fifty. A month! I don't need to pay any more. I hurriedly write out the address, hiding myself from the pigtails. What if they see it and run to Grand Vasilkovskaya faster than me? I slam the magazine shut, hand it back to the violet lips and jump out of the university.

I'm pretty sure that the place is probably not all that, but, damn, one hundred and fifty karbovantsiv per month in Kiev, five minutes from the uni, I'll happily live in a closet. It's probably already occupied. Although the ad was posted today – a small glimmer of hope.

I march under the sunny Grand Vasilkovskaya, smiling about future freedom. Now I'm studying in Kiev. This isn't a dream. I saw the professors and classmates with my very own eyes. Blonde Sasha with glasses and brunette Maria, with tightly pursed lips, both with short, dishevelled haircuts, ask how old I am. Sasha is twenty-five, and she rushes off home, because she has a seven-year-old daughter who also has a first of September today.

Maria will be eighteen in November, and she wants to go to the library while the books still haven't all been taken.

And I'm approaching the address, with its wonky handwriting.

I get to the entrance. There's a cool smell of chicken broth with peas and a sour aroma from the bin, which reminds me of childhood. When I was three years old, we lived in Kiev behind the zoo. Our block smelt like this. I wanted to live in Kiev even more. Flat number one. First floor, of course. Tall wooden doors, all the way up to the ceiling, which were painted blue during Khrushchev's reign.

I ring the doorbell. Doesn't work.

Knock. Knock for a while. I really want to live in Kiev, five minutes' walk from university for one hundred and fifty karbovantsiv a month. From the flat opposite, the neighbour comes out wearing a flowery dress, holding a shopping bag. She advises me to look for Nana Masha in the park. My Kazakh nana goes by the same name! It's definitely fate. Livening up, I jump and head for the park. I'll find Nana Masha, even if there are as many people there as there are at the Republican Stadium, when the rides are packed. Actually no, if there are that many people, she's going to be kind of hard to find. What if she's on the rides?!

Luckily, there are mainly straight-out-of-the-oven, unfamiliar-with-each-other freshers with bottles of beer and shy smiles. Just one netsuke, in the form of a hunched old woman with a headscarf and a grey jumper, is sitting on the furthest bench in the small park. Getting closer, it is impossible not to note that indeed the old-as-earth-itself lady looks strikingly like my old nana. Only about a hundred and fifty years older. Questions arise: did this nana have a husband, and if so, was he old like Gandalf? Were there children? If so, they are probably long dead, way before the war. Yes, old ladies don't age well in cities. My nana in her Kazakh village marches across her garden with a shovel for her ripe watermelons (and melons) and simultaneously rakes out potatoes from underneath ripe gooseberries. That's why she looks one hundred and thirty-five years younger than this one. This one eyes wary students in the park, from dusk till dawn, I bet, shaking her head in disapproval. She doesn't agree with their shy wariness, or their choice of beer. "Should have gone for Stella, not Fosters," she's probably thinking.

I sit down next to the old nana on the bench. She turns her head in my direction.

"Hello, Nana Masha!" I say emphatically, triumphantly. If this isn't Nana Masha, then I admit – I made a mistake, am looking for housing, maybe you know someone who's renting out. You, for example.

"Eh?!" quacks the old lady, not taking her dark eyes away from me, shaking her head untrustingly.

"You wrote an ad about renting!" I say, taking it up a tone.

"Ow d'you know I'm Nana Masha?" Her lips start quivering, and her face shows fear. Oh no no no… Nana Masha, you got the wrong end of the stick, for the love of God please don't be scared. I'll explain everything.

"I'm looking for housing." I point to myself. "Did you write an ad?"

The students with beer turn their heads.

"Ahh! Housing!" She's got it, thank God.

"Mine ain't all that," concludes Nana.

"So what! At least it's really close to the university," I say more quietly, the park full of competition.

"Also, I got a cat. 'E craps," the nana continues, shaking her head. She doesn't like that he craps. Well, that's fair enough.

"I also have a cat. They love doing it," I say. You won't dissuade me, Nana. I've got you, like a shoe on a hook.

"Well, you so badly wanna move in, 'ava look but you won't like it. You chepurnenka." Nana begins to rise, leaning on her stick.

She called me "chepurnenka". Me? The topest kind of neatness and prettiness? She is also blind, I note.

"No worries, I'll like it," I say and give her my arm for support.

"Wait a…'ow didja find me?" She freezes, putting her hand on my elbow, as if she won't get up from the bench till I confess why I randomly want to live at hers under any conditions.

"Neighbours said that you'd be in the park." I smile radiantly.

"Ahh, neighbs." She takes hold of my arm, and we go to exit the park.

She untrustingly shaking her head, and me minding my speed and trying hard not to jump for joy. It is especially hard to do as we walk past a group of those freshers with beers. I just proudly put my head back, like a pleased cat with a huge herring between my teeth.

Of course, during my short, seventeen-year-old life I've been to places I wanted to urgently escape straight away out of. For example, our nomad neighbours in the Kazakh village of my nana. With a small kitten in my bosom, I ended up in their house of seven rooms, none of which were being aired out at all. I walked past the aligned rooms in the corridor, like compartments on a train, one after the other. I was warned that in the corner of the rooms there was rat poison. Suddenly, from the room in front, a huge rat pranced out along the corridor with big black-button eyes and disappeared into the last room. The poison doesn't work, in other words. The house was filled with the smell of mutton fat, gone-off cheese, unwashed bodies and rat fur. The thick air entered through my nostrils right into my stomach. The stomach thought it was a sausage that entered, not air, and turned on the process of food digestion, which caused me to vomit. I guessed the same air caused my kitten's diarrhoea. Liquidy. "The cat's shat itself!" I shouted jubilantly and flew out of the house. That was the last time I was that excited to leave someone's house.

All in all, the home of Nana Masha is in a much better condition than that. For one, her ginger cat Ginger chooses to do his work at least not on my bosom. And you have to agree with me, that's better…

First, the old lady spends about fifteen minutes sorting out keys. She has five locks and five rusty keys, which turn very stiffly.

"Let me help you," I cry out, waving my hand at the risk of yet another storm of suspicion. My unshaking hands manage the job a lot more quickly. Finally, the sacred door bursts open and we find ourselves right in the kitchen.

The acrid smell of feline faeces comes crashing into my nose. On the kitchen table, in the half-dark room, sits the cat himself. Ginger, and very ugly. He sits next to his very own heap. I hope it is his own. I wouldn't ever dare accuse Richie of going to the toilet everywhere. This is living proof – not everywhere.

"'Ats Ginger," says Nana Masha. As if this explains why he's on the table, and also why there's a heap next to him. But a point to Nana for manners.

"Yeah, I guessed," I say out loud.

"Ow' d'you know tha's Ginger?" The old lady stirs, shaking her head.

"Well, because he's ginger." I smile. Her suspicion continues to touch me.

I open the blue door from the kitchen to where I assume is the bathroom.

"Tha's the toilet," she says.

Or the bathroom, I think. "Is there, somewhere…" I continue, checking out the bathtub, piled up with dusty, dirty cans of different sizes. I can't bring myself to turn on the light. Out of the bathroom there is another door, which definitely leads to the toilet. I mentally cross myself and pray to Lord Jesus, pushing the door. Darkness. Turn the light on and…

Well, compared to the kitchen, not bad. It's obvious which room is visited more, I think. More or less a white basin, which flushes well. The depressing dark-blue-coloured walls don't turn me off as much as the pile of empty jars, which have obviously been there for about the last thirty years.

She must be around two hundred and two, flashes through my mind.

"Where has she been washing herself all this time?"

"Where do I wa—"

"You wanna wash, you get a blue pot, warm water and wash." She guesses the rest of my question.

I return to the kitchen to look at where she's pointing.

On the greasy, oil-drenched stove, stands a big blue pot. The bottom of the pot has a darkening hole.

"I should tell Katka I'll be going to her halls to wash," I note. I also decide that I won't be eating at all. Better to spend money on theatre tickets and vodka. I'll just snack, and not at Nana's, definitely.

"Also, place is rich wiv roaches," says Nana, shaking her head, as if she's in doubt that she's rich with cockroaches. But there is no doubt for a second. I open the door of the old, dilapidated chest of drawers, and these same cockroaches run across my hand, to my elbow, then drop to the floor, scattering in different directions. Maybe they're playing hide and seek, and one of the roaches in the chest is "it". I slam the door, not checking if there is a cockroach left counting, and swear to myself never to look in there again. No point in disturbing cockroach fun. We walk into the living room.

"'Ere's your bed. 'Ere's mine."

And dontchu mix 'em up, flashes across my mind.

"And thas' my man. 'E died in the war."

I cautiously look around, to see if there is a corpse, lying or sitting somewhere, of her deceased man, who died in the war, but see only two beds. She mentions her man because I do check out the dusty photographs plastered on the wall, like in our school newspaper. I look around warily for the man, but still only noticing the small bed, covered with a long grey veil, a fading picture on it. But there is a lamp above the bed. I have a faded feeling vaguely resembling a sense of comfort.

In the evening, before I fall asleep under the bright lamp, I read *The Twelve Chairs* and don't notice either the snoring old lady, or the noise of passing cars, or even the occasional cockroach falling onto the pages. Then I want to go to the toilet. I put my feet into slippers. Even the crowded bogies running up my legs don't break my solid spirit to stay in this room, further from my parents. Besides, I can scream, jump and stamp my feet in the midst of the night as much as I want, throwing the full-of-life insects off. Nana won't hear anyway.

CHAPTER THREE

How Ukrainian Mothers Gasp

A sunny September morning. The rays fall onto my pillow and onto my ear. I squint. Monday. Today, after uni, I'll roll over to Katka's. She'll be waiting for me at three, at the tram stop. I'm staying in Kiev at Nana Masha's till Friday. I lazily turn from side to side, burying my nose into the pillow. The pillow smells of Ostap. Pictures of yesterday's meeting: passion on the bench at 3am near the boiler house, then his whisper, that we will be well behaved and will see each other as much as possible. On my left breast there should be two wine-red love bites, and his neck, covered in Gorbachev's birth marks.

Trembling knees. An urge to spread them further apart, to numb the shakiness, which was interrupted by the movement of drawers and Mum's steps up and down my room. Something was being searched for, unsuccessfully, because she started looking into the most unpredictable places. Between books. Think about that for a second. A person looks for keys, a wallet, her favourite scarf – between books. Or in the bottom drawer near the balcony, where for three hundred and eight years she has kept her bridal dress, and two blue-chequered quilts. No, not there? And now maybe in my laundry basket full of underwear. Wallet and keys in my pants and bras... Oh my God, oh my God! There's...

Crawling home at five in the morning with the rustling sound of kisses in my ears, I didn't hide my drenched-in-youthful-passion underwear. Mum's shocked gasp echoes through the room. That one, which Ukrainian mothers make, when we were rolling around in dirt and poo, and we were only sent to the shop for a loaf of bread. Normal mums gasp like this: "Ah!" A short sigh. Ukrainian ones like this: "Ghaah!" Air in the throat. Lots of air. If you're going to sigh, then sigh well. Ukrainian mums' philosophy.

Mum has been for seventeen years, and especially in the last year, proving to her friends and family that her daughter is a naismyshlyonneyshaya (meaning "the smartest ever" and clearly spelt and pronounced with all prefixes and suffixes). The girl who would never "bed" herself with any kind

87

of Ostap, and would, as she repeatedly announced herself, save her virginity for her future husband.

Did I really announce that? I wonder sleepily, during Mum's steel speech.

I feel a strong storm of shame and a strong storm of annoyance. Shame, because I didn't hide everything, as I should have, so that Mum wouldn't find out about everything so stupidly.

Annoyance, because she's looking for her keys in my pants and generally putting her nose in my things, into my private life, thinking that she has a patent for that virginity. As if she is my future husband, and I am needed untouched by her, else I'll be stabbed, like Circassians who live in Nagorno-Karabakh, or wherever it is that wives are needed untouched, else they'll be stabbed. Not the best reason to describe to Mum the full depths of my feelings and passions of the three-person tent.

My eyes are closed. Half sleeping. A sensation, or a vision in my head that there is a fight between responsibility and sensitivity for the microphone. The microphone slips and falls onto the sleeping boy – sarcasm. It's him, who says with a deep voice into the microphone:

"I wanna know what you forgot in my laundry basket."

I feel Mum's piercing gaze on me. The only thing that's mine in this house is the dirt under my fingernails. Never in my life will I ever, silly dirt-bag, prostitute, who has nothing better to do than to walk on my hands and be thrown into a ditch under a fence (Mother lives in a world where ditches are always near fences), dare to speak to her in a similar tone and voice, and in general, I should get out of the house swiftly before she whips me with a belt on my behind. The eyes can't open right now, else I'll see Gorgon and turn into stone.

I firmly request myself to stay quiet. I have no strength to cry, to scream and run from here, even in a naked state. Mum leaves the room. Before she can light her cigarette, I walk into the kitchen, fully dressed, and sluggishly ask for one hundred karbovantsiv to get to university. Mum, not turning her head, takes out some money from her purse and throws it on the floor. I catch her sharp venomous gaze, loudly saying with my eyes "I hate you!", turn around and walk out of the house, without the money and not slamming the door.

I leave with the hope that Mum has the whole day to understand the idiotism of her behaviour, and also to realise that I'm not little anymore, though I do need a hundred karbovantsiv to get to university. I walk along the street, flooded with September sun, past the market to the stop. Under my dark shades, tears fall, my cherry mouth slanted sideways from kissing, and I just want to sing that the holidays have begun, and I am no longer sixteen, but seventeen. And it is now, not back then in the three-room tent, it is now that my real adulthood actually begins.

Damn them all! I'll hitchhike to Kiev. Could go straight to Ostap's halls instead of Katka's. He is my boyfriend after all, and I need his support in these difficult times. Although I don't know where his halls are. I just need ten karbovantsiv for some oatmeal.

I hitchhike to university. I don't have to look for where Ostap lives. As at lunch, after Microeconomics, Dad appears at the windowsill. Dad puts two hundred karbovantsiv in my coat pocket, and we turn to the window.

"What's happened?" Dad asks the window.

I cough and say: "Mum found out that me and Ostap…" I cannot find the words. What is it called, that Ostap and me do, when I'm talking to Dad? I'm seventeen years old, and nobody has taught me about that. I clear my throat and continue:

"About me and Ostap. He's my boyfriend, I love him."

I rattle on. "And he loves me. And she said all these horrible things to me and threw money on the floor."

I feel like an adult now, and free. Yes, Ostap loves me. And I am not a prostitute.

After a long pause, Dad asks: "And Ostap, is he going to marry you?" I can feel Dad is choosing his words with care. He doesn't want me to run away along the uni corridor and dissolve into the crowd of students passing by.

"He says we have to finish university first," I say, and sense unease around the conversation about "marriage".

I recall how once I asked Ostap shyly:

"At what age is it best to get married, in your opinion?"

Ostap answered matter-of-factly: "Well, no younger than twenty-seven."

And I felt that same unease.

I would right now, I thought sadly, although I knew he was right. And I bet his parents wouldn't call him a prostitute all this time, till twenty-seven, if he didn't get married.

Nevertheless, Dad nods in approval to my answer and adds: "Well, be careful, Little Brush."

I want to giggle and tell Dad that condoms are only twenty karbovantsiv per one, so he shouldn't worry. But I stop, thinking that my dad is awesome actually. And he calls me Little Brush. Just like when I was a kid. My eyes fill with tears; I throw myself onto Dad, who gets confused. I want to say "Thank you, Daddy!" but the spasm in my throat doesn't let me say anything. And only the group of students walking past, the flurry of translator-interpreters, keeps me from sobbing.

Coming out of uni that afternoon, with my dad long gone, I realise: it's not worth slicing your veins open if Mum shouts at you in emotional anguish. She has her own responsibilities and sensualities in her head to deal with, and sarcasms too.

I hurry over the sunny square, scattered with people, past the Republican Stadium, to tram number ten towards Borshagovka where Katka's halls are. With the intention of telling her that a great event has happened in my life: Mum found out about Ostap and me having sex. And with a proposal to urgently get drunk and cackle about this event.

"I brought vodka, three cucumbers and oatmeal," I say, getting off the tram, while she is waiting on the busy platform. "Got to drink ASAP."

We walk towards the exit when I say:

"This time I definitely screwed up big time."

"Kapets! What happened?" Katka stops dead in her tracks. A man immediately crashes into her and slurs out soaring words. It's not enough for Katka to flutter her beautiful, small, light blue, bead-like eyes. She also has to stop in a crowded place, bring wrath to passers-by, and repeat, ignoring their wrath:

"This time you definitely screwed up big time?" With the emphasis on the word "this". As if it could be worse than it already is.

But nothing more serious has ever happened to me before, therefore her reaction does not make any sense. In a normal situation, I would have replied something like, "It's not necessary to stop drunk passers-by over this," fluttering my small, dark brown eyes.

But I shut my sarcastic mouth, because I know: Katka will listen.

I answer seriously:

"Mum found out about Ostap and I, then threw a tantrum, stating that I wasn't her daughter no more."

Within half an hour we slowly cover what should be a ten-minute walk to Katka's halls, stopping and waving our arms about. Katka listens and looks at the trampled path in front of us.

"Kapets…' She repeats her favourite saying. "My mother would've hung me. Why the hell are they like this…" She searches for the right word. "Narrow-minded, is it?"

"Exactly," I say.

"What difference is it to them; it's not like I'm getting pregnant, catching some disease, and the main thing is no one's even raping me," Katka continues.

"Yeah!" I say. "But we've got to suffer, not knowing happiness, according to them. If you're so worried that I'm going to catch chlamydia or a baby – sit down, explain the dangers normally and I'll decide for myself."

"Aha! Yeah right!" says Katka.

"Anyway, I've decided: I don't want to live at home right now. Dad thinks I'm at Nana Masha's. Are you going to have problems because of me?"

"Who's Nana Masha?"

"Oh, later. Are you gonna have problems?"

"Do you have your passport on you?"

"Always. How would I get to my uni otherwise?"

"Then everything's gonna be fine. Don't attract too much attention when you come in, and if they ask – show your passport, say you're on the secfac. Golden rule: never give your passport away to them. Understand?"

"Secfac. God, that's a bit of a rude word, isn't it? Where's that?" I say.

"Faculty of Secretaries-Referents," Katka explains. "It's like Business Administration," she adds.

"A-ha," I say.

"Yeah," continues Katka, "all new faces at the moment. Lady at the desk isn't stopping anyone."

We get to Katka's halls of residence.

"Let's chill here for a bit more. Tell me, how have you settled in? If you live with girls, I'm guessing we won't be able to chat with them there," I suggest.

"Then let's go sit. That's another half an hour," she replies.

We are sitting down on a bench, which still has bits of paint on it. On the part where people usually sit, there is one crooked bar. There are supposed to be four of those. Following the unwritten law, we sit on the back of the bench.

"I live in a room with three beds," Katka begins.

"Wow! And how are the beds in bed?" I giggle.

Katka corrects herself:

"In my room there are three beds."

"Three beds there are with you, I get it," I say.

"No, they are there. But living there are only two of us, me and a girl," Katka says.

"And we live with them," I add.

"No, we sleep on them. And live in the room," Katka says.

"You live with the girl, and the beds live with each other," I say.

"We live, and they're just...there," she says.

"They just...love to eat," I add.

"But we sleep together," Katka points out, raising her index finger.

"Be sure to use protection," I caution, waving my finger in reply.

Then, my imagination throws out a rectangular person with short hands and legs, like a bed, with a face the shape of a pillow. I don't know what Katka's imagination shows her, but we both start having fits of laughter, after which I finally find out that, in the room with three beds, live two – Katka and Lika. Lika is twenty-two; she has three guys. Lika shares her sexual knowledge with Katka: anal sex is better when drunk. It's sooooo awesomeeee! Giving a blow job is better after chewing a strong mint chewing gum, and vaginal sex is better avoided. Or with a condom, but men don't like condoms. You mustn't let them come inside you, but how do you stop them? She doesn't say. Or better on the first three days of your period, or the last three days. Then there's no need to pull out. Also, a slice of lemon really helps, slipped into the vagina after sex (which explains the endless bouts of thrush Katka and I get after receiving this information).

It's important to note that Lika's sexual experience isn't enriched with the knowledge of what the guy has to chew for a better cunnilingus, and how to make him want to do it, and where to find a partner who loves condoms, will keep an eye on your cycle, and will not come inside, when you don't ask him to. For that knowledge, probably, a bit more experience is needed.

Nevertheless, the anal and oral sex really perked my ears up. "Mint chewing gum?" I say, rocking back on the bench.

"Yeah. Better to alternate with hot tea," says Katka, rocking in time with me.

From the outside, we look like two giant sparrows, swaying on wires from the wind.

"Listen, she should be collecting money for these consultations."

"That's exactly what I say to her. She knows so much, ka-pets."

"Ahm...sorry for asking..." I sniffle my nose. "And in case you put this same chewing gum up your bum, how will the anal sex be then?"

Katka rocks with laughter, and if I hadn't grabbed onto her, she would have dropped off the bench.

"Chewing gum in the bum..." Katka chokes, "and hot tea in the mouth, let him run backwards and forwards..."

Her last words she mouths with her lips, as the rushing hysteria doesn't give her any more strength to breathe in air to talk out loud. I am giggling.

"By the way, a few guys come over sometimes," says Katka, finishing her laughter.

"A few guys?" I repeat.

"A few guys," says Katka.

"A few is more than two," I confirm.

"More than two, yes. Four," she answers.

"That's interesting," I say.

"And I like one of them," says Katka.

"Ah! I see!" I prick my ears up.

"Yep...like that," says Katka.

"Well, tell me, who are these guys?" I say.

"One is called Amir. He's like Vick – good to chat to, but he's a mate."

"Mm." I nod in understanding – we know what mates Vicks are like.

"The second one – Pashya. This one doesn't enter anyone, just loves to philosophise. He's from Kholmysty, by the way!"

"Wow! What's his name?"

"Sergei Pashko."

"I was his older buddy at school! He's three years younger. Why is he not at school still?"

"He left home on philosophical grounds. He wants to quickly learn to be a secretary, make some money, open a coffee shop, philosophise and smoke some shisha. He always says, in every person, both a woman and a man are present."

"I was just thinking about that today." I light up.

"You should chat to him, he'll tell you lots of stuff, he's cool," Katka replies, and continues:

"The third – Seryoga from Kryvbas. A depressive blond. Lika's got her eye on him."

"Eye," I repeat after her. "Just one, or both?"

"Both, one and the other," Katka agrees.

"The mint and tea heaven will scatter his depressive thoughts," I say.

"That already happened," Katka says.

"Already?" I ask.

"And anal heaven too," she says.

"I thought you guys only had your first lesson today!" I say.

"Well, what about yesterday? Or the day before? What else do you think there is to do here on weekends?" Katka says.

"Yeah. Looks like I got here right on time then," I say, scratching my head.

"The fourth one is called Slavo," Katka continues. "He looks like a cat and has an erotic chain on his hairy chest. Just like Rudi, actually."

"Hairy?" I ask.

"Hairy," she replies. "Take heed."

I put my hands up.

"She's already studied the hairiness of his chest," I say quietly, in the direction of an old lady coming towards us, pulling her perhaps-bag on wheels.

"See, how good it can be to dig your way into a sack of pears," I add.

Katka aims her fist at me jokingly. I raise my arms again and act up even further: "Na na. Only with Amir and Pashya and only conversations about friendships and philosophy. I won't speak about chewing gum and pears even with Pashya. And with Slavo I'll just turn on the cruise control eyelash fluttering."

"You're not even his type. He doesn't like girls with big boobs," says Katka.

"Says the girl with massive ones," I say.

"And that is why I think he won't like me either." Katka sighs. "He got with some other girl, also Katka with big tits. He was wasted yesterday; told me he broke it off completely with her."

"So hey, now he's yours," I say.

"No, I doubt it," says Katka, prying a chip off the bench.

I look at the chip, and scream to the lady walking off with the shopping basket, in the distance:

"Katka's in love!"

"Idiot!" Katka shouts, trying to push me off the bench.

"And Katka's definitely, truly in love!" I shout again, dodging her waving hands.

"Shut up you fricking…Ka-pets." Katka jumps on me and throws me to the ground.

I'm squealing with laughter.

"In the halls, there are windows, which have a tendency to let sounds through," she states, rolling me on the yellow maple leaves, stretching my hoodie over my eyes.

"Did you see how Nanny was really surprised that you're in love?" I continue, choking with laughter.

"She even jumped! *Help*! I'm being dispossessed of my prized hood!"

"I'm gonna dispossess you of your eyes in a sec!" snuffles Katka.

Dishevelled, with sparkling eyes, we are lying on the grass and in the leaves.

"Five pm. See the crowd leaving the building?" says Katka.

"Time to booze," I say.

CHAPTER FOUR

First Student Night Goes Wrong

The next morning. I wake up in the third bed. The first thing I remember: trying to find out what the secret to Lika's orgasm was. It took me a long time. At what point and from what moves does it happen? My tongue was about to fall out, and I had enough of gazing up her wide spread hips above my face. Lika's face was on the other side of me; I could feel her fingers, tongue, it felt like there was so much of everything... I'm not a very good lesbian. Fooling around, yep, but after that, no. I liked Seryoga's gloomy, cynical stare. Lika and I danced, caressing each other's breasts, and he looked on, as if he were being given the best blow job in the world, and he didn't really want it, but couldn't do anything about it either. And he's about to sneeze and that's it.

I don't want to get up, crashing nose to nose with Lika, heating up the kettle. I don't want to talk about porridge and salo and not look her in the eye. I want to...

Lika stops snoring. She wakes up. I hope she'll be the first to get up and leave. She's the one who's got lectures to go to, not me. My first one is at twelve. Sensible Katka has already left.

I decide not to wait for Lika to get up. I rise, pick my jeans up off the floor, tuck the bed in, down two mugs of water and get out of there, firmly and quietly shutting the door.

The same bright orange maple leaves, the same half-destroyed bench with its nanny and shopping bags.

I sit down on the bench. The conflict with Mum feels so far away, as far as how Dad used to walk away from me picking mushrooms in the forest, going all the way to the thicket. I smile, remembering our mushroom-picking trips.

We had to get up extra early, while the fog was still in the forest, among the trees. Get dressed up warm and leave quietly so as not to wake Mum. Dad would disappear for a long time, so long that I'd start doubting whether I had come with him in the first place. And the same now. Was there a conflict with Mum, or did I make everything up?

Someone who made me laugh a lot yesterday was Pashya. Among the fun, he declared, deadpanned: "There are boys and girls in everyone's head."

It's his fault, by the way, that I gave in to Lika's attempts. I laughed for ages, and he kept reinforcing to me the idea that responsibility, sarcasm and sensuality definitely live in my head. He claimed he could actually see behind my back a huge green room, and they were definitely all fighting for the microphone. Two doors from the room led to the balcony, the left, my left eye; the right, my right. Here, I noted to him that between them should be a fireplace with two chimneys for my nose, and underneath the balcony doors, a wide hole along the skirting board – the mouth. Katka and Lika cackled with laughter, while Pashya carried on talking straight-faced, looking through me. It felt like he was almost about to wave to somebody behind my back.

Now I really am observing my head like a green room. There is definitely something whining there, pricking and not letting me enjoy the lightness of the morning. I imagine the conversation between sarcasm and sensuality: "You whining again?" Sarcasm would say, grimacing like Ostap. Sensuality has the face and figure of Liv Tyler. She sits on the shore and looks onto the lake with bullrushes.

"I cheated on Ostap," she would reply. "Now he's going to leave me."

"Don't tell him anything. That's not even hard for you to do. Your whole life you've only been able to handle an hour and a half of conversation with him," Sarcasm would reply, and I start to find it comical that an Ostap-lookalike in my head is advising me not to tell him anything.

Ostap promised that we would meet whenever we really wanted to. Today is already Tuesday.

"What are you doing here? Scared of Lika?" I hear Katka's voice.

"Ohh…it's so good that you're here, in this world," I voice, genuinely happy.

"Also, you're a drunkard," says Katka, putting one foot on the bench.

"What are you doing here? I thought you had lectures," I say.

"We've got half an hour's break. So, I came here to munch. Come with me?"

"Lika's there. I'm not going."

"What, are you ashamed? Haha. Yeah, Lika was your sweetheart last night for sure."

"Oh please, don't remind me," I say, groaning.

"Don't fret, I just saw her. She waved. Said that you're so good, that you knew to get up early and get out. Or else she would never have got up and would've been late to her favourite lecture on printing."

"Oh really? Was she embarrassed too? Yesterday she was a totally different ball game, right? She's probably embarrassed she didn't orgasm. Ahaha," I say and become lively again.

"So, she slipped out behind my back?" I continue.

"Looks like it, yeah. Hehe. Let's go, then. I've got some salo. Gotta do something with it," Katka says.

"Want me to make some porridge with it?" I say, rising from the bench. "Epic thing."

"Euw, that's gross. I've hated porridge since childhood," she says.

"Who was talking about the porridge you were fed in childhood? Porridge with salo is my own personal invention. You weren't fed this stuff, even at school. And if you've got some onion…"

"I have," says Katka. "Hm…I will have to try; I'm hungry."

"Let's go. I'll teach you," I say, and we walk into the halls.

"Lika is smart," I say, lowering my voice, so that the darting hungry students won't hear. "She managed to get Seryoga jealous of her with me. Remember how reluctantly he left to go home?"

"Agreed. She once said," Katka replies, "this is how strange she is: if her boyfriend is having sex in front of her, then she isn't jealous. But if he wants another girl and has fantasies about her, then there's nothing worse."

We walk into her room.

"Hm, I see the point," I say more loudly.

"I get the feeling that she realises Seryoga might like you. But because she did you herself, she doesn't have to feel jealous. Better he feels envious and proud about his Lika," says Katka.

"Interesting tactic," I say, trying to imagine whether I would ever sleep with a girl in front of Ostap. I feel crazed. Then I imagine that I should sleep with all the girls whom Ostap might like, and I start feeling even worse.

"Oh, it's all muddled up on an empty stomach," I say.

"I also want to eat."

With salo, onion, oats, knife and a pot I go to the kitchen at the end of the corridor.

The corridor fills up with the smell of fried onion and salo.

Twenty-five minutes later, back in the room, Katka is at the table with an empty plate of leftover porridge. She says:

"Wow, this is epic."

"I know," I reply, with a sense of importance. "And it's so filling. You won't want to eat till lunch."

"Ka-pets, this is now my breakfast. It's sinfully cheap..."

"Happy to help." I smile.

"Listen, Katka," I say. "I need your support on something."

A knock on the door.

"Girls!" bleats Amir, opening the door. "What smells so good?"

"Amir, we're busy!" snaps Katka.

"Ah, understood. I'm leaving." The door closes.

We spray with laughter.

"He thought we were still here with Lika," I say.

"Yeah... You know, I actually once had a dream that I was making love to a girl...it was you, I think..." says Katka, the corner of her lip twitching, which makes me think: she is feeling shy.

"Kat, come on, don't." I sob. It seems her eyes sparkle with a shy distress, but after a moment, she says in a sombre voice:

"Come on, spill the beans. 'Cos of Mum again?"

"Because of Ostap." I sigh, letting go of the uncomfortable feeling.

"I'm worried he'll find out about last night with Lika. You won't say anything, right?"

Katka pours herself more porridge. Finishes eating it. Another two minutes go by. "Gonna go put the kettle on. You want tea?" she answers.

"Yeah, why not." I shrug my shoulders.

"Be right back," she says, disappearing behind the door with the kettle. Katka vanishes. Maybe she got upset that I didn't find her dream all that impressive? Maybe she took Pashya's philosophies about guys in girls' heads seriously?

I am slightly irritated to be left on my own with these wonderings, jerking my leg and staring at the table. The tablecloth covering it. Breadcrumbs, an opaque salt dispenser, two different plates – one red with white polka dots, the other white, with lilac flowers. I saw the red and white one filled with potato stew at Katka's house. Katka complained that this one didn't fit into any one set back home. I should also bring all the inappropriate mugs to Nanny Masha's.

At last Katka returns with the steaming kettle, interrupting my creative thoughts about decorating Nanny Masha's kitchen with garlands.

"Please never mind my absence," she says. "You know I always carefully think over my answers, before giving advice."

"Ah, yes, that's right," I say, catching on. Sometimes I end up forgetting what I've asked, while listening to her breathing down the phone, to my question: "What's your thinking?"

I always want to reply for her: "Thick and slow."

On the other hand, I'm lucky to have her. This person thinks, before giving advice. I, for example, never do that.

"This is what I think. You should tell Ostap about Lika." She pours boiling water into the mugs.

"Are you mad?" I say, moving my mug to the kettle.

She's still deeply into Ostap, up to her hair roots! And here I am, pricking my ears up, listening to this cat singing lullabies! Or, I think, she's up to her ears into me. That's my sarcasm thinking. I think I'm going crazy. Go to hell, Pashya.

"You have to tell Ostap," Katka continues, stretching to the shelf for the packet of tea.

"Because, it's not like you slept with a guy, but just played around with a girl, drunk. It happens. It's not serious. And secondly, if Ostap doesn't come to see you either today or tomorrow at uni, then let's go to his on Thursday ourselves. I know where Vick lives. You know he got into the Academy too? You don't even know that, see."

"Yeah, I know," I lie. I am annoyed that I find out about this not from Vick himself.

So, to change the subject I say: "Why did Ostap, having got into Shevchenko, decide to go to the Academy with Vick? This I'll never know."

"Because at Shevchenko it was an evening course that he got into, and at the Academy it's a full-time course, every day, five days a week, as for any normal student," Katka replies.

"So, he would have gone to the evening one for a year, then I'm sure they would have transferred him to the full-time one," I reply.

"Well, his dad's got connections at the Academy – he's considered a big fish there, whereas at Shevchenko he'd have to prove to everyone again that a brain does exist in his head. I think it's because of that," Katka replies.

"And plus, it's handy because now Vick lives near him.

"He'll definitely tell us where Ostap's room is. How's that for a plan?"

"Unexpected. We could go to his halls. But I'm still not sure whether I should tell him about Lika. I know him. He gave me such a hard time for walking around Kholmysty with Vick..."

"Listen, kapets, you're surprising me," Katka snaps. She is quite snappy today; I make a mental note.

Katka puts bits of black tea into the mugs and then pours boiling water into them, then announces: "You're a free girl with your own opinion. Vick, by the way, is upset that you don't ring, don't visit, and you're never home."

"Katka, damn it, who taught you to brew tea like that?" I take a teaspoon to stir the water. She laughs.

"One thing when he's just a mate, and another when I know, and Ostap knows, that he's head over heels into me."

"I always brew it like that, if there isn't a teapot. Amir is also my mate, and if I start dating Slavo, I'm not going to stop talking to Amir," says Katka, sipping her tea. Two tea leaves lodge on her top lip.

"I still think Amir and Lika are different kinds of mates to make out with. You just weren't that drunk or that tempted by her dances," I say, catching the bits of tea leaves from my mug, and lining them up on the tablecloth.

"You don't know much about me and that sort of dancing," Katka says, lifting one eyebrow. I feel faint that I don't know her types of dancing all that well.

"And Amir," she continues, as if answering a question in biology class. "He's in love with me too. Plus, he and Slavo are friends. This doesn't stop them from having a laugh at breaktime and after studies. And you've cut Vick off completely. You and he didn't have anything?"

"No, thank God we didn't," I answer.

"So, it's decided. On Thursday, we go to Vick's. I'm coming to visit a friend, and you're coming along for the company. And there we'll decide who's going where and who's looking for whom."

"All right. On Thursday," I say, thinking. "Although if we find Ostap, I'm still not saying anything about Lika."

Katka sighs. "Why are you so damn careless?" her sigh says. Out loud, she summarises her lecture: "I wouldn't start a relationship with a lie."

"I know. But in this case the relationship will end entirely otherwise," I say.

"Well, it's up to you. I've got lectures now," she replies.

"Yep, I'm running off as well. Listen, Katka, is it OK if I come to yours to stay for the week? Nana Masha's is only good for storing my microeconomics book, you know."

"Why are you even explaining yourself? There's the bed, take it, live it. Everyone loves you here; you're fun, and actually, you're my friend." She smiles.

"Thank you, buddy!" I say, pecking her on the cheek.

"And with Lika we'll have a drink and laugh about it," I add.

CHAPTER FIVE

Visit to Goloseyevka

After lectures I go over to Nana Masha's. I mop the old, tattered floor, previously red wine coloured, put new bedsheets on my bed.

"I'm going home till the end of the week!" I shout to Nana Masha. "And from next Monday I'll be staying here overnight," I lie shamelessly.

Nana nods her head untrustingly, as if I am going to the front line, and she doesn't believe that I will return. So that she believes, I leave her ten hryvnas and my book on international law, and I dash off to Katka's.

On Wednesday, at break, Sasha asks me: "Osha, why do you keep bringing the same notebook every day?"

"Buy some beer, and I'll explain," I answer.

"I'm with you guys," exclaims Maria with the sharp nose, wearing a cap.

That evening I crawl back to Katka's halls late, stinking of eight per cent beer "2000", with my head full of thoughts about Sasha, the coolest girl at uni.

At night I tell Katka and Lika, finger pointed at the sky, that at twenty-five, after having a family, Sasha went to study, her child being only eight years old. And the way she mocks our elderly gay English teacher is hilarious: "Oh, my goody goodness, Sasha, the worst kind of smell is body odour mixed with deodorant, oh my goody goodness eughhh!"

Then I also say that Maria is the spitting image of Napoleon Bonaparte in a skirt. Sharp nose, black hair peeking out from underneath her hat, short and ruffled. She's small, with long, tightly shut lips, ready to go on the offensive against the whole world in a heartbeat. But it doesn't suit her. Because there isn't an attack. But the look is there. Sasha christened Maria – Lil' Crow. Now, Maria is Lil' Crow Bonaparte.

I've only seen her in a skirt once – on the 1st September. She prefers baggy trousers with pockets on the knees, and all kinds of quilted jackets and waistcoats with blue tops, orange T-shirts and long sleeves the colour of tarmac.

When she laughs, she doesn't stretch her lips into a smile, but lightly opens them exactly the right amount, for air to pass through, which is used for laughter. It looks like she's about to whistle. Or that she would be happy to smile widely but doesn't want to show her teeth. Maria is interested in girls.

I advise Lika to get to know Maria, and get a pillow on my head, then giggling, fall asleep.

That Maria is now the image of responsibility in my head, I am scared to mention even after four bottles of "2000" beer.

On Thursday morning I wake up early and forget that I have drunk. Leaving halls, I remember the biology lesson about hydrocyanic acid, which wakes an alcoholic up after exactly five hours. Nope, the girls don't remember this from biology class, and stop in their tracks to hear this important detail.

"What are we deciding for today?" asks Katka on the steps. From here we go in different directions.

"My lectures end at four," I say. "Maybe you could come to my uni?"

"Mine finish at three. That all works. From yours the twenty-one bus goes to Goloseyevsky," says Katka.

"Let's do it," I say. "There is something wrong in all this, don't you think? Why hasn't he come to visit, not even once? He knows the address."

"Who? The bus?" Katka smiles.

"Witty." I smile sourly in reply.

Katka chuckles and says: "Drop it. Maybe he's got lots of lessons and has decided to booze it up with the rest of his halls."

"Yeeeah… I don't like any of it," I say, straightening my notebook under my arm.

"I have to run," says Katka, pecking me on the cheek before leaving. "And don't think so much. You'll see, tonight everything will be different. And go get on your tram now."

The bus journey from the uni to Goloseyevksky where the Academy halls are, turned out to be stuffy, long and irritating. I stubbornly didn't want to pay the fare, although I still had thirty karbovantsiv in my pocket. But, giving in to Katka's mumbling and grumbling, I rolled my eyes, giving the conductor some change. After an hour and a half, we got to Goloseyevsky sweaty and jittery. The path to the halls led through a forest, and the bad mood was blown away by the wind.

"Oh-gwow," says Vick quietly, chewing something.

"Vick, we desperately need the gash bucket. Where is it?" I say.

Vick swallows whatever he was chewing and blurts out: "Just like that, right on the porch, around the corner on your skis, out of the blue, no hellos, no hugs, three months later you come to tell me you need the gash bucket."

Katka and I burst out laughing.

"Vick, you haven't even changed after so many years," I say, cuddling him and squishing his cheek, just the way he hates it.

"The gash bucket is at the end of the corridor to the right," he says with a doomed look.

"Though you didn't have to drag your asses all the way here. Why aren't the woods a gash bucket for you? With fresh air as a bonus."

Giggling, we head for the toilet. Vick wasn't joking.

The combination of dark blue tiles gives an awful effect to the room. I decide not to breathe until I leave.

"Would thou like some tea, ladies?" Vick asks, when we run into his room, greedily breathing.

"We brought vodka, but could start with tea," I say, catching my breath. "That was one horrendous gash bucket."

Katka has tears in her eyes and says nothing. Then she looks at the four beds.

"And where are the other three?"

"That's how you should have begun, with the vodka. Everyone's a few halls up at Vera's for her b-day. I was meant to change and go there. But I'd rather drink with you."

"Hurrah!" I say.

"Pickled cucumbers, bread, salo?" Vick offers.

"Wow!" Katka is genuinely surprised.

"You guys are economical. By Thursday our shelves are already empty. If not for Osha's porridge..."

"The porridge sounds kind of disgusting," says Vick.

"Osha, come, conjure it up. We brought porridge with us," says Katka.

"With pleasure," I say. "But first drink, then afterwards give me a piece of salo and twenty minutes. And if you've got some onion lying around on a Thursday…"

Vick winces. "I'm not promising that I'll be able to do any more than try it," says Vick.

Twenty minutes later Vick is gobbling up the porridge with onion and salo, and the vodka is almost all drunk.

"You're not far from Stapler, I bet," Katka asks, observing four books above somebody's bed.

"Well, how do I put it? We're in block number three – he's in the eleventh. Another two kilometres through the forest from here. Are you trying to tell me that you're going to trudge to Ostap's? He's probably boozing. I saw him this morning with a bottle of beer and drunk happy-puppy eyes."

"We're not trying to tell you that," I answer.

"Are you serious?" Katka asks quietly, as if she won't be heard in the room, with four beds.

"I want to sit here." My tone doesn't tolerate any disagreeing.

"Wonderful," says Vick. "So, you sit here, and I'll get the second one in." Vick flies out that very second, as if he is scared that we will change our minds and leave to go to the eleventh halls. Katka continues to look at me with a question in her eyes.

"Listen, why the hell did we even rock all the way up here?" she says quietly, sitting down next to me on a chair, as if Vick might not have gone anywhere, and is eavesdropping behind the door.

"Don't even try and argue." I fidget on my chair, exactly the same as Dad when he wants to show assuredness in his opinion.

"I don't want to go to his. Like an idiot. And he's boozing there anyway. Where am I meant to look for him? Two miles away. And what am I meant to say? I missed you so much, here, smell my vodka, and I even brought Katka along. And anyway, he's boozing there, don't you get it?"

"So why did we even rock up here?" Katka keeps asking.

"You blocked me," I let slip. I want to say that if she wants to see Ostap, then she should be honest and own up, and then leave to go to his. And I'll sit here with Vick. But then that would mean that she could leave for real, meaning I'll have to get really upset and not come to her halls to stay over. And I already agreed with Nana Masha that I'd be coming next week.

So, I say soothingly: "To booze with Vick. He's a safe guy. You said yourself, he's been upset with me for the last three months and all that. He seems to be doing just fine in my presence; it looks like he's cooled down now..."

Vick bursts into the room. Noisily puts down a bottle of blackcurrant and a pack of Marlboro Lights.

"Wow," I say.

"Yeah, you're minted," says Katka.

"And quick-footed," I say.

Vick opens his mouth to say something witty but shifts his attention to the blond guy who has just appeared in the room, with a mean face and puffed-up red lips, like a pissed-off kid.

"My face also goes red and unwelcoming when I have a drink," I quietly say to Katka.

"Vick! Vera's waiting for ya. I already tolja," he explains with a strict, fatherly tone, and puffs up his lips even more.

"Proha! I get it. Buh-I-ain't-makin'-it," Vick replies. "Proha! Have you tried porridge with salo?"

"Ay, Vick, Vick, Vick. You're a numpty, Vick. Nu-umpty," says Proha, and he leaves, slamming the door behind him.

"What a friendly young man. Ple-eased to meet you. Very pleased." I bow to the closed door.

"Why are you a numpty?" Katka asks.

"You went and got vodka so quickly. You guys have a shop around the corner or something?" I ask.

"No, no. I asked this dude to go to Vera's room, whose birthday it is, to slyly tell Proha, in his ear, that Vick is waiting for him outside and that he is asking for a bottle of vodka and a pack of cigarettes."

Katka and I exchange glances.

"And Proha took a bottle from someone's b-day for you?" I ask.

"And didn't even tell you to do one?"

"Imagine that," says Vick, puffing his chest out.

"That's a real mate," says Katka.

"To him," I say, toasting.

Proha bursts back in again, slamming the door behind him, and with

107

a clatter, drags a chair over, sits on it and says: "Pour me one, then. I'm too curious, what Vick's secret is."

"What secret?" asks Katka.

"Vick, I'm wasted, so I'm gonna say erything I think, right in front of 'er," says Proha, sliding his chair towards the table.

"Don't, Proha," Vick says, handing Proha a full shot of vodka.

"Nah, you listen. Vera's waiting on ya over there. And you're here doin' fuck all."

"Why is this fuck all?" intervenes Katka. "Vick has mates over."

"Proha, stop being a girl, have a drink with us for being such a good friend to Vick," I say, touching my shot with his, before downing it in one. I get the feeling that it is because I downed my shot in one gulp, and not because I uttered a muffled toast, that Proha looks straight through me, slowly nodding his head, as if he is struck by a realisation of something important. He finally says: "Y'now, Vick, firs' I thought that this is her." He indicates Katka with his full shot glass.

"She's kinda prettier. But then this one spoke, and now I get who is she."

"Proha, stop chatting rubbish! God you're such a mug." Vick puts down his empty faceted glass.

I giggle. "He's so funny. So, who is she then, tell me?" I ask, looking over at Proha.

"Dontchu laugh," says Proha, continuing to spill vodka.

"Fucked so much with a guy's head, that he ain't even goin' to Vera's birthday now. You're comin' and goin', and he coulda had a normal chick. She likes him, that's bait!"

I am startled. "So that's what's up," I say, turning my gaze over to Vick.

"Osha-Osha, don't pay attention. Right, Proha, let's go talk. Need a smoke."

He takes Proha under the arm. Proha lets himself be picked up, finally downs his shot, spilling half on his collar, loudly thumps down his glass, and they both leave the room.

"How does Vick change from Ukrainian to Russian so easily?" I say to their tracks.

"Damn, what does he want? Vick's got his own head on his shoulders," says Katka, warming her glass in her hands.

"Shouldn't have come," I say. "Stopped him and some Vera girl from hooking up…"

CHAPTER SIX

Unfinished Convo

"Babe, it's a stop. Do you want anything?" I hear Denis's voice above my head. I look up with a blank stare.

"Were you asleep? Water, sandwich? I see you're not eating, not drinking, only looking out the window."

"Oh, no thanks. My bag is full up with Mum's chicken drums and eggs. I'm fine for now," I say with a sleepy voice. Please go away. And since when am I Babe? I see him off the bus with a gaze and go back to my memories.

The next day, on Friday, turning down beer with Sasha and Lil' Crow Bonaparte, I thunder off home. He'll definitely ring today. Because since that sweet night, five long days have gone, and I've got so much I need to tell him. For one, that I was round at Vick's and we were too shy to come to see him. He'll say I'm stupid and next time I should definitely come over, that his halls are number eleven, and he'll tell me his room number. And I'll come over to stay with him, as much as possible.

Eight o'clock in the evening. I'm watching TV, after showering, in my dressing gown. He doesn't ring. Why? Maybe he found out about the visit to Vick's? Again, that feeling that I made everything up, just like back in school. That in reality there is no love or affection between us. The love and affection that every couple around seems to have: a fiery brunette Olesya, hair trimmed into a plant-pot hairstyle, is being picked up in a green "merc" by a chubby Ruslan in a peony jacket; a petite blonde Anya with a ponytail is being picked up by a similar-looking small blond Slavik, without a ponytail though, who's older than her by three years and recently found a job; Sasha is racing home to make burgers for her husband, who is hurrying home for dinner. And even long-legged, lanky Ella rushes off for her photo session with a broad-shouldered, long-haired photographer with sensual lips. Lil' Crow walks to the library with her underachieving stunner Violetta with pearl blue eye shades. One off to get books, the other to ogle.

Only I am trudging home alone on Fridays. Why do I need the library, if I have a boyfriend? Although I don't really know anything about him, and he doesn't even meet me after lectures. And we don't laugh on our way home about our management lecturer Tiagotinski, who during one lesson manages to say all of his favourite words – "in principle, in general, sort of thing, so to say" – one hundred and four times. I don't fly to lectures the next morning half asleep, but shamelessly happy, and I don't grumble: "We were at it again all night."

In general, I think I need just one little thing – a call from Ostap. The world hasn't turned upside down in five days, and nothing has fallen out of it. I can bravely look Mum in the eye and say that I'm going to Ostap's, coming home late, and there's no need to worry. We love each other, and you, Mum, are silly and wrong. Next week we're going to the circus together. Or to the theatre. Then on Sunday I'd ring Katka, proudly telling her that I'll be staying the night at his, she doesn't need to wait up for me at her halls and can envy me. And she can get her erotic charge out onto hairy-chested guys.

Instead of all this, it's getting dark and I'm sitting in a dressing gown, watching *Have I Got News for You*, my ironed blouse and jeans hanging on the back of the chair.

"Well, where is your Ostap, then? It's already half eight. You're not going to his today?" Mum asks, sitting on the armchair opposite, wearing a yoghurt mask, cucumber circles covering her eyes.

I squeeze out the worst possible answer in this situation: "I don't know."

Waiting for yet another pun to finish on the TV, Mum replies, "Mmm-yes. Interesting, no?", and leaves the room to wash her mask off.

The conversation, to my relief, stops, but in my head, it is only just the beginning.

I glumly think of myself as the gullible one, and how he's most probably using me, having already found himself some kind of blondie or the like. One who lives closer and is chattier. I want to cry, but I tell myself: no bawling. Get a grip; go and find out what the deal is. He's not going to ring. No one rings decent girls at this hour. Am I his booty call or what? I won't be kept on a leash next to the phone till eight at night.

"Where are you off to at this hour?" Mum's voice echoes from the bathroom.

Her tone doesn't promise anything exciting.

I want to leave the house even more. Go somewhere, where I'm treated like a normal person. And not where my one-sided love for Ostap leaves an un-washable stain on the reputation of my family.

"Gonna go to Katka's," I answer.

In response an accusatory silence.

The street is warm, summer-like. It smells of burnt leaves and the freshness of pine needles.

I'm going to go and tell him everything. About him not ringing me, about me going over to Vick's to find out where he lives, and, generally, that Katka persuaded me to do it all.

I decisively march towards Ostap's block. A minute later, Ostap's mum welcomingly opens the door and says that he's waiting for me in his room.

Definitely not – I think – if he were waiting, he'd have rung.

Again I'm at his closed door. I hear the loud howling of the Doors. It's true; he's waiting.

I carefully push the door. If I had kicked the door open and launched a brick at the mirror in front, Ostap still wouldn't have heard me.

He would lie there, like he's lying now. With his eyes closed. I sit down next to him. He doesn't even flinch. He probably went to ring me, but then fell asleep.

I gently caress his cheek with the back of my hand. He starts blinking. Softly pulls me to him. I listen to the beating of his heart. So cosy here.

First, we talk, and then you can do what you want. Actually, to hell with everything. Tomorrow we'll find out, or the day after that.

I sink my lips into his neck, as if I want to suck all of his dreams out.

Like on the "Go!" signal, he takes my face into his hands, crazily covering my cheeks, eyes and lips with his kisses. I tease him for a long time, turning away from his attempts to undress me, unbuttoning his shirt with my mouth, kissing his neck. Finally, he manages to get to my breasts. I feel his lips, and don't allow him to kiss them, and then he pulls me to him with all his might and loves me till midnight.

I return home once again. With love bites in all the right places. Quiet sighs, muffled moans. Also, my head is full of timid thoughts that something isn't right – I can't orgasm. Why do I pretend that I do? Or maybe I do, but I don't know about it? Maybe when you masturbate, the orgasm is so bright, but when you're making love for four hours, you simply feel good all the time? He fell asleep again and didn't walk me home.

A similar scenario the next day. This time, not waiting for accusatory looks from underneath the yoghurt mask, I leave home at 6pm. Ostap is watching TV. He drags me under his covers, like a boa constrictor's prey. Then, pants are flying out from underneath, and shirts too.

CHAPTER SEVEN

Señor Watermelon Yoza

The parents drive me to Nana Masha's on Monday morning. We grab some bread, cottage cheese, chicken and tomatoes. They are surprised about the low-cost rental price of the flat. Continuous knocking on the door. Despite warnings that the "hut stinks", my parents wrinkle at the entrance and their eyes roll upwards. Mum turns her gaze from Nana Masha to my bed. Coming to her senses, Mum starts laughing:

"Well, at least you won't be bringing any lads over, nope!"

Nana Masha eyes my parents.

Observing a cockroach on top of the ragged tablecloth, Dad clears his throat: "Olga, maybe you could come home for a bit?"

I cross my arms on my chest, stand next to the deaf Nana and shake my head disapprovingly. At that moment we look similar to two Winston Churchill British Bulldogs, which would have looked great in Dad's car, if we were a hundred times smaller.

"I'll put down some more poison for the cockroaches, clean the floor again and everything won't be so bad. I've only got another four nights here," I say.

"And anyway: Grand Vasilkovskaya, no alleyways, no elevators, you couldn't think up a safer place. Plus it's a five-minute walk to uni."

The parents exchange glances. Mum sighs. Dad puts his hands up in response. Then they unpack the groceries on the chair, the only more-or-less clean surface, and leave.

Shutting the door behind them, I feel a soaring feeling of freedom and want to sing about flying walks along alleys in May.

After a lively spring clean and many monologues from Nana about her husband who died in the war, I am bored. Monologues, not because I am silent, but because she doesn't hear anything I am saying, or hears stuff that I am not saying.

She also refuses to give me the keys to the flat. The inevitable possibility of constantly knocking on the door and yelling through the keyhole causes me even more deflation. How am I supposed to get in, if she won't hear my knock? Climb through the window?

A knock at the door. Nana Masha is sitting on her bed, watching a film, completely still.

"Someone's knocking!" I shout with my remaining strength.

"Eh?!" she asks, turning her head.

"Knocking on the door!" A note of frenzy in my shout.

"Someone knockin'?" she asks again.

"Yes!" I shout, nodding and feeling a crunch in my neck.

Nana gets up to open the door. I am surprised that she doesn't try to find out who it is first. What if they are burglars?

With agility uncharacteristic of a two-hundred-year-old woman, Nana Masha copes with all five locks and the latch, and a huge creature enters the flat, like a wide wardrobe with a head.

It is a person who is two, or even three, times wider and one and a half times taller than Nana. From afar she looks like little Piglet in a hanky next to a giant Winnie the Pooh, who seems enthusiastic about life, perhaps a sugar rush. His glimmering eyes scream: "Honey!"

Winnie the Pooh dressed in a dark green jacket. Above the dark green jacket perches a large, round head. A hairy watermelon. Maybe he's off to a masquerade, and this is his costume, Señor Watermelon? A hairy thick fringe. A face of some sort of Caucus origin, hard to guess which.

"Hwhy har you shouting, madam?" Watermelon smiles.

"Nana tormenting you, hyes? Hshe cannot hear hanything…"

"Yeah, I have to," I say sheepishly.

"Thas' Olga," says Nana. "I've got meself a new lass."

"Ahh, Olga, that's hgood name, listen. Listen, h-so good that hshe took you in, least someone hear when I knock on door."

"Are you her relative?" I find myself asking. Watermelon laughs.

"Ha'm not a relative…"

"I'm a watermelon!" I want to finish for him, smiling further. He continues:

"I hwant to buy this flat from her. And make shoe shop here. And she so old and mysterious."

"Nana! Tomorrow you got to go to housing office!" He shouts right into her ear.

"For wha'?" Nana replies aptly.

"See, when she h-wants to hear, she hears hstraight haway," says Señor, half voiced. And shouts in full volume to Nana:

"You heve to sign papers, that you don't mind selling flat. I already bought you new one. We see it h-later. I show you. It's close bhy."

Nana nods, understanding.

"H-Listen, help us, no? Come with tomorrow."

And again, to Nana: "Olga come with tomorrow, help you read papers."

"I've got lessons." I wave my hands. "I can't."

"What h-time you sta-hart?" he asks.

"At ten."

"There you have to be at eight. Listen, help us, ha? She is tormenting so much, not want to sign nothing."

"Fine," I say, shrugging my shoulders.

"Ah, angel. H-I invite you to restaurant! But you don't think hanything hof it, I'm honest and married man. You honly helping me, and h-I take you to restaurant. My name Yoza, by the hway."

I smile, raise my hands again and say: "How can I not help an honest, married man..."

The next morning turns out smooth like butter for Yoza. From the morning, he has polished hair, a thick scent of cologne and a facial expression as if he is about to break into loud, excited singing. He shows us Nana's new flat. The flat is near Vladimirskiy Market, with light green walls and without cockroaches. So far.

On the way to the housing office, Nana tells me that it is very good that I have come with her. Because she is scared that she'll be "played with and left without a flat".

"You won't be left without one, Nana Mash. He showed us the flat," I say loudly, looking around the empty morning street.

At the office, she signs everything. In reality, he won't be able to upset a babushka with trembling hands. I wouldn't let him. I reread the contract. I am not suspicious, but I make sure to read the clause "The Buyer is obliged to provide equivalent housing" and calm down. With the papers signed, we have to queue up.

The noble feeling that I am helping Nana persuades me to skip my first lecture.

After the second lecture I bump into Katka.

"A-ah!" I yell. "A Talking Tomato!"

Katka silently laughs. It's from our favourite joke, about two tomatoes in a fridge.

One: "Brr, it's cold!" The second shouting what I yelled, bumping into Katka.

When she finds something really funny, she first laughs silently, and then slowly takes in more air and laughs more. Something like this: silence, open mouth, "ah!" sound, silence, mouth open, "ah" sound, and so on. A similar sound to that of crows in old Soviet cartoons.

"Is the bandana for conspiracy, so I won't recognise you?" I ask, leading her to the side of the corridor, into a wide hall. I observe her bandana, red with brown daisies.

"You look charming," I admit, and stop near the window opposite the dean's office.

"What are you doing here? Have you come to a gathering of hippies who listen to Tolkunova instead of Nirvana?"

"No, for God's sake," says Katka, wiping her eyes, wet from laughter. "It's fashionable these days. Lika taught me." Katka raises her eyebrows importantly, squares out her shoulders, and only the dimples near the sides of her mouth, which haven't caught up with the rest of her, give away the fact that she is amused. "I came for an interview. I might be taken on as a department secretary through some people I met. Just for half shifts at first, and perhaps full-time after graduation."

"Oii that's aaaawwwesome!" I scream. "Now we'll definitely see each other every day! Wait. Are you not enrolling next year?" I start worrying.

"That's the thing," said Katka, lowering her voice. "If I manage to get a job here, then after two years I automatically enlist on the course I want. Without any competition or any fuckery."

"Oh, my days!" I shriek. "Good luck, mate! I'll be keeping my fingers crossed for you. And my toes as well."

"Keep them crossed. Listen, do you wanna go for a walk?" says Katka.

"Yeah, of course. And you can check out the wreck that I'm living in."

"Is it that crappy?" she asks.

"That's not even the word. Can I come over tomorrow? I want to wash in your shower!"

"Listen, this is ka-pets. To hell with your Nana, just come to ours today?" she says.

"Thanks, I would come today, but someone has invited me for dinner; I can't say no, I already promised."

"Who?" she stirs, her left eyebrow twitching upwards. "Ah, Ostap?"

"Not that kind of someone."

"Katerina Marchenko?" calls out a plump blonde of about forty years.

"Come on, Marchenko-Farchenko, break a leg. I'll be waiting at two o'clock and tell you everything then."

"Whatevz!" Katka sighs, and confidently strides forwards.

"Nana ish complaining 'bout h-you," Yoza throws into the direction of my seat, reversing his six Series BMW nto Grand Vasilkovskaya, from the back yard of Nana Masha's.

"Complaining?" I scrunch my face into the shape of a tube. How? The Nana whom I skipped my lectures for, with an aching heart looking over her paper signing, whom I poisoned cockroaches for, scrubbed cat tracks off the table, licked her floors clean plus soon to use her leaky pot for hygiene purposes... This same Nana is complaining?

"But in the morning it's all good and fine to skip with me to the housing office. How is she complaining? Why is she complaining?" I say.

"She s-hays that you have turned into real pest. First you took two people to house, preh-tending they parents, but really your clients, and then even brought over gipsy."

"What gipsy?! I told her it was Katka! My friend. Why gipsy? She's got blue eyes and pigtails."

"Says, h-wrapped in handkerchief gipsy. She doesn't h-see good. She can't h-see what h-eyes Khatka has. Pretty one? I have friend."

"Listen, what the actual—?" I clap my knees in annoyance. "That's Katka, my old classmate. Her 'handkerchief' is for fashion."

"Ah don't pay hany haattention, she's wary, she have nothing better to do, she mek up story. She decided that you t-hargeted her in park. We go to my h-friends quickly, OK?" Yoza confidently swerves through the alleyways of Kiev.

"I need to quickly print h-something. H-you want pizza? I get some."

I open my mouth, to once again rebel against the completely unfounded suspiciousness of Nana, but answer "Of course!" about the pizza and the "need to print a little bit at friend's". I put Nana to the back of my mind. Yoza stops by an off-licence, jumping out of the car. I don't mind about the pizza. I pat down my weekend outfit. I am hungry, like a real student, having not made any porridge at Nana's – I couldn't find any pots without holes. The idea to eat after lectures, so that I won't be grabbing everything at the restaurant, seems appropriate. And if I dig deep down into my soul, I find hope: we're not going to the restaurant...that's why! What do people wear there? I look at myself once again. I'm wearing a sporty black combidress with long sleeves, and black trousers. This is the only thing I have that looks smart. On top, I'm wearing Mum's autumn cream overcoat and my favourite attribute of every self-respecting Soviet lady – a handkerchief over the neck. In the overcoat I feel confident, but I will have to take it off in the restaurant. And would the fairies sitting at the neighbouring tables (in my mind, Kiev restaurants always have undressed fairies at tables. Always), would they be able to guess that it's just a sporty aerobic suit, bought at Vladimirskiy market for two hundred and twenty karbovantsiv? If yes, then the ground would have to swallow me up.

In addition, I remember long-legged Ella. When she found out that I was going to a restaurant, she bulged her eyes out in surprise. On the one hand, as if she wasn't expecting that I'd have a busy private life outside of university. On the other hand, it could have been: "Oh my God, she's going to a restaurant in an aerobic suit! I've *got* to tell Olesya!"

The worst thing is that now I have the feeling that even Yoza knows that I am in an aerobic suit, even though I haven't taken my overcoat off. In general, I am not sure about the restaurant.

The door swings open, and Yoza, rustling with his bags, bulkily falls into his seat and says: "I bought mushrooms, pizza, coo-cumbers, a jhar of holives, and bottle vodka."

"Wow! And vodka?"

"Well, we drink little bit then go to restaurant. I need half hour to do something at friend's. We go?"

"Ah, of course," I say.

Yoza is climbing the stairs to the third floor, and holding his breath, he tells me about his plans to open a shoe shop by the name of Top-o-the-Number.

Jumping forwards, I'll say that he wasn't lying. In the place where Nana Masha used to live, a shop did indeed open there with that name.

Chapter Eight

Snail in a Watermelon

"Y-hou drink, drink," mutters Yoza in his friend's narrow kitchen, pouring me the fifth shot of melon vodka, and I'm wondering when he's going to start printing.

"And when are you going to drink with me?" I say, looking at my shot glass being filled.

"H-I behind wheel, listen. Why you not h-eating? You h-eat," says Yoza, sliding a plate of pizza in front of me.

"You know who y-hou don't remind me of?" says Yoza.

I freeze. The awkward moment has arrived, when a married man tells compliments of weird honesty to a young girl.

"A crocodile!" I find myself saying. "That's well observed."

Yoza emits short squeaks and I realise this is the way he laughs.

"My ex." He puts his fingers on the table, thick like sausages, wrapped in dark sleeves, staring at me with his black watermelon seeds. I realise he's stopped laughing now.

I carefully place my shot glass on the table. Yoza jumps up to the sink, grabs a cloth, turns his back to me and starts scrubbing the hob, telling me:

"She was so sad, she h-always crying to window, that I married, and you so heppy and h-always joking."

Always joking. I just think sadness is not the best way to deal with screwed-up situations...

I'm done for. An Honest Married Man (HMM) who urgently needs to print something at a friend's flat on the way to a restaurant. Easy. Well, I happen to have a plan.

"Let's go, I show you something," says Yoza, pulling my hand, marshalling me into the hall, dropping the cloth into the empty sink.

"Scared of blood?" I ask, reluctantly giving in.

"Why h-you ask, ah?"

And before I can explain why he doesn't need to drag me into a half-black room, if he's scared of blood, he lightly pushes me onto the sofa. His clothes are on the floor. He rubs his bulky body against me, trying to shove his tongue into my mouth. As if somebody is trying to force feed me a snail, I giggle and say:

"I can't, Yoza." I turn away from the kisses. I'm laughing, at how he can't cope with my sports aerobic suit. It's got to be taken off through the legs, and he thinks it's a top!

"H-you don't be scared. I don't have big one. H-your boyfriend never knows. I clean," he whispers, encompassing me with his pickled mushroom breath. Or snails?

Jesus, Yoza, my dear, in which country were you taught to look after ladies so hhh-gallantly? If I were your lover, I'd also cry all day at the window. I wouldn't even know what to do if I was your wife. Probably wave my arms about from morning till night, shaking my head, like Nana Masha. Or maybe Nana Masha is his wife? I'm smiling. This would explain a lot.

Anyway, at least I don't have to show my manners either.

"I'm on my period," I say emphatically, like a cub scout in a line-up, stopping my trousers from descending lower than my knees, widening my eyes as if I'm offering him to have sex in a lifebuoy.

"Ah nah you lie." Yoza stops his kissing attack.

"Here," I say, again unceremoniously, finding the string from my tampon and putting it to his finger so he feels it. Convinced. His face shows sincere remorse while I boldly crawl out from his wet, deodorant-sprayed bulk. In the nude, he actually looks like a hairy slug, and his jacket, thrown into the corner of the room – his watermelon rind.

"And you don't worry." I straighten my hair in front of the mirror in the hallway. "In a few days we can come here again, get better acquainted, and you can actually take me to a restaurant." I say the last words in a harsh tone, like an erratic lover. He doesn't start demanding blow jobs or any other silly stuff. Otherwise I would have had to parry him with the tracery lamp or the half-empty bottle and end up hitching a ride at nine in the evening in an unknown part of Kiev.

"…Y-hou don't get upset that I jumped h'on you like some hungry moron," says Yoza, parking his car opposite Nana's house.

"Well…you didn't eat that much, did you?" I say, chewing on my lip, not interrupting my thought process about being able to make the last tram to Katka's halls. Just got to nip back to Nana Masha's, tell her I urgently need to stay with my friend, pack my stuff and never come back here again.

"And I congratulate you. You have good taste," I declare. Vick has heard this joke about fifteen times. I once read it out loud from a flip calendar of the year 1992.

In Yoza's six series BMW there is a stabbing series of squeaks. Laughing he is, bless him.

"Ah you smart one. Ah joker. Ah clever, clever." He is hugging me with one arm, and gripping the steering wheel with the other, still laughing and looking at me. I'm not smiling.

"I'm gonna need another bottle of vodka with two chocolate bars for the emotional distress," I say. And this isn't a joke. I'm really gonna need that, as now Katka's halls are the only place in Kiev where I can stay safely.

And add with a smile:

"Gonna booze with Nana. I want to soften her."

"Ghe-Ghe. Good idea. You h-wait here, Kitty." Yoza jumps out of the car and heads for the off-licence, pacing quickly. What an idiot. He's falling for it. What boozing can there be with a half-dead nana?

"Well, see you tomorrow." I peck him with tightly shut lips, and with great enthusiasm jump out of the car, although not before grabbing the bags with vodka and chocolates.

Eugh, horrible. I shake my head in the darkness near the door. Am I his Kitty? Blegh. I shudder with my shoulders and start drumming the door.

"Me sister's comin' over tomorrow. I'm gonna need the bed," Nana announces, as soon as I walk through the doorway. She is once again shaking her head, almost as if she isn't sure whether her sister really did need a bed or not.

"Excellent!" I yell, nodding, and head to the bed, to where my rucksack is.

"Sister can come over now if she wants," I add.

After five minutes, I am hurtling along lit-up Grand Vasilkovskaya, past the Republican Stadium, to tram number ten via Borgashovka, having freed up the bed for the arriving sister of Nana Masha. She is most probably shaking her head all night, wary that I will return and, with a way only known to her, cause her problems. Of course, there is no sister to come over. It was my parents and Katka who built up a whole Agatha Christie-type mystery in her murky, lonely head. Is she Miss Marple after all, or not Miss Marple?

Two months later I did visit her new flat, which was above Vladimir Market. I didn't have to knock on the doors for long. Nana Masha opened the door and I felt relieved that Yoza hadn't conned her out of her flat.

Now I'm racing to the tram. My bags are cheerfully clanking with jars of mushrooms and gherkins and rustling with leftover pizza and chocolate bars – to charm Lika and Katka. They'll die of laughter once they hear the restaurant story, sprinkled with Yoza's accent.

Just won't be able to tell Ostap how operation "Living near the university for one hundred and fifty karbovantsiv with cockroaches, poo and pots" didn't go well.

Otherwise I would have had to mention Yoza's pickled breath too.

CHAPTER NINE

English Test

October. Evening. Monday. Katka and I are walking in Goloseevo forest. We have a mission: to deliver Ostap's English test, which I have completed for him this weekend. He asked, you see.

"Tenth," says Katka. "That means the next one has to be the eleventh, if the halls are numbered logically."

"Then it should be behind those oaks and the turning. Another half a mile," I say.

"Listen, with these drunken shenanigans I keep forgetting to ask, did you tell Ostap that we went to Vick's?"

"N-no." I pensively observe the lit-up tarmac, which is wet.

"What the hell, what are you guys even up to together? You spend all your weekends together," says Katka.

"Same old," I reply. "I don't know; I see him, and my knees start giving way, and I can't speak till he…well, till he feels good. And when he achieves feeling good, there's no one left to talk to; he falls asleep."

"Doesn't he even walk you back?" says Katka.

"You and Vick say the same things. It's only next door I have to walk to," I say.

"Yeah but, what the hell, you've already almost been raped," she says. She lightly shrieks at the last word. She is right, my friend Katka. But I will never admit it to her. Because it's Ostap we are talking about. And Ostap is like an orange – he might be too sour and not ripened, but he is mine and I am not letting it go or sharing it. So, I say: "So what, a drunk guy walked into the lift. My own fault. Should have taken the stairs."

Katka is silently concerned.

"Well, that's the way he is." I gesture with my hands.

"He don't walk and he don't talk. He thinks that I should stay with him all night. Then we would spend Sunday together too. But I can't – Mum wouldn't understand."

"Did you do the test for Sunday?" Katka changes the subject.

"Yeah, in the morning. There was nothing to do anyway: two exercises on passives and one on the future perfect tense. The sooner I give it to him the better," I say. My confidence is melting with every step.

We're silent, just the double thumping of our autumnal wellies on the ground. It's easy to tell that Katka is wondering why I'm such an idiot. And I'm thinking that I don't like the idea of visiting Ostap. Katka pushed me into coming to him, and now she's saying that I've finished the English test too early.

Another pressing feeling is that I'm breaking our normal Saturday routine. Almost like if I decided that instead of sex on Saturday, I'd invite him to eat pancakes at my parents' on Sunday. And any other activity, except for sex, seems criminal. As if we are forbidden to travel to each other's homes without warning, being seen in halls, popping in for breakfast, meeting up in a cafe, going to the cinema...

We pass the turning and are close to the halls. About twenty paces away, two figures emerge: a lanky one and miniature one – a young man and girl. My heart skips a beat, like it skips every time, when I see lanky figures. And if the glasses are shimmering, then my stomach by tradition turns into one big butterfly and tries to flutter out of my body. The figure isn't only lanky but shuffling. There's no doubt. Ostap is with a girl. They get closer and look past us, as if we're drinking tea with booblick in Borshagovka, and not walking towards them. I'm not looking at him anymore, nor at the girl, and just want one thing – to keep walking, go unnoticed and run like the wind to the nearest bus stop, jump on a bus, go to Katka's halls and cry for a long, long time into Lika's dressing gown. These emotions create a huge lump in my throat and give me cotton feet.

Something inside of my head starts screaming, like a drunk, if a vodka van had crashed in front of his eyes. Although drunks don't scream, their voices are hoarse.

We walk past one another right under a lamp. And here Katka recognises Ostap.

"That was Ostap!" she says.

"Yeah," I utter.

"So, what's up?" she asks me. "Osha, are you guys completely...? Ostap!" she shouts to the whole forest.

"Katka, leave them."

"Ostap! Damn, you're both so weird."

I like that Katka is surprised by our behaviour. This gives a hint of normality between us.

I turn in Ostap's direction. Ostap also slows his pace and stops. Turns around.

"Yeah, I'm Ostap."

All four of us fall silent. They are there, and we are here.

I, for example, have turned to stone. Katka doesn't know what to do. The whole absurdity of the decision to come to Ostap's without warning gets to me. I hate Katka. Not Ostap, for some reason. Well, for one obvious reason, really.

I hate Katka. For pushing me into coming, for being so stupid and not understanding that we don't have a normal relationship. Ostap does what he wants, and I build myself around it, not putting everyone in an uncomfortable position in the middle of the street on a Monday evening. Maybe there's nothing between him and the girl, but he pretends (or doesn't pretend?) that he didn't see us, and now I should be angry. It's not like he asked for that test to be done and delivered urgently in one day. He expected it this week on Saturday. We would have met up on Saturday, as always. Now it's unlikely we'll meet ever.

"We brought you your test!" Katka shouts, with annoyance in her voice.

"Cool. Did I ask you to do that?" he replies.

A huge dragon arises inside of me, emitting a heartbreaking cry, spewing out fire. Fury. I confidently walk up to Ostap, take my backpack off my shoulders, get his book out, shove it under his arm and tell his chest:

"Th-there."

Turn around. Don't even glance at the girl. Pretty or not? I am curious. Fury is blind.

I take Katka's hand. Straight ahead.

Whether buses to Borshagovka are going from where we are heading to, we do not know. We end up having to change three times. Jumping it each time. We get home by midnight. The doors are locked, the warden sleeping. We have to throw stones at our window on the second floor, calling Lika to help, so she can open the doors for us. I climb up on some metal thingy. Slip and fall on my ankle. The metal thingy punctures a hole in the bone of my leg with the sharp end. It takes around three months to heal. The scar is still there. I don't go to his the next Saturday after that Monday. And he doesn't ring.

At the end of October, I find a cosy room in the People's Friendship area, at Aunt Sonya's for thirty pounds a month. Now in the morning I cook porridge in an enamel orange polka-dot pot, without holes, of course, and take showers and baths behind a curtain covered in dolphins, with lights and in the warmth. Aunt Sonya's two-bedroom flat smells of geraniums and buckwheat soup. I have my own work desk, a cosy green desk lamp and a small fish tank with red, yellow and blue fish. I do my work with pleasure and go to uni on foot. An hour and a half each way. It's good for the figure, and with the money I save I buy textbooks. On Saturdays and Sundays, I'm at Kholmysty and go over to Katka's parents'. Vick comes round too. I don't talk about Ostap. I think that Vick knows from Katka. Because he doesn't ask.

CHAPTER TEN

Beginning of Christmas Lent

Christmas Lent is approaching, and I decide to fast. I'll lean out some more. Although, my jeans are already falling down as a result of walking to and from university. What if I bump into Ostap in the street? He'll see how thin I am, and fall in love with me with a new-found strength.

Independent life without fun drinks with Katka and her friends affects me deeply. I crash into religion. Not into walking to churches and placing candles in front of icons, but into my own organised religion, which includes reading prayers in the first hour of waking up and before sleep. I decide that my soul is dirty and sinful because I succumbed to the devil, giving myself to Ostap. If I could have held out and taken God seriously earlier, then I wouldn't be running to Ostap right now; he would be the one running to me. Reading prayers includes sometimes three kneels, sometimes six and sometimes twelve.

Aunt Sonya can probably hear how I am praying, because once in the morning she asks me where I got my deep faith.

There is a bug in my head. The image of Maria Bonaparte speaks to me more and more. I forget that this is an idea, born from a psycho-lonely Pashya at Katka's halls.

I see the green room, and there is a steering wheel, and behind it right now stands the responsible Maria Bonaparte in her monarch robes.

Maybe to the monastery?

"Why not," she answers. "I wonder if they let you into the monastery during Lent?"

I am hit with hope. If I am going to the monastery, then I won't see Ostap till the New Year. He will miss me, find me, kiss me, love me and make me happy on New Year's Eve. That's when I come out. On New Year's Eve it will be a year since we got together.

Maria Bonaparte, like the snow queen, is already in her royal robes. Sensuality begs her to go and say goodbye to Ostap. She isn't reacting.

"Saying goodbye is necessary," Maria Bonaparte suddenly says.

"And we have to show: now I rule this kingdom. By the way." She walks along the green room, Sarcasm and Sensuality staring at her.

I decided not to go to the monastery. Lent is tomorrow already; I should have gone sooner. Instead our room with Aunt Sonya will be our monastery. It's quiet, cosy. We can pray as much as we want. I want. We'll go and see Ostap, saying that we're leaving for a month and have come to say goodbye. I insist on a short visit.

I suspect that something isn't quite right with my head.

So, on Saturday, the twenty-seventh day of November, I leave to say goodbye to Ostap. I will arrive after nine. Either he or his parents will definitely be home. I hope that it will be him. Obviously.

I'm in a fur coat. It's fashion. I inhale the light scent of perfume from underneath my collar. Make-up. It's nice to look attractive again. Calm. I haven't just come to say bye. I'm leaving for a noble cause. My heart beats steadily. Maybe I don't love him any longer? I don't feel anything at all. I ring the doorbell. Silence. Then the rustling of trousers. Ostap's lanky figure appears. An exciting odour. He's so close. I want to hug him.

I look him in his eyes and remain silent. This should have an effect.

"Wow," Ostap says under his breath. As if I just told him that eggs on the market have doubled in price.

"I'm not staying long," I say, confidently stepping through the doorway.

"Lady, you must be here for Vick, I presume?" he says, backing away and shutting the door behind him.

"No," I say, and understand that he knows about the visit to Vick's.

"Well, if anything, he's here. Whooping me in chess for the third hour running," he says, walking through the dark corridor. I take my shoes off. Vick isn't an idiot. He's either hanging out with me on Saturdays, or at Ostap's.

I walk into the room. Vick and Ostap sit in the lotus position.

"Know how to play chess?" Ostap asks.

"Yes," I reply, sitting on the table opposite the bed.

"Oh, Osha, hey!" Vick's voice sounds as if I look about thirty stone heavier. I smile mischievously. I know what he's thinking: I gave up, came to Ostap's myself, forgetting about a girl's sense of pride, and here is Vick, happily getting in the way. And I'm annoyed, Vick is thinking, just like at cub scouts, when our keeper lets in a goal, and the whole bench of supporters are shouting: "Damn it! Such a shame, uh well, uh well, uh well!"

"I was only passing by, really, and thought I'd come in," I say, shrugging my shoulders.

"Tomorrow I'm leaving till New Year's."

Ostap stops sitting and staring at the chessboard, resting his chin on the palm of his hand. He's looking at me, as if the queen is on my forehead, and he has to make a move, to bring down the knight. If I mention the weather, he'll never look. And if I say that I'm leaving, he'll look. Here. Now he's looking.

Vick drops the intention to whoop Ostap at chess for the third hour running, also intently covering me with his serious gaze. As if he's a doctor, and I'm complaining to him about my aching liver, especially after eating a fatty sausage. This expression of exaggerated pity doesn't suit him – he looks like an ugly bear with clumped eyes and a pug nose. But Ostap suits every face. He's so tempting with his unbuttoned shirt in large chequers, draped over his T-shirt. If not for Vick, his bed would have long been creaking before my departure, and the monastery, so to speak.

"Vick, so good that you're here!" I say. I really mean it.

"And where are we keeping you from?" asks a stone-faced Ostap.

"The monastery," I croak, staring at his unbuttoned shirt. Get a grip, Osha! "Well, I won't get in your way," I say, coming to my senses. And then briskly adding:

"See you in the New Year, friends."

And I leave.

I left! I want to roar with joy, like a whole crowd of football fans at a match, in ecstasy! I score a goal in the deciding match. I tap away at the wet tarmac with my heels. The excitement is too strong to go home and fall asleep in half an hour. I hurry off to Katka's house.

With Katka it is fun. We drink some beer. Her mum makes a first-class cheese. We eat all of it. And the next day, we begin fasting together.

CHAPTER ELEVEN

Christmas Lent Interrupted

Two weeks after the start of Lent, it is Rudi's birthday. We are in his cosy three-bedroom flat with Ostap, Vick, Katka and Zhuka, and half of the class.

Everyone is eating, drinking, laughing. I'm sitting on the sofa, bored. Almost asleep. Alena Sensuality wakes up in the green room, creeps up quietly to the remote…and catches Ostap's sad gaze behind Maria Bonaparte's back. Either his gaze is sneaky-sad, or his desire has started to burn in one place or another, but I notice joy in his eyes. Maybe because I came back from "the monastery" earlier than he expected?

Everyone goes out to smoke. Katka, who is doing Lent with me, goes to the toilet. I'm the only one in the room. One on one with the table, which is bursting with yumminess. I'm not staring at the fried chicken. It's the chicken staring at me. I'm holding myself back. I'm not staring at the stewed potatoes with the tender pork; they're staring at me. But I still hold myself back, very tightly, grappling a napkin. And then I see them.

"Pancakes stuffed with cottage cheese and raisins!" I exclaim to Katka, who has returned from the toilet.

"How do you know they're sweet?" asks Katka. Katka's voice turns even glummer from the Lent abstinence.

"What are the raisins in the cottage cheese for? What do you think?" I reply. The next second: bang, I take a bite. Katka gasps in and out, sighing just like a Ukrainian mother.

Maria Bonaparte screams in my head: "Fear God!"

Katka mutters, "What are you doing? We'd been holding on for so long," and waves her arms around, two wrinkles on her forehead.

And if she hadn't muttered anything, maybe I would have stopped after one piece.

But as it was, I wanted to spite her with another piece, and another.

How I hated her back then, so much that all five pancakes with soft cheese and raisins ended up in my stomach in one swift moment. Katka is paralysed with shock. I imagine how my sarcasm, full of strength and energy, hits Maria Bonaparte properly. In the face, and she flies back all the way behind the sofa. Alena now sparkles with emerald tones, cackles and says:

"Now take me to Ostap."

Pashya would have been proud, had I have told him about my green fantasies.

I open the balcony door. They're arguing about where to celebrate New Year's, and smoking.

"Osha," says Zhuka. "Year after year, eleven years running we have the same argument on Rudi's birthday: where to party for New Year's, at Tolly's or Rudi's?"

"Have you come to look down on us?" says Ostap, taking in a drag.

"Can I have a cigarette?" I say, holding his steely soft gaze. How does he do it?

Everyone chants the letter "O" in harmony.

"And anyway, let's drink," I add.

Everyone sings the letter "O" more loudly and animated.

"Good on ya," says Rudi.

Katka comes out to the balcony and murmurs:

"You held on for so long – two weeks."

"Hello, Osha, finally," says Vick.

"Take a seat. I'm happy for you," says Tolly.

"Drink some vodka and don't forget that you've still got everything in front of you," says Rudi.

"In front of me? How very poignant, Rudi, now I'm gonna be smoking out this saying all night," I say, lighting a cigarette from a quiet Ostap. Our eyes meet for a second, telling each other "I hate you" – "Oh really!", and then part again back to friends.

"How about I bring some vodka, and we'll all pop one here?" says Tolly and he is already squeezing behind my back to the door. I lose my balance and would have dropped, but Ostap's long arms catch me. His palms slip from my hands up to my elbows. I cling to him, my back to his front. Rudi brings over an ashtray; I flick the ash and feel Ostap's lips on my forehead. His strong arms and soft lips speak libraries of words.

"At least do not drink a lot today," I tell myself under my breath and try to turn to the direction of my flat.

"No, tonight you don't live there. You live over there." Ostap's offhand words take us to the direction of his place. The wind romantically blows in my face. Today I'll tell him about Lika, about the visit to Vick's and Yoza. I'm scared.

"I have champagnske," says Ostap, sitting in his favourite lotus position and folding his hands in place to hold his chin. Déjà vu. I'm sitting in the same pose, opposite, and remember that if he has champagnske, then he was expecting my arrival and also wants to talk.

"Bring it. And the glasses," I say, shrugging my shoulders.

He pulls out a bottle from under the bed, and two plastic cups from his pocket, not taking his eyes off me. Our gaze connected by an invisible electric current.

"It's a bit warm." Ostap opens the bottle carefully and looks at me. "I thought I wouldn't see you until New Year's."

"I always liked how you take out a bottle and open it with one hand, and with the other not taking your gaze off me," I say.

"I'm listening to you intently. With both hands," he says, and pours the warm foamy liquid.

"What are you going to listen to?" I ask compassionately, taking a full cup.

"The truth."

"And you don't want to tell me your truth?" I ask.

"Sure thing. Ask me," he answers.

"Who's the girrrl?" I ask.

"Lera. Course mate. A friend. She loves me, I don't love her. We were walking from the Colloquium."

I think to myself that he and Vick pick up girls at the Academy with such boring names.

"The opposite direction of your halls?" I ask.

"She asked me to walk her." He shrugs his shoulders.

"And you can't even walk me." I am stung with jealousy.

"Oh, here we go. What don't you like about my bed?" He jumps up pointedly. The bed creaks loudly and woefully.

"There, there," I say, raising my eyebrows. "Plus, your place is packed out with parents in the morning, plus my mum is in shock, that same morning."

"How old are you?" Ostap sighs.

"Unfortunately, we have different mums. Mine doesn't like it when I don't sleep at home, and yours does," I answer. But I do agree with him. My mum has to understand – it's safer to stay at his place.

"Our mums are different. That's fortunate, don't you think?" says Ostap, and we start laughing.

"OK, another truth," he says.

"I thought we would meet up in Kiev. What was the point of shooting the breeze all night at the beginning of studies?" I give him a serious look and bite my lip.

"Um, you see..." He rubs both palms on his knees and looks at the floor, as if there are loads of different words scattered across it, and he has to find the right one.

"I come home on Friday. Only political science and international law in my head. Mum's stewed potatoes, cow's tongue in the garlic. We sit down at the table. Dad pours a drink and says: 'Well, Ostap, go on, tell us all, what have you learned?'"

I burst out laughing, just like every time when he switches to Ukrainian, speaking in different roles.

"After five hours, I climb into my bed," he continues, "I shut my eyes and glumly think: 'Tomorrow is Saturday. Oshka's coming.'

"Well, now you," says Ostap, his softening eyes sparkling under his glasses.

"What do you want to know?" I shy away for some reason. Ostap holds a pause, just like when he's about to say something important. I am about to say the truth. And then I can jump on him.

"I want to know everything that I don't know, but Vick knows." Ostap's voice chills. "I want to know what even Vick doesn't know. And I don't know, but can tell by the face." He looks me in the eye. "I don't want my girl to lie to me," he adds more softly.

And I am hoping my guy will talk to me about silly stuff. But I don't say it. I nod. Throat feels dry. A sip of champagnske. The moment of truth. He knows that I have lied and haven't told him everything. Is he reading my mind? Or Vick, maybe Vick.

"Right, I'll start by saying that I would love to tell you everything that Vick knows, if we had more time than just Saturday. And Sundays, sometimes. But after five days I want to eat you. Slowly."

Ostap smiles.

"Afterwards it will be too late to speak," I continue. "After four hours we're both sleepy, and you instantly fall asleep." Ostap nods.

"Now about what Vick knows. In the first week of September we came to the Academy with Katka. And went round to his. What Vick doesn't know: we went to his to find out where you live. Vick said that he saw you in the morning with beer and I decided that you wouldn't be happy seeing me. Our second visit with Katka to the halls confirmed my doubts."

Ostap nods, but I catch no guilt spark in his eyes.

"What neither Vick nor you know..." I sigh deeply. There's still time. I can still decide not to say anything and leave it all as it is. "Is about Lika and Yoza," I blurt out.

Ostap widens his eyes with interest. And I continue, no longer looking him in the eye, talking to his socks:

"Lika lives with Katka. In the first week of studies, I fell out with Mum over...well, that's a whole 'nother story. Mum found out that me and you... you know..."

This topic is harder than I thought.

"Say it how it is." Ostap interrupts my stuttering.

I say it how it is. Ostap grunts, then I continue.

"In short, we fell out. I went to Katka's halls. We got drunk. We partied. And whilst dancing with Lika, we fooled around, and when everyone left, we..." I start to shake. Ostap's eyes darken. He stops nodding and looks at me, as if he is looking at the middle of my forehead. I feel so lonely now.

Ostap is silent. I've lost him. What was I thinking? Ostap is possessive.

Actually, no. He threw Katka on her shoulder blades, ate pies at Pushi's, walked some Lera home.

And I am very understanding about all of that.

He's a man.

And I – a woman.

And I also have a right to make mistakes.

"Next story," he says hoarsely.

"Now Yoza," I say.

Taking a proper deep breath, I tell him about Yoza. Honestly. Even about his watermelon rind under the shade and the forcible tasting of snails... Ostap isn't laughing. Ostap slowly rubs his brows, and slowly moves his toes in black socks with their small hole.

The story is over. Why isn't he falling over with laughter, like Lika and Katka? Lika even started hiccupping, when I compared Yoza's tongue to a snail. That's it. It was a good Ostap. Now he is Lera's. Vick can dance the Lezginka quietly in his room. Katka will sigh with relief – neither she nor I managed to win Ostap over.

On the other hand, I feel lightness. Now there's nothing to hide or be scared of, that he'll find out about from Vick or Katka. And such a pleasure when he's listening!

I need to make up more stories every weekend.

I want to return back to Rudi's for the birthday, when Ostap was looking at me from the other side of the table. Then pressing his lips to my forehead.

Ostap pours the remainder of the champagnske.

"Walking in my favourite socks, knowing there's a hole there," he says. I freeze. Is he really going to start insulting me? Damn, it isn't my fault, well not the second incident.

"But," he continues, "now I can sow them up and drag them further, like new."

"That's some comparison..." My tone is contemplative, as if icy, but sounds pitiful.

"Not the best," Ostap says. "I'd like a hole in my favourite shirt, on the left side."

I smile with relief. He is off the hook.

"Well, here's to the repair of the socks and shirts," he says.

He kind of tainted everything, but also didn't really taint anything. I nod and take a sip of champagnske.

"And now, the maintenance," says Ostap, and he puts down his empty cup on the floor. "Usually it's done like this." He wipes his lips with his sleeve. "The guy kinda invites the girl to the restaurant, and then they go off to shag."

"Ah, that's how it's done? I didn't know, you see, an honest married man, a deaf, blind granny."

"And I want you to know. That's exactly why I ain't showing no melancholy."

I satisfyingly fall silent.

"And you didn't have to tell me about Lika. It's a girl."

I raise my eyes. And if she's got a whole army of men in her green room, who look like Ryan Gosling, like my sarcasm does?

"Oh yeah?" I say. As if I didn't know that Lika is a girl.

"And if you did it with some lad, fooling about, then am I to know?"

"A lad with a lad…that's different," he says.

"You could get pregnant?" I smile.

Ostap bursts out laughing, like a five-year-old kid, who manages to pull off a magic trick with his finger. I love his laugh. Then I'm a kid too.

Like a caterpillar, he crawls towards me. I'm hugging him around his feet. I pull mine out and hug his waist. I whisper to his lips: "I won't do it again."

CHAPTER TWELVE

From the Memories Box

On 1st January, we are heading back from a friend's. Night. Silent snow falls on my hat. My cold hand in his hot hand. No gloves. I want to be at his. I want to keep the hat on. We rush. We are in the lift. Kiss. He is thirst and I am water. I am lots of water.

He quickly copes with the lock. The door squeaks open. It's dark in the hallway. I lean on the door and close it. Heart is pumping. He touches my face in the darkness. He finds my mouth. He kisses it greedily.

Unwraps me from my coat, like an ice cream from its wrapper. He doesn't touch the hat. The same fantasies. I am on the floor. The fur coat gently caresses my back. It's wet from the snow and my back is hot from... Everything happens in silence and quickly.

While he's breathing in my ear, his mum comes out of the bedroom, turning the light on in the hallway. We hastily cover ourselves up with the coat. The light instantly turns off and his mum walks back into her room. We're giggling in the darkness, barely touching lips. I know that he's happy.

CHAPTER THIRTEEN

Auntie Sonya's Illness

In mid-January, at six o'clock in the morning, a dishevelled Auntie Sonya bursts into my room, with a red face, and starts babbling separated syllables:

"Dali – Laka – kama – tapa – titu…"

I was fasting all day yesterday, and on an empty stomach, I get incredibly scared.

Maybe I have overdone it with the prayers and the evil spirits have moved from me over to her? Maybe these spirits are from family portraits, which hang on the walls in the flat?

Twenty years ago, poor Auntie Sonya had a tragedy. Her nineteen-year-old son was hit by a car and was killed. The housekeeper, Miss Elvira, told me this story in a whisper, and I started to feel really sorry for Auntie Sonya. My heart broke every time I saw how she looked at the curtains with eyes full of tears. The calm beautiful face of her son, who looked a lot like our famous actor Andrei Mironov, mockingly pierces me with his gaze from both walls of my bedroom every morning. I am overtaken with a feeling of guilt for being alive. Like in the fairy tale from my childhood, Mashenka in the Bear's bed.

A year after their son's death, her husband died of a heart attack.

Judging from the furniture in the flat and the German ornaments, her husband earned good money and even travelled abroad. For example, a stick with pink and yellow feathers for wiping dust. I have never seen feather dusters before. I assume they were unheard of in the Soviet era twenty years ago. He worked with some secret services; exactly which ones, I don't know.

What is important is that Auntie Sonya's life stopped twenty years ago. She stopped cooking food, cleaning the flat. Her sister Lucy, a buoyant frizzy-haired brunette, had to hire a housekeeper for thirty pounds a month. The elderly housekeeper Elvira – a fine woman, plump, smelling of milk and pies, around twenty years older than Auntie Sonya – comes over on Mondays, Wednesdays and Fridays. She cooks food, cleans the flat and takes Auntie

Sonya out for walks. Auntie Sonya has two favourite activities: searching for new pills to increase her energy and watching soap operas.

Not one of the series is shown without Auntie Sonya's acknowledgement. Auntie Sonya's whole day consists of waiting. Waking up in the morning, she begins to wait for Elvira. Elvira comes at seven to cook semolina porridge. They'll talk about the weather, and about yesterday's soaps. Then Elvira starts wiping dust and vacuuming. Auntie Sonya starts waiting for me to get up at eight in the morning. She wishes me a good morning. I have upset Auntie Sonya dearly by not watching the soap series with her.

Hearing that I pray, she started being wary of me. I don't blame her for that. After tidying, she and Elvira go out for a walk. Then Elvira will cook lunch: brisket soup, either with rice or buckwheat, and Auntie Sonya will watch yesterday's soap rerun. She'll eat, chatter, and nap. And then it's nearly time for dinner. At five in the evening, having cooked dinner, Elvira hurries home for the start of the soap, so that she can discuss it tomorrow with Auntie Sonya.

Buoyant sister Lucy comes round at eight in the morning on Tuesdays and Thursdays, filling the flat with her loaded, chesty voice:

"Did you see yesterday how Alberto drove one into Victor's face? Blegh, he's so slimy. Where did they find such a lousy actor? He's just *right* for this part!"

Seeing that Auntie Sonya is still in bed, Lucy usually exclaims:

"Wait, are you still in bed? Sonya darling, I don't know, but is it really that difficult to get up and cook some porridge for yourself?"

In reply, Auntie Sonya is silent, and I, walking past on the way to the bathroom to brush my teeth, say hello to her. Auntie Sonya's eyes fill with tears.

"Sonya, darling, it's better for you." I can hear through the bathroom door.

"You purchase all these tablets to have more energy, don't you? Well, what the heck do you need it for? You don't even come over to visit me. I, for example, wiped the floor this morning and feel alive."

Auntie Sonya replies in a neutral tone, hiding the sadness in her voice:

"I haven't lived for twenty years, Lucy." On the word "Lucy", her voice shudders. "And you know that," she ends in a whisper.

Walking past her room to mine, I see that Auntie Sonya looks at the window curtain, mourning.

Sister Lucy waves with her hand and goes to the kitchen mumbling under her breath:

"When she wants to eat, she doesn't suffer, but when it's time to dust, she rolls her eyes in sorrow. What kind of person is this? Lord, give me strength."

Hearing this dialogue twice a week makes me giggle every time.

So, that morning, usually pale Auntie Sonya, with a mane of straw hair, like a queen, bursts into my room with a red face, as if straight out of the bath, mumbling unconnected syllables. After which, she starts whimpering pitifully. I, just woken up, frightened, yell:

"Auntie Sonya, what's wrong? Have you gone crazy? Get out of my room!"

Auntie Sonya looks around frightened, and walks out. Behind the wall she is babbling and sobbing. What do I do? Sister Lucy!

"What, did Auntie Sonya not warn you? She gets bouts of hypertension every three months. Give her cold water. I'll be right there."

Half an hour later, Auntie Sonya is taken to the hospital – right opposite her window, the one she was looking at mournfully at eight in the morning on Tuesdays and Thursdays.

An hour later Sister Lucy rings and says: "Olga, Auntie Sonya has been examined; you're looking after the house now. They're hospitalising her for three weeks."

"Poor thing. Of course, by all means." I'm full of compassion, then it suddenly dawns on me.

"Miss Lucy, I'm scared to stay alone. Can I call my friend Katka?"

"Your friend Katka? But how are you going to pay? Ah, you're scared. Yeah, I can't sleep at all at her place either. OK. You're a serious girl, a female friend is allowed."

Me, serious? I've urgently got to stop morning prayers.

That was Friday. Immediately a plan forms. I'm off home. Tomorrow I'll see Ostap. I'll invite him to live at Auntie Sonya's. To make love in a quality, most probably German, bed belonging to Auntie Sonya, which probably doesn't creak either. The thought of it takes my breath away. I call Sister Lucy again:

"Miss Lucy. My friend Katya can't come. It's a long journey for her to get to uni. Could I invite my boyfriend? He's very careful."

A silence. I bite down on my bottom lip. I shouldn't have said about the boyfriend. But in three weeks, she'll come over and see a man in a towel and will die from surprise. Finally, the phone asks:

"You have a boyfriend?" This information doesn't coincide with the ritual kneeling for prayers three, six and twelve times every morning.

"I do," I admit, guiltily of course. "For a year and a half already."

"It's kind of surprising. And why don't you get married?" Miss Lucy asks.

"We'll finish our studies, then get married straight away," I lie.

"Has he proposed to you?" A glimmer of hope in Lucy's voice.

"Not yet." I really want to be rude to Sister Lucy right now but want to live with Ostap for three weeks even more.

"Well, all right," she announces.

"I won't say anything to Auntie Sonya. Let her think you're with your friend Katka, so she won't worry."

What's there to worry about? That we'll break the bed? I really don't like Sister Lucy. But I have to be nicer to her. Three weeks with Ostap! Woo!

CHAPTER FOURTEEN

Three Days in Auntie Sonya's Flat

"We're not drinking," Ostap says, leaving his shot of vodka. I obediently nod, gathering up the empty plates, and stand to do the dishes. He comes over, lifts the hem of my silk robe, tucks it into the belt, and I feel him getting onto his knees. The rippling water runs from the tap. His kisses below my knee. Then the other. Higher. His hands run higher up. Under the robe's belt. My back bends under his fingers. His hands wrap around my stomach. He kisses me higher and higher towards my back. I turn the water off.

"Let's go," he whispers, and I return from the heavens into Auntie Sonya's cosy kitchen.

The first night on Auntie Sonya's pull-out sofa. A blanket isn't necessary. Turning off the night lamp isn't necessary. Shutting the doors. Putting on the Doors on high volume. None of it is necessary. I greedily look at him. The light from the lamp allows me to see his open lips, his gaze from top to bottom. He grimaces, as if he is in pain. That means he feels very good. I claw into his hips; I am trying hard. He cannot take it – gently pushing me onto the sofa. The main thing is to fall gracefully. I can do it – what were all those aerobics classes for? My boob is half lost in his mouth. Wow, what a big mouth! I smile. A sudden movement. A sweet pain. No more room for smiles. Auntie Sonya's pull-out sofa doesn't creak.

During the night we wake up to a rustling noise in the flat. The red numbers on the digital clock show zero two thirty-one. The floors creak; I hear irritable mutters and whispering. I break into a cold sweat. Is Auntie Sonya back from the hospital? At zero two thirty-one? Not one prayer is being uttered at this point. Ostap's breathing is almost inaudible.

"Are you asleep?" I ask in a whisper.

"No," he answers back in a whisper.

"Can you hear it?" I ask.

"Yeah," he replies, feeling for the switch on the lamp.

The strange noises die down. The rest of the night is spent with open eyes, turned-on lights, and no sleep.

In the morning, putting a mug of steaming coffee in front of Ostap, I say:

"That was her son that woke us up last night." I sit opposite him with my mug.

Ostap looks at me questioningly.

"Have you seen the portraits?" I continue. "One is her son, the other her husband. The son died twenty years ago, the husband a year later. She remembers them every day. She's probably not letting them go to the other world. So, they're in anguish, that we slept on her sofa. Nobody's shagged on it for twenty years, I bet."

"What are you on about?" says Ostap, blinking. I can feel the disappointment in his voice. He's switched to Ukrainian. Meaning he's going to try to sound clever.

Sarcasm hisses in the green room to Alena: "For once she was allowed the mic outside of bed talk – to chat such bollocks! Quick – turn it into a joke!"

"What are they teaching you at Humcoll?"

"Why do you call my university Humcoll?" I say bitterly. My college is called the Economic Humanitarian College at the Kyiv State Linguistic University, but Ostap likes to call it the Humcoll.

Ostap sighs with frustration, as if he were trying to explain something to an eight-year-old.

"Imagine, child. Baba Claudia and Baba Valia are sitting on the bench. Osha and Ostap are passing by.

"'There, you see,' says Baba Claudia, 'the couple is walking: she is at the Linguistic University, and he is at some sort of academy.'"

"Some sort of humcoll sounds simpler, I reckon," I say. "But anyway, tell me, why didn't you end up going to Shevchenko Uni? You could have studied there for a year on placement, then transferred to full-time. And no chicks would have been annoying you."

"Everyone knows my old man at the Academy, and at Shevchenko there's a lot of knobs driving around in Mercs."

I once again feel like I am asking too many questions.

He finishes his coffee, gets up, puts his mug in the sink.

"I get it. Humcoll, so let it be Humcoll. Leave it; I'll wash it myself. But let's sleep in my room tonight. I'm scared."

Ostap nods. Kisses me with coffee lips and goes into the hallway.

"I'm going to a stand-up gig today with mates. Be back evening time," he says, tying the laces on his shoes.

"Good." I pretend that I don't care.

Why didn't he tell me earlier? Why isn't he taking me? What friends? I won't ask. I'll wait.

For me, evening time is 7–8pm. Sometimes nine.

Ostap comes back at 1am. I have to point out here, the night life of Kiev in the nineties is non-existent. There are places to go to, of course, but not without a thousand dollars, a gun and a heavily made-up chick in a short skirt. I am sure Ostap would sooner be dead then end up in a night club.

So, by 1am I have drunk half a bottle of vodka, smoked five cigarettes, waving away various thoughts from my mind. He was robbed in the street, beaten up, and he's lying there, drunk, unconscious, with broken glasses, and a cracked shard is poking him in the left eyelid. Hearing the creaking on the floor of the flat, I loudly say:

"Please do come through to the kitchen, fellow comrades affected. We can wait together."

The noises stop. I read aloud, "Our Father," and drink more vodka. I'm losing my mind. What am I supposed to do? I want to scream so loudly, like the boy in black trousers and a white shirt from the film *The Legend of Tim Tyler: The Boy Who Lost His Laugh*. This amuses me.

I look out of the window for the tenth time. Leaning against it, to see the whole street. An empty part of the road, leading to Auntie Sonya's hospital, lit by a street lamp, and bare trees swaying in the wind. Terrible. More vodka. And more smoking.

I'm shaken. What happens if he ceases to exist? I would just die. Or turn into Auntie Sonya. I'll hang his portraits all over the house and watch soaps for the rest of my life. Bloody stand-up.

I imagine a scenario a la Pashya: Sarcasm weakens and lowers the remote even further. He isn't drunk and isn't asleep. Alena and Crow whisper. What are they whispering about? Black trousers and a white shirt flash by the remote.

Sarcasm looks at it and smiles helplessly. The boy's black eyes, wide open… He's about to start screaming. Alena and Crow cover their ears…

At that very moment, a knock at the door. Then a short ring of the doorbell. I stub out the butt into an empty can of salted peanuts. Open the door, and without looking to see if it is Ostap or not, walk off into my room. Take off my dressing gown and dive under the duvet. Fearing that I won't warm up without him, I'm shaking. Glad that he's alive.

He comes into the bedroom, smelling of oranges. He leans down and tries to shove a slice from his lips into my mouth. I don't open my lips.

He climbs under the duvet and puts his hands under my T-shirt. I take his hands away. He realises that I'm upset. Sighs and walks out to the kitchen. There he will see five butts and a half-empty bottle of vodka. With that thought I warm up and fall asleep.

The next morning, he appears in the kitchen, when I am already finishing my coffee. With the tone of Elvira asking Auntie Sonya whether the semolina porridge is tasty, I ask: "How was the stand-up?"

"Good," he answers, suspicious of my friendly tone. I notice his eyes quickly widening and instantly narrowing.

"Laugh lots?"

"Uh-huh." Ostap goes for the coffee jar.

"I'll be off, then. Lectures finish at two today. I'll be home by three," I say and peck him on the cheek.

"Mine finish at two as well. Let's meet here and go for a walk?" he says.

"Take a key. I found an extra one yesterday. Didn't think to look for a second one before."

Now with complete trust, he takes the key. The happy hungover beams in his eyes dance around, celebrating how good it is that there are no tantrums.

I bet he'll go to the Academy and tell yesterday's friends how calm his girlfriend was this morning.

I get home on the last tram from Borshagovka at 1am. In the kitchen, the smell of smoked cigarettes and an empty bottle of vodka. He is lying with his eyes shut, the table lamp turned on. His eyelashes trembling.

"You see," I say, "how crappy it feels."

He doesn't move, but his closed eyelashes keep trembling. I undress, curl up in a ball next to him.

"I guess there's no point offering you an orange," I say to his forehead. He's silent. Another night gone to waste. I want it to be like the very first one.

In the morning, I brew coffee. Ostap reads the newspaper and is nodding to something.

"And why are you getting mad?" I wave my hands about.

"You can and I can't? I spent most of last night on the balcony, and it's cold there. I was worried you'd get robbed, beaten. And you came back like it was nothing and didn't even apologise."

Ostap grimaces, as if my words had made his mouth go sour. Finally, he says in a low voice:

"I can get robbed, beaten; and you can get raped on top of that, and if you try to resist, even killed. Get the difference?"

He sits and calmly rubs his chin. I am silent, seeing the difference.

"I get it," I say, "but my nerves also have to be taken into account, no?"

In reply: silence. If I'm an idiot and don't get that I could get raped, and if I try to resist, then even get killed, then I've got to remember once again what he already said. He's not repeating it. Mechanical waves.

"I don't want to live here for some reason," he announces in a tone that's as if he wants to try out a new diet, without bread or sugar.

"It's boring here. I've got melancholy." As if he's saying his stomach has got bigger and won't fit into his jeans properly.

I'm silent. He folds the newspaper and goes into the hallway to put his shoes on.

"Fine then!" I shout from the kitchen. Eyes full of tears.

Thanks, for brightening up three whole days. Only another two and a half weeks to go.

"God, child, you're such a dummy," I hear from the hallway. The door slams. I jump up. Why slam the door? He's left. I feel dumb.

The next two and a half weeks, I live alone. At night I shut myself in my room, praying for a long time and sleeping badly. On Saturdays and Sundays back in Kholmysty I don't go to Ostap's. He doesn't ring. Brutal. He knew how scared I was. And he knew why I acted like that.

Of course, when he came at 1am, I should have told him that nobody does that. Or sent him straight out the door. Or slapped him and called him a wanker. But I pretended that everything was fine, then hurt him three times over.

CHAPTER FIFTEEN

A Meeting at Grand Vasilkovskaya

Mid-February. Two o'clock in the afternoon. Cold. Grand Vasilkovskaya is cloudy. Wind. Outside the university, students are darting about with cold noses, in coats with wrapped-up faces. I'm miserable. I walk into the direction of Lybidska. If you felt like it, from there you could get on the twenty-two bus, and go to Goloseyevsky In the hope of meeting him. Could go over to Vick's when the hope fizzles out. Raising a point that using the forest as a toilet is too cold right now. I want to see Ostap so badly, much like a recovering alcoholic urgently needing a drink. A shot. With one eye at least.

Next is the impossible. You couldn't make this up in a Brazilian soap opera of even the cheapest kind. Pashya was explaining that this is a common phenomenon: my energetic field is bigger, so I felt how our fields touched. By about a hundred metres. Blimey, on our fields you can even play bio-energetic football briskly.

In general, my eyes habitually search for Ostap among passers-by. A slim man walks past with glasses. Not him. Ostap looks twenty years younger. And this student has the same winter coat, the same protective colour. Not him. This one's without glasses. And there, in the reflection of a shop window on the opposite street, another one is pacing. And this one has glasses, and a protective coat, and even his stance, like his shoes weigh about twenty kilos each, just like Ostap's. And even the habit of keeping his hands in his pockets while walking. Crazy. And I'm walking in his direction. There is my red coat in the shop window, getting closer to him. Let's see, who this joker is, with the same stance as...oh mmmy...

"Ostap!" I almost crash into him.

"She walkssss, not noti-cingggg," Ostap sings, wrapping himself in his frosty vapour.

"What are you doing here?" I ask him, dumbfounded.

"Oh, y'know, wanted to take a walk in your neck of the woods." The voice of an unflustered human being. Only the corners of his lips just giving him away.

How is it possible? I want to go to his, and he has already come to me.

"Beer, now. Soon as I see you, I want to drink," I say.

"So, what's up?" Ostap smiles. "I know a great place. We just have to walk to the other side and get a cab."

"A cab? Someone got their scholarship," I say.

"Someone talks too much," he says playfully, hugging me, and we head for the crossing. He came to me. Did he really miss me that much? I'm going to attack him with kisses in the car.

Half an hour later, in his room, we are shoving our hundred layers of winter clothing off each other in a frenzy, under the loud sounds of the Doors.

His hot hands, my cold ones. The same moles in the shape of a comet. He should work in a perfume factory. There will never be another war in the world.

Like two puppies we are biting, rubbing, squeezing each other. His eyes. Without glasses. He looks intently. Maybe, of course, he can't see anything, but I never ever want to break eye contact. Always, always to be in his vision. It is getting dark. I whisper:

"Go on then…"

He shakes his head and smiles. Teasing. His eyes shine in the twilight. I am about to cry. His sweet, sweet moan.

"Finally…" I whisper to his lips.

I'm over the moon I can make him feel that good.

At ten in the evening, I'm pacing his room with a fork and a can of stew, in his shirt and boots with tractor soles. He has humongous-sized feet.

Ostap lies looking at me, his hands thrown underneath his head, watching me with genuine interest, as if I'm about to act something out of *Hamlet*.

"Come live with me," he says. "I've got another shirt."

I'm smiling, chewing, and I say:

"I'm living."

Suddenly it dawns on me.

"Damn! I've gotta ring Auntie Sonya!"

Ostap chuckles.

"You're paying her thirty dollars a month, to then report back to her?"

"Stapler, make something up. She's so not normal. She'll think that something happened to me. She'll have another hypertonic seizure."

"When you're asking me in that shirt." He gestures with his hands.

"Well, it's not funny, is it?" I whimper.

"Get dressed." He shrugs. "The phone booth is just outside the halls. But you'll have to pretend that you study here. Make a dumb face... How is that a dumb face?"

I burst out laughing and think that he doesn't value his Academy enough.

CHAPTER SIXTEEN

Honeymoon and A. Glyba

We have a honeymoon. We run home after lectures at around three o'clock and have fun romping in bed till late at night. At night we pounce on Ostap's food supplies – stew, salo, bread, pickled gherkins. Even with late-night eating my trousers start to become loose. The happiness continues for two and a half weeks. Exactly the same duration as our stay at Auntie Sonya's. And it would have carried on for longer, if once during break in the halls of residence, a pair of fat lips with freckles hadn't asked me:

"What course are you on?"

"Economics." Ostap taught me to reply in pure Ukrainian, calling it just the economics course. He argued that nobody's gonna believe that I am from agriculture; my face is "too katzap".[3]

Ostap lives in a world where faces from the city are all katzap faces, and those from the villages are Ukrainian. I'm Ukrainian after all. Though two generations in Kazakhstan washed the Ukrainian language out of the family. I don't try to argue with him.

"And who's your assistant principal?" the lips ask.

"I don't know," I answer. "Do I have to know that?"

In reply the fat lips with freckles laugh in a masculine bass.

"Show me your passport, please. Tomorrow you'll get it back from the head of residence."

I obediently hand over the passport.

Should I have handed it over or not? Ostap doesn't say.

Should I have said I'd forgotten it?

What if they don't let me in? I really want to go to Ostap's.

"Why did you give them your passport?" Ostap looks at me unnervingly, the pupils in his eyes darkening.

3   An offensive epithet of Russians used by Ukrainians. Literally – like a goat (Rus. "kak tzap")

"Damn it, they wouldn't have let me in!" I answer, frozen in the middle of the room.

"So what they wouldn't have let you in? Now they're not going to give you your passport back." Ostap looks serious.

"Why are you freaking out? I'll get it tomorrow from the head."

"Don't! Even! Think about it!" Ostap shouts. I've never heard him shout. "Wait for me." He lowers his tone to a normal, firm voice, one that doesn't tolerate any bickering.

"Don't go to your lectures tomorrow. I can't not go, I've got a test. Wait for me. I'll ring you myself."

I don't go to my lectures. Why did he forbid me so severely from getting my passport? Am I a little girl? I'll go myself and collect it. And I'll prove to him that I am a completely independent being. I imagine Ostap's surprised face, and decisively leave the room.

I knock on the door with the sign "Head of Residence A. Glyba." Glyba means "a boulder" in Ukrainian. I thought I'd warn you now.

"Yeah?" roars the voice behind the door, sounding like Taz from *Looney Tunes*. I open the door warily.

Starting to feel like the little Tweety Bird from the same cartoon.

Behind the desk sits an actual boulder of around thirty stone, in a jacket, on top of it a fleshy mug. That's exactly how I remember the head of halls number eleven. A Kholmysty person. A hill. I leave the door open just in case. What if I need to call for help? I realise that nobody apart from a pair of freckly lips will come for help. And that's not good help.

"I left my passport here at reception last night," I begin in Ukrainian. Boulder doesn't give me any of his attention, writing something down.

"Can I get it please?"

Silence. I'm standing at the open door, looking at Boulder's hand. His hands resemble sausages, and the ballpoint pen with its blue lid looks like a chopstick.

Is it going to talk to us in this lifetime at all?

What a freak, good heavens. Just look at the nose – it's like a bristle for painting the ceiling white.

"Should I come back later?"

"Close the door," blurts the boulder.

"From inside or…?"

"Stop fannyin' around. Close the door and come closer."

His tone and the absence of a "please" starts tickling my tough student nerves. I shut the door and make a small step forwards.

I don't like this piece of work. I'll just be rude and get the heck out. He can pickle my passport for winter and then stuff his face with it. He'll have to give it back sooner or later. But Ostap may get in deep crap for this. No wonder he told me not to go. And I went anyway, so now I've got to behave.

What if Boulder tells me to suck it? Eughh!!

"Well, explain yourself," sighs out Boulder. "You spent a night where?"

"In two oh five," I reply honestly.

"At Sokira's?" He lifts his hairy bushes above his eyes.

Wow! The head of residence knows Ostap by his surname.

"At Ostap's," I agree.

"He-he." His eyes light up, like five-year-old Alex's from nursery, when I, a five-year-old too, led him behind a cupboard and lifted my dress, showing my panties.

"And what were you doin' there? Maths equations?" he asks, smiling dirtily.

"Of course. What else?" I say in his same tone.

"Interesting, interesting." He puts his pen down on the table and his red eyes remind me of my babushka's boar, Boris, when a she-pig on heat was let loose in his cage.

"Maybe you can show me, how to do maths? I went to school a long time ago: I've forgotten."

Not surprising that you've forgotten, I think to myself. To shag such a misunderstanding you've got to wrap everything, from mug to toes in a cumbrella. And yourself too. It's been a while since he was not only in school, but also in a bath, and in front of any kind of mirror.

"Y'know what you are? You's B…"

I fly out of his office, not fully understanding what I wanted to say with the letter "B", either Boulder, bullshit, "cumBrella" maybe. I dart to the stairs, tears pouring down my face in anger as I run to the eighth floor.

*

I'm sobbing for the third hour in a row. The end of love from lunch till dawn. The end of stew with pickled cucumbers at night. And Aunt Sonya will probably kick me out now. I'll have to live in halls. She can find another tenant. I freeze: Ostap is going to kill me for going to the head's office. He'll get kicked out because of me. Mama!

Ostap bursts into the room. I stop crying. He slams the door. Chucks my passport onto the bed. Feverishly tearing everything from us that we put on in the morning. I am his peach.

After a few minutes, not more, with eyes still wet, on the floor, with a softened Ostap, I ask hesitantly:

"Has the war started or something?"

He lazily smiles to my left breast, wiping the sweat from his brow, looking into my eyes and quietly says:

"You're my girl."

I want to cry again. We hug. I try to beat away the vanilla atmosphere:

"How did you get the passport back from that ugly mug?"

"That's why I went to the Academy, and not to Shevchenko," he says lazily.

"Why?"

"Saba told me ages ago. They catch chicks at halls, take their passports." I feel a little awkward that he's ignoring my question but listen with interest about "chicks and passports".

"In the morning, if the girl puts out, she gets her passport; if not, she won't see it till she does. One was going there from spring till autumn. She gave in."

I'm silent. My tears have dried up.

"You're only telling me this now?" I quietly ask.

"I told you, child, don't go anywhere. You didn't listen." Ostap lifts himself up, as if he's about to do push-ups on me.

"Well, if you'd have mentioned that, I'd have listened," I say, crawling away from underneath his arms. "Didn't want to make the mechanical waves?" I say, getting up.

Ostap sits on the bed and doesn't say anything. His victorious facial expression dissolves. It dawns on me:

"You were testing me? Would I have put out or not, to that freak?"

Ostap gets up sharply. Turns to the window and pulls his trousers on.

155

Does his zipper up. I stand two steps away from him in one denim trouser leg, staring angrily at his back.

He wasn't checking me!

"I just took it." Ostap finishes my thoughts. I am stunned. How is that possible?

"Remember the telephone booth, which we called Auntie Sonya from? I dialled my dad: 'Head of Residence here!'" he yells in his dad's voice.

I giggle. Ostap stays serious. A pause. I pull on the other denim trouser leg. And my bra.

"I made a bet with myself." Ostap breaks the silence once again.

"That if he gave me the passport when I get to…" Ostap pauses again.

My God, why is he trying to drag it out?

Why isn't he speaking in specifics, and most importantly, quickly?

It's time I get used to all his pauses.

"But if he is still on the phone with my dad, then…" says Ostap and pauses again.

"Then what?" I can't hold on any longer.

"Anyway, I lost," he says, not taking his eyes away from the window.

Lost? Why did he lose? I remember the victorious expression on his face, which he had burst in here with.

If Glyba didn't have the passport that means that I slept with him, but because the passport was still there, I'm good.

But then it turned out that I'm not good; I'm a fool, because…I'm a fool. While we were shagging, it was good, but then I blurted out nonsense.

So what? He must accept that I get different moods. I want it to be like Marilyn Monroe said: "I'm selfish, impatient and a little insecure. I make mistakes, I am out of control and at times hard to handle. But if you can't handle me at my worst, then you sure as hell don't deserve me at my best." Or our good old Bunin said something like that to love a woman means to love her tantrums and fat thighs."

Yes, but it is hard to love a suspicious woman.

Oh, what have I done?

"Stapler, can you speak to me and not the window?"

Ostap is silent.

"Did you notice that awesome sunset two minutes ago?" he says, turning his joyful face around. I smile sheepishly.

"Now it's overcast," he adds. "I have melancholy."

"When will the melancholy be over?" I inquire in the tone of a relative talking with the doctor in charge.

"I don't know." Ostap still looks at the window. It's dark and heavy snow falls.

"Do you want me to leave?" I ask quietly.

"Do what you want, child." Ostap sighs.

"Stop her," whimpers Alenushka in my head.

He won't stop me. You know him.

Fine, I'll go to Auntie Sonya's, wag some nerves.

I put on my sweater. Boots. Coat. Backpack. Quietly close the door behind me. And now, I am melancholy too.

I walk past a pair of taunting freckled lips near the entrance. All your fault, Screwship.

Get out on the street. The cold frost stings my nose. Snowflakes on my eyelashes. Crap! Forgot my passport. I stop. I want to return. To cry again. To ask for forgiveness. But if I keep shamelessly appearing, all too katzup like I am, in front of the freckled mouth, Ostap will have problems. I can't keep returning before every lecture to the head's office, trying to get my passport and calling him "B".

Happy days are over. Now I just want to grieve. I walk along the snowy path, knowing that he's looking back at me. I don't turn around.

I shove my chilly hands into my fur coat sleeves, as if into a muff.

Walking, keep walking. Let him miss me. The making up will be something, when I come to get my passport back. Or maybe he'll call first, and then it will be awesome. There's so much to look forward to. Apart from the conversation with Auntie Sonya. We'll find another Auntie Sonya. And anyway, I want to live in halls too!

Maria does, and she pays two hundred and twenty karbovantsiv a month. That's three pounds! A bit more than Nana Masha's. And she has a shower, and a kitchen. It's cheaper, and no crazy people burst into the room in the morning in a sick condition, and no spirits creak the floorboards at night.

I should complain about Mr Head of Residence Number Eleven, A. Glyba. So that Ostap can get chucked out of the Academy or his exams written off?

Next is a truthful conversation with myself.

"I've always wanted to ask, are you going to talk about you-know-what to him?" says Osha-Bonaparte. "We've been together for a year now."

"He'll leave us straight away!" Osha-Alenushka answers.

"I want to remind you of an article we read the other day." Bonaparte paces the green room, folding her hands behind her back.

"Women who don't reach orgasm, are at risk of all kinds of sexual disorders and tumours. And also," she spins around on her heels, nonchalant, and strolls in the opposite direction, "they face mental health disorders."

"And what is a mental health disorder?" Bonaparte barks the last words into Sarcasm's face.

"What?" he shouts back in reply.

"You know what! A mental health disorder means that you and I will disappear from this room!" she shouts to his face. An echo thunders in the green room.

"Only naked Alenushka will stay. Na-ked!" She turns her drilling gaze to Alenushka. "You'll end up like the Truth!"

I made up the Truth when I was ten. Back then, once, I admitted wholeheartedly to Dad that I bunked off art school and went to the woods instead, for which he hit my back hard with a belt. The pain made everything dark in my eyes, as if someone switched the light off for a few seconds, but I didn't utter a sound. That's when I had a vision of a bald naked Truth, with hanging breasts and unshaved legs. She looked around my room with sad eyes, and said: "Why do you need me here, when I'm like this?" And flew away somewhere.

From then on, I do not admit to anything.

If I'm honest, my mental state was destroyed a long, long time ago, judging by how scared I am to tell him even two words. Truth or not.

If I did reach my orgasms, I wouldn't be affected by his melancholy. I get a great deal of suffering from him and a tiny drop of happiness. Without climaxing. Then these drops of happiness are enough to last me for the whole of spring.

I'm still walking along the snow-covered path. Looking at the snowflakes falling onto the tips of my boots, melting. And on my hair, and collar. And I realise that next year, or maybe next Saturday, I'll have to admit to Ostap that I simulated all my orgasms. And he'll never understand why I did that.

CHAPTER SEVENTEEN

The Apple

"You stunned me, and upset me so." Auntie Sonya sits, stately, on the sofa. I am washed, in a bathrobe, with steamed cheeks, sitting on the edge of the armchair in her living room.

"Your room has everything you need," she continues. "And you prefer to live in student halls, where the hygienic conditions leave one wanting more. I heard they get fleas and bedbugs." Auntie Sonya spreads the hem of her flawless robe.

"They even have snakes," I blurt out.

"What's that?" Auntie Sonya asks.

"I said everything is fine there, hygiene and a shower, a clean bed." I lie unashamedly, remembering how I had to wash in cold water at night, throwing my right leg over the sink, cursing the Academy with all the names under the sun. The toilet, however, is better than Vick's at number four.

"And there are no fleas there," I add. And that's the utter truth. It's not like I'm itching or anything.

"Maybe you heard that twenty years ago," I continue. "My friend needed help with English prep. I couldn't invite her over here, so we decided it was better that I went to live at her place," I say and only then notice Auntie Sonya's chin is quivering. Like a belly dance. Chin dance.

"How can you say that? Twenty years ago..."

"Auntie Sonya, I didn't mean that. Really. Ten, twenty-five, it was a long time ago, when fleas existed in halls."

Auntie Sonya's chin is still doing shimmies.

"Well, if you like, I can leave if I frustrate you so much with my absence." I hang up my hands.

"I wouldn't like that," she says more calmly.

"I would like for you to live here, in your room, to study and make your mum and dad happy."

"I want that too." I sigh deeply.

"Get to the dean's office to find out about halls! First thing tomorrow!" Sarcasm yells. I'm going to disappear if we keep namby-pambying with this sixty-year-old child. Bonaparte will get fat, take over the remote, start praying from morning till night, and you, Alenushka, won't have any space here either.

"OK, OK, don't shout," says Bonaparte, raising both of her hands in the air. "Tomorrow we'll go to the dean's office. Let's go to sleep. We have to get up at six."

The next morning, I get up at six in the morning with the alarm. Pray for an hour. Then to the shower.

"Good morning, Auntie Sonya!"

"Good morning." Auntie Sonya is already up. Hm, she is up an hour earlier? Maybe I woke her up? To the kitchen. Damn! I don't even have a crumb to eat. Apart from oatmeal. I think of the tinned stew at Ostap's halls. My heart aches. Not right now.

Today is Thursday. I go home on Friday. I'll lunch at uni, and for dinner I'll drink some tea. Right in the middle of the kitchen table, covered with a cloth in blue chequers, there is a huge green glass vase with red and yellow apples.

I want an apple. Right now. What do I do? I swallow my running saliva. Oatmeal is good. But I want an apple so badly that my gums start to itch. Two weeks on stew with pickled cucumbers. Do you know what I mean?

I imagine a plump green caterpillar on Sarcasm's shoulder. She is shouting in Sarcasm's ear:

"I want a yellow apple!"

After lectures I'll buy exactly the same one and put it back in its place.

"Stealing is bad!" says Bonaparte, but nobody is there to listen.

I grab the apple and head for my room, past Auntie Sonya's. I walk by quickly, not turning my head, as if I've forgotten something – to put my socks on, for example. I sit on the bed. Catching my breath, I take out the apple, and discreetly, with tremendous pleasure, sink my teeth into the yellow, crunchy skin, sucking in all of the juice. I start to rock, stealthily sucking it like a lollipop.

I come to my senses when I hear snippets of Auntie Sonya's conversation on the phone. Auntie Sonya's voice sounds quiet and nervy.

"Lucy... I recounted the apples...eleven... And now... I didn't take any... Ten...what am I supposed to do now?"

160

A bit of apple lodges in the back of my throat. Crap. If I had waited a minute longer, then upon hearing this conversation I could have put the apple back. But now...

I come out of my room as soon as I hear her put the phone down.

"Auntie Sonya," I begin at her door. "I really hope you don't mind, I took an apple. I wanted to buy the same one after lectures and put it in its place."

"Yes, you took the apple," says Auntie Sonya, not taking her eyes from the window. A lot of window-staring lately.

"Please forgive me, I was going to replace it," I add, feeling like a spit on the floor.

"Why didn't you ask first?" Auntie Sonya asks a completely logical question.

"I hoped that you wouldn't notice," I say really quietly.

"I will forgive you." Auntie Sonya turns to me. "But you have to own up to everything else you've taken without asking."

"I haven't taken anything else," I say, leaving the guilty tone behind, raising my eyebrows.

"See, you're making me sad again. Who, then, do you suggest took my onion and sugar? I trust Elvira more than myself. Apart from you, nobody has lived here since I came back from the hospital. I know, because I don't eat that much onion and sugar."

"Wait, Auntie Sonya. I don't like tea with sugar, and apart from oatmeal on water, I don't cook anything here."

"I don't know what you do with it, Olga-dear..."

"Hey, this won't do." I raise my hand. "Sorry, Auntie Sonya, I took the apple. For the first time. I've apologised. But hanging the onion and sugar onto me is not fair. Fire me. I'm packing my things."

I return to my bedroom and start to pack, picturing myself in an onion necklace with sugar sprinkled all over my head and shoulders, like dandruff.

From the other room I hear sobbing and mumbling. She is on the phone again, but I stopped listening, so I don't know with whom or about what.

The front door clicks open with a set of keys, and Elvira enters the flat. She asks Auntie Sonya something, then hearing the answer, she runs straight into my room.

161

"Olga," she wails. "Have mercy on me, an old hag. If it wasn't you, then it must be me who took the sugar and onion. I've never taken anything in my life. But are we really going to fall out over something so petty? You know how attached she is to you."

"Elvira, darling, I swear it wasn't me. If I admitted to the apple, why would I need to deny everything else? Maybe nobody took anything, maybe it just seems like things are running out so quickly, but actually things are running out the way they're running out. I'm upset that she knew I had nothing to eat and put out those apples on purpose. You have nothing better to do, Auntie Sonya!" I shout into the hall over Elvira's shoulder, who gasps and grabs my hand, as if I have shouted with it.

"Get up and do some tidying." I walk around Elvira who keeps gasping, enter Auntie Sonya's room and continue in a calmer tone. "Make some soup for yourself, at least once in your life. Take those portraits off the walls and sign up for knitting club." I just can't stop now, it seems.

Auntie Sonya's chin does chin dancing again and she looks at me with horror, as if I am sentencing her.

"It was impossible to sleep here. Your floor creaks at night. That's why you're afraid that I'll leave. You're frightened. You need to let them go and start to live a real life. Your own. Not mine or Elvira's. And not twenty years ago."

Auntie Sonya is sobbing and I return to my room.

"Olechka, you know that she is not well," Elvira whispers.

"I know, Elvira. I'm still moving out." I hug her.

"I want to be alive, not sick."

Outside the green room under the balcony I can hear whistling and the sounds of applause.

My bag is packed. Under the pillow lies an apple core. Should I get it out, in front of Elvira, or leave it for her to find?

At that moment the front door opens and Sister Lucy authoritatively marches into the flat on her heels.

"Where is that shameless girl?" I hear her steel voice from the hall.

"Come to me, my dear," I mutter angrily.

"Shame on you!" She appears at the door of my bedroom and hastily speaks with her painted crimson lips.

"Not only does she hang around student halls with God knows who, she brought men over, whilst Auntie Sonya was in the hospital. Sonya, darling, I didn't want to tell you…"

I can only imagine how, in the next room, Auntie Sonya's red eyes open wide and her chin quivers even more.

I laugh confusedly. Like a parrot trainer would laugh, if after three hours of repeating "Good parrot" the bird announces "parrot wanker".

"And she's laughing! How dare you!" exclaims Sister Lucy.

"I'm going to have to ask you to stop insulting me," I say calmly.

"And she's even asking!" Lucy flares up even more.

"Are you reporting this over the walkie-talkie?" I say curiously.

"Shame on you!" Sister Lucy bursts out. "To even think about living with my husband before marriage… And then she tries to believe in God. Look at her. Us three together are more holy than you, and we don't even believe in anything!"

I'm standing silently in the middle of the room with my zipped-up bag in one hand, an apple core in the other. Sister Lucy occupies the door, hands by her sides, like a feisty aunt at the market, as if a salesperson sold her short half a kilo of cucumbers and she busted him.

Elvira stands between us, confusion on her face. From the hall I can hear sounds of sobbing from Auntie Sonya.

"Lucy, darling," says Elvira tentatively. "She's just a girl."

"A girl? Types like this were excluded from the Communist League back in my day."

I want to say something rude about the Communist League and leave. But nothing anti-league comes to mind. I decisively swing my bag over my shoulder. Clasp the apple core with my fist and confidently stride towards Sister Lucy.

"Let me give you some Communist League exclusion," I say, tossing the apple core in my hand.

"Oh, my God, what is she…" Sister Lucy's voice is full of hysterical notes, as if she is exercising the sounds. She may need to shout "Help!" She edges into the hall, presses her back against the chest of drawers.

"My darling holy Sister Lucy," I utter through my teeth. "What is that, shining above your head? A halo surely?"

Sister Lucy puts her hand over her balding chestnut crown and moves away from the doorway. I walk past her.

"Are you finished? Have a snack."

I put the apple core on top of the chest and open the door. "Goodbye." I close the door behind me. Quietly and firmly.

Elvira, Auntie Sonya and Sister Lucy are left behind the door. They have something to talk about today, and all month. They'll discuss what to do with the unfinished apple. How outrageous it is for a girl to live with an unmarried man. How hygienic the student halls are. How much sugar and onion are used monthly. Maybe they'll even skip tomorrow's repeat of the soaps. They'll be feeling the taste of life for a few more days or weeks. Then it will all go back to normal.

On the bus it dawns on me: was it Ostap who took the sugar and onion? I pull my gaze away from the frosty window. How could I, after so many years, not suspect him once? Although why would he need an onion? And sugar, well... When? In the morning, on the way into the hall, in between his words "God, child, you're a dummy" and tying his shoelaces?

Hm. I'd love to ask him one day. I dreamily shut my eyes. OK. Even if he did steal the sugar. At least because of this onion and sugar I ended up in an awesome place.

PART THREE

Revolt

CHAPTER ONE

An Awesome Place

"Here's the key to the room seven hundred and two. Nobody lives there right now, but there soon will be people." Caretaker Ludmila Ivanova puts the key on the edge of the table. She is tall and slender; I can see that even though she is sitting at the table, in a brick-red suit with a barely noticeable neatly applied terracotta shade of lipstick, not Sister Lucy's way.

I don't believe my ears, nor my eyes. Just this morning I was rowing about an apple, and in the evening I'm already holding the key to my own room in student halls, three stops away from Goloseevsky. Three stops from Ostap!

"So, I can go and see the room?" I dance a little with impatience.

Ludmila Ivanova leads with her neatly plucked eyebrows and shrugs her shoulders.

"Olga, it's your room. Have a look if you like. Move in if you like."

"Thank you." I grab the key from the table, in case Ludmila Ivanova changes her mind and decides to take it back.

What was I thinking before?

Why didn't I ask about the halls before? Ostap was right – I have the mentality of a girl from Humcoll.

I climb the stairs to seven hundred and two.

Jumping up excitedly. Up to the third floor I bang the drums, and by the seventh I'm blowing into a tube. In the corridor I clatter my feet, as if I'm heading to the whole point of my existence, and not to the students' dorm.

The eighth of March, eight days later. A Blue Door. Seventh floor. Slightly out of breath. I don't use the lift. As I don't have time for aerobics. I open the door – a big window. Next to it – a table. Two beds either side. I open the window. Maybe there are people that exist like Pashya, who can read people's minds. I now see everything. Among the laughter, squealing and mumbling. Eight days already. A hundred years ago, the caretaker gave me the key. One hundred years ago there was a scandal with Auntie Sonya over an apple. One hundred years and one day ago, I left Ostap's halls. Now I am alone. I can sleep here, or not sleep here. I can move the beds together, or not move them together. I want Ostap. Laughter behind the wall. As if they're laughing at my stupid hopes.

Only three stops from Goloseevsky. International Women's Day. The day when men give flowers to their women. He hasn't popped in. And it's unlikely that he'll bring a flower today. I'm sure in halls number eleven there is someone to do that for. And anyway, he's getting ready for his session. Like last year for his exams. Of course, he'll pass with flying colours. Otherwise, what would his dad say?

Last spring, we met only twice – in the cellar and when I got the rose and a pink hare. And then in May before his birthday I heard some rumours regarding shoulder blades.

The open window lets in the thick scent of early spring. I turn on the lamp, brought from home, sit down, take out my diary to write about how lonely I am, and why all these love feelings are so stupid.

I look at the lamp-lit table. Tears drop onto it. I realise that Ostap doesn't love me. And I have two beds, which can be moved together. While I'm waiting for the end of the session, he's laying another Katka or Lera onto her shoulder blades. And not in any hurry to give me back my passport or a flower. Miserable. I want to run and jump onto him. It's still only five in the evening, all of the snow has melted, and the sun is shining. But Pride is getting in the way. Pride is a bird, so hairy it looks like an eagle. It sits on my shoulder, all ruffled up. Not letting me go to him.

If only it was like Valentine's Day – we accidentally meet in an unexpected place. In the queue for cigarettes, for example. Maybe I should take a walk around Goloseevsky. What if I meet him? What if he's with somebody?

If only there was a knock at the door now, and it was him. I would have been silent for so long, then taken advantage of him on the floor. Between the two beds. Or him me. I don't mind.

A knock on the door. I can't breathe. A horde of thoughts flashes past in three seconds, like a pack of rats in an underground tunnel.

"What if it really is him?" one rat mumbles, running past.

"You've met once already..." another says.

Maybe I felt the field again, and Pashya is right? So what he doesn't know where I live? Katka knows. Vick knows. Maybe one of them told him? Absurd, but things like that do happen. I really want to see him.

Although I always want to see him. When I am tasting the soup I made with sunflower oil and admit that it's not as tasty as my mum's made with pork bone. When I'm sleeping, when I'm sitting at lectures or doing homework, when laughing with Sasha in a double lecture, and when coming home for the weekend. Especially when I'm coming home. That's when I really hope to meet him at the bus stop, in the queue to Kholmysty.

I really, really want it to be him. Please. Please, can it be like this? Even for the last time. I'm tired of thinking about him and tired of being unneeded only three stops from Goloseevsky when it smells of fresh, lightly melted snow.

I open the door. Spring's sunset is reflected in Vick's radiant smile.

"What's up, sunshine, were you crying?" The white teeth hide behind the curtains of Vick's thick lips.

"Yeah, imagine, sunshine is howling. Doesn't want to set without you. Go ahead, sunshine, get on with your setting, he's here." I nod to the window, wipe my face with my sleeve and shut the door.

Vick laughs and hugs me. That's who appreciates my sense of humour. I sniffle. I'm tired of waiting for Ostap. I want to live. I can see how Vick suffers without me. Why do I need to see one unrequited love, while being in another unrequited love myself?

"Vick, let's go to Goloseevsky, find Ostap and smash his face in," I say to his shoulder.

Vick laughs, but this time not whole-heartedly.

"He's upset you?" Vick frowns.

"No, he just forgot. And I'm waiting for him to remember." I sob.

"Does he know you're here?" he asks.

I shake my head "no".

"Last time I saw him was eight days ago," I say, freeing myself from his embrace.

"Take a seat on the bed, the table, the windowsill, I've got it all." Vick obligingly sits on the bed next to me. "We didn't end very well. You want tea?"

"No," Vick replies.

169

"Didn't end very well, and now I don't know what to do," I say.

I take a pillow and lean against the wall on it. Vick takes the other pillow and does the same.

"Theoretically," I continue, "I'm a girl."

"Theoretically, yes."

"And I should have enough pride not to go to him." I climb off the bed and sit opposite him, grabbing the pillow. I haven't forgotten that although Vick is the face of concern, he is also a face of interest.

I want to have a heart-to-heart, but don't want to give out false hope. Vick is interested in my smile and eyes my movements around the room.

"But on the other hand," I continue, "waiting is lower than making the first move. What do you think?"

"I agree," Vick blurts out and energetically nods.

"I'm tired of being in the position of a silent lady." I continue: "Who's waiting, when her prince finally arrives on his white horse and shags me? And then disappears. On the same horse, mind you. How do I know, maybe he found a new one ages ago, and I'm sitting here doing nothing?"

"He's got someone, some kind of Lera," says Vick. My heart drops with a deep whistling sound. Downwards. I even hear how it lands with a soft thud.

Like a watery lump of dirt. Onto the bottom of the left heel.

"But he doesn't love her, so they're friends," he continues. "Like me and you," he adds.

My heart bunches up into a ball and climbs back up with the help of a rope, back to its place. Phew. Doesn't love her. Friends.

"Or?" says Vick.

I look at him questioningly. What "or" Vick? What "Or?" I want to answer.

Actually, I like Vick.

I imagine how reproachfully Alenushka looks at me, wiping her tearful eyes and nose with a handkerchief.

"Vick, if you knew how happy I'd be to fall in love with you," I say.

Vick sighs heavily.

"You're everything that makes for perfect company," I continue. "You understand me even after half a word, I can talk about my periods with you, and how bored I get at international law seminars. If it was love, we would have been married a long time ago, and I would have given birth to your kids. Would have."

Vick's bitter grin tells me it would be good if that had happened.

"But what can I do?" I wave my hands. My tears dry up completely. "Just like you with your Vera, the one whose birthday you were at. You can't just start to love her."

"Yeah, yeah." Vick looks at his fingers. His eyes no longer emit sparks, and his smile no longer reflects the sunset.

"I flew to yours, skipping. I thought if you'd see me in such a happy mood, something would definitely wake up inside of you, something different."

"Yeah, I guess love doesn't depend on moods. Leeeeuve. Listen, I'm sick of that word, let's talk about something else."

I get up from the bed and walk over to the open window. No sign. To hell with it…

"Let's talk about you. How do you find my new room?"

We burst out laughing.

"Let's do a house-warming party?" he suggests. "We'll call Katka. I haven't seen her in forever."

A knock on the door. The laughter stops. Please, not Ostap. Actually, so what? I open it. A short, blue-eyed blond.

"I'm Yuri," he announces, keeping his hands in the pockets of his designer jeans.

"Osha. Vick." I point to myself, then to Vick.

"Also, here are Roma and Sergey," says Yuri, looking at me with remorse. "Osha…sounds Asian," he says. "Kinda esoteric."

"Olga. It's a nickname. Just stuck from when I was a kid." I laugh.

"OK, Osha-Kosha. And which one of you has moved in?"

"Me," I answer. "And he's come to visit."

"Cool. Boyfriend? Friend?" Yuri waves his index finger in the air between Vick and me.

"Friend." I smile.

"Vick, yeah?" Yuri confirms, taking a look as he leans in closer to Vick.

"Vick, yeah." Vick nods.

"Vick, no offence, but I'm glad it's Osha who's moved in and not you. We don't got no girls on this floor." He turns his head to the right and shouts, "Not any *normal* girls, I mean!"

"Friends," he continues, not waiting for an answer from his right. "Let's booze, smoke weed, have fun in other words!" He shakes both his sleeves, like a conductor on the final chord. "Let's celebrate Osha's house-warming."

"'Course. I get you." Vick shrugs his shoulders. "I came here with the same."

"If you want to be OK, do the boozing every day." Another stranger piles into the room, tall, with frizzy black hair. He stops in front of me, rooted to the ground.

"Hey, Romka!"

He glances over at Yuri.

"She, she's moved in, not him!" Yuri is smiling, as if he were saying that both he and Romka had received a crate of ice cream.

Romka turns his gaze over to me, then back to Yuri, before finally howling:

"Blo-onda! We got a neighbour! We're saved! Spring ain't come for nothing!"

Yuri is howling something as well, and they jump onto each other, hugging, jumping as if the score is two nil to their team.

Vick and I exchange glances.

"I'm guessing that Blonda is Yuri?" I say to him. "Because I'm not."

"Well look at that, she is able to guess things," says the second stranger, waving his hand in my direction, as if I'm a monkey who's politely thanked him for a banana. "Ah – I'm Romka. But everyone calls me Madona. With one 'n'. But I'm Romka."

"Does the third one have a girl's nickname too?" I laugh.

"Yeah, looks like you guys have it rough without girls." Vick smiles.

"No. Leonard is our writer," announces Romka-Madona. "He wri-hites t-hings!" Yuri throws his index finger upwards and puffs himself up for effect.

Leonard appears at the door, turning out to be even taller than Romka, having to duck down to come in. He looks like a well-fed six-foot-six Mongol.

"You look like a Mongol," I say to Leonard. "You look like a gipsy," to Romka, "and you are Raymond Paul's grandson," I say to Yuri.

"And you look like a Kazakh," they reply practically in one voice, including Vick.

An eruption of laughter.

A woman's unhappy voice is muttering something from the room next door. Yuri loudly shuts the door and sits opposite Vick and me.

To be honest, this situation is much safer with Vick around. Romka and Leonard drop down on either side of Yuri.

"Let's smoke her out, lads," Yuri offers. His eyes shoot all over me. And it's not hard for me to figure out why he wants to smoke me out.

"I wouldn't advise her," Vick says glumly. "But you can bravely smoke me out."

"Who are you to advise? I've never even smoked weed." I lazily lean against the wall.

"Have I not seen you drunk?" Vick throws over his shoulder. Sounding intimate. "I can imagine what would happen if you smoked, ha."

Yuri's eyes light up even more than before. "Never smoked weed..." his eyes are saying. "That's like taking a virginity." His eyes start popping with questions. How drunk had Vick seen me? Am I sleeping with him? Am I sleeping with him when drunk? Or am I making myself out to be special? And if so, then what kind of special? Drinking till four in the morning or getting laid after the second vodka shot? Getting laid after the eighteenth? Getting laid with someone whom I like or with anyone who comes along? Do I pass out right at the table and end up in bed? My own or someone else's? Ha, my dear Yuri's youthful thoughts, you are so clear to me.

Two hours later. Window wide open. A thick cloud of smoke.

"Imagine if instead of money there was shite," says Yuri, taking the last drag of the tightly rolled spliff. A cackle of laughter. We're not just cackling, we're crying and creasing with laughter.

Romka, amused, says:

"Imagine, going to the bank with a sack. For shite!" He cries out the last words, as if begging for change in a train carriage.

We're all laughing. Yuri mutely chuckles with laughter, as if a bone has lodged in his throat.

"A plastic one. So nothing leaks out. Or with a diplomat," Vick announces with a resounding bass. Everyone's face is scrunched up, smiling, as if they're happy, good-willed Asian bee-keepers.

"Everyone comes over and helps themselves to a shovel of shite." Then Yuri's laughter turns into a shriek. "For pocket money!"

"Oi, imagine on the bus." Romka creases, guffawing, not able to say a word.

"Pass this over to the driver..."

Another wave of hysterical laughter.

"The driver's in shite, the people are in shite!" Yuri squeals.

"And chicks!" basses Romka. "The more shite a guy has, the cooler! Mm... I can smell the shite on him!"

Everyone is blaring.

"Shite..." Yuri repeats. "Shite smells all kinds of different. Green ones with one scent, brown with another..."

"Chicks can be different too," I say. "Some who go for shite, some who don't."

Yuri again throws me a half-serious gaze.

CHAPTER TWO

Misunderstanding

Two-and-a-bit months later. May. Four in the morning. My room. I'm sitting on the windowsill in a light-purple gown. On the two pulled-together beds lies Yuri in his pants. I'm looking at him guiltily. Yuri has been trying to usher me closer for the last five hours now. Yesterday we were celebrating passing our exams; ahead are two days of break.

He came over with photos of his trip to England to pick strawberries. And when I went out to the kitchen, he moved the beds together.

Sometimes he's able to kiss me. And there was even a time, between two and three in the morning, when he was able to distract my attention with well-placed kisses on the neck and the face, and unravelling my gown, even getting to one breast. If Ostap had seen this, he would never speak to me again. He doesn't speak to me anyway. This is all for Katka's shoulder blades. I forgave him. Right?

Around three in the morning, I decisively get up from the bed, adjust my gown and climb onto the windowsill. Looking at him guiltily. Behind the window, the sunrise is purpling, like the colour of my gown.

"You need to be placed in a museum," Yuri squeezes out huskily. In his voice, a lot of distress and a little surprise. He can't believe that in life, there are idiots like me.

"Why a museum?" I don't give in. "If I don't cheat on my boyfriend, what's so museum-like about that?"

"Where is he, your boyfriend? Where?" Yuri jumps up. "He hasn't been here once in three months."

"He's studying." I shrug my shoulders, looking at the sunrise.

"Vick's studying too. And why's he here almost every day? You're studying. I'm studying. Everyone's studying. And boozing, with who they want, shagging, with who they want. And where they don't want to be, they don't come. You think he doesn't booze and shag in his halls?"

I hide my sorrow badly.

175

"I see him at home," I lie.

"Come on, Osha-Kosha." Yuri tiresomely waves his hand. "You made everything up. You're showing your unapproachability."

"No I'm not!"

"You've already proved it," continues Yuri. "I want you so bad that my eyes are turning black…"

"That's because it's still dark," I smile.

"And soon I'll stop wanting you." He ignores my attempt to joke my way out. "Because it's morning already; I'm tired and bored."

I turn to the sunrise again and say nothing. It's true, you can't prove anything.

"At home I too had a…" he pauses. "Misunderstanding."

I turn to him. Finally, he's going to share his secrets with me.

"We were together for a year and a half."

Like us, I think.

"I went to England for half a year. To pick strawberries. Came back. She's married. She's got a kid, f— knows from where. And I, like a mug, thought I'd take her with me to England. We'd live it up." He quietens, then adds: "She's a bitch. She got knocked up by him before I had even left, can you believe that?"

"Maybe it's your kid?"

"Now I'm here, she's with him," Yuri continues, ignoring my words. "And with a kid. So, what, am I supposed to shut everything up and not shag anyone?" The last sentence sounds like a slogan.

"It's all so simple for you, to shag, or not to shag. And feelings? I can't, without feelings. I liked you, so we kissed. If it had sparked, like with Ostap, then there'd be no question…but that probably comes around once in a lifetime. I don't want anyone apart from him. If he hadn't ever been here, I'd happily want somebody. But I can't." I shrug my shoulders.

I feel like I have a fever. Yuri sighs. Nodding, he understands the important part. He gets up. Jeans. Hoodie. Shoes. He dresses well.

"You'll see," he says over his shoulder. "That's not love. It's a mis-un-der-stan-ding."

And he shuts the door behind him.

To hell with him. Like I really need his opinion. He's unlucky and thinks everyone gets the same. I look at the full sun, without rays above Kiev. And I don't hurry to agree with myself. I'm not sad that I didn't give in to Yuri's persuasions and caresses. I'm sad because I'm in an awesome place, without Ostap. He won't come and won't say that the darkest time of day is before sunrise. Here it is, sunrise. But my soul doesn't lighten.

CHAPTER THREE

My Real Sunrise

"Ah, your lectures are over then?" I say sleepily to the standing-in-the-doorway Ostap. His eyes happily jump from behind their lenses in his glasses, like brown fish in a mini aquarium.

"Yeah-huh." He stretches, proudly smiling.

"Congratulations, then," I begin. Ostap tries to shove a soft rabbit toy towards me. Another one?

"All passes and excellents," he whispers to me seductively.

"Wow! Good thing we didn't see each other for three months, then," I reply. His smile doesn't leave his face.

And why am I just standing there, as if charmed?

I'm going to say everything to him. What do you call these kinds of meet-ups, once every three months?

I don't want him to think that I've turned into a grumpy old hag.

All right, you can tell I'm now a cobra. Stapler doesn't even need a pipe. But actually, he did come to me. He didn't forget, he came.

I'm an idiot.

"Come in," I say.

Ostap happily chuckles and walks in. I go straight to the kitchen. If I had said to him that he was a complete twat, that I cheated on him and that actually I got pregnant by another man ages and ages ago, he would still have happily chuckled all the same.

"Let's go swimming," he announces to the flat at large.

"Oh! Let's go!" I freeze. He's never invited me to go swimming at eleven in the morning. The forest, in the bushes, that's obvious what for. Swimming – no. Must be progress. Just like a real boyfriend to his real girlfriend.

"Don't stand in the doorway. Go to the kitchen and put the kettle on, and I'll look for my swimming kit. Don't be scared, my parents just left..."

"I know, I said hello to them."

I go to my room and get to work in the wardrobe, in the hope of finding my swimming kit.

"They went to meet Uncle Lyosha," I shout from the open doors of the wardrobe.

"He's going to live with us for a few days. The train is only at 1pm, so they won't be here before three."

"I came to yours yesterday at eleven at night," says Ostap.

"Your dad opened the door and said: 'Ostap, pull yourself together. Olga is asleep.' I apologised and thought to myself: you're chatting breeze, Anatoly Vitalyevich. I sat on a bench and waited. I thought, maybe you're out, you'll come back and I'll tell you everything. So, I had to wait till eleven in the morning. After your parents left."

I don't believe my ears. Ostap slept on a bench because of me? He waited for me? I bet he thought that I was cuddling up to someone all night; maybe he'd catch us in the act. So much attention. Even lost my breath from all of the happiness behind the wardrobe door.

"You can look for your swimming kit now if you want, but we're going in two days," he adds.

"What?" I have dived out of the wardrobe, full of plans to find it in the other wardrobe.

In reply Ostap is silent and tiredly pulls off his new squeaking shoes. My plan of finding the swimming gear flies out of my head. Ostap importantly heads for the kitchen. I follow him. He sits. I sit. I watch, how he gets up, finds matches under a tattered newspaper near the hob, turns the gas on, puts the kettle on it. He shakes the jar of coffee. I know the more questions I ask, the later he will answer. Just like a crashed computer: the more buttons you press, the slower it loads. Ostap continues to silently shake the jar of coffee. I wait.

"Maybe I'll take a shower whilst you do that?" I don't stop myself. "So much news in three minutes, I even broke into a sweat in surprise, and I don't need to look for my swimming kit."

"Dad was given a holiday to Odessa for twenty-one days," he explains to the jar of coffee.

"Riight…" I stop at the shower.

"So, if it's shared in half, two people can go for ten and a half days."

"Uh-huh…" I say, and realise that I don't know at all what to say next. I stay quiet. Looking at Ostap. Ostap looks at the jar, as if waiting for it to reply. Is he inviting me to go on holiday? I need a shower immediately. Then to take advantage of him good and proper, right there in the kitchen, and then confirm everything.

"So, you're saying that I'm going on holiday, a white suitcase in my hand, looking for a boy to kiss?" I ask Ostap in his ear ten minutes later.

Ostap is stuck to the linoleum floor with his sweaty back. I'm lying next to him. His arm for my pillow. The crumbs dig into our bodies, but do not spoil the romance.

"Do you have one?" he asks, getting his breath back from my pounce on him.

"Have what?" I ask.

"A white suitcase," he replies.

"What, are we going alone, like completely alone? No friends or parents?" I lose my breath again.

"Scared?" he asks.

"No," I lie. What am I going to tell Mum?

"What's Mum going to say?" he reads my mind.

"She shouldn't…" I shrug my shoulder, which is lying on the floor.

"She doesn't know that we haven't seen each other for three months. She thinks that I've been coming to yours."

"And where have you been going?" he asks.

I laugh. How cute is he? Not only did he live on a bench outside my house all night, inviting me to the trip of a lifetime, he's even jealous lying on my kitchen floor with lowered trousers and his back covered in crumbs.

"I met some awesome girls," I reply. "We meet at the Oaks near the dance floor, or at the Parapet, every night. There are five of us including me, and we're always laughing."

"Yea-ah?" It's hard for me to make out whether he likes the fact that I wasn't studying in the evenings like he was. And he was expecting me to be sitting at home, waiting for him to finish his lessons and ring me? It's not like I'm tittering about with lads at the end of the day.

"Ah, you noticed that we're lying under the table?" he asks. I chuckle and get up.

"So, what's up with these girls?" he asks, brushing the crumbs off his trousers.

"We all became friends after a lesson at uni," I say, wrapping myself in my gown.

"You know one of them, anyway," I say, taking out some mugs from the kitchen cupboard. "Katka. The most annoying one, you know her."

Ostap grins.

"Then there's Mira. She's always complaining that we don't pour her enough drink. 'More!' she yells. But she is a good laugh. Not like Katka. You know Tasha, my ex-classmate. Tasha is special; we have to drag her home every night. She gets wasted. But she introduced me to Ally." My eyes light up here obviously, judging Ostap's smile in reply.

"So, we're sitting on a bench with Tasha in the Oaks. Coming towards us is Sita with this Ally. We wave to them. Sita waves her hand, like a normal person, while Ally jumps on the nearest stump, rips her white fleece off and waves it with fury, like a pirate flag. And she's actually tiny."

I show him how Ally waves her fleece. Ostap laughs. I like telling him about new friends. Let him know that I don't only live and breathe him.

"Sita is also small, hilarious. Though she falls into depression a lot. When she drinks, she squeaks: 'Girls, let's chill, everything's cool!'"

"Sita is friends with Lena Bone-sy. Surname Bones, but we say Bone-sy, because she's scarily thin. She's seeing Limur and does drugs. I should introduce you to all of them," I say, sipping coffee.

"No, you shouldn't." Ostap cuts me off, also sipping coffee.

"What? You don't want to meet my friends? It's so awesome to have a bunch of friends, Ostap. You can laugh as much as you want and never get bored. Tell me, why do you hardly have any friends?"

"Why the hell do I need a bunch of extra friends?" he says.

Suddenly I don't want to talk about my friends. Hm. Maybe I shouldn't have said that they fool around with drugs and demand more vodka? That means that my friends are all alcoholics, drug addicts, and greedy.

"So, you sat on the bench all night waiting for me?" I switch.

"I sat, lay, and slept. Woke up – 9am. Back is killing me. Went around the corner, bought some cola. At eleven I went to come over again, to get on your dad's nerves. And then I saw your parents leaving for the train station."

I am silent, stupidly smiling and squinting like a cat in the sun.

CHAPTER FOUR

The Sunset Becomes Cloudy

"No way. Over my dead body." Mum gets up from the table, collects all the dirty plates with a crash and places them in the sink.

She adds to that the noise of the strong stream of pouring water.

Dad and I silently observe her actions.

"That's it. I said no," she continues. "No holidays. Ostap will get over it. He can go on holiday with his mum."

We're silent. Dad looks out of the window. I bite down onto my bottom lip.

If she doesn't turn the tap off now, I'm going to throw all the leftovers from the plates onto her.

Relax. You know what she's like.

Also, I want to cover my face with my arms and cry.

"It's only five hours to Odessa," says Dad to the vase of fuchsia on the windowsill. "Uncle Lyosha and I could drop you off in the car. And you can come back on the train or whatever."

"Are you completely bonkers, or what?" Mum turns off the water, spinning round from the sink.

"He's going to drive his daughter to a dump! And the shame! First let him marry her, and then he can take her wherever he wants. No."

Mum spins back round to the sink and turns the water on.

"She isn't getting my blessing."

That's very bad. A mother's blessing is an important thing.

Ow, shut up you high-flown thing in my head. A mother's blessing, shame, disgrace. I want to shag!

"Mum, can you speak to my face?" I say.

"You!" shouts Mum. "Be quiet!" The words fly out of her like bullets. "Disgrace!"

Hope Uncle Lyosha doesn't hear. Good thing he's gone to take a shower.

"No need to humiliate me!" I shout, flying out of the kitchen into my room. I am steaming. I want to smash something. Why does she speak to me like that? Because I'm her daughter, does that mean she can insult me with nasty words? And anyway, I'm not her property! I'm my own! I stamp my foot. I'll go out of spite! I jump up. No matter what happens, I need to go! My cheeks are burning.

In the kitchen, I can hear Dad's voice:

"Tammy, you're acting like a kid," he says calmly. "She isn't little now; she's capable of making decisions. If we don't support her, she's still going to go..."

Mum was probably getting ready to shout something else upsetting and high flown, but out of the bathroom comes steamed, wet-haired Uncle Lyosha, Mum's big brother, wrapped in a yellow dressing gown – Dad's. With a striped towel on his shoulders. A kind, good-faced uncle with a square face and joyous eyes.

"Who's happened?" He asks his favourite question.

Not a sound comes back from the kitchen. I shout from my room:

"My boyfriend's inviting me to the seaside. Mum's not letting me go, Uncle Lyosh!"

"Why, Miss Tammy?" Uncle Lyosha calls everybody either "Miss" or "Mr".

In reply, only the sound of water is heard and the thundering of the plates being placed into the cupboard.

I want to reply that she's embarrassed to admit that her head is twisted, that's why she isn't letting me go. Come on, Tamara Semenovna, say: "My head is twisted. I need help from a specialist dealing with people's heads, but I never see these specialists because I prefer to take everything out on my daughter and husband." Well!?

I didn't notice that I was whispering all of this out loud. Wow! Looks like me getting help from a professional wouldn't go amiss. I am my mum's daughter.

"Let 'em go, so they'll relax after their lectures, why not?" says Uncle Lyosha, taking a seat at the table, wiping his hair with the towel.

"Lyosha, you know what kind of person that boy is!" In Mum's scream, funnily enough, there are notes of compassion. Uncle Lyosha definitely has an effect on her like water on an unwashed pan.

"Oh, as if I don't remember my Sveta at seventeen?" He speaks in a good bass. "That age, Tamara darling, they're not going to date honest academics. What's he like? A bad guy on a motorbike? With chains and bandanas?"

"He passed his exams with flying colours, Uncle Lyosh!" I shout out again.

In the sink, under a strong stream of water, once again the pan begins to rumble.

Oh, now to wash the clean pans.

It's a disgrace to turn round and look a healthy, common-sensed person in his eye. Instead, scrape the tiles and whitewash the ceiling. Wash the curtains, even buff up the windows.

"So, Mr Toll, you're saying it's five hours to Odessa?" asks Uncle Lyosha.

"Five, if we leave in the morning." Dad nods keenly.

"When do you need to leave, Miss Osha?" asks Uncle Lyosha loudly.

"The trip starts tomorrow!" I shout excitedly, not believing my ears.

"Where are you going to sleep?" Mum shoots out her last ammunition – an appeal for healthy, common sense.

"I'll drive five hours there, and Uncle Toll five back." Uncle Lyosha shrugs his shoulders. Then, louder:

"Well, ring your bandana biker, tell him to be outside the flat tomorrow, suitcases in hand!"

I squeal, jump up and clap my hands. I fly out of the room and jump onto Uncle Lyosha's neck. Run around the table. I hug Dad so much that his neck gives a crunch. I turn round to Mum, intending to straighten out her neck too or even just to peck her on the cheek. Mum continues to wash the pan, not looking in my direction. Fine. I shrug and run to ring Ostap. She'll get over it.

Happy, I whisper to Ostap over the phone that we're leaving tomorrow at five in the morning, to meet tomorrow outside. I immediately hang up the phone. Through the door of the room, Mum peeks her head and hisses:

"You just wait. You'll come back and I'll set you straight. You'll see."

And with a crash she slams the door shut.

Would be nice to mace her round the head.

It's not nice to think these things of your mum.

Not nice to use a mace, but nice to dream about it.

184

Big Changes, And Not Only In The Green Room

CHAPTER ONE

Love and Hatred in Silence

A large, gold-plated pillar with the inscription "Kholmysty" appears in the front window of the bus. At the top of the pillar is a stork's nest. I was seven years old, when my nan, seeing the nest with the stork, said "Good sign". My heart froze back then. Still to this day it freezes every time: if there is a stork, it's a good sign. There was no stork. Little did I know that my babushka actually meant that the gold-plated pillar looked like a well-made sign, that we were entering Kholmysty.

Mum's hissing in my head. It's time to pay for everything. Sea, sand, prawns, love till the morning. The family with an eight-year-old girl next door sneakily observed us in the mornings. Probably asking themselves: married? And where is the ring then? Creaking beds! We do have strange holiday places. For those who've done with lovemaking. Or for those who want to catch a break. For prostitutes and old men. For everybody else, the creaking of the bed or love on the floor. Love in the sea. I remember the whispering lips, "Come here!", and sweet sensations in the water.

I blush from the memories. This all happened. Every day. Before breakfast, lunch, dinner and before sleep. "What if there is a war tomorrow?" he joked, catching his breath. I laughed. Happy, carefree. And once, a hasty question: "Do you love me?"

A careful silence. His damp eyes in the moonlight. The crackling of cicadas.

"Yes."

I am at his disposal till the end of life, and if he doesn't want me – then to a monastery I go, to pray for his happiness. But he wanted me. He was there. He said it.

And now home, to Mum.

A week later, I'm sitting at the kitchen table in front of an open window. Smoking. Parents are at work; Uncle Lyosha is in Kiev working. I'm howling a sad Ukrainian song "The Cherry Orchard". I always howl it when I feel rough.

I stop at the usual lump in my throat at the words "I want to live, because I love".

My ears ring for a few seconds because of my loud singing. I grab the phone. For the eighty-first time I dial Ostap's number. And for the eighty-first, and the four hundred and twelfth time, nobody answers. For a week now. Mum isn't speaking to me. As if I don't exist. Maybe she's lost her voice, while I was in Odessa. Or she's numb.

I sit carefully, looking out of the window, going insane. I'll go outside till five in the evening. Girls' laughter, vodka, cigarettes will blunt the stinging desire to see him, backhand him, and then somewhere in the woods or on a rooftop, scratch his back, leave love bites on his neck, real bites on his shoulders, and try not to strangle him to death while he's having an orgasm. I saw that in a film once.

Two questions are tormenting me.

Where is he?

Why did he not say he was leaving?

OK, have a two-day break from me, but he hasn't been home for a week now, and because of him, I'm not speaking to Mum.

I jump off the table. In the hallway, the clock shows 5pm. In an hour Mum will be home, and my presence here will be very unnecessary.

The thought of seeing her today, just like for the last six days, even being in the same room as her, suffocates me.

Shower, make-up, jeans and a T-shirt. I open the desk drawer, by habit pulling out two wads of cash: two hundred. One hundred is enough for five menthol cigarettes, and if I take the other hundred, I'll have enough for blackcurrant vodka.

I eat a spoonful of cottage cheese. And not because I want to eat, but so that there is something in my stomach before the vodka. I don't want to ring Katka. Pleasing her that Ostap has forgotten me. I walk to the Oaks. I will most certainly meet someone I half know, who isn't interested in my relationship with Ostap. Maybe Tasha.

"Osha, you got a cigarette?" Tasha shakes her leg, sitting on the nearest bench.

"And you should have some matches," I take out the five cigarettes from my back pocket, freshly bought.

"I should," she replies, taking out a match from the box, warmed up in her hand.

Before we can ask each other our introductory questions and limp under the effect of the cigarettes, I see two men approaching us. One is tall, thin, with glasses, and the second stocky, with a shiny chain on a trim neck. They climb the stairs leading to the Oaks, and they're staggering.

"Who are those misunderstandings?" says Tasha, letting out a stream of smoke.

"Ostap," I say. "Staggering. Drunk as a skunk. And Rudi. Not staggering. But also drunk as a skunk."

Ostap drunk in Kholmysty, and not in the village, helping to water the courgettes? The last crumbs of justification, that his whole family packed up and went to his grandmother's, scattered.

All I have now is his tall figure, hands in pockets, gleaming eyes. He's staggering and getting closer. Tall, skinny, like a middle finger.

Should I tell him that I'm insulted? As if we share a flat, car, kids and expensive mattress?

I'm going to act as though time has passed and I haven't thought about him once.

Ostap and Rudi stop in front of us. Are they going to start rapping to us or something? I imagine them as two oaks, and I'm observing the ants crawling over them.

"I got a feeling these might be the girls," says Ostap over Rudi's shoulder.

"Yep, that's them," says Rudi, and he nods.

"And maybe, you girls are drinking vodka as well?" says Ostap.

"Yes, we are," I say for both for us.

"I think they've given in," says Ostap to Rudi. Again, over his shoulder.

"Yep, they say they're drinking."

Half of the plastic cup of vodka quickly and powerfully hits me in the head. The tablespoon of cottage cheese hasn't been enough to quench that amount of alcohol. It's difficult enough as it is for me to speak in the company of Ostap. And now there's an iron lock hanging on my lips.

"Time to get out of here," says Ostap to no one in particular.

Tasha and I glance at one another, shrugging our shoulders, as we get up.

We trail after Ostap and Rudi. From the side it might look like the boys are taking us out, and I feel like a little cow.

"Osha, these alkies, they are not creepy, are they?" asks Tasha in a half-whisper.

"Nah! Others could be, but these are my ex-classmates. They are OK," I reply.

I know what Tasha means. Will they not get us drunk and take advantage of us? But I myself will take advantage of Ostap three hundred times first. And Rudi...he'd be very surprised to meet a girl that doesn't want him. That will be the day. It's written on his face: "Come on, surprise me. Don't let me fuck you."

"What you doin' for Independence Day?" asks Tasha. We've been sitting for an hour already on Ostap's balcony, smoking and drinking vodka and Coke.

"Don't know yet." I shrug my shoulders. The truth is: hope that Ostap will drag me out somewhere. But I don't confess that to Tasha.

"Let's get the girls and go to Krechatik to party it up?" she says.

I agree. Loudly. Let Stapler hear and know that I've made plans.

"Where's Stapler gone?" I decide to ask the question that has been bothering me from the moment Ostap left the balcony.

"I'm gonna go check," I say to Tasha.

"If you're not back in five minutes, I'm going home."

I find Stapler in the bathroom. In trousers and a T-shirt, with closed eyes, up to his ears in water, he looks like a meditating young monk. Drops of water on the lenses of his glasses. I lower my finger into the water – cold.

"What are you doing, idiot?" I ask.

Ostap is silent. I turn the tap off. Slap him on his cheek. His eyelids begin to tremble. Meaning he's conscious. Anger starts to brew inside of me. Not only was he missing for a week, God knows where, he drags us to his house, then gets into the bath, not paying any attention to us.

He's downed a lot of vodka and he's cooling off in the cold water.

And I don't care. What kind of attitude is this?

It's my fault. Following him, like some young cow. Where's the respect?

190

He loves me. Meaning he should respect me. Behaving like a young cow, or not.

Ostap grabs me by the waist, spilling the bath water onto the floor, dragging me into the bath.

Maybe he really was a cobra in his past life?

In the water, I try to breathe in, and not taking anything in, I screech from the cold, falling onto him and instantly sobering. I wallop him on his cheeks. He presses me into him, shutting my screeching mouth with a kiss. Pulling my arms behind me. I turn away from his lips, giving him a strong bite on his neck. And that's kind of hot. Who cares if in the cold water you can catch cystitis?

CHAPTER TWO

The Last Drop Into the Tub, Not Onto the Umbrella

The next morning. Mum's voice in the kitchen. The door opens a little; with a heightened tone, unclear, a voice carries through:

"Your daughter is just like you!" she shouts. Picking the right moment on purpose, when the door opens?

"All scatty, dirty! And she doesn't care about anyone but herself!" Her shout fills the whole flat densely, leaving no space, like a choir in a church. Dad calmly replies:

"Do you understand that you're making a scandal because I bought the wrong type of sausage?"

I understand that Dad is in the hallway and about to return to the shop to get the right type of sausage.

"And you never buy the right type of sausage! Because you never listen!" Mum shouts.

Fury brews inside of me, and the front door slams. Dad is gone.

"First of all, why shout?!" I shout. "Secondly, why shout so much over a sausage?"

The kitchen reigns in silence.

"And thirdly, why shout all kinds of nastiness?" I finish more quietly. I'm breaking the rule of not getting involved in parents' arguments. But the argument includes me, so I'm getting involved.

Hurried steps from the kitchen into the hallway. Mum bursts into my room. Her eyes emit sparks. Eyebrows bent from anger, like the bent roof of a cottage, rolling pin in hand. I think she's going to hit me. I need to get dressed. Or at least take up a vertical position. I quickly sit up on my pillow, wrapped in my duvet.

"You! Waste of skin! How dare you butt into our conversations!" Her ringing voice cuts my ears right through with an invisible drill.

"Hard not to butt in, Mother, when all I can hear is your voice, ringing in my ears!" I shout, burying myself in the depths of my bed warily.

I'm angry. Decisive. Fearless. If she hits me – I'll jump up and push her into the armchair. The duvet will fall off. Let her see me how she sees me.

"You! You!" Mum, by the looks of things, isn't warming up to sing a famous Russian song by Philipp Kirkorov, but struggles to find the right words, and her face turns scarlet red.

"You shameless slut! Slagging around wherever, with whomever! She goes on holidays! I can't stand you!"

"Oh really?" I scream in reply.

"And you and Dad made me with a finger, a few months before the wedding?"

For a moment, Mum's face turns to stone, and mine to glory. For a moment. I once stumbled upon their marriage certificate. They married in April '78. And I was born in August of the same year.

"*Yyou*...disgusting, fffilthy little girl!" Mum's words are like a jackhammer in the neighbour's wall.

"You egg! Eggs don't teach chickens! You can pack your bags and go and live with him, with your Question Mark! Only he won't take you! You won't be getting my parental blessing! He does not love you! He has you where he wants you, and you fold in front of him, like a doormat, no! Eugh! I curse you! You're no daughter of mine!" Mum continues to scream and turns purple. I don't want to see her face. I close my eyes, head in the pillow. Her voice echoes in my ears. The echoes struggle to find an exit, the words repeating and repeating.

The scream finishes after an eternity. Fearing that she's going to whack me with the rolling pin, I open my eyes.

Mum isn't here, and I can hear her steps getting further away into the kitchen, and the frying pan starts to hiss again. At least she didn't whack me with the rolling pin.

I need to get out of here. Did she really just curse me? How can I live with her under one roof?

Otherwise, she won't respect me. And I'll have to leave under really humiliating circumstances.

But to where?

To the unfinished cottage. There's a house there with no doors or windows, but it's a house. It has a roof, it has walls, and it has gaps for the doors and the windows too. I'll walk there. I contemplate calmly, as if I'd planned this long ago, last year. I'll go for a week. And then to the end of the summer, Independence Day, to student halls. Too fast.

Taking my prayer book, matches and a blanket. I write a note: "Be back Saturday. Don't look for me."

CHAPTER THREE

What Is Above Ostap's Head?

In the country, in the house with no windows or doors, but a house, in the morning of the third day: I want to go home. To shower, to my bed. I want to eat. Normal food. Fried eggs and sausages. To sleep on a pillow. My body aches. It's a wooden floor. In two days, I've slept once, on a haystack.

In the secluded country town, at night, on the first night, I hear the roar of a motorbike. It stops nearby. I quit attempting to warm myself up and shoo off the mosquitos.

I listen. August Ukrainian nights aren't hot. I stop struggling to start a fire with wet branches and logs. I stamp it out with my trainers.

In the place where the bike has stalled, I hear men's and women's laughs, the clanging of bottles. Cigarette smoke? Really close!

What if they decide to shag in one of the nearby houses?

And what if they saw the fire? On the other hand, they don't know who is there or how many of me there are. After an eternity, the motorbike booms and leaves in the direction of the woods, with squeals and laughs.

I'm freezing. I shake, holding a half-empty matchbox, to light the fire again. Behind the wooden wall, rustling and grunting. Wow! A boar? A grunting dog? A drunken hedgehog, left behind from the motorbike? It's not funny. My heart is pounding on an empty stomach. The grunting disappears into the darkness, but I don't strike a match till morning.

It is dawn. On the horizon, a hay barn. I'll walk to the barn, wrapped in my blanket, take some hay, come back, lie on the floor on the hay, and sleep well. How far an it be to walk? Upwards, top of the hill.

The top of the hill turns out to be a four-hour walk. What looks like one hummock with the hay barn on top turns out to be three bald hummocks with the hay barn on the fourth. Between the hummocks are deep ravines. I have to walk around them on the dusty road to the right. The dusty road stretches out, five kilometres per hour for four hours – twenty kilometres. What's an adventure without obstacles?

When I get to the hay barn, the sun is at its zenith. I climb up onto it – it is almost as high as a two-storey house! Else I wouldn't have noticed this construction from the window of my house. Before I can properly think about this, I fall into a deep, child-like sleep.

I awake. The sun is setting. Around the hay barn – cows. A horse walks around; there's a man with a moustache and a hat. I tie my blanket around me into a knot. I slide off. A calf darts to the side. The man's eyes! He accompanies me with his look for a long time. Maybe he thinks that I am a haystack spirit? Or a hermit, eating hay? Or that I was on a date with a combiner, and maybe fell asleep and the combiner went to harvest at six in the morning. He could be imagining anything. Or maybe he isn't thinking anything, and is just admiring my tightly fitting trousers, humming the Ukrainian tune about two oaks on the hill into his moustache. I look round twice. Once, with a smile; the other, without. As if to say, these things also happen, see.

I return back to the cottage at night. Tired. Wanting to eat. I dig out some potatoes from the vegetable patch. Make a fire. Pour in the potatoes. Carpet the floor with hay straws and take a nap. A rustle wakes me up. This time, the rustling of the rain. In the pitch-black darkness, the fire is lightly burning out. The potatoes have burnt. Again, till morning I grind my teeth, this time on the hay, although I am praying, so that I won't be afraid of the smoking boars and the grunting motorbikes.

On the morning of the third day, I realise that I can take it no longer. In an hour I read all of the prayers in the book, raising my voice on the Sleep of Death prayer.

I pack the blanket into my bag, along with the prayer book and matches and head in the direction of my parents' house.

After walking one hundred yards, I arrive at the main road. A car emerges. After a second, I recognise the number plate. After two seconds I recognise Dad behind the wheel. After three seconds I don't recognise Mum with a grey face. Both the car and I stop. Like two cats, not wanting to provoke a chase.

In Dad's eyes: "Thank God!" In Mum's, a guilty, tormented look. Her eyes are saying, "I know I was wrong, but leaving the house is too much."

Too much?

I go up to the car and get in.

"Good morning," Dad says clearly and starts to reverse the car in the direction of the house. So, they didn't come to water the crops. They were looking for me.

I did tell them I was coming back on Saturday though.

"Good morning," I mumble. My first words after the argument with Mum. My mouth is dry. I enjoy breathing in the smell of the family car. The scent of nuts, apples and cigarettes. Awkward. They're not telling me off. I'm happy.

We go in silence. A pleasant sadness. A rural morning landscape out of the window. I fall into sleep. Home and dry, I think.

Dad drops us off outside the flat and goes to work. Mum and I go up in the lift in silence. I study the burnt floor in the corner. I feel the same awkwardness and happiness.

Mum opens the door and walks into the kitchen. She puts the kettle on. A Kholmysty resident's favourite thing to do – under any circumstances – put the kettle on. I follow her to drink water. We sit at the table. I drink water; Mum drinks coffee.

"Forgive me," she utters in a voice with clear diction. I stop hiding behind my glass, put it on the table. A spasm in my throat. I hastily cover my face and start to sob into my immediately wet palms.

"Everything I said and did," Mum continues, "I said and did because I wanted to protect you. But I give up. You are my child, no matter what you do with your life. I've decided that."

She speaks slowly, which isn't like her at all, seeming as though there is a clear speaker inside of her, and not a history teacher.

"The only thing I want to say now, honestly: I don't believe in your relationship with this boy. I don't see his respectful attitude, which you so deserve. I don't see flowers, communication, and a desire to meet the parents. After all, you spend the whole night with this person, all ten days. My dear, my sunshine, love! I never thought to tell you the one thing: do love. You are allowed."

I stop sobbing, as if I am injected with a big dose of sedatives.

"To love is extraordinary! It's a gift! And with this feeling you are richer than him three hundred times! But you don't have to express your love the way that you do. There's no need to drink vodka and run to him on every call. Draw! Write! You're my smart sweetheart! You finished five years of art school! You've written poetry since you were seven years old."

I wouldn't call that poetry! I want to throw a reproachful look at myself and burst out laughing. I turn serious instead. I'll read and fix Mum's doubts after.

I can love. She's right.

It dawns on me that all the suffering is because I wanted to show my love through physical attachment. No attachment – lots of vodka. No vodka – fasting, prayer. That's why out of all the buildings in our town one hundred and fifty are churches; the rest are beer bars. Also, one hundred and fifty of them. And only one basket-weaving club at the House of Culture in the name of Karpenko-Kary.

How else do I express myself? To paint, go fishing, mushroom foraging, chess. Look at Dima Skvortsov, for example. From year three he was going after Dasha, and still had time for yacht club. And we still all thought he was cool.

Not one conversation with Pashya felt as deep as Mum's words. Mum sits next to me and embraces me. I feel better. She understands – I love him; I'm not a slut.

"Maybe he loves you," she says. "And I just don't see it, no?" She shrugs her shoulders. I sob into her shoulder.

"I judge by old measures. What do you think of your relationship?"
Good question.

"I don't know." My turn to shrug.

"Sometimes he behaves like there isn't anybody closer in the whole world."

Our night talks flash past: the "Yes" dropped by the sea, the jealousy for Vick, and the honeymoon over at his halls. Love scenes flash past too. And both of us are serious, as if for the last time, as if tomorrow is a war indeed.

"And sometimes it's like," I continue, "I just don't understand anything."

Here are long weeks and months stretching out in my memory, waiting for his phone calls. And Yuri's sentencing: "mis-un-der-stan-ding" as he slams the door.

"You're both just young and silly," says Mum. "You have feelings, but what to do with them, you've yet to learn and learn."

"Maybe." I sigh with relief. At least somebody knows that there is something to do with these feelings.

"Right," she says. "You're a big girl, eighteen years on your head; you'll figure it out on your own. These last two days hurt too much, paying for my lack of indifference." Mum smiles sourly.

"I am ready to check whether he is serious, but my attitude to him will not just change overnight."

Her voice has a note of the previous history teacher, and I cringe.

"Until I see that he really does love you. Tell him all of this. And give this to him too." She takes a big orange from the vase and places it in the middle of the table. I understand that she has read my diary.

I blush, and then smile. Well, what else to do if you run out of ideas for where to look for your runaway daughter?

"OK," I say.

After a beat, Mum says:

"Go over to his. He's worried that you've disappeared. We called. We called everyone."

My mum is advising me to go to Ostap's?

The phone rings.

"Speak of the devil," Mum says. "That is either him, or Vick. Vick rings every two hours."

I go over to the phone. Certain that it is Vick.

"Is that you?" The delighted voice of Vick. "Idiot! Where did you get to? The whole of Kholmysty has been on the lookout for the last two nights."

"It's me, Vick. I'm home. I'm a fool."

"The main thing is you're alive. Have you called Stapler? He's discombobulated." Vick emphasises the last word. I try to imagine a discombobulated Ostap. I fail to do it.

"Not yet. I'll go to see him now."

"Go, go. I'll come over after lunch. You can tell me where you've been, OK?"

"OK."

To Ostap's at eleven in the morning, jumping up with an orange in my hand. Mum has sent me off. If Mum had supported our meetings from the beginning, letting me stay overnight, for example... I stop smiling. How would our relationship have panned out?

I probably wouldn't be hiding from Mum in different flats with cockroaches in cupboards and in heads. And, maybe, if it isn't love but God knows what, then it would have ended naturally by itself. Although how it would have ended naturally by itself, it's hard to imagine. And what is even harder to imagine is that it isn't love but God knows what.

I'm happy that Mum didn't support our meet-ups from the beginning. I'm happy that I left home, and that he was worrying, and now I'm going to his. Now, I'm not the only one who thinks that he's my boyfriend. Maybe he really is my boyfriend? Strange contemplation. "You're both just young and silly, and you don't know what to do with your feelings."

In his room, it's as dark as usual. Windows taped over with the same newspapers. The Doors are playing. I turn on the light. The red Kewpie dimly lights up the bed. Ostap lies on the bed, fully clothed.

I open the door to the balcony. The daylight slashes across our eyes. I sit next to him. Placing the orange into his hand. He looks at me indifferently. As if it's not me who's come with an orange, but Tolly Pushka with a plate of pies, and he's just already eaten a whole tray of them.

"That's from Mum," I say. "She said that you must be really worried."

Ostap's eyes are heavy. Finally, he says:

"That's why first she rang Vick, then Katka, and then everyone else, and after everyone else rang me, and asked me if I knew by any chance…" He raises his eyebrows. "By any chance, where you were."

I frown, like a guilty schoolgirl.

"I think, maybe she doesn't get enough of your attention," I say, picking my nails. "She complains that she doesn't see you at our house at all, that you don't want to be her friend, and that she doesn't know you."

"Mhm," he says. "Vick is the opposite, on the other hand. He comes over, drinks tea with your mum; that's why ringing him comes naturally."

"Well." I gesture with my hands. "That's how it is. What's stopping you from coming over to Mum's and drinking tea? You went to Pushi's mum to eat pies."

We're both silent. We're not speaking about the right things. Where has he been all week? My mood is getting ruined. I don't want it to get ruined. I want to leave. But he doesn't ask, where I've been, why I left, and the conversation feels unfinished. And Ostap lies there, eyes closed, as if the conversation is over.

I start to feel upset. I remind myself of the main changes after the talk with Mum. The decision to not react to his mood swings grows bigger inside of me. I don't want to be upset and finish his thoughts and feelings for him. Mum can't change me. I can't change him. I should tell him, straight and honest, at eleven in the morning, and then go to live the way I know how.

Find other ways to express feelings.

"You disappeared for a week and didn't say anything. I called you. Lots. I was worried. At home, the situation was grim. Mum wasn't speaking to me because I went to the seaside with you.

"Then you appeared. Drunk. Rude. Shagged me in the bath, like a slut. In the morning, Mum called me a slut. I packed my bags and went to our countryside dacha in Bezradychi. I left a note that I'd be back on Saturday. But they were still worried."

Ostap continues to be silent, eyes closed. He only frowns his forehead slightly, as if I have caused him a headache with my words. Maybe I have a nasty voice?

"Above my head there is no umbrella," he says. "There is a tub above my head. And the last drop landed the day before yesterday."

Then he adds:

"I'm melancholy."

It's pointless to continue the conversation.

Had I heard these words before, my heart would have shrunk, as if I'd been roundhoused into my solar plexus. The world would have collapsed, and the ground would have disappeared beneath my feet. But the decision to live, the way I know, to make mistakes and not to pretend to be the ideal girlfriend of Ostap wins. So, I get up and say:

"Well, you know my phone number. Where I live, you know too. When the melancholy passes – ring, write, come over. I don't have anything else to say." I step over to the door. And add:

"I'm sorry. For everything."

He's silent. I exit. Without a ruined mood. I am surprised.

CHAPTER FOUR

Independence Day

Independence Day coincides with my spirit. I don't need to wait till eight in the evening for Ostap's phone call and I don't need to make plans. I don't need to worry that Vick will come over and Ostap will be upset. Everything is in Ostap's hands. Phone, when the melancholy finishes. Establish friendly relations with Mum. Warn me when he's going to disappear for a week.

I love him, but I'm not pathetic.

If not for the situation on Independence Day, everything would have stayed on a cheerful note.

After two weeks I would have gone over to Ostap's and our relationship would have panned out differently. But that Independence Day threw me to the top of adulthood, like the older kids throwing the cap of a five-year-old right to the top of the pine tree.

Tasha and I stop at the bus stop. I dance about; I'm happy. My parents have given me money and allowed me to stay the night at Tasha's friend Barashka's, in Kiev.

Mum's shoes, one size too small but they suit the hoodie and flared jeans. Before reaching Kiev, I realise: I cannot take another step in them.

"Let's go to Barashka's. She'll defo have spare shoes. And then to Maidan for a concert," says Tasha. "Remember the road where we're sleeping tonight."

Yeah… If not for Mum's shoes, then I could have been sleeping anywhere that night. I wouldn't be going anywhere today; I'd be lying dead somewhere in a ditch, stinking, still to this day.

Six hours later. The hill on Maidan. I'm lying face down on the grass. Around me are poll rees and the hum of drunken youngsters. I was bellowing from six in the evening. Can't get up. Clocks strike ten. Four hours of lying down. People walk past. They're laughing. Some at me, some between themselves. Some stop by, pick me up, unfold me and press into my stomach. Further along, a voice:

"Val, leave her. She's wasted."

"Damn it, we've gotta help her," Val replies.

"She's wasted, it happens."

"Leave me, Val," I exclaim, ready to kiss her with gratitude, but not wanting to give off my vomit scent.

"I can't stand or walk," I moo.

More attempts to induce vomiting, then Val is in despair, carefully placing me on the grass, and leaves. I clearly remember how I ended up here. We were sitting close to Krechatik, in an alleyway drinking three-star cognac. Counterfeit. We didn't eat. It's my own fault.

I fidget on the bus seat. Unpleasant to remember. But I have to. The point, which turned the outlook of my world upside down. The point, after which the power in the green room shifted from Sensuality to Decisiveness. The Day of Independence from Sensuality in my own head. Ready.

"Hey, get up." Someone touches my shoulder. I raise my head. More help on offer? The face of a man with a responsive expression in a Berkut military uniform[4]. It is chiming eleven.

"Can't," I say. "Want water."

"One sec." The guy shouts into the poll trees: "Zheka! Bring water! I found a girl!"

Zheka, also in a Berkut uniform, brings a bottle of water. They lift me under my arms and sit me down under a tree.

"Poor girl." Zheka looks at my grass-and-mud-stained face, giving me water. "Where are your friends?"

"They left," I say, unsticking my lips from the neck of the bottle.

"Probably," I add, and drink some more. The water makes me feel better.

"Maybe try to puke," offers the first stranger.

"Nothing to puke with." I shrug. "We didn't eat."

"Wow, you're something…" Zheka is emphatically concerned with my condition.

"How could they leave you?" asks the first.

4   Ukrainian Riot Police – 'Berkut' (Eng. Golden Eagle)

"Me and Barashka went to wee," I say and hiccup. "Into these birch trees. She managed to get up, and I didn't. I pulled my jeans up, lying down." I giggle gullibly.

"Come, let's help get you up." They grab me, as if I'm wounded, and stand me up on my legs. Professional. We went over this at Basic Military Training at school.

"You standing?" asks the second.

"Standing," I say, staggering.

"Vovan, let's take her for a wash," says Zheka.

"You're so kind, Zheka and Vovan," I say, looking into their faces. They are smiling frostily. I think to myself: that's luck. There is a God in this world.

We go through the dark streets, up the hill. In the direction of Hotel Ukraine. Zheka and Vovan in front. Me, obediently following. Just like a few days ago, behind Ostap and Rudi. Guess I am a young cow. We pass the poll trees. Pass a drunken crowd of youngsters. They shout, having fun. Into another alleyway. The yard of a multistorey block of flats. A dark entrance. The doorbell rings in the door on the ground floor. A scared woman, hair in curlers. Zheka shows her his Berkut ID.

"Good evening," he says loudly. "Apologies for the trouble. This citizen needs help. She needs your sink."

I burst out laughing.

The woman and the Berkut men retain their serious facial expressions.

"Please, of course," says the woman.

I go through the corridor into the bathroom, pass a huddled family. They look scared and I think of Stalin times. Or maybe, several families. A communal flat?

I stare into the mirror above the sink. Their frightened faces aren't surprising. Mine is swollen and red from tears. The mascara washed away long ago. At around eight o'clock, I imagine. My flared jeans and hoodie are covered in dirt and grass stains. Hair hangs like wet icicles. Dad is a thief, Mum's alcoholic, and I ran away from a kid's shelter, dreaming of piercing my nose and eyebrows and to perform on stage shouting about fire, like the singer Linda, but I don't have any money. Though my shoes aren't tight anymore.

"Guys, thank you so much," I say when we go back outside. Washed and fresh-faced. Tears reappear.

"Come on, leave it. You not cried enough yet?" says Bear, taking me under my arm. "Come, we'll take you to the metro."

I follow obediently, holding on. I don't cry. Passing a building site, we turn to a bench.

"Let's have a fag. Still got time," says Bear.

"How old are ya?" asks Jekyll.

"Eighteen," I answer.

"Little. But a grown-up." Bear eyes Jekyll for some reason.

"Got a boyfriend?"

Jekyll sits up on the back of the bench. I stand facing Jekyll. Bear is walking in the direction of the building site, and utters over his shoulder:

"Be right back."

"Probably do," I answer. "Though we got into a row."

Jekyll stretches out a hand, holding a cigarette.

I spark up. Behind us, I hear Bear's footsteps approaching. His hands grab me from behind and tightly press me against him.

"Building site over there. No one's about."

"Oh," I manage to say. Bear is gripping me tightly, and Jekyll jumps from the bench straight onto my lips, with kisses. "Operation: Snail Returns?" I try to turn away.

"Listen, love," Jekyll says in a low bass, breathing cigarette smoke into my face.

"We ain't had a bird in years. We ain't letting you go." His face gets angrier.

"Keep tossin' and turnin', you'll get shut down with a rock to your head. You'll only be guessin' what we did to ya."

"If you even come to your senses," Bear adds into my ear.

I sober up. What happens next, I remember with particular clarity. Though I couldn't get my head round all of it. My brain is swimming. What do I do? Nothing but a building site all around, night-time, nobody will hear me. Who's going to save me, if I'm being raped by patrolling Berkuts? Least they washed me. I mull the situation over in my head for long after. To shut them down with a rock. But only one of them. Wouldn't have got away from the second. Cotton legs.

Maybe complain about them? But, firstly, I can't remember their faces properly. Tall, thin, both snub-nosed.

Secondly, I've heard stories in Kholmysty about what happens to girls who report. Who's to say that the police in Kiev aren't like that? Here are two walking bits of evidence – in Berkut uniforms. And where did they take me to wash myself? That lady looked around forty-five. I remember. I don't remember the house.

I remember me crying. Asking not to touch me. I lie that I'm a virgin. Doesn't work. Though they promise, only half the tip, it won't hurt.

What's up with rapists persuading to only put "half the tip" in? Do they take a special course, What to Say Before Raping? Yoza must have attended that one too.

I say I want the toilet. They let me go, ten steps away. To the fence of the building site. Maybe I could run away? Even to hide. I walk to the fence and pray. I pray. I start running along the fence. Then, I am jumped on, either by Jekyll or Bear.

"That's it, now that's it," he says heavily, breathing evil at me. "Piss here. No need to pull your trousers back up."

I pray. Stones in my back, under the stones, concrete. What a place to get raped. Didn't they scuff their knees up?

Jekyll and Bear were taking it in turns, twitching; all the while I could see the sky, full of stars. To see Him among the stars now. If He doesn't see me now, when I need to be seen, then there really isn't anybody there, apart from the stars. I think.

"Can you stop crying?" says the twitcher. "I can't come like that."

I laugh weakly. A request to stop crying comes through, because the victim's cry distracts the rapist from getting pleasure. And I was thinking it was turning you on, that's why I'm crying.

Strangely, I don't get slapped, as I am sure the laugh sounds as distracting as the cry.

When everything finishes, I hear all about how much of a good girl I was, and that it wouldn't be bad to meet again.

I could have even taken their number! They offered it. Could play along, convince them that I liked it, and, sod it, snog them goodbye. Then pay Karamaz and his gang to rape them somewhere in the deep forest, film the whole thing and blackmail them till old age, and not let them get any money for haemorrhoid medicine. Instead of this, I pull the dirty jeans up over my scratched and bloodied waist, and mutter:

"You bastard creeps. Don't have children, because they'll be bastard creeps too. And when you do have them, remember when your daughter gets raped. Or your girlfriend, or your sister. By some other bastard creeps."

"She's got a tongue on her..." says Jekyll.

"Well, if you don't want my number, don't take it. But I did actually like you."

"What-the-f—" I think. So, this happens too. After threatening to shut the victim down with a rock, the person genuinely regrets that feelings of sympathy aren't mutual. 'Least they didn't beat me. And let me go in the direction of the metro.

I walk. Ostap, you are not the only man who has had sex with me. There are two others... Jeans rubbing against the scratches on my waist. I sourly shrug my shoulders.

Getting on the last Obolon train, to Barashka's. The clock on Maidan Square strikes midnight.

The picking up from the ground, washing and raping took exactly an hour. In the reflection of the metro windows, even in a sober state, my face looks around twenty years older. And now, at midnight, with dead eyes, I look like a dirty old hag in a hoodie. People turn their eyes away. And my scratched waist hurts too. Curse Berkut people. But probably not all. Surely there are some guys among them who don't rape twenty-year-olds. Must be.

CHAPTER FIVE

Here's to Good Cognac, Normal Toilets, and Confident-in-Themselves Berkut Men

"Osha." Tasha's frightened voice sounds through the phone.

"Where did you go yesterday?"

"Oh! It's you?" I say. "Where? Was getting raped, obviously, what else? But it's fine, a ten-minute job. The rest of the time I was lying in my own urine and howling, like a beluga whale."

I am horrified by my own casual tone.

"You were…what?"

"Oh, come, let's meet instead, and I'll feed you with all the details," I reply.

"My God, that's horrible," Tasha says. Her cigarette burns between her fingers; the ash falls by itself. She listens to me, widening her eyes at some parts of the story, her jaw dropping during others.

"Imagine me telling my parents," I say, burying my foot in the sand.

"They just started to trust me. They gave me forty hryvnas instead of the usual ten to go out."

"We were a mess," she says. "I was led under my arms, and Barashka completely lost her memory. She remembers that she walked to come and get us, and when she came, she forgot what she came for. And we didn't get anything from her slurring."

"No point now." I shrug my shoulders, stepping onto the buried stone with my big toe. "From 2pm we were drinking fake cognac with no food. Obviously, our brains fried. And we were drinking equally – shit loads. My legs were knocked out. I'd never had that before. I'm glad we got out alive. How many people poison themselves with that fake dirt? People walked past, trying to help us get up, and then giving up in the end. And when I was on the metro – I looked down at my hands – I had none of my rings. Felt my ears – earrings gone too. When? I was just crying, I never passed out."

"Daaamn, gold?" Tasha gasps in horror. At the loss of the gold jewellery she gasps louder than at the rape.

"Yup. Mum's present for getting into uni," I reply. "She'll notice. I don't feel bad, just that I'll have to make up stupid excuses."

"We'll muster up something. I'll help you," says Tasha. "What happened after the metro?"

"Barashka's parents took me in," I reply. "How handy it was that my shoes were hurting. Otherwise I wouldn't know anywhere to go in Kiev except Baba Masha and Totya Sonya. Where would I have gone? Back under the fence, used as a doormat under some other dick."

Natasha giggles dryly.

"Thank God," she says.

"No," I reply. "There is no God. I checked." I smile dryly back. "But there are plenty of stars," I add. And, to change the subject, continue:

"Barashka's mum was freaking out, thinking what kind of places her daughter chills at. I looked horrid. They gave me a towel, sent me to the bathroom, clean T-shirt, put me to sleep on their fold-out bed. In the morning, I woke up from the hissing of the iron. Her mum was ironing my washed jeans. I burst into tears."

"So sweet of them," says Tasha. "Listen, it's grim, getting raped."

"You been there?" I ask.

Tasha nods.

"And I was sober," she adds. I shift my gaze away from the sand to Tasha.

She continues: "Dressed like a real lady, in a blue chequered dress. Waiting for Sita at the dam. I never heard him; he came over, covered my mouth with his hand from behind, and just hissed 'Chshhhhhhh' in my ear. Quickly found everything by himself, shoved it in, jerked a few times, came, and that was that. I look around, darkness all around, nobody anywhere. How did he move about so quietly? Perhaps wrapped his shoes in cotton, I don't know. Only my pants covered in sperm."

"Didn't even introduce himself." I giggle.

"Exactly. Could have said something, apart from 'Chshhh'. And his thingy was so tiny, probably embarrassed to show it to anyone. And then he legged it, ashamed, I bet. Drip. It didn't really hurt, just felt horrid, as if someone came and pooed, right under my nose."

"Into your pants," I say.

"Ew. Into my nose," she says.

We burst out laughing. Begin to feel better.

"I was raped too. My best friend, Vovka," says Sita that evening, flashing her slanted eyes in the darkness. We have gathered near the Oaks, all five of us: me, Tasha, Sita, Mira and Ally. The benches are arranged facing each other. The first toast is for Bear and Jekyll not to ever be able to get it up again. Tasha is assuring us that five girls is a huge power, and that if everybody wishes it, then that is what will happen.

"And me," says Mira, holding out her cup to Tasha, who is pouring the next round of vodka. "On some crates. One drinking buddy."

"And me." Ally sighs faintly. "Classmate's husband, five years older than us, my godfather, actually. He got drunk too."

"Oh-wow! Let's go in order." I liven up. Rape stories combined with vodka shots take my heaviness away.

My nerves are tickling. Like when I was a kid, in hospital, everyone telling each other scary stories, or their first sexual experiences. As it turns out later, for some of us, rape was our first sexual experience.

"Sita, you first." I point at Sita with my plastic cup.

"What do I say," Sita begins. "I 'as hanging out with some mates. It 'as time to be gone. My bestest friend came to walk on me home." We giggle. Sita's Tatar accent with mistakes sounds cute and always brings smiles to our faces. Sometimes we don't correct her.

She continues: "We sat at the same table at school. He wrote me love notes and stuff. He loved me, he'd assure me. So anyway, he is walking me home. He calls me over to his to give me coffee. To say like, where are you going in that state, come, sober up at mine. We went to his. At home, his mum was snoring in the next room. Younger brother asleep in the hall. You'd think there isn't a safer place to drink coffee. We're sitting in his room on the bed. I put the empty mug down; he's already piling on top of me, placing something cold against my face. I look with the corner of my eye – a knife. He says: 'I'll kill you, then my mum, then my brother, then myself, if you don't give yourself to me. I'll kill you, and then rape you anyway. That's how bad I want you.'"

"I cried, begged," Sita continues indifferently. "I was thirteen-year-old virgin. Not only did it hurt, there was a puddle of blood on the cover, he didn't get off me all night, and I got pregnant too." She weakly slaps her hand on her denim knee.

"His religion restrained him in his hometown Tashkent, so when he moved here, he got to the freebies. I got pregnant with twins. At thirteen years. They'd be five right now."

"Moron." I shake my head in horror.

"Abortion?" Tasha asks.

"What else am I meant to do?" replies Sita. "Hide from Dad in the basement with two kids? You know my dad: he is a Tatar, he'd have killed him. Killing him would be just fine, but he wouldn't let me outside ever again."

"Cra-azy," I say, and smile enthusiastically. I like it; killing is fine, but not being let outside again – that's the real killing.

"Yeah, Osha and me are the same," says Tasha. "Parents find out, they'll ground us in the village to weed parsley and plant potatoes till we're thirty."

"We'll have to drink to our school friend not getting it up again too," says Tasha, lifting her warmed-up cup. We drink. And light up.

"Listen, maybe I should go and get tested. What if they've infected me?" I say, fearfully.

"What!" Everyone shouts in one voice. "You'll get ripped off, before you even walk through the door," adds Ally.

"They said they hadn't had a girl for years…" says Tasha. "Believe it. And if its syphilis or gonorrhoea, then it will show in two weeks anyway."

"Yeah, and if you do go, then it will get round to Mum somehow," says high-cheek-boned Mira with her green cat eyes. She smokes by squeezing the cigarette down between two matches, so that her mum doesn't smell and suspect anything.

I'm scared. I hope that the Berkuts really didn't have any girls in years.

"Now I'll tell my story," says Mira. "Mine isn't so dramatic. Thank God, I didn't get pregnant. But was at it for most of the night. Anyway. I got drunk. Everyone left. He, jokingly, without any conversation, pulled everything off me and said he wouldn't give me back my clothes till I gave it to him. I say to him, looking around: 'Where? Here?'

"And around us are only empty plastic crates for beer. So, Osha, I definitely know what a scratched waistline is."

"On crates?" I howl.

"But actually, he didn't come either." Mira smiles. "I just started singing songs and laughing through tears. Stuff like 'Yellow Submarine'. He tried and tried, then failed. Gave me back my clothes, and I left. I was humiliated, but smiley, humming the same happy rhythm in my head."

We giggle.

"Well, we should drink to him never to be able to come," says Tasha, leaning in for the half-empty bottle.

"Wow, brutal," I say. "Imagine how many girls he's going to just rub against."

"Well, then let him come into his trousers as soon as he thinks about sex," says Tasha cheerfully, pouring vodka into the cups.

"That's a great one," says Mira.

"So, all his money is rinsed on nappies."

We drink. Ally sparks up.

"And my godfather," she begins, "has a massive c***."

We laugh at her joke. Especially in Ally's broken Ukrainian. Ally's family moved from Kazakhstan three years ago, so her Ukrainian is funny indeed.

"You can fit thirty pigeons onto him, huh…" She searches for the right word. In reply, fits of laughter.

"And so, he uses this prong." Ally listens to us laughing. "Yes. And he was my godfather. Husband of my classmate. She ran off to Spain, and he was missing her. I came over to his on her birthday. We got wasted, obviously. And he started babbling, 'Ally, babe, I never loved anybody as much as you.' I asked: 'And how did you make the kids, with your finger?' I froze and instantly regretted it. That's when he showed me his 'finger'. Dragged me from the kitchen, crazy eyes. I'm tossing and turning, I'm only little. He throws me straight onto the bed, covering my mouth with one hand, and with the other shoving in his vile thing. He could have taken my pants off. I had to move them myself, so that he wouldn't push the pants up into me… I couldn't walk for two days. And he just stunk so bad." She cringes, as if she'd smelt a dead rat.

"If he'd paid someone for sex, nobody would fall for it. But me he managed for free. Good for him, honestly."

We sit and stare into our empty cups.

"Wish I could kill them all, those idiots," I say.

"What should we wish for him," Tasha sings sarcastically.

"Two kids, godfather, classmate's husband."

"Should just forgive them all and live happy," says Sita, flashing her moistened eyes.

"I'll introduce you to Pashya, that's a wise kid. He says: 'Whatever you wish upon someone, it comes back to you.'"

"Pashya again. I saw him at Katka's last time in student halls. Spill the beans," I say, biting my lip.

"To not forgive – is basically to keep on clambering over the same feeling of hatred," says Sita. "It's so heavy. When I spoke with Pashya, that's when I forgave my rapist. As if a whole new life had begun, and I could do anything. I felt a touch of God."

"Hm." Ally scratches her head. "And if he's going to rape others the same way?" She glares angrily. "You forgave him, and then another one will come for coffee and will be left with two twins at thirteen."

Sita shrugs her shoulders and at this moment Ally's anger is more human to me then religious Sita's shoulder shrug.

Sita continues: "I was young and stupid. You can't change the situation, right? It's what happened. Allah will punish them."

"I don't like that logic," says Ally. "God doesn't punish everyone. Look at Karamaz, how many he's raped, and nobody's punished him. Not until he killed the whole family with ten-kilo weights and shagged their dead mum with her smeared skull, in front of her daughter. No God interfered with any punishments."

"Yeah." We all sigh, remembering the horrible story, which engulfed all of Kholmysty a few years ago.

"The girl got out alive, Vorobey let her go, whilst Karamaz wasn't looking," I said. I knew the story quite well. Karamaz used to go to karate back then, the same club as me. I clearly remember the white faces of the girls, when the trainer told them that evening what had happened.

"And her sanity?" says Ally. Again, nothing to say. Ally is right.

"The best defence from hatred," Sita carries on, "is to leave everything for Allah's will. God, in your language."

"I agree," says Mira. "God isn't silly. He sees a few things."

"He doesn't know or see jack. Your God or Allah," Ally says quietly.

I'm silent. I remember the indifferent starry sky, above yesterday's building site.

Tasha pours the last of the vodka around. Soon we'll be going for the second bottle.

"For the soul, ovissly, as Sita says," says Tasha.

"Forgive eeeeveryone, let go, pray, light a candle and live happy," she concludes, staggering, sipping cola from the bottle.

"Well." Mira nods. "Forgive in the soul but fight for justice. If there is a way. And if not – drink and chill. Rather than carry the anger inside."

"Yeah, that's better," I agree. "Justice, just like love, can be fought in many ways. Like Mum said: to love doesn't mean to sleep with your lover from the get-go. You can write a poem in the local newspaper, or an article, make a movie script. If there's no way to tell the police – draw a caricature and send it to the magazine *Crocodile*."

"Or drink and chill," Mira adds again.

Ally shuffles around on the bench. She shrugs her shoulders.

"Well, maybe," she says. "I would still just pick up a bat, with spikes, preferably..."

"A cosh." I help her.

"A cosh," she repeats. "And then smash his skull to smithereens, then the other. Then pull his balls, left onto one ear, right – onto his chin. I'd shove a log up his ass, the one with bark, and kick him on...under a tram. And then I can forgive him."

We roll around in laughter. Ally bursts into a fit of laughter too.

"Ally, that would be one awesome cartoon!" I crease with laughter. We giggle, spilling vodka on our jeans. Laughing with tears. And not because of Ally's imagination, almost falling off our benches, but because we've been laughing for so long, and we're still having so much fun together.

"Ally, enrol onto a film directors' course, and shoot a story, please," I say, raising my cup.

"We have to warn young girls."

"So they don't drink dirty, fake cognac by the gallon," says Mira and raises her cup.

"And they should build toilets on the Krechatik," says Sita, lifting hers.

"Girls themselves should build toilets there," Mira adds.

"So, if we fall, it will be in a public place, where the cleaner finds you, and not on a hill amongst trees, where drunks and rapists in Berkut uniforms like to hang out." I catch on.

"It should just be good guys in Berkuts," says Ally. "The ones who girls will give themselves to anyway. I heard abroad; they send girls to soldiers on Saturdays. So, what if they're prostitutes? What if they just like soldiers?"

"Anyway," Tasha sings in a drunken voice.

"Forrr goooood cognac, well-built toilets all over Ukraine, and especially on the road to Odessa, there's this one…" She squints, her eyes dangling on above her nose, covering her mouth with her hand, manicured red nails. "And confidenttt aand sssecure men in Berkut."

We drink together. If somebody close to the Oaks was reading in their bedroom at this time with an open window, they'd have thought we were competing over who had the best joke.

"And also, girls, let's have a rule," says Mira. "If we drink with unknown company, then we drink first three shots, and then just tiny sips. Nobody watches you after the third one."

"Exactly," we agree, downing everything in one gulp.

PART FIVE

Age Of Responsibility

CHAPTER ONE

The Decision to Become a Different Person

The next morning, I conclude that yesterday only Mira said something smart – we drink the first three shots and then just tiny sips.

If we hadn't got drunk, nothing would have happened.

I prepare to make a decision. For the first time ever.

I drink tea, and tell myself in a calm voice: I don't want that anymore.

Also, I want to get rid of the obsessive image of Pashya's green room. I take a pen, bring out my diary, which I haven't written in for about two hundred and eight years, and write:

I'm tired of it. Once again, my head is filled up with characters that Pashya made up, instead of myself. They argue. When they argue, I can't make a decision. Look.

This is Sensuality. I call her Alenushka. She hands the remote control to Sarcasm. I call him Slava because I love Vyacheslav Butusov, the sexy rock singer. And this is Responsibility – Crow Bonaparte. Don't ask. You have to meet my course mate Maria who looks exactly like Crow and Bonaparte.

They sit on the sofa.

"Yesterday I was disappointed in Him," says Alenushka.

"And us in you," Crow and Slava reply in one voice.

Alenushka gives up the remote control. Whoever holds it controls the green room. All this time Alenushka has been controlling me.

"Let Crow control. She's ugly. And insensitive. She won't get us into trouble."

Crow taps the microphone. Adjusts her tuft of slicked hair.

"Lord, our God, forgive our sinful souls." She clears her throat. "Save us and forgive us and lead us into your everlasting kingdom. Amen."

Slava collapses nearby, in shorts and headphones. His index finger is impatiently tapping on the play button.

"Oh, these chicks. I'm turning on the music," he mumbles.

"As if it's not enough for there to be more blokes present in a chick's brain than chicks themselves," Crow cuts in. (Here I completely agree with her.)

"And that would have been just fine." Slava won't give in and continues: *"They would be lesbians and they'd shag strictly women and make decisions strictly with men. Would love to have their company here."*

Alena and Crow look at him in horror.

"Guide us onto the right path." Crow finds herself. *"We've sinned against you, lots. It's all because we're unlucky in relationships. Our relationship with Ostap just won't gel. Help us, please. In return we promise to fulfil the Ten Commandments. Namely:*

"First: Never overeat.

"Gym exercises, dancing three times a week, fasting every two weeks, complete exclusion of alcohol and unhealthy drinks such as tea, coffee, fizzy drinks and juice. We don't drink them anyway."

I hear Slava mumbling, *"What utter crap. If we don't dethrone her within the next month, I'm jumping from the balcony."*

"Be quiet, I'm asking you seriously," Alenushka whispers.

"What if it helps to bring back Ostap?"

"What? Not drinking fizzy drinks?" Slava is losing his composure.

"So, all in all," Crow interrupts, *"I look over the list of commandments and this is what I've decided: a. No swearing. Maybe it's because we use foul language that our relationships don't gel."* Crow eyes Slava.

"Exactly because of that!" Slava shouts, not opening his eyes.

"b. On Saturdays we don't do anything. No homework. And all chores on Sundays and Fridays," says Crow.

"That's what I'm talking about," says Slava, remembering how Crow used to appear on Saturday laughing-with-friends nights and mumble that on Monday we had a seminar on international law or that in four weeks we had to hand in the thesis.

"c. We promise to love Mum and Dad. No matter what they say and do," says Crow.

"That's not difficult." Alenushka sighs. *"Parents are sorted."*

"d. No killing," Crow continues.

"Ah! Exactly!" Slava jumps up, widening his eyes. *"That's a very useful decision! I've said for a long time: it's time to sort out this killing-people mess, or we won't relax with any Ostap."*

"I understand your irony," Crow continues in a low voice, with her leather cap on.

"At first glance, we haven't killed anybody. But remember those ten hatchlings we taught to fly with our second cousin Marat…they crashed to their deaths."

Slava rolls his eyes.

"And also…"

(I put down the pen. Take a deep breath in, and begin writing again.)

"e. We promise: not to wish death and trouble upon rapists. If we want to be good and to get Ostap back, we have to find the strength in ourselves to forgive."

Silence overcomes the green room. You can hear Slava chomping on his chewing gum.

Alenushka says, "I'll try." And pulls in her knees.

"f. No stealing," Crow continues. "Money from Mum's purse, for example."

Slava silently lifts his arm in agreement.

Crow turns over to the next page of the notebook. "g. No gossiping and no offensive mocking of friends or teachers."

"That's too much!" says Slava, taking off his hat. "Friends are fine, but there's so many teachers to laugh at."

"You can do it kindly," Crow replies. "And lastly: h. No jealousy towards Ostap being with other girls. If he's happier with another, then that is God's will. We're happy for him."

Alenushka grits her teeth.

Crow announces: "I insist we write out all the commandments into the Bible. There is a page for notes in there."

"Why the Bible?" Slava's face shows fright.

"Can't we just write it on paper? In a diary? Why do we have to ruin a book?"

"In the Bible," Crow repeats.

"At least you are allowed to mock the teachers, and I'm not allowed to be jealous," says Alenushka to Slava.

End of diary entry.

CHAPTER TWO

Magnificent Itty

"Look at Osha, girls. Everyone's smoking, and she isn't," says Violetta. She produces a stream of smoke, releasing it into the twilight of the room in which we live with Sasha. Sasha broke up with her husband over the summer, her daughter is being taken care of by her babushka, as the school is around the corner from her house, and we're living in halls in one room. Sasha and I are both so kind and accommodating that we get break visits from Violetta, Yuri, Roma, and anyone else who doesn't want to smoke out their own rooms.

"I would honestly smoke, if I wanted to," I say, enveloped in smoke. I'm telling the truth, or I'd have broken a commandment about not bearing false witness and I would have moved further away from my secret objective.

The smell of cigarettes is mixed in with the smell of sausages, sweat and worn shoes. I am determined not to be irritated by the smoke. Firstly, it's no worse than the smell of shoes and sweat, and secondly, the irritation of smoke doesn't fit into the Ten Commandments. The lit cigarette in my presence shouldn't spoil my mood. For a whole month now I've been going to sleep with a prayer to bring back Ostap's love, waking up at six in the morning with the same prayer, exercising. I don't drink, don't smoke, and at gatherings at halls only drink tea and water. I don't pretend that I drink vodka. I just announce: "And I'll have some water" or "Me – tea". It's not like I'm going to lie. It's a commandment. Whoever has refused to drink vodka in a group will know how much easier it is to just pretend that you are drinking it. Mira knows. She suggested I take small sips in unknown crowds. But I have commandments.

I complete all my homework. On Friday, I go to Kholmysty, to teach aerobics. Yes, I returned to work in the House of Culture in the city of Kholmysty to teach aerobics. On Fridays and Sundays. Tomorrow is Friday, by the way. On the way to aerobics I carry an emaciated backside and straightened shoulders, taking in the native surroundings – maybe my love is heading towards me from the shop, maybe he's sitting under our willow near the boiler house, or smoking in the Oaks. Maybe he'll look out the window. Maybe he'll take me for a non-drinking, non-smoking, noble somebody, on my way to work. Everything is for you, my love. For you I eat oatmeal porridge and salad in the morning, nuts and bananas for lunch, and for dinner, aerobics and a glass of water. For you, I don't have any extra kilograms and my life is in order. In the morning and in the evening, I wish you wellness with my prayers – happiness and joy – as if those aren't the same things. I promise not to be jealous, also twice a day, no matter how well your life pans out without me. Without me! I am without you. Sometimes I want to howl. Or sing Masha and the Bears "My heart is without you, like a wild bird without a sky-yyy." To the whole flat, when the parents go to the market for plums to make jam.

I enjoy independence from alcohol, nicotine and munching. I don't want anything. Euphoria. I watch some pastor's speech on some religious channel. I want to sing along and clap my hands. Throw my positive energy around. I share his ecstasy, forcing myself to keep still, and not let out the wails and tears of joy.

That Friday night, I am walking home after my aerobics class with a bunch of trainee girls. Something in the fresh forest air tells me it will happen tonight. I will bump into him. I always get this feeling though. It doesn't work. But today is one month since I wrote "the deal" in the Bible book.

Passing the willow tree. Noticing a guy's tall figure on the bench I straighten shoulders, suck in my flat stomach, and tread softly. I listen to twelve-year-old Tanya's chatter about her strict maths teacher and look at the bench out of the corner of my eye, almost with the back of my head. Is it Ostap sitting there? I would love him to see me now! I'm tender, like a birch tree, and I have smart conversations with my students. Well, not exactly students, but they learn aerobics from me and I teach them.

He'll want to hug me, kiss me, I'll walk past, and he'll be suffering and... Is he sitting there or not? In the dusk I can just make out the shadows. Three big guys sit on the bench, one taller than the others. The familiar light-coloured jacket. The figure's glasses flash... My heart doesn't skip a beat but starts beating pleasantly and joy flows through my body.

This is what the life-giving Holy Cross can do. He sees me walking, with girls, they're asking me childish questions, and I'm listening and answering clearly. He hears my voice. I'm slender, confident in myself. Such a grown-up. Doing work, other than studies. Gorgeous. He appears a month after when the Bible had promised. A clear sign.

The next day, after getting paid, I go shopping to get chicken and washing-up liquid. I'll spend money on things other than vodka and cigarettes. I've earned it myself. I'm proud.

"Osha!" A man's voice interrupts me from namby-pambying. I look around. Tolly Pushka. Katka and I used to tease him with the words from the famous song "Tolka, Tolka, Tolka, ain't enough!" The 27th September, which was yesterday, was Toll Pushka's birthday! Every year the whole class would celebrate it together. And where there's the whole class, there's Ostap.

"Toll!" I exclaim. "Happy birthday!" I've never been happier to bump into Toll Pushka.

"Ain't enough, ha!" Toll runs up to me, catching his breath.

I giggle.

"Met you just in time, ha. I was going to ring Stapler, so he'd give me the address, so I could at least leave a note, ha. I rang all last weekend. Nobody's picking up the phone, ha. You're working, I heard, on the weekends. Anyways, listen. I've invited everyone to come over today, at three." Toll waves his mighty hand, as if he's studying to be a blacksmith, not a dentist. "We're going up to the woods next to school for shashlik. My sister marinates a killer shashlik, have to say, ha."

For shashlik! One of the most exciting outdoor activities of Kholmysty is to have shashlik, barbecued meat on skewers, outside in the forest.

Ostap's got to be there! Ostap'll be there! Please, find out who'll be there!

The sun comes out and my dress becomes blindingly white with bright daisies. "Wow, that's interesting!" I say. "I'll definitely come. Who'll be there? What about Katka?"

I want to ask about Ostap, obviously.

"Twenty-five people are coming," answers Toll, looking back at his house. "And Katka, and Vick, and Stapler, and Rudi, and Juka, basically everyone. Only my sister won't be there, ha."

And he runs off.

And Stapler!

Everyone will be drinking, and I'll be sitting with water and a carrot, like an idiot.

And Stapler! Stapler will be there! Stapler!

Keep an eye on Alenushka. I can picture her running around the green room in ecstasy.

And Slava taking the mick out of Crow: "Wow, what is that on you? Scales, burning in the heat."

Crow wears a knight's helmet, with a shield, and instead of a sword – a remote control.

"You tryna pass for Motherland Monument or Ilya Muromets, the knight from our ancient fairy tales?" says Slava.

"Maybe you can have one drink, Comrade Ilya Muromets?"

I walk home, excited and giggling.

CHAPTER THREE

How Osha Kissed Katka

"Rudi?" asks Katka.

"No," answers Toll.

"Stapler?" she asks.

"No, ha," replies Tolly.

On the sunny soft pine hilltop, licking and biting down her bottom lip – oh she loves doing that – Katka stands blindfolded with a blue bandana covering her eyes. We're playing a game. The leader, Toll, points at people one at a time, and the blindfolded person, Katka, chooses, blindfolded, whom to kiss.

Katka made her choice. She was kissed. Now she's guessing. Surrounded by the remaining twenty-three people.

"Vick? But his lips are bigger," Katka thinks out loud.

"Sweeeetie," I purr and smile slyly. "You didn't recognise me?" The next second, Katka screams: "Beeeetch!" She rips off the bandana, finds me in the first row and darts towards me. I jump up and shoot off into the thicket. We run around the pines, the classmates – who've fallen over from laughter – Katka launching pinecones at me, and dry branches, which she manages to grab on the run. She gets me, I squeal, then jump into Ostap's lap and cover myself with his hand.

"I'm really sorry that you liked it!" I wail, trying my hardest to ignore Ostap's scent, which is driving me crazy, among the flying pinecones.

Katka pulls me by my leg, pouring pine needles all the way up my back, since pinecones kind of hurt. The woods shaking with the roaring laughter of twenty-three different people. Ostap gently shakes the needles off me, which is very sweet.

"Osha's turn," announces the leader Toll.

"Why me? She didn't even guess right," I say. I really don't want to break away from Ostap's dizzying underarm.

"Everything's right," Toll explains patiently, regaining his senses faster

226

than anybody else from the laughter. "If she had guessed right, then you'd be leading. But you have won, so you get to be kissed. The leader is Katka."

So, my turn to stand blindfolded.

"This one?" Katka shouts in my ear.

"Don't shout. I ain't deaf. And no," I reply.

"This one?" she asks in a calmer voice.

"Definitely not," I reply.

"Maybe this one?" she sings.

"I'm fine, thanks," I say.

"You're choosy, aren't you?" she says.

"Well. Not like some, getting excited over a kiss with a freaking girl." I gesture with my hands. "Mistaking them for Rudi and Stapler. Ouch!" I'm startled by a kick coming from Katka's direction.

Laughter.

"This one?" she asks.

"Listen, point to a normal one."

"Well, this one's normal," she says.

"Well, go on then."

Silence. Muffled footsteps. I tensely look down from underneath the bandana covering my eyes, in the hope of seeing shoes and guessing their owner. I can't see. The kiss. I purse my lips. You never know whom Katka considers normal. A familiar softness. I relax my lips. So sweet it hurts. Savouring it, I carefully drink his lips. The kiss is prolonged. I stop. The lips retreat back. I smile with an open mouth and a stupid smile.

"Yy-yeah, normal," I elongate out. "Can I have more?"

"That's enough," says Katka. "Now guess."

Everyone waits.

"So, now I am the leader, and Stapler will be guessing?" I say.

"Wow!" everyone shouts; some clap.

"Spot on, spot on," says Rudi in the first row.

"Experience and practice are the keys to greatness!" I say. No need to act like an experienced man though.

"This one?" I point to Juka.

"Yeah," Ostap agrees.

Laughter. Chortling. I didn't need to walk around Katka for long.

227

A subtle kiss on the lips.

"Hm, is it VyVy?" says Ostap.

A friendly chuckle.

"Well…not Rudi, and not Vick… They've got bigger lips." He gestures with his hands.

"Bugger," Katka says with a laugh and shakes her head in disappointment.

"Maybe, Katka?" he says.

He wove Katka into his "VyVy" list!

My God, so much joy, I am embarrassing myself.

CHAPTER FOUR

The Last Relationship Showdown

"Not even some champagnske?" says Ostap. We leave the woods and find ourselves on the hill. Night-time Kholmysty is flickering with lights at us. It seems smaller than ever, my childhood town. More lights though. Under my feet the pine needles rustle amicably. Behind I can hear Katka's squeaks, Vick's bass and Toll's laugh. We climb down and head in the direction of our nine-storey block. I've got to get to the sixth entrance, and he to the first.

"Stapler! Are you going to Toll's?" Rudi calls.

"Maybe later, gotta drop these bags home," Ostap replies.

"Come on then, we're waiting for ya," Toll shouts.

"And nobody's asking me," I quietly complain.

"Reckon we're together, don't they?" Ostap shrugs his shoulders.

"And are we?" escapes from my mouth.

The main thing here is not to utter a load of silliness, looking with in-love, languishing eyes.

Please, please, can we go and drink some champagnske?

How is this going to look? I don't drink all day, and when left alone with Ostap, I instantly get hammered on champagnske?

If I don't drink a little today, then that is the extreme of the extreme – and the extreme is fanaticism, and I'm not a fanatic.

"Well, I wanna drink champagnske and find out," Ostap says quietly. Our gazes meet. Mine, guilty, like a student who hasn't prepared for class, and his, like a physics teacher, asking the question "What are transformers?"

I think he's angry. Does he really know about the rape? Nah, he's still not cooled down from my runaway to Bezradychi. Of course, the running away. And the week-long absence before the running away? Not a word about the rape.

"Let's not get drunk?" I say quietly and tenderly.

"And not smoke," he whispers.

On the darkened street, passing the first porch on to the sixth. The route is much quicker than I would have liked. I'm flying! And normally, on the way from the shop, or from dance, from uni past his porch, my chest would tighten up. Kind of like a dog who's lost its owner.

We hold hands.

Ahead of us, a conversation.

Sweetness.

I'm a different person – sober, not smoking.

I smile. The autumn forest air has wrapped itself around the night of Kholmysty.

Ostap's bag cosily rustles with a bottle of champagnske and a packet of nuts.

And the sleepy birds are tweeting that we won't be going to Toll's today.

So little is needed for happiness.

Why do some evenings not last an eternity?

The bottle of champagnske emptied. We sit on the bed in our usual poses facing each other. An unpeeled orange on the stool.

Instead of the red Kewpie, a bright table lamp shines. The conversation doesn't cross the finish line. Take the orange, Ostap! He's completely forgotten about it. I carefully concentrate on the conversation. Right now, he wants to know why my parents rang Vick, and not him, first. And why I didn't tell him that I was mad at him.

"You can come here, kick the mirror, rip out my balls, swear all over me. But run away every time you get angry..."

I smile. I'm happy to get permission to rip Ostap's balls out from Ostap himself. I think he loves me.

I reply: "My parents rang Vick because they know him. And you, to them, are someone whom their daughter really likes. But they don't know who you are and whether you would care."

"What, am I supposed to turn up at your old man and mum's yard, saying 'Howdy, it's me, the bellend, who waits for your Olga to finish her walkies with Vick hand in hand in Kholmysty'?" he snaps. "I don't want my girl to be walking round Kholmysty with some other dudes. My girl – is mine."

"So why don't you walk around Kholmysty with me, hand in hand?" I shout back.

"Where?" he shouts.

"For a walk! Round Kholmysty."

"What's wrong with home, does it stink?" He gestures.

I roll my eyes. Give up. No, obviously it doesn't stink. I change the conversation to another topic. "Mum says: no need to act clever, best to act silly. I don't know where to stick her advice."

"Act," Ostap interrupts and drills into my eyes with his stare. "But not actually *be*."

I shrug. He's right. And if he knew about Independence Day, he wouldn't be drilling me with his eyes.

"So, I can talk about stuff with you, if I'm angry? I thought you were not a big fan of mechanical waves?" I say.

Ostap breathes in deeply. "When you've got something to say, it's gotta be said."

Hm. Logical. How did I not guess it myself?

"Why did you disappear for a whole week?" I say into the empty glass in my hands.

"How was I meant to know that you'd notice? You've got heaps of girlfriends, you're busy, maybe you wanna disappear with Mum to the country for a few days, or drink rum and Coke with Katka on the Parapet."

"Yeah, maybe I do. But maybe I wanna know where you are too. Or not?"

"I didn't think about that."

Pure and simple.

"I don't walk around with Vick any longer. I thought you'd noticed," I say, as if that's the right answer in physics class. I place down the empty glass next to the orange. "I get it, you don't like it. Before, I used to think that you didn't care."

"Cheers." Quiet and clear.

"Sorry." Mature.

CHAPTER FIVE

Euphoria. Now Everything Will Be OK

At five in the morning I creep back into my room, after a second taking off of my clothes, which smell of the forest, the shashlik and Ostap. I jump under the covers into bed, covering all of myself including my head.

Though I think my parents may wake up from the overwhelming happiness that has dawned in the flat. My heart pounds crazily, as if I've drunk ten cups of coffee. I want more and more. Today after dance I'll definitely go and see him. I hope he'll be in halls tomorrow morning.

Did I imagine it or did his eyes really spark when we kissed? A tear...does he really love me that much? His lips. I would have savoured and savoured them. His scent. I'd swim in his arms.

How did I get like this? I'm not normal. I don't need anything for myself. As long as he's all right. As soon as he closes his eyes, he begins to moan. How helplessly he buries himself into my chest, and presses against me with his cheek. I'll never admit to him that I don't orgasm. I don't need to. To cross that line. I can't. Is this love? But everything will be fine. I think he's got like this too. The same as me? Signing a contract with God, not drinking or smoking in return for me? Is he an idiot too?

I won't find out. I wish I were Ostap for just one hour. Who is it, inside his head? What does his sensuality and sarcasm look like? Does his responsibility talk strictly in Ukrainian, like Taras Shevchenko?

How do I find out if he loves me lots or just so-so? I won't be able to. I'll never be able to. So scared. I only know about my feeling. I am stuck with it. And I'll take care of it.

How do I sleep when I'm overexcited? It's my own fault that I'm simulating it. Can't admit that I need it longer than him. I don't want to lose him again.

Now everything is OK. Like this. I'll tell him later. To live only like this: no drink, no smoke, no walks with Vick, and on the weekends only Ostap, studies and aerobics. Everything will be OK, now I definitely know this.

It's good to have fun without vodka.

The passionate kiss with Katka! She squealed so much. "Maybe Rudi, maybe Stapler?" Stapler-Scrapler. You wish. And he put her in the same list as VyVy.

I wanted to laugh, like Maria Bonaparte through a restrained smile, as if I was about to whistle.

PART SIX

Age Of Sarcasm

CHAPTER ONE

Sarcasm Tidies up

Three months later, on the 6th January, year 1997 on the roof of a nine-storey house. Frost. Frozen fingers. I put on a glove. In the other hand, a lighter and a cigarette. Shaking. From the cold. From the anger, hatred, disappointment and many other feelings unknown to me. Can't seem to cry. Light up. The glove slowly slips onto my freezing hand.

So? Happy with your God's deal? Happy with quitting smoking? Quitting drinking? Come on, pray to your God, let him sort out his dumb, arrogant, ignorant head. And let him sort out my dumb head too.

***k off everyone!

My head starts to ache. I imagine how slumped Alenushka and Crow are. And the speech of Sarcasm Slava: "This New Year brings enormous change. I no longer trust the women in my head. I've had it with your waiting for a miracle. Miracles don't exist! Downstairs, on the ninth floor, lies the lanky proof! Mugs exist, one of which we spent three months on.

"Stapler this. Stapler that. Oh. Ah. Stapler will like it. Screw your Stapler! He's climbed in, laid his legs out with his stinky socks and smudged his bogeys on the wall, your Stapler. And you grovel before him. Both of you. Idiots.

"From this moment," his voice sounds ceremonial again, like in a class formation. "No more Staplers. The rules are as follows: First, we drink, as much as we can fit in."

The balcony roars like a stadium full of fans.

"We smoke, as much as we can fit," Slava continues.

Another roar.

"Socialise only with those whom we can shag or laugh with. Except for Stapler!" He lifts his finger in the air.

"Everyone else can flush themselves down the toilet. And your nerdy Katka too. We only hang out with my friends. Mira, Ally. Understand?"

Alenushka and Crow shrug their shoulders.

"Yes."

"Yes."

"Good." Slav softens.

"Can I smoke?" Alenushka asks.

"You must," Slav answers. "Now get in your miniskirts, put on your make-up and pour some vodka. Let's have some fun. New Year's. Ally and Mira have left, and we're going to halls. Sasha should be coming."

CHAPTER TWO

What's Happened?

"Osha. What's up?" Sasha enters the smoke-filled room and goes across the room to open the window. I glance over my shoulder.

"Wow, what the hell? Four butts in the ashtray. Are you OK? You don't smoke, remember?"

"It's Stapler," I reply, like Mum when she used to indicate to a picture of a ladybird.

"Stapler? But you drew an awesome portrait for him. He looked exactly like that picture."

"Yes," I say. "I gave him that portrait. But this is his real portrait."

"Right." Sasha sighs, sitting on the edge of the bed near the table, as she undoes the top button of her coat.

"What's happened?" she asks.

I put down the pencil. Fifth cigarette. The sixth one to Sasha. We light up.

"What do you think," I inhale, "a guy could say receiving his portrait from his girl, in which he looks just like his picture?"

"Wha'?" Sasha opens her big blue eyes, with long curly eyelashes.

"You really wanna know, yeah?" I tap the ash into a peanut can.

"Yes," she says.

"Am I such a mug?"

Sasha raises her bushy eyebrows above her blue eyes. I gaze at her face with pleasure like a masochist at the painful cut on their palm. Her face looks like the sun – round, with plump lips and spiral curls heading outwards.

"What a village." She exhales smoke. "Wait. Rewind, you were so happy soaring home on New Year's. What happened?"

"That's exactly what. Nothing happened. Today is what day? Sixth of January. Why am I sitting in halls and not home in Kholmysty, celebrating Christmas with my boyfriend? Because I don't have one." I gesture with my hands, as if I'm checking to see if it's raining or not. "That isn't a boyfriend.

That is an empty space. An empty space, two years of mucking me around. On New Year's, we had our two-year anniversary, and he didn't give a crap."

"No way." Sasha looks untrustingly. "You guys are always falling out. You'll make up."

"No no, Sasha, that's it." I move the ashtray away.

"We haven't fallen out. We were not together on New Year's and the next five days after that. I'm an idiot! Such an idiot. Dragging myself all over Kholmysty with his portrait in my bag, figuring out where he is. After twelve I bumped into Zhuka near the big Christmas tree on Parapet. She said that all the classmates were partying at Tolly Pushka's. Am I not a classmate? She said they only wanted to get the boys together. Even Zhuka knows that they only wanted to get the boys together!" I slam my fist on the table. "Ally was calling me to go to Moscow, and Mira to Odessa!"

"Well, yeah." Sasha shrugs her shoulders.

"He's just trash, damn it, I've got no words, no strength. Anyway, the boys-only party has continued up to this day. Today I lost it and decided: the portrait isn't going to be at home, reminding me the person I buried two years of my life on. If he doesn't ring on New Year's, doesn't write, and doesn't consider me a human being, then this portrait – is trash, and I'll give this trash to him. I'll shove it into his postbox, into a crate. I'll treat him how he has treated me."

I put out the dead cigarette butt.

Sasha sighs and doesn't say anything.

"Do you want tea?" I ask tiredly. As if instead of speaking, I'd run ten laps around the halls in the frost.

"No, come on, finish your story," says Sasha, wrapping herself in her unbuttoned fur coat, throwing one leg over the other. "I have a suggestion afterwards."

"OK," I continue. "Anyway, he ended up being at home. I kicked the door open and into his room." Here I smile smugly. "He's lying on the bed. Listening to his stinking Doors. Football on the TV. In the darkness. Red Kewpie on his lamp. Everything is just like it always was, damn it, I just want to puke. Maybe he'll wank over the Kewpie and calm down. What's the point in having a real-life girl? I give him his present. He stares at it. And I at him. He's questioning with malice. I'm affirmative with hatred. I won't be taken

240

for a ride again; that it's my own fault, that I don't understand it, that I can't comprehend it. He says: 'Am I such a mug?' And I leave."

I spark up a cigarette. The cold room is silent.

"Yep, Stapler, you're a mug," I continue. "He is. And I've had enough of being the idiot. Chasing a mirage in the desert. If you don't love a girl, let her go. He's already proved to everyone, to Vick, that I gave myself to Ostap and not him, and Katka, that I forgave for the shoulder blades, and parents, that I don't need to be friends with them, I'll run to him anyway. What else does he want? Fuck it, it's over. I went up to the roof, sparked up." I wave towards the ashtray, explaining the butts. "And I decided to not suffer no more."

I raise my eyes up towards Sasha, as if only just noticing her. "What did ya wanna suggest?"

"Let's go to my girl's village. They're inviting us. My brother Slava will be there, it's Christmas, loads of vodka, pies."

"Nah, I'll sit here, smoke thirteen cigarettes and cry about Ostap."

Sasha furrows her eyebrows.

I smile. "I mean let's at least have some tea for the road."

241

Chapter Three

Real Cheating

Two days later, I'm on a minibus from Vydubychi to Kholmysty. My mind is noisy and drunk. The nonsense of Sasha's country house in Uhabovo village sweeps past me. Behind the huge wooden table in a half-pitch-black shynok (Ukrainian pub), opposite Sasha and me, sit Tanya and Sveta, two large ladies, both with immense manes of hair, looking like famous Soviet singers.

"Right, lasses, I'm off to find me pals. When you's coming home, call me," says Nazar, evaporating into the midst of the shynok, filled up with people.

"Fifth bottle of vodka, second cucumber. Where are our boys?" says Tanya with large breasts and dimples in her cheeks. In the bar, it's cold. The vodka doesn't give much.

"Gonna get drunk in one and then off I go to shag this bloke round the back," says dark-haired Sveta, nodding towards a guy with a large nose in a long leather coat and a cap, at the bar.

"My sister's godfather," she clarifies. And this relationship is supposed to explain her intentions?

Soon, in front of us is only Tanya with her dimples.

We leave the shynok to have a smoke, and a short-haired Zoriana comes up to us, with the same large-breasted attributes, and guffawing with a chesty laugh, she tells us: "Your Svetka is over there! Hehe! Aha, I can't even…go check yourself. It's all there." She points to a wide tree behind the wooden pub, where somebody is moving in and out of the shadows, flashing their light-coloured underwear from under a fur coat and a leather jacket.

"That other one's Andrey," Zoriana says through guffaws. "And that one's your Svetka…" She can't squeeze anything else out of her from the laughter.

Really though, what other reaction could there be from an adult woman, seeing two familiar figures getting it on?

"What a village," says Sasha, cringing. And I don't really get it. Is she talking about Zoriana, Sveta with Andrey or just generally taking in the beautiful night view of the village? At the end of the day, literally, they are getting it on in the shadow of the huge tree, which rises above the shynok. Smoke is pouring from the chimney of the shynok, snow all around, and the full moon lights everything up.

We walk back six kilometres to Sasha's village, Uhabovo. The moon has spilled pearl sour cream all over the snowy fields.

The vodka has aired out in the icy wind. Kisses with brother Nazar after every three steps. Can't escape catching a cold sore. I slip. Fall. Nazar falls onto me. We kiss for a long time and laugh. Sasha and Tanya sing drunkenly way ahead of us.

"Oooosha! Nazaaaar!" reaches us from a distance.

"Let's go. We'll sort it out at home," he whispers dirtily. Such a nice boy with blue eyes and curly hair and manages to dirtily scare off a lady like that.

At home the lady doesn't give in. We kiss for a while on the sofa and then part ways to sleep in different rooms.

On the minibus, I realise: I have a crush. Else I would have given myself to him.

Why am I drawn to rudeness? I shrug my shoulders. And if I hadn't had a crush, then why would I need to sleep? I'm confused.

From the bus stop in Kholmysty, I stumble home up the frozen mounds. The snow crunches underneath my boots. A cold morning. Dry. Empty. Ostap's windows look unwelcoming. Stapler, I no longer care. I kissed Nazar and it felt good. And today I'll ring Vick.

"I was thinking, why not invite you on a date?" I say to the phone, sprawled across an armchair, throwing one leg over the other.

Silence. Then: "Osha, I'm choking. Good evening, firstly."

"Exactly, Vick, exactly," I purr into the phone.

"What did you just say there?" he says.

"Cinema or that bench in the park?" I say.

"Hm, well the cinema is warm, but I've got questions and no time for cinema."

"Bring cigarettes?" I say.

I spark up with Vick's lighter.

"I need it once a day."

Vick quacks. "Maybe we should try the cinema first?" he says.

Vick rests his foot on the ice-covered, snowy bench in the oaks.

"I don't want to. Nobody's home at Katka's. I've got keys. Let's go?" I say.

"Nobody's home at mine either," he says. "That's not the point."

"I'm sorry, I don't recognise you in your full-body make-up. Are you Vick?" I answer.

Vick doesn't smile and says: "What's going on with Ostap?"

Everything is serious for Vick. Boring.

"Nothing." I shrug my shoulders. "Fell outta love. It happens. He turned out to be a pig and a jackass. I don't really love a pig and a jackass."

"Are you sure?" Vick looks like a serious, ugly version of Mishka the Bear from the 1980 Olympic Games.

"One hundred per cent," I reply.

"Let's go to mine," he mutters, taking his leg away from the bench.

"I don't love you yet, Vick." I don't move from my spot. "Don't think that I've fallen out of love and instantly fallen in love with you. But I'm giving you a chance. Maybe, it wasn't love. Some kind of disease, maybe. I want to find out. Or else I won't ever know if I can love you or not."

"You can," he answers, giving me his hand.

How I want to believe him. I do like his self-confidence though. And his waist is bigger than mine; shoulders, hands. Plus, he's built like he's supposed to be. Like Ostap, he fits my heels. Right under them.

Do I really have to recall the first time with Vick?
Yes, I do.
For the same reason. To understand the mistakes.
I've got to tell myself the truth. Especially that truth, which I don't want either to tell, or to recall.

"Don't worry 'bout it, I'm dry as well," I say into the almost pitch-blackness. Vick freezes. I can feel his cold sweat all over me. I hear his fast heartbeat.

"Should I just go hang myself now?" he says.

He sits on the edge of the bed. Gets dressed. The outlines of the wardrobe, the table, where we prepared for the maths exam. Through the net curtains, the windows of the house opposite. Ostap lives in that house opposite, in the room with the newspapered windows. Vick's room is spacious, simple, and easy to breathe in. Not Thumbelina visiting a mole at all. Yet, I am actually Thumbelina visiting a mole.

The curtain calmly flutters.

Ostap isn't here.

Ostap is a rat. No need to whine about Ostap.

I'm fully clothed in the middle of the room. Observing Vick lacing up his shoes in the darkness. I suppress my irritation and feel sorry for him. It's actually kind of sweet.

He copes with his shoelaces, walks up to me. Hugs me. I hug him back. We stand hugging. Me with eyes open, facing the open window. He with eyes closed, facing the closed door. We should really swap places. I can't see happiness in the open window, even though my eyes are wide open. He sees happiness with closed eyes, facing the closed door. I know his eyes are closed.

"Let's not do it like this." Vick breaks the silence. "Better when we're ready. We've got to get used to each other. I waited two years. And a bit. I'll wait a bit more, OK?"

"OK." I nod.

"I already feel really, really good." Vick strokes my hair. "Let's just be together."

"Lets." Still, with the same disinterest. I get him though. I'd trade all the nights of love with Ostap for the days filled with just being together with Ostap. Every day.

"And anyway," Vick continues. "I had this one girl in halls..." He sighs. "I need to get myself checked out. What if I give you something? My uncle works in a sexual health clinic."

"Wow," I say, "I've never been to a sexual health clinic. I'll come with you."

I continue to look out of the window. Not happy, not sad. Just empty and light. I have Vick. I didn't really need to work hard on getting him. But now, until I want it, nothing will happen between us. And bonus: we'll be together every day. I'll speak in riddles, and he'll figure them out. He will say how much he loves me. Silly boy. And I'll be smart. And his uncle works at the sexual health clinic.

Somebody in the green room wants to go to the room without the windows. And reckons the real cheater has her eyes wide open.

Suddenly, Sarcasm's voice in my head clearly bellows: "Next time I'll be the one shagging Vick."

I shudder.

Chapter Four

Osha and the Hippie

A month later, spring arrives. I'm in halls, on the windowsill, cheery: the dust dancing in the sunbeams. When did the snow manage to melt, why is the sun shining, and why is the room so hot?

Alex from the second floor stands in the doorway, with the question: "Do you have sugar?" Blond with sneaky eyes. A guitar in his lowered hand. He looks like Keswick. I don't like blonds. From the bottom of my soul I realise that I actually love them, but it pains me. Did he come all the way from the second floor to the seventh for sugar?

I feel for the jar of sugar on the table, not taking my eyes away from his thick lips. How convenient – the table near the door. He takes the jar, barely touching my fingers, slyly smiling, and disappears next door. Yuri and writer Sergey finished their fifth year last year, and both went to England. Votsa and Romka now occupy their room. So, he is friends with my neighbours.

Vick is in the country today. Helping his nan to dig up the fresh soil.

In three seconds, I muster up a plan.

"I've got a bottle of vodka lying around, the girls from aerobics gave it to me. Do you wanna fry some egg and salo and have some booze?" I say, widely opening the neighbours' door.

"Ooooshaa! Oh, my days. Obviously!" says Votsa. Votsa wears a T-shirt with the word "Sepultura". He pronounces the letter "s" with a whistle. It really suits him. But I don't want Votsa. There are things we talk with him about, he isn't stupid and we're friends. In one of our heart-to-hearts, he told me: "A penis is nothing, it's piece of meat. The real penis is inside a guy's head." And he knocked his temple with a long, solid finger. With someone like him it is either love or friendship. I'm not ready for love.

In the middle of our room, at the table sit Roma, Votsa, Alex, Sasha and me.

On the table – a pan of fried eggs with salo, some chopped Bulgarian pepper, and a whole litre bottle of vodka. The girls from aerobics love me.

We start to drink vodka from the mugs. And we eat. Laughing. The guys talk about the new breathing technique they've learned recently. It's called hyperventilation. It's when you breathe, breathe and breathe deeply and constantly, and in the end, you feel an orgasmic rush through your whole body.

I touch Alex's thigh with my knee. He responds with a questioning look back. I agreeably widen my eyes and raise my eyebrows. He squeezes my knee with his large, childishly white hand.

A knock on the door.

"Oh, you're here."

"Vesnitskaya!" yells Votsa.

"I recognised you from your scweams. So youw the ones fwying salo and eggs, the whole of halls smell of it," says Vesnitskaya, unable to pronounce her "r"s, which burr pleasantly.

"I know you," I say. "We were watching the Doors in 209 last week, and you came to the sound."

"Yes, that's me. The Doows make me cwazy."

"Who's in 209?" Votsa asks, taking an interest.

"Vesnitskaya, sit down, have some eggs and vodka. Here's your mug," I say. After some short organising and lugging another chair over, in between jokes about eating and drinking eggs of different kinds, Vesnitskaya sits opposite Alex and looks with her moist eyes into his sly face.

"I don't know who's in 209," I answer, not taking my eyes off her. "They watch videos there, for those who aren't lazy."

The guys continue their conversation about 209.

"You again, me old hag," says Alex, not taking away his hand from my lap.

I inquisitively raise my eyebrows. "Your girlfriend?" With difficulty I tear my gaze away from her, and glare at him.

"How can I explain," Vesntistskaya answers, giggling. "We are kind of, yeah, but lately we've been needing a thiwd one." She kneels her cheek against her palm.

"I'm interested," I say. And interested I am in whether she understands that his hand is on my knee.

"We're hippies," explains Alex.

"Like, how?" I ask.

"Hippies are those people that live how they want, with whom they want, and they don't owe anything to anyone," explains Alex with his thick lips. The sneaky eyes dart between Vesnitskaya's moist eyes to mine and back.

"Well, that's like me." I shrug my shoulders. "But I'm not a hippie."

"You're a hippie." Alex affirmatively nods.

"I don't think so," I say. "We'll see."

"Come join us today," he says quietly. I look at Vesnitskaya. She hears everything and mysteriously smiles.

"Well, we might as well check, as my ex used to say." I bite my lip. "You pour us a drink, mister."

He's dismissive with her. And she doesn't mind. Why? I imagine myself in her place: opposite me sits Ostap with Katka, his hand on her lap. It feels sickening. Nope, nobody can go to the room without windows. But if she doesn't mind, then let's go and see what all the fuss is about. Soon the opportunity occurs. Votsa and Roma take Sasha into her room to acquaint her with Sepultura.

Fearing that they'll burst back in, I shut the door and lock it. We're left alone, just us three. Alex grins. Vesnitskaya puts her bony palms and thin fingers on the table, as if it isn't a table, but a piano, and she's about to play. I catch her solemn-moist gaze, intended for Alex. Alex walks up to me. Takes in a drag from his spliff, for a blowback. Here, in halls, I found out that a spliff is a cigarette with marijuana, and a blowback is when one person, in this case Alex, puts a spliff into his mouth with the roach on the outside, and the second person, me, takes in the smoke which comes out of the roach.

I take in the blowback with my lips. While I'm taking it in, Vesnitskaya, like a ghost, silently gets up from the table, walks up to us, and gets down on her knees. She starts doing everything to him down there. Alex and I, finishing with the blowback, start kissing. She, still on her knees, climbs under my short skirt, and also does everything to me down there. I'm OK with that. I'm ready, he's ready. Now my turn with him, Vesnitskaya, and you can smoke some marijuana.

I get tired jumping on him. Take the spliff from Vesnitskaya, swiftly pull off her jeans and offer him to her. Vesnistakaya willingly, gracefully sits herself onto Alex. But, barely starting, she begins to look like a limp bag of cherries, and announces: "Guys, I don't feel so good. I'm going. You do it youwselves."

She leaves, and we spend a long time doing it ourselves...

The next day: depression. Instead of spring, into my life comes Vesnitskaya. A feeling of poshlost. A Russian word, meaning meant to be done with a style, but comes out brutal and tasteless instead. Posh lost. Where are clean feelings, where are in-love guys with guitars jumping up and down beneath windows? Instead of this, guys jump from one bed to another, with other random girls, in front of their own. And I am just a random girl in my own life scenario. I am not a hippie for sure. I am the girl who looks out of the window and sees the grey clouds, smells burnt porridge and hears the crows.

I still feel stupid having to lie to Sasha in the morning: there was some grass left to smoke and I passed out, as if, and they were being noisy by themselves. As if. She believes me. What a village. Having smoked the second cigarette, I give in and go to Vesnitskaya's upstairs.

"I'm depressed. Does it ever hit you?" I ask. We sit crouched down, in the drying room near the balcony. Smoking is allowed here.

"What, thiwd person? Yes, it's hitting me," Vesnitskaya agrees, and takes a selfish toke. "I twy not to give in."

"Is he your first?" I ask. The words in the drying room hang in the air. As if we're in a movie about an operation.

"You sewious?" She smiles. "I just look young. My fiwst was a giwl." She dreamily turns her gaze to the window, covered in pigeon marks.

"I had guys after, but it was just out of intewest. Guys hurt down there, if you know what I mean. Too big or too fast. Alex is the fiwst out of the guys whom I have loved. He does everything properly in bed. It doesn't hurt. He lets me do it with giwls, and I let him do the same thing."

"Do you love him?" I whisper in surprise.

"I don't know. Kind of."

"Then where's the fun in watching him do it with someone else? I wouldn't be able to do that with my first."

"You see," she says, blowing out smoke. "He's still a child. He's fooling awound. Finding out about the wowld. He'll gwow up. And he'll become a fantastic man."

"And when he becomes him, you think he'll need you?" I ask.

"I think he will. Evewy hippie needs a giwl, who allows him."

Hm. There's something in it, and there's something missing in it too. I think. But I say out loud: "That's rubbish. I guess when we fall in love, we all say rubbish."

CHAPTER FIVE

Osha and the Tramp

The depression lets itself go the moment Votsa noisily piles into the room that evening with a tall guy in a cowboy hat, with a scarf and juicy lips. Every day the lips get juicier.

Sasha and I are distracted from our card game and observe the smiling stranger in the scarf.

"Votsa's here with the son of Ostap Bender," says Sasha.

Votsa erupts with a howling laugh. He laughs and points at the stranger with his finger, shouting out: "Exactly, the son!" We smile and look at them. Getting his breath back he says: "Sashka, you worked him out."

The stranger immediately smiles with his thick lips and looks at Sasha and me.

Votsa adds: "Girls! You've gotta play cards. With this one."

"And straight up for kisses," says the stranger ceremoniously, in the pose of a music show host.

"Come on, then," we say with Sasha in one voice. We react to the lips.

"If I win, and I'm winning, then I choose who to kiss." Votsa disappears, as it seems, sighing with relief.

Sasha wins. Her choice isn't varied. It's not like she's going to be kissing me. They kiss.

"My name's Benjamin, girls," he announces, licking his lips.

"Sasha," she says, stretching her lips into a smile, which looks false.

"Olga. Osha."

"Osha. Hot name. Something Asian about it."

"Aha," I keenly agree. I want to kiss those lips. I am a hippie after all. Fight fire with fire. Or else today-tomorrow will I start running up and down the halls' corridors, eavesdropping to see whether Alex is laughing behind closed doors, playing his guitar with his half-child's hands, munching eggs and salo, downing it with vodka from a mug and all the while grabbing onto someone's knee...?

Benjamin wins the next game. We kiss. For a long time. As if we're drinking.

I come back to my senses, when Sasha clicks the lock from the other side. For a moment I tear away and whisper confusedly: "Where's Sasha? What do we do now?"

He answers with a new wave of kisses. Within half an hour I'm on top of him; he's whispering that I'm very fine, like his first love.

"And you're not as fine as my first love," I whisper back in reply. And add: "Though in truth, I never peaked to the real sweetness with him."

"What, you didn't orgasm?" he says, surprised.

I nod in reply. And why's he so surprised? I am the only girl on the planet who doesn't orgasm from sex. Am I?

After a couple of minutes, I receive my first sparkling, sharp orgasm. So that's what it means to help the person out, tell them where to stroke and how wet the finger should be.

"So, did you enjoy it with your first love?" Benjamin asks smugly, throwing his arms behind his head, demonstrating his smooth-shaven armpits. Smooth-shaven?

"No." I smile calmly, getting up, taking my dress from the floor. "Orgasms are good, I won't lie."

The smile doesn't fade from Benjamin's face. This is the kind of person that you'll never be able to assure is a freak and a moron.

"Can I stay over? There is a party here on the 7th floor tonight; I'm worried it might finish late," he says, not changing his tone, as if we're still discussing my first love and good orgasms.

"No, you can't." I slip on my dress. "At night I'm with Votsa. But we can go to the party."

"Ow. I'll be quiet." He shapes his lips into a tube and begins to look like a duck in love.

"That's annoying," I purr, straightening my hair, facing the mirror. Why do I need a tramp in my room? Even if he does have shaved armpits and the desired skills to give sparkling orgasms.

In the evening we rave at the party. Benjamin leans me against the chilly wall, clasping my face with his hands and kissing me greedily. Good. We probably look awesome in the darkness of the shimmering dance floor. But you still won't be able to sleep over, Benjamin, boyo. Well, you'll know for future reference: you play cards for kisses after the party, not before.

CHAPTER SIX

The Walk Around Krechatik With Bender's Son

The next morning, Sasha, as always, leaves for her double session of lectures. I'm late, as always. Benjamin bursts into the room in yesterday's clothes, at eight in the morning, with the words: "Don't go to lectures today. Look at the weather! Let's go out."

I confusedly fasten the zipper of my yellow skirt in front of the mirror, turning my gaze towards Benjamin, then back to the mirror, then to the window. Benjamin shuts the door and sits at the table. The weather is sunny, the air has sprung. I don't want to go to lectures. My head is buzzing from yesterday's party. A powerful orgasm flashes past: me on top of Alex. Wait, am I getting confused? Why is everything on top and with orgasms lately? I remember the sparkling one on top of Benjamin, and in the laundry room for some reason on top of Alex too. When did I do Alex too?

Being a hippie is good. Fall for one – find another. Am I always going to keep getting erotic guys without complexes? What if I end up getting AIDS? And what if suddenly everyone gets sick and tired? And what if they start calling me a slut? Do I give a crap, if I feel good? AIDS I do give a crap about, actually.

I'll stock up on condoms.

Guys don't like condoms.

What do I care? I'm still in a woman's body.

No time to think about that.

"Well, let's go," I answer, and slip on my sandals.

Benjamin jumps up from the chair and whispers: "Don't put any panties on."

I sense fun. I obey.

On the way to the stop Benjamin declares he wants to smoke. I stash the last five hryvnias in my bag. Today is Friday; at six I've got aerobics in Kholmysty. In response I keep quiet.

With his trench coat waving across the ground, he walks up to a person who's just bought cigarettes in a kiosk. I lean against the newspaper kiosk opposite. The person listens to Benjamin and, as if he's been hypnotised, takes out a cigarette from the packet. Benjamin says something, waving in my direction, and with the other hand takes out another three cigarettes. I feel my face burning. Horror. I turn away and look at yesterday's edition of *Pravda*.

Benjamin calmly walks up with two lit cigarettes, and hands me one.

"He lit them for you too?" escapes from me.

"Yeah, I have a talent, I know." Benjamin smugly shrugs his shoulders. "I can get by without money in any situation. I got here from Zhitomir, not spending a single penny."

I mentally pat myself on the back for the stashed fiver.

"For a real rainy day, I've got this." He takes out a hundred-dollar bill from his pocket.

"A hundred dollars?" I exclaim.

"Quiet, babe, quiet. That's ten dollars. The second zero's cut out from a magazine. You can't tell, right?" Benjamin smugly sniffles his nose.

I look more closely. And it's true. The border of the cut-out zero is incredibly hard to see.

"I've got a talent," he says again. "Got it from my dad."

"Ostap Bender – dad?" I stare at the bill. He laughs and doesn't say anything. Maybe Ostap Bender isn't Ilf and Petrov's creation?

"Bus is here. Let me hide the note," he says.

We jump on the bus heading via "Moscow Square – Maidan Square". What am I intrigued about? A hundred dollars? Bender's talent? Or Benjamin?

Shame. He jumps all his rides and nabs cigarettes. At least it's fun.

A real player. And nothing to play me with. I can only be walked; I really love that.

Krechatik Street near Maidan is flooded with spring sunshine. Benjamin stops me, turns me around to him and passionately kisses me. The passers-by, maybe not used to seeing such street antics at nine in the morning, crash into us, sigh, mutter something irritable under their breath and walk on.

"Let's go, I'll introduce you to my friend," he says intimately into my lips.

See, he has friends. Yeah. I bet he's a drunk. I'm dying; I want to meet them so much. And the way he kisses! Should I go out with him for a few weeks? He'll become a better person and marry me?

Oh God! I'm already in love. Alenushka, get away from the remote, dummy.

We come to a stall in front of Krechatik metro station, filled up with CDs.

"Baldie, hi!" exclaims Benjamin into the empty tent. From underneath the stall dives out a bald, middle-aged man.

"Hello." He shrugs, and dives under the stall again.

I don't think he likes being called Baldie.

I glance at Benjamin with caution. He could end up getting it with the sharp end of one of those compact discs. And he'll deserve it, in all fairness.

Benjamin ignores the unfriendly Baldie and walks around the stall. I walk away towards the ice cream stand, as if I'm suddenly interested in the variety of sundaes. Out of the corner of my eye, I note Benjamin excitedly waving his arms around to Baldie. Whether Baldie is listening, I can't tell with my side vision.

"Osha!" shouts Benjamin.

I walk over tentatively. Benjamin hugs me and comes behind me. "He's gonna put on my favourite song!" he says like a five-year-old boy who's got a new motorbike, and Christmas is still ages away.

For the first time, I hear Professor Lebedinsky's song "I'll Kill You, Boatman".

Later on, whenever I hear this song, the flooded-with-sunshine Krechatik will pop into my memory. The hustle and bustle of people, the deep bass of Lebedinsky's voice emanating through all of Ukraine up towards the sky, and the young insane tramp with shaved armpits, whom I want to run from by now, hugging me from behind, purring into my ear about his intention to kill some kind of boatman. I ignore my wish to run away and, squinting, sing along with him.

Then, the song sounds: "In heaven and in hell!" shouts Benjamin in delight, and the same words are carried throughout all of Kiev, as if the whole of Kiev is one big disco club. Baldie has powerful speakers.

Between Benjamin's groin and my bum we're holding some kind of cucumber. Am I doing that to him or is it the song?

"I want you," sounds in my ears, drowning out the next line of the song.

He drags me by my hand through an alley, to a street parallel to Krechatik. How can my squinting eyes disagree? There is that horrid building site...

The same way a psychopath enjoys the torment of his victim, so do I relish my own fear, walking past the building site, where I was raped, half a year ago. I feel a wave of sadomasochism coming on. I want to mock, belittle and use. The desire is so strong that it becomes hard to walk. While Benjamin looks around in search for a secluded place, a cellar or a bench among bushes, I pull him to the entrance of the nearest five-storey block of flats. Is it here that the woman with curlers in her hair lives, on the first floor, where I washed my face?

The building site won't do, too much space and too public. We choose a space near the bins between the third and fourth floors and start to selfishly caress each other.

I start to feel something animalistic, something unknown. Him caressing me is comfortable; I'm not wearing any pants. His hand lives under my skirt. I get down on my knees, a few tricks, and a muffled groan. Two things: there won't be a part two, and I immediately need a drink to wash it down. The man-thief. The man-on-the-ball. Stole my powerful orgasm. From the top floors, the doors burst open and people come out. We're forced to go downstairs.

I leave feeling angry, with a sweet aftertaste in my mouth. I should have spat it out. Onto his shoes. He wouldn't be annoying me right now with his smug whistling and would be looking for a fountain instead. So, he's washed and shaved; I'm bored. Nobody is stopping me. Back to the stall. I become hungry.

I bet he's hungry too. Should I run before he starts to squeeze out money from Baldie for beer and perepichkas? Perepichkas? The best sausage pasties served at Krechatik. I know!

I squeeze his hand and whisper into his ear: "I'm going to the toilet."

"Go on, babe. I'll wait for you," says Benjamin, and he turns back to Baldie.

I go. Merge with a crowd of tourists. Look back to the stall. In my bag I squeeze my fiver as if it's a lucky charm. If only there wasn't a queue for tickets. Two people. Nerves – like strings. What's wrong with me? Is he going to chase after me and, instead of a ticket, convince me to buy beer? I'm handed a ticket, along with change. I run down the escalator, as if being chased by a herd of Benjamins.

I hop into the carriage.

Freedom! Friday. Going home. Running away from a chain: hippie – tramp – rape – what's next? My turn to rape somebody?

I'm coming for you, Vick. Coming to your boring attempts at making love, at the end of which we'll be silent for so long, smoking your cigarettes. It's dull with you, like at a lecture on international law, which I consistently attend in the hope of finding out something breathtaking.

Nobody was home at Vick's that evening. But there was a huge mirror opposite a large bed in the parents' bedroom. Vick decided that I love him, because I was happy for four whole times. And I decided: no more tramps. And no more hippies. And also no more fictitious orgasms. And no more gifted ones either. To anybody.

And I also thought: how scary it'll be to go to the STD clinic now.

CHAPTER SEVEN

I Am Different

In the morning I wake up and realise: I'm different. I want a different look. Not long, wavy mouse-coloured hair, but a short haircut, with an ash-coloured shade. And to sing songs about zombies. Like the Cranberries.

In the evening, Vick is in shock.

"Who are you?" he asks, not daring to come in.

"I'll be like this only for you," I promise for some reason.

I admire my haircut in the mirror. Ostap will like that I changed my appearance when I was with Vick. As if it isn't me at all. And if we make up when the hair grows back, I'll dye it back to the mouse colour.

Since when is this about Ostap? I frown.

Just thinking.

Well don't "just think".

Instead I think that I look like a dyed gay boy in a dress.

"Well, I'm used to it," says Vick. We both stand in front of the mirror. He looks at me, and I at myself. I turn my gaze to him and say: "Wanna do it near the rubbish bins?"

We bang one another next to the nearest bin. A conversation in my head: why am I drawn to trash?

Because I'm bored.

I wonder what Sarcasm feels about Vick?

Interest and power. Self-love blossoming with daisies.

Thereafter, boredom. He's about to fly, and I'll fly, and again I'm bored. A man?

I'm not doing Vick, but the man in my head is?

Meaning, I do not love him.

"I don't," Sarcasm responds. "I'm not very good at that."

Next is Pashya's nonsense: "Disgusting, unnatural sin," concludes Crow.

"Vick should be with Alenushka, or me. And not Slav. He's a man."

"Oh fine, fine!" Slav replies, and turns to Crow – pointed arrows in his eyes and a stuck-out haircut.

Crow gasps.

I think he's about to fly. Thank God, we thought we'd be banging here till tomorrow.

"You're so full of beans," says Vick behind me, gently hugging me around the waist.

"Spring, probably," I say. After taking his hands away from my waist, I pull up my jeans.

"Were you the same with him?"

I hear his question in my forehead. I stop zipping. He instantly regrets it: "Sorry."

I turn to his almost-black eyes. Fasten my zipper. He sees an ocean of feelings in my eyes, when actually it's completely empty.

"With whom?" I smile. Vick happily smiles in return. And once again thinks that I love him. Because we did it four times yesterday, once today near the bins, and then I asked him "With whom?"

And I think: at least with Vick I don't want to get drunk.

"I'm tired." I interrupt the flow of his hung-up thoughts. His facial expression turns into that of a worried bear. I am not tired, but I do want to be alone. Got to listen to my thoughts about sexual orientation. Wince.

"One cigarette and we go home?"

"No cigarettes. I'm tired."

At home, I pull off my clothes, taking my time in the shower, then shut myself in my room, diving under the duvet, as I bring the lamp to my pillow. Really want to note down this crap about sexual orientation. Then show it to Pashya! Where the goddamn is he?

I write in my diary:

Crow says to Slav: "We (meaning Crow, Slav and Alenushka) are a woman in our mind and body."

Slav answers: "Do you think others have only men or only women in their heads? What is heterosexual about a woman who has sex with a man just to feel power over him? (Good question.) And a gay man with a head full of women, in love with another man with a head full of women, doesn't he stand as a prime example of heterosexuality?"

(Good question.)

Crow, widening her eyes, replies: "And how are you then supposed to atone for your sins? What are you supposed to say when confessing?"

Slav, smirking: "Sod off with your sins! You're the damned prototype of a lesbian Maria in a cap!"

Crow erupts.

"What's a sin? I, Slav Butusov, a man inside a woman's head, want a man. How much does this make me a homosexual? Explain that to me."

(An even better question.)

"Then why don't you love a woman?" asks Crow.

"Well," Slav stretches his lips out into a tube, "I did have fun."

On the screen in the green room flashes of Lika and Vesnitskaya.

"You didn't love them." Crow narrows her eyes.

"No, I didn't. A sporting interest." Slav shrugs his shoulders.

"I thought that feminine women, fragile and weak, only have women in their heads," says Crow.

"Ah, these women actually mainly have sarcasms. Example: Ally. Opposite example: Vick. I think his head is filled up with chicks only. Those ones that shag Andrew behind the shynok in Bugrovo."

"Then what about Strong Woman?" asks Crow.

Slav smiles. "Oh, I love giving an answer to this one. Is Strong Woman not strong because she wants to defend the weak girl inside herself? Have you noticed that strong girls are cry-babies? And a big, tall man? Is he not big and tall because there is a weak creature inside of him whom he is desperately protecting?"

Maria-Crow is fuming.

Slav continues: "With someone like Vick I only wanna be buddies and nothing else. Your Alenushka took him. I just don't love him. I guess the women in his head are just not my type. I like them with fantasy, with edge."

"Aaah!" screams Crow. "What if we're a lesbian?"

Slav rolls his eyes: "We need a new word to identify sexuality. Is Ostap a woman in his head or not? Heterosexuals, lesbians, gays, these are all obsolete terms. We are personalities. We love those personalities in other people's heads whom we like the most. It's like with nationalities. Imagine: you populate an island with one person from each nationality. They remarry and have a child each. How many nationalities do they end up with?"

What would Pashya have said about all of this?
Where is he now?
And how am I supposed to sleep?

CHAPTER EIGHT

A Meeting Fatale

Vick and I are always together.

Vick is at my doorstep at 10am on Saturday.

I go to halls with Vick on Sunday night.

Home with Vick on Fridays.

Outside university with Vick after double lectures.

To the spring in the woods with Vick, for water, when I'm fasting.

Vick bakes pancakes for breakfast on Sunday.

Mum and Dad are happy.

Me kinda too. Though the sex isn't varied, it is regular.

And always ends well for me.

Once on a bench under the willow, his "I love you" heard mine "and I love you".

"I love you" over the phone, and when meeting, like a greeting, and as a farewell, with passionate kisses, in the shop, at the bus stop.

For helping me carry my bag from halls.

For surprising me with his visit on Tuesday evening.

For bringing me a cake.

Crow loves Vick.

In halls they love Vick.

The janitor – for the completely unnecessary but very pleasant packet of cookies.

The neighbours – for the cigarettes.

Girlfriends – for the cakes.

Vick and me.

With him it's easy. Free. I don't stiffen, when introducing him to friends. I don't worry about the awkward pauses, the unfriendly tone. He leaves me to my girlfriends in the evenings and appears at the right moment with a packet of cigarettes and even a bottle of vodka.

"Where were you before?" I sigh.

"Been weaving around you for two years." He throws his hands up.

Spring goes by. Once after lunch on Sunday, at the end of May, we're at the bus stop. Waiting for the bus. On our way to halls. Vick is further away with two bags. I'm closer to the road, putting my hand out to hitch a ride.

I look around. Anyone I know to travel with?

In front are two teenagers and a woman with a bright-red head of hair.

Behind...life has stopped.

"You?" I say powerlessly.

"Yes. And you – aren't you?" replies Ostap.

"Yeah, tell me about it, cool right?" I say, running my fingers through my short ash-coloured hair.

"Dope," he agrees. Alien from Pluto. And I'm only talking to him because I conjured him up by foretelling it in coffee grounds.

A car stops near us.

"To Vydubychi?" I say confusedly.

"Get in." The driver shrugs.

"We've got bags, open your boot please. Vick!" I call.

Vick brings the bags to the boot.

Ostap stares. Between us the open door of the car. For him, my eyes are empty. But there is an ocean of feelings.

"Have a pleasant trip," he says quietly, smiling dryly to the sun.

"It is a pleasant one," I reply, smiling dryly. I get into the car.

"Who?" asks Vick in the car, wiping his sweat off with a handkerchief.

I'm silent. We drive off. Meaning Vick didn't notice, and I don't need to explain why I'm silent for the whole journey to Vydubychi.

I stare out of the window.

Ostap saw us together.

If any feelings towards me have stayed, then right now, he's in a lot of pain.

And my feelings for him?

And me?

CHAPTER NINE

Night Tea Hut on the Outskirts of Town

Once in August at midnight, actually a week before my birthday, Ally, Mira, Vick and I stumble upon a strange place. On the outskirts of town, near a bar called Mimino, which is closed on Mondays, we find an inconspicuous wooden sign, on the door: "Pashya's".

Pashya! So that's where he is! And he's even open at midnight!

Behind the bar, the only lit-up area in the room, sits a completely fresh, lanky Pashya with his same spiky blond hair, pale skin and freckles. There's a thick scent of Indian tea and also something sweet. Pashya! So, he did open a tea hut!

"Good evening, strangers and pilgrims," he says, throwing a glance at my wide smile.

"Send us some tea to drink," says Ally.

"Here." He waves at the wall, lined up with a hundred tin tea cans with labels. Vick gasps. Typical Soviet cans of Indian tea with the picture of an elephant.

"You're just like me!" I laugh, looking at his blond haircut.

Pashya calmly looks at me.

"And we aaa-re?" he drags out.

"It's Osha! From Katka's dorm in Borshagovka, remember? I've cut my hair and dyed it."

"Olga." He smiles. "You've changed."

I'm laughing. "Yeah, it's Olga, Olga. So, this is where you are, wise guy. I've got so many questions for you."

"Where did you get all of these cans from?" Mira interrupts.

"Been collecting them since childhood," he says simply. "Everyone knew about me collecting them, so were giving me their empty cans. Parents, friends, friends of parents, friends of friends. I've dreamt of a tea hut since I was little."

Open-mouthed, we read the labels, with large handwriting, in black pen.

"Any booze?" Mira blurts out. Mira doesn't stand on ceremony, and something is always blurting out of her.

"My house doesn't sell alcohol. That would disrupt my energy," Pashya replies indifferently.

"So, you don't give a crap that we urgently need a second bottle." Mira smiles.

"Absolutely correct." He shrugs his shoulders.

"And if it's our own?" we reply in chorus.

"I realise that I live amongst imperfect people, with whom I actually prefer to communicate, so your drink does not disrupt my field but, on the contrary, contributes to a more productive creation of humus."

We glance at each other and burst out with laughter.

"What?" says Ally. And looks over at me, as if I am the specialist on soil.

"We've got vodka. Can I get some mint tea?" says Mira, as she heads to the furthest corner to a dark brown table.

"Four," I add, heading towards her. I'm happy. This is whom I can talk to about Slav and Alenushka in the green room.

"The tables are tea-coloured," I contemplate out loud. "Someone went a bit tea-mad when they were a kid."

"Wow! There's shisha here!" Mira raises her voice from a dark corner.

Two hours later: the tea hut owner's monologue in the dark corner with shisha and mint tea for five: "I live alone. I don't intend to multiply in this life. A human is imperfect and serves as a material for higher beings. We have to move and be at one with the earth. From this mix, you get mould matter. And from soil you get the materials to create the new sixth race."

"Oh God, where did you read all these horrors? You can't be taking Strugatsky and Azimov literally..." I say. Shamelessly lying, because I've never even read science fiction. It's my dad who has twenty-three whole volumes on his shelf at home.

"And anyway," I continue, "what will your soil be made out of if everybody stops multiplying?"

"You should first read this book, and then we can discuss it," says Pashya, carefully placing a book on the table. Does he offer it to all visitors? The book is of a dark green colour in the dim light. The title is unambiguous – *Analysis of the Aura*. The book's author – Pavel...

"Girls! He's written a book!" I point my finger at the cover. "Part one? And it's in different parts?"

"The next one will be *Analysis of Urine*, after that, poop…" says Mira.

"*Analysis of Blood*," adds Ally.

"Sweat, saliva," I add.

"Anal is zis of Zaura," says Vick.

We roll around laughing. Pashya is indifferent. It seems he's used to such reactions.

CHAPTER TEN

Beginning of a New Life

The next morning. A phone call. Vick's babushka has fallen ill. She didn't feel too good before, and now she's even worse. Vick has to go and live with her. For a week at least.

In a week's time, the results from the STD clinic will be ready. I know, I know, we've left it till the last minute.

I listen to Vick, opening the book near my pillow. "Today is the beginning of your new life," promises the first page.

Rubbish, I think.

The conversation with Pashya last night.

What soil? What analysis?

Rubbish, I think once again.

We decide: I'm not going. We'll have a break from each other. I'll see Katka and Tasha, who have completely dropped out of contact, and I'll also go to the country with my parents.

My parents are preparing to go to the coast. That's what they announced, when I got home, having said goodbye to Vick at the bus stop, telling him five times that I love him.

Dad: "We're going to go to the coast in three days."

Mum: "What do you think? You won't get upset, will you?"

"Why get upset?" I say, not raising an eyebrow.

I want to scream for joy. Dance around. Grab someone by the hands and start spinning! My head feels light.

"Well." Mum guiltily shrugs her shoulders.

"It is your birthday. It's just, Dad was offered a holiday, and later on we won't be able to take a break. You know yourself: country, potatoes, and everything."

"Mum, come on. Am I little?" I say, really believing that I'm such an adult, and so serious. "Anyway, I'd have disappeared from the table in the evening, and this way you won't get upset."

"Yeah, that's what we thought too," says Dad.

"You're a big girl now. And Vick – is a serious guy."

"Oi! Careful! You don't blab that Vick is in the countryside! Give me that remote!" shouts Slav.

"Give me that remote!" wails Alenushka, as they both jump on a startled Crow, rolling to the floor and… The remote is in Slav's hands.

Actually, Pashya said that people in your head is a completely normal thing. He also has three of them. He also said that this happens to the chosen ones. It would be good to find out a normal person's opinion. But a normal person's opinion I can guess myself.

"Better change the Chosen's surname. To…" Mira taps her nail on the table.

"Mediocre!" Ally clicks her fingers.

"Completelynormal," adds Mira.

"Completelynormalbutverystuckup," adds Ally.

We laugh, dampening Pashya's spirits. Then he philosophises.

"Where are you off to?" I ask my parents with ease and interest. I ask, but I'm actually dreaming about how I'll call the girls; we'll have a festival.

And maybe guys too.

And we'll call him. Bored with Vick. I want to booze and laugh, like before.

"I'm leaving this room!" Crow complains.

"Stop dramatising," says Slav.

"Why not hang about instead? To help to make sure nothing cocks up this time?"

Crow turns around, as if she has been offered some vodka, and has been fantasising about a shot of anisette for some time now.

"I've helped you to move on from Independence Day," explains Slav. "Our orgasms are fine. So, we can manage the remote control together."

Crow and Alenushka smile. It feels peaceful.

Crow says: "And anyway, it scares me that Vick's glued on his surname. All my life I've dreamt of being Olga Vysochenko."

Joy, excitement, a revelation of feelings towards Vick, from the sudden feeling of freedom. I savour it.

An emotionless face. I pretend that I'm listening, paying attention to where my parents are heading.

I miss all the details of their departure. After a five-minute reply describing the resort, specifying the time they'll be leaving and the meeting point, throughout which I regularly nod and nod, the question "So where are you going?" would sound suspicious.

In the evening, Dad's on the floor playing himself at chess.

I ask him; he is less suspicious than Mum.

"Remind me again, where are you going, Skadovsk or Yevpatoria?"

"Tatarbunary," says Dad, raising his glasses.

Almost guessed it right.

"Ah, when?" I ask cautiously.

"In the morning, on your birthday. Here we go, I thought we went through this. Are you OK?" Dad is disheartened.

"No, that's what I'd thought. Cool!"

Damn it, no more questions! To the kitchen immediately to put the kettle on!

Chapter Eleven

When I Was Born

Ostap appears on the day of my parents' departure, like a cake for my birthday.

In reply to Vick's sad "I really want to see you", I say, holding back my wickedness, "Me too!" And run to the shop, skipping. Liar, liar, pants on fire.

The sunlit street is covered in blossoming linden trees. I've got a bagful of cucumbers, vodka and flour to make cake. I'm nineteen, after all.

He comes towards me. Like in a fairy tale. Rudi next to him. I try to make out the joy behind his glasses. Eyes glistening. Excitedly. You can even make out his nervousness, if you notice how much he's trying not to press his lips together, and they only tremble from doing so. You can even hear the sound of bells and the tune from "Bitter Sweet Symphony". But this is only audible in my head in the given situation.

"Hey!" Rudi and Ostap say.

"Hey!" I loudly say.

"You're happy," says Ostap, eyeing me, as if he'd been doing an experiment on me and finds an unexpected result.

"Share," Rudi says.

"I'll share," I say. "Come over today for my birthday. At mine."

"Yeah?" Ostap looks at his watch for some reason. Is there a calendar there? Is he pretending or did he actually forget?

"Where?"

"To mine. That way, remember?" I point towards the entrance to my apartment. "At three. Parents have gone to the coast." Here I jump up, which makes the two of them smile.

"OK, we'll be there," Ostap replies.

We part ways. I walk, bag swinging from side to side, as I try not to look around and imagine the bewilderment inside of Ostap's head. How am I inviting him in the morning, in a sober state, to my birthday?

On a day when Vick will definitely be with me. Do I really want to make Vick that angry? Or jealous? Maybe we had an argument? Or maybe…?

I skip further, jumping up. I haven't felt so happy since Tolly Pushka's birthday. I should walk around more with shopping bags.

Everything is kind of falling into place.

I wa-ant to si-ing! Ah, I feel so bitter and so sweet! But at the end everything's gonna be all right! Bob Marley said so.

He probably has someone else. I shouldn't get hung up on him and shouldn't let myself feel miserable.

I'm not going to tolerate any more depression or tastelessness instead of Alenushka or Gosling.

He doesn't have anyone. The way he was looking at me!

But a year ago, he looked at me exactly the same way, and then he went back to his life without any vacancies for me beside him.

Three fifteen. The doorbell rings. Mira and Ally. They present me with two litre bottles of blackcurrant vodka, gift-wrapped, and tied with a bow. They see a large bouquet of daisies on the table. Terrified: "Did Vick come?"

"No, Rudi and Stapler."

"Rudi is stapled? Wow! I've got to see this." They walk into the hall, and I run into the kitchen to unwrap the bottles and put them in the freezer.

The doorbell rings again. Tasha. Another bottle of blackcurrant and some perfume. The doorbell once more. Sita and Ogurchenko bring a toiletry bag as a gift. Inside is a bag of marijuana. They say they grew it themselves. And giggle profusely.

The sound of smashed glass. Anzhelika Varum assures the whole flat that it's nobody's fault.

Squeals. Laughter. The girls' – high pitched. The guys' – reverberating, low.

Doorbell. Tolly Pushka has brought his classmate Vitya Electrov with a tape from the latest stand-up contest show *Kah Veh eN*[5].

"Today there'll be lots of funny dudes," says Vitya shyly. Generally, he isn't shy one bit, he just speaks that way.

I love both – the stand-up and Vitya Electrov.

[5]   A popular comedy show, where two teams compete with their comedy skills. Literally translated as "The Club of Funny and Witty". In Soviet and post-Soviet countries it is recognised by the name Kah Veh eN.

I'm nineteen; my head is full of joy, adventure and determination to have it all.

It's midnight. I'm smoking on the balcony. The creaking of the door. Ostap comes out.

"Meeting on the balcony, take five," I say.

"And where's your boyf?" he asks. By habit, he's ignoring my joke.

"Do you see him here?" I reply. I put my face up to the soft breeze.

"I don't. But I feel his presence everywhere." Ostap shudders in disgust.

"When there's lots of guests he usually hides in the closet and sits there for three days," I say. Ostap isn't smiling.

"Ostap." I blow out the cigarette smoke. "It's your own fault. Don't push it."

Silence. We smoke. Looking into the night stillness.

"Well, yeah, probably," he finally says. Was he wondering whether he was guilty all that time? If only I had his confidence.

I'm silent.

"Even the guilty have a final word," he says after a whole century.

"You want to get a final chance to throw around some mechanical waves? Bubbles, or whatever you call them." I shrug my shoulders.

"I do." He nods.

"I'm listening." I take an interest.

"Not now. Let them leave. Happy birthday, by the way."

"Thanks."

See, why do that? Now I have to wait God knows how long, for everyone to leave.

Quiet. Morning. Around five. Everyone has left. In the emptied hall, on the floor, we sit on our knees, embracing. Ostap and I. With drunken in-love eyes I search for the pain in his fixed gaze.

"Did you fall out?" He breaks the silence.

"No, his babushka doesn't feel well," I say.

"And what, so Olga Anatolyevna didn't go to support the love of her life?" he asks.

"No, she didn't."

Silence. I can't hold his gaze, so I look at the floor.

"Everything's exactly like last time, no?" I say, observing the pearl nails on my toes. "Sitting on a digger. Shovelling."

"I'm thinking it's time to buy a bulldozer," he says.

"What's happened, Stapler?" I ask.

"What, me?" he answers. "I'm not dating anybody and I'm not performing a perfect image of love to the whole of Kholmysty."

"You never performed one with me either," I say. "And you didn't date me really, if you think about it." Then I raise my index finger to the sky, just like Ostap does, and mock him: "My friend, to have sex takes two hours max, but what to do for the rest of the time?"

"Vick told you that, yeah?" Ostap looks sour.

"What difference does it make, if he told me that or not? You're the one who said it to him," I say.

"I spoke to Vick in his language. I tried to convince him for two years that he didn't love you." He shrugs. "But he won. Son of a bitch."

"Flattering. And you know how to be jealous," I say.

"I do." I just about hear his faint reply.

"Well." I stretch out my legs. "Now you know, how I felt once upon a time in May before the last ever school bell in my life."

"I've already paid for that with all of your hand-holding and jokey kisses with him, and all of his visits to yours. And your parents' phone call to him, and not me."

"Mm-yeah. Paid," I say. "Betting on Katka and me to win the lottery with Vick. Is it not better to play some football instead?"

"You see." He scratches his chin. "You're Osha. Out of a hundred, ninety-five will chase after you. The other five will be three gays and two of them impotent."

I smile.

"And I'm always gambling," Ostap continues. "Will that girl go for me or not? You're a girl. And I'm a guy. Get it?"

I'm silent. I get that football isn't his strongest side here.

"So, what are we going to find out?" I say.

"I don't know. I'm drawn in..." he replies, connecting his toes together. Simple and charming.

I squeeze out: "Me too."

More silence.

Ostap drives his finger across his empty glass.

"What are we gonna do?" I ask. And answer straight away: "Actually, it's easy to solve that." I look at the bed.

"No!" A dry reply.

Silence, as we listen to his finger slipping across the side of the glass.

"What?" I say. "I think it's ideal. I've got a dummy boyfriend, who walks me everywhere as much as he can. And you appear once every six months. Blow my mind for two hours. Then back to your busy life, where there's no space for me even on New Year's, and off I go back to my dummy boyfriend."

Why did I have to return to somebody? Couldn't I be alone?
Better to be alone, than with random people. A well-known saying.
And the depressions, when you stayed alone?
The depressions are from a lack of Ostap, and not from loneliness.
Well, that's what I think now.
While we're there, we can check in London, whether the depressions are from loneliness or from a lack of Ostap.

Ostap nods his head. It dawns on him. "Ah, that's where we got stuck. I didn't invite you for New Year's."

"Finally! We've grappled it." I liven up.

"Come on, where would I invite you..."

"...There were only guys there," I finish. "How about agree to meet me the next day? Or warn me? And I wouldn't make plans for the next five days? And wouldn't be running around the whole city with a question mark lodged in my eyes. What's this mania – holding someone by their strings, and not using them one bit?"

"Yeah, I was a mug. I told you, I was a mug, but you still left."

"So that's what you meant!" I smile. "And I thought that you didn't like how I drew you."

He's laughing. "You drew me great," he says quietly. "Thank you. That portrait was on the wall but I felt like crap every time I looked at it. So, I took it off and put it in a safe place. I was sure that you wouldn't forgive me."

"Sure? You should have checked. I'd have forgiven you. Should have found the right words, written a song, requested a poem over the radio. Use your smart brain. But there wasn't a you anymore. As if you never existed. It was easy to get me back then. Bring some oranges and say 'I'm sorry.'"

And now I'm with somebody else. And you're basking in proud loneliness.

I think we've figured it out.

"I'm sorry." He looks as if the words slipped from his lips completely accidentally.

Fluttering my eyes, I look at him. Not believing my ears, obviously. What is there left to say? And I'm silent.

"And here's another reason, why any desire to make up turned into a 'no'," he says cheerfully, as if he's found the missing button from his shirt. He takes out a photograph from his chest pocket. Touching. He brought it with him. On it are my breasts in a grey-blue bikini. Well-kept, tanned. From my last birthday.

"I stole it from Vick," he explains. "Last year I went over to his after we got back from Odessa and stole it. Recently I came over, and he shoved a pack of photos at me. On every one you're kissing, cuddling."

I grin. Vick's habit of photographing all of our movements irritates me.

"And again this photo's there," says Ostap. "He shoves it at me, proud. He printed it again. That time we met at the stop was like a knife to my balls, and he shoved a whole pack of evidence on top of that."

"Strange, he's never showed me the photos," I say.

"He'll give them to you on your birthday. A photo album of your lurrv story," says Ostap.

"Are you taking the piss?" I say, painfully regretting everything with Vick.

Next, we're silent. I want to cry.

"I'm sorry," he whispers again.

"I forgive you," I gratefully whisper back. "And I'm sorry."

Ostap shakes his head negatively.

"Can't." He puts his head in his hands. "I can't."

I'm dwindled. All this time I was the one on the horse, and here I am, jostled down with a stick. How can he not forgive me? This is my movie. I'm the one who's upset. Does this mean there won't be a sequel?

"It'll pass," I persuade him, like a medic to the wounded. "Mine passed. It hurt. And it passed. And yours will pass."

Ostap is hushed. This is probably how it feels to perform mouth-to-mouth resuscitation on somebody who has drowned, and not see any results for all of your effort.

I stare at the clock on the wall. Half eight. I want to sleep. I want to sleep with Ostap even more.

I feel an assured desire to be with him. Why now? Because he's in pain? And because its half eight in the morning, and nobody could possibly lie at this time? Or because behind us are many hours of conversation about our relationship? I don't know. I know that if there is even the tiniest, microscopic chance, I'm ready to fight. With no sleep, till my parents come back.

It doesn't matter. What matters is that I don't love Vick, and that the sudden meeting with Ostap on the day of my birth is the best present for me.

"Let's forget everything." I tiredly look at him. "I was hurt too. You think it's nice to feel yourself in the shadow of someone else's life? You coming round for two hours once a month, then me mulling this meeting over in my head, till it gets stale." I pause, sighing. "Let's be together?"

"And Vick?" His words hang in the air.

"Vick had it coming." I shrug my shoulders. "I'll speak to him. I don't love him."

"He told me different." Ostap smiles sourly.

"He's silly."

We're silent once more. I lose hope again. It's saddening to look at the nothing-to-offer Ostap. I want to smoke and sleep. I want water and vodka. And I'm upset. Like a child, whose ice cream's been taken away.

"When I was twelve," I say, "I wanted to go to the cinema with some friends. I liked this boy Lodkov back then. He'd hold my hand during lessons; I was so happy. Mum let me go, but at the last moment decided that I should sit at home and draw instead, and not hang around with friends in cinemas. Since then I haven't liked sitting at home, or drawing.

"Now I feel a lot worse than that day."

I walk out onto the balcony. Eyes flooded with tears. Now is definitely not the time to cry. In the morning, in the heat, while the air is still fresh, and especially after a sleepless night.

Behind my back, the door creaks. Ostap is next to me. With the photograph and a lighter.

"I want to burn it," he says.

I shrug my shoulders. Do what you want. I opened up more than I needed to. Burn it and leave. And don't torment me anymore.

No means no.

And I'll still talk to Vick.

I don't want to be with him.

Who needs this circus?

"I want to burn it and start all over again," he says, and inside of me everything sweetly compresses together. I want to breathe in deeply, but fear I'll miss a second of what he is about to say.

"As if this photo, and what I heard from Vick the other day, didn't happen."

I turn around to face him. He continues: "And there were no Katkas, or shoulder blades. There was just you and me." His voice sits on the word "me", and he continues in a whisper: "And there was New Year's, and oranges, and a three-bed tent..."

I sink into his whispering lips. And the next moment I can feel just how tightly he is able to embrace. And not let go. I want to dissolve into his arms, gently stroking his neck. And here are those familiar seven moles in the shape of a comet.

Next, everything happens. The trembling fingers, burning the photograph. And the ash, scattered from my balcony. The bed. Hot hands. Kisses. Kisses. Lots of prolonged kisses.

Kissing – the meaning of life.

Then sleep. Joyful eyes and silly laughter at midnight in the kitchen. For some reason with a cup of coffee. Two days. Asleep, giggling and kissing.

I feel as if I have been born.

CHAPTER TWELVE

Vick Returns

In the morning on the third day, the doorbell in the flat rings. I open one eye. See the sleeping face of Ostap beside me and shut my eye again. I'm not home. No time for ministers. A saying from my favourite movie. I'm sleeping. Tomorrow.

The doorbell rings again. Longer. Definitely not Aunt Valya. She usually presses the doorbell twice in short bursts. Maybe she's in a hurry? She was going to bring some apples and tomatoes over today. Maybe she's rushing to give us the tomatoes, or else they'll rot? I'll pop over after.

The doorbell rings for the third time, longer. Ostap lazily stretches over, sleepily saying: "Who is that?"

"Don't know," I whisper. "Neighbour, probably."

"Not Vick?" he asks.

"Vick?"

Damn, I didn't think of that. Can't be. He's still got two more days with his babushka.

"No, not Vick."

They ring again. This is not Aunt Valya. It's more persistent. And only Vick is more persistent. A friend wouldn't be so pushy, although has something happened?

I did unplug the phone. Vick could have got back earlier with the results from the STD clinic.

I feel like a piece of cloth, tied to a tree in the North Pole, being blown away by the wind. My gosh, what's it going to be? Gonorrhoea or syphilis? I imagine telling all of this to Ostap. And he's all like: and I wondered why my member started to fall off and my balls are blue.

How does it show up, this so-called syphilis?

Lika said that you get pimples on your stomach. And Nietzsche went mad in his old age from syphilis. Better to hang myself straight away than to tell Ostap anything. Never, ever again without a condom. God, you do exist, right? I'll believe in you once again. Dirtier, than to be raped. I didn't check myself. What if I've been pumped with some form of something-or-other?

"I'm going to check," I whisper, feeling nauseous from the fear. "Something might have happened."

The doorbell rings for the fourth time. Long, so very long. I find my green dress and crawl up to the eyehole. Slide the metal cover to the side. An empty corridor. Phew, thank God he's left. Whoever it was. I go back to the room. Ostap is pulling on his trousers.

"Let's have breakfast," I suggest.

"OK."

In the kitchen, I take my time washing my hands with soap. Then put the kettle on. Ostap's sitting on a stool, drilling me with his stare. The doorbell, once again. Two short rings.

"That's Aunt Valya," I say and fearlessly walk up to the door. I see Aunt Valya through the eyehole, already leaving. I run out – to grab the tomatoes with apples so she won't scare us anymore.

"Aunt Valya, wait up!" I shout to her.

"Hello, sweetheart." In front of me the towering figure of Vick. Aunt Valya's door slams shut and deafens my request to wait up. I become angry. I try to walk around Vick and continue the chase for Aunt Valya's garden fruits, but he takes me by my shoulders and places me in front of him.

"So, how did you sleep?" he asks. A grey face, eyes burning with anger, and his jaw creaking. It sounds like his teeth are about to crack. Is that my teddy Vick-the-melted-chocolate eyes? And still I don't feel scared.

"What do you want?" I grumble through gritted teeth.

"To talk!" He throws up his hands, as if it's obvious what people want in these situations.

"To talk, you need to arrange a time, and not to ring the doorbell eighteen times. Psycho. Cool down, and then we'll talk."

I push him out of the way, and I'm only able to do so because Vick doesn't struggle. Along the way, I hit the button for the lift. The lift door opens. I ring the bell to Aunt Valya's.

"Olechka, dearest. I popped in, brought you tomatoes. Aren't you lonely over there?" says Aunt Valya.

"Thank you, Aunt Valechka, I'm not lonely. Friends are visiting. There's

280

never a dull moment really." I look in Vick's direction and see an empty corridor. He's about to go fight Ostap! I hurriedly accept her tub of gifts and mutter: "Got to run, the kettle's boiling." I turn to catch up with Vick. Vick once again appears near the lift. Enraged, resting his fists on his hips.

"So, you slept well, yeah?" he says.

With a crash, I put down the tub of tomatoes. Would love to throw them over his head. I imagine what he would love to throw over my head. I press the button for the lift again. The door once again obediently opens. I push him into the lift, pressing the button for the ground floor, with the words: "Cool down, then we talk."

The closing doors shut out the look of a hurt teddy bear. I walk back to the flat, angered, suppressing my pity for him.

I was ready to talk. Why try to break in the door?! Especially two days early. Bloody verifier.

He suspected, because I didn't pick up the phone.

Ostap sits here still, on the stool in the kitchen.

"Was he here?" I ask.

"He was here," he replies. Condemnation in his voice. To hell with you all. Like girls, for God's sake. I'm silent. The kettle boils and whistles. I stretch over to the cupboard for the cups.

"What did he say?" I ask.

"Walked in, in silence. Walked out in silence. And slammed the kitchen door."

I nod. Brew the tea. Put the cups on the table.

"Want a fry-up?" I ask.

"No appetite," he replies.

"Stapler, don't feel sorry for him. I'll talk to him. He's a psycho. Why try to break in, as if it's the end of the world?"

"Well, yeah, yeah." He nods. "I should pop home, tell everyone that I'm alive."

"I need to go and visit my parents' shop too. They asked me to check up, make sure everything's in order. If you want, we can go right now."

"You promise me," he says.

"What?" I ask.

"That before you go to the shop, you'll speak to him. I want to know

281

that everything's in full strength, not just some drunk jibber-jabber."

"With pleasure." I smile and stretch over to kiss him.

"No." He pulls away. "Not before you speak to Vick. No."

"OK-OK." I'm stunned. "I'm running now. Finish your tea. How long you gonna be? Come on, hurry up, let's go."

He smiles.

CHAPTER THIRTEEN

The Final Break-up

"Vick, jealousy – is the fear of losing what doesn't belong to you," I say, putting on a smart face.

"Osha the philosopher," Vick responds.

I smile. "Not me. That's Pashya. We went to see him recently; smoked some shisha, and that's what he told us. Looks strange on the outside, but sometimes he says smart things."

We're sitting on the bench under the willows. I've got an explicitly cheerful expression on, not worried by Vick's puppy-dog beaten-up eyes.

"Remember, he gave me that book to read? I thought that it was the trashiest of trash, but it says in it that the main thing – is love, no matter what. Do you see?"

"Vaguely." Vick frowns, but looking interested.

"Mum says that you can love, without the need of having a relationship. Draw, sculpt, build, dig, write, express, generally in different ways. I only vaguely understand too, but I see that it works."

Vick stares through me, gritting his teeth.

"Vick babe, I'm sorry. I thought that I loved you, but I don't think I do. I just loved to be loved."

"Do you love him?" he asks, ripping out a blade of grass, clamping it between his teeth.

"Yes." I look at him guiltily.

"Super," he replies in an extinguished voice.

"Sorry," I quietly say to his shoulder.

"Give me Pashya's book. My head's exploding."

"I will." My heart squirms.

"By the way, the results came back," says Vick.

I freeze. Listening to his gritting jaws.

"Come on then, tell me," I moan, clenching the hem of my skirt.

"Clean, clean. Why're you nervous? Afraid you might infect Bender?"

Shut up about the flat adventures in the halls!

"I told him everything," I say, with the expression of a straight-A student, who's handed in her assignment, plunking onto the bed. My dress waves around, baring my legs. At that moment, Ostap's mum walks in, delighted with my arrival, holding a plate of cherries.

"Osha, cherries for you. Have some." She puts the plate of drupeson the table, shielding her eyes from my naked legs, and walks out again.

Ostap clamps his lips together.

"You can't just walk into my house after half a year of us breaking up and collapse on my bed with those naked legs. Mum thinks that you're Vick's girlfriend, and our faces should be unhappy."

I, not changing my smile, sit up and pull the dress up over my knees.

"That better?" I ask.

Ostap continues to be serious and soundless. I stretch over to grab some cherries. "Have a cherry," I say, feeling stupid.

He turns away. I put them back onto the plate. The smile disappears from my face.

My mood is deteriorating rapidly.

What's wrong now?

I broke up with Vick. This time, actually, I feel sorry for him. But I'm happy that Ostap and I will be together.

I came over to share my happiness and end up bumping into yet another melancholy mood.

Now I see that I've come at the wrong time. I should have sat at home, suffered a little longer.

But he did tell me himself to come and tell him everything.

Ahh, I just don't get it. Any of it.

"What should I have done? Come back a week later? You told me yourself to come, soon as I had spoken to him," I say.

"It's too early for fun. You caused pain to two people," he replies.

Wow, would you just look at this male solidarity that's awoken in him. Was it not he who stole my photo from Vick and burnt it with pleasure?

I'm getting out of here. He'll calm down, and then he can call me. No need to delve into his melancholy.

I get up. And leave.

I got happy too early. I should have been sad. And what if I'm bored of sadness? Behind the smile was my pity for Vick and the regret of the relationship that I'd started with him.

Everything returns to its place. Silence and a sea of misunderstandings. Well, fine. That means I don't need either of them. Also, of course, the fear of the results hid somewhere beneath all of this. Never, never, never again do I want to experience this kind of fear. Something is telling me that this was a warning and that next time I won't be so lucky. And what's the point of this risk? You lose out either way.

Even if you end up clean, you feel like there's a coffee stain on your skirt. And now there's that feeling of fear, that Vick could randomly spill the beans about everything over a pint of lager after table tennis.

A dog with hurt eyes, just like Vick's, walks past. Once again, my chest aches. His eyes were so sad. Why do I need all of this? If I had wanted freedom, I should have just had fun by myself. Why did I need to start up relationships, and encourage them? Stupid, stupid, stupid. Ostap is right. I'm stupid.

And what if Ostap's only with me out of pity too? Feeling sorry for me just the same, using me and then leaving me. Arranged a truce, not because he loves me, but just to get back at Vick for all of the "lurrv stories".

I stop.

Everything is clear as day now. This is how it is. He wanted to get revenge. Now he no longer needs me.

CHAPTER FOURTEEN

Who Needs Me?

"He needs me, to fix his pride," I say that night to Tasha. We sit in my kitchen, drinking blackcurrant vodka. Third bottle already.

"Brushed off a good man, and now I'm buzzing again. Know what I mean?"

Tasha nods, knowing what I mean. Sita, Ally and Mira also know what I mean.

"Why d'you need 'em anyway?" says Mira. "They're both idiots. Did they even give you any gifts? 'Love' they call it."

I get that talking with Mira about feelings is a huge waste of time.

"Well," Ally adds. "Be happy that you got rid of them and live your life in happiness. You'll find better."

I also get that talking to Ally has not much point either.

"I don't agree," says Sita. "It'll be fine till you wanna shag again. And when you do – you'll have to run to one of them. That's how it is for me, anyway. Osha, just have them both. Why tell Vick that you don't love him? Have one in the morning, and the other in the evening, till you find a proper one."

"Hm," I reply. "I could just lie, but I can't lie to Ostap. He sees straight through me. And when he sees that I've lied, he instantly stops calling and falls into his melancholy."

"I also don't agree that you should throw your guys around," says Tasha.

"Although in Kholmysty you need superpowers to keep them both secret. All it takes is a friend of the mum, godmother, in-law, or friend of a friend of someone that someone knows and immediately with great pleasure hand you over under the nearest walnut tree. That was what happened to me."

I listen to Tasha and realise that there are a lot of walnut trees in Kholmysty. And I think that there is something in all of that. But also, something missing. I spark up.

"This is what I suggest," says venturous Tasha.

Her eyes shine excitedly from the vodka, and I don't understand when she manages to drink so much.

"No, let's all have a drink first. Then I'll give some advice."

Aha, so that's when. Before every piece of advice. Ally fills up the shot glasses.

"This is what my babushka did, when she was pregnant with my mum. It was near impossible to figure out who knocked whom up in their village. And Babushka was the one who got knocked up."

Tasha picks up her shot and says: "To the rrright decision!" And downs it in one.

We clink glasses and drink up.

"And so," she says, chewing a cucumber. "When Babushka realised that she was pregnant, she had two lads milling around her. So, she decided to check what kind of person each of them was. She told them: 'I love you, but I'm pregnant by someone else.' Just to see the reaction. The first one told her to eff off straight up. The second said: 'If you love me, we'll raise the kid together.' Happily, luckily, he turned out to be the father."

"What, they had paternity tests in the villages back then?" interrupts Ally.

"Well, according to Babushka's legend." Tasha waves away. "But you are not even pregnant. After, just confess that you wanted to test them."

"Nah, that's a sadistic method," says Ally.

"Our village girls are proper advanced, right?" says Mira.

"Can't you make up something simpler?" says Sita.

I start to think. "I like that idea," I say.

"Alenushka, don't! Drop the remote right now. It's stupid," Crow demands. Alenushka clasps the remote and with a screech runs around the room, jumping from the sofa into the armchair.

Slav puts a leg out and trips Crow, who falls, and the others loudly roar with laughter.

"Top us up," I say. "I'm going to make the phone call." I clap my knees. "We'll start with Vick."

"Well, that is interesting," says Sita.

"The tzar knows what she does, don't get in her way," says Tasha.

"Let's drink." She clinks everybody's glass and drinks.

"Well, let's see what Vick says. Stupid idea but sounds like..." Ally shrugs her shoulders.

"Vick isn't home," says the disgruntled voice of Vick's mum.

"Mum, give me the phone." Scuffling down the phone.

"He… Hello." I hear Vick's disturbed voice.

"Vick, get here, now. There's trouble," I say, and notice that I can hardly move my tongue.

"Are you crazy? Where's your head at? It's 2am?"

"No. It's here. And I am in trouble," I babble. "I'm pregnant. By Stapler. But I love you. Yeah." I tear up my voice, as if crying.

Silence down the phone. Then, Vick's steel voice: "I'll be there." And he hangs up.

With the beeping phone in my hand, my face is confused. "Said he'll be here," I say.

"Decisive," says Sita.

"Means Ostap's gonna tell you to do one," says Tasha. "Let's drink."

"And if they both want to marry me?" I say, scared.

"Then, Osha, you'll get married," says Tasha, handing me a full shot.

"Mm-yeah," says Ally. "I wouldn't take Vick's hand though. He doesn't even know that you've got to wait two weeks to see if you are pregnant."

"Hah…that's true. Well, what if he thinks it's from before?" I contemplate.

"No, he doesn't think that. Your Vick does-not-think," says Ally.

"Do you really love me?" asks Vick. We shut ourselves in the bedroom. From the kitchen comes Tasha's drunken singing, and Sita's, singing about winter cherries. The clocks show half past two.

"It's true," I say, slurring my words, tongue-tied.

"When we broke up, I remembered your eyes, and my heart ached so much. And in the evening, this happened."

Keep on lying, go on.

What else is there to do? Too late to say that you're joking now.

"I'm sorry, Vick," I continue. "I don't know what to do. I'm lost."

Come on, be happy: it's happened! Now he'll fall on his knees to propose to me. I'm sure he has the ring with him too. He's prepared it, probably, three months in advance. He's probably jubilant that he's won me over from Ostap. Now, not only is he marrying me, he's going to raise Ostap's baby, too. Ostap will hate him twice as much. Cushty.

Be quiet. I don't understand anything. Do I love him or not? I'm just drunk.

"We aren't," Crow and Slav say in one voice.

"I'll marry you," says Vick quietly. People usually speak in this tone when saying their last words at a friend's funeral.

"But I won't booze with you. We'll raise the kid together. And now, get some sleep. And stop drinking."

"And you? With me?"

"No, today I won't be with you. You're drunk."

"Vick, please. I'm lonely and scared."

"I don't care. Your job today is to sleep and not drink. And to think of the child. Sleep." He unfurls the cover. I obediently lie down and close my eyes. Let him think that I have fallen asleep. He tucks me in. And walks out. The front door slams shut.

"See, hand your man a trump card, even a kitten like Vick will turn into a sabre-toothed tiger," I say a moment later, in the kitchen with another shot of vodka.

"At least he said that he'd raise the kid," says Sita.

"And quickly vanished," says Mira. "Back to his mum, probably promised to be back in ten minutes."

"Exactly," I say. "I don't believe either one, or the other. If it weren't for Vick, Ostap wouldn't be chasing after me so much. And Vick felt that I was in his hands and turned from a soft bread bun into a stale rye bread. He's the one who showed the photos to Ostap, where we're kissing. Why do that? They're competing. They hate each other, and they use me to fight over."

I'm starting to feel miserable.

Ally says: "Why even do these stupid experiments? Why listen to Tasha? Just look at her."

Tasha's eyes perch above her nose. It seems as though she's staring at something on it. "Wha— tash…girlzz…lezz drink…"

"Yeah…Tasha's had it," says Sita, to everybody's laughter.

"Right now, I understand one thing: I won't be putting Ostap through this bullshit," I say.

"You understand correctly, Comrade Novoseltsev," says Ally.

The next morning, or more precisely at lunch, sorting the hangover with two warm glasses of water, a shower and tea, I decide not to be silly. No more actions. The only action: to ring poor Vick and admit that it was an experiment.

I was insane, acting under the influence of alcohol, and the questionable advice of my friends. This is awful. I truly feel ashamed of myself.

No phone calls to Ostap. None at all. I have girlfriends. I'm learning English. I can draw. Wince. I could help my parents in the countryside. I wince even more.

"I don't want to," I say out loud.

Don't want it, don't do it then. That means, English during the day, then play, later in the evening. And don't muck anybody around. Because my brain feels like it's melting.

On the bus, the only thing that can be heard is the whirring sound of the engine.

Later, I don't remember Ostap, all the way up to the night of the disco.

More about him at the end.

Later, I don't think about Ostap.

Later, summertime walks in fur coats around Kholmysty.

Ostap hasn't rung since then.

So, I don't have to reminisce about Crep?

God knows what that was.

That is exactly why I have to remember Crep.

Oh, Crep.

How did we end up in a relationship?

How do I avoid stuff like Crep in London?

If everything is clear with Ostap and Vick, who loved whom, then Crep...

Did I love him or not?

And is it true, if he hits you, it means he loves you?

And what do you mean "hits"? Hits physically, like Crep, or hits morally, like Ostap?

PART SEVEN

Lover Or Loving?

CHAPTER ONE

Make a Wish

Crep appears in my life one October evening. Two months after the experiments.

From a crowd on Moscow Square for ten whole seconds, he is the answer to my tormenting question: will I meet somebody, someone, apart from Ostap?

Three hours earlier I look out of the bus window, which is covered in rain droplets. I realise that I am hurting from Ostap, the rain, and the winter ahead, and that I should stock up with guys, so I won't freeze in the unheated hall's dormitory.

But if I'm being serious, there just isn't a suitable replacement. How I really want to meet somebody better than him!

Someone...normal.

Let it be not crazy love, from which, actually, you get ill. But let us communicate two to three times a week, and not once in six months. At least.

And let it not be Vick, so that I don't get the feeling that I'm sleeping with my brother.

Let it be a man. A real, normal man.

Let us do everything together that normal guys do with their normal girlfriends: go to cafes, theatres, meet in parks, throw autumn leaves at each other, shove our noses into each other's ears in queues, selfishly munching on perepichkas and sipping cola on Krechatik square.

So bored, how insanely bored I am with the silent, proud, condemning utter lack of communication. Just fed up with it. Like a ringing in the ears.

I want to meet someone, who'll treat me like a normal girl, a girl who has the right to make mistakes.

We can then laugh about the mistakes together and wag our fingers at each other. But continue communicating. Because deep down in my soul I am good, and I want love, and everything that I've done is from a lack of attention. From a lack of a normal, real, loving and beloved man next to me.

I don't want to be ignored for a year, because of one mistake. That's cruel. That is very, very cruel. Better to just hit me, for God's sake. I agree to forgive him right now for everything, just to be together. I just need the guarantee that he won't disappear from my life for half a year, won't fall into his melancholy. That he won't be disappointed in me once again, in my silliness, in my contemplation of ghosts and in fooling around with the cherries, flashing my knees when I should be feeling unbearably sad instead, with a sense of guilt for the years lived and mistakes made.

But there won't be this guarantee, and nobody's even invented these guarantees yet. So that's enough of Ostap in my life. I have enough of him in my head, in the shower. That's it. I'm full. I want to live. He's like my favourite wound on my knee, for which people feel pity. I want it to heal.

I love him. Still. Clichéd tears. Clichéd snuffling with my nose, looking at the clichéd droplets on the window of the bus. I realise that I can't go on like this and won't. For my own sake.

It is then, on the bus, for the first time, that I want to treat myself with care.

And enough of waiting for closure!

There will be no closure with Ostap. He is Stapler. He likes to hold his girls down. We don't know how to end relationships out loud. We have to guess it for two whole months, or however long I will last guessing. Ostap won't change his attitude towards me, but I can change my attitude towards myself. That understanding, that love, which endures the thick thighs, the tantrums – I can give it to myself.

And he can remain silent and sulk in the room with his Kewpie on the lamp, with the newspapered windows.

And as much as I would like to have gone there, however much I would have liked to be with him, and even better to live with him, I need to live my own life, be on this bus, look into this window and be myself.

That night, I knew what I would do.

Firstly, as always, drink.

Secondly, go out, meet people, visit friends.

On the way back to students' halls, I buy cheap vodka, and I place the bottle in front of Sasha, who is writing her assignment.

"Oh gosh. Again?"

I nod, pouting my lips.

"Vodka? Warm vodka? Sick! I'm in," Sasha howls, throwing her pen down onto the notebook.

In two hours, we are in the right state of mind, knowing where we need to go next.

We're going with Sasha to her old chubby classmate Ruso's!

He invited us round just yesterday for chicken. Let's go! Time to start living.

I put on my favourite red jacket, with a locket on my chest, and then brush my grown-out, freshly dyed blonde hair. It's already shoulder length.

My favourite pair of high heels, black trousers. Bold and pretty, which is enough for a new life start, as far as I'm concerned.

"Less' go," says Sasha with her red lips.

Moscovskaya square. The tops of people's heads can be seen hurrying past. The figure of a tall brunette in front of me. The top of his head not visible. If only I had a stool. But I don't carry around stools.

I stop, rooted to the ground: pale skin, keen brown eyes.

"Wow," I say, interestedly.

"Yeah, exactly," he replies. "Going far, girls?"

"Well, you know," I say. "Depends on what you're baiting us with."

"Can bait you with a car." His eagle nose stays prominent. "Or with a pager."

A practical approach. But even I'm sick from the romance.

Sasha is laughing heartily with a brunette beside us.

"Do you have a boyfriend?" he asks conspiratorially.

I look around and whisper: "No. My name's Osha."

"Exotic. Crep. And how old are you?" he asks.

And why don't I feel like I'm being interrogated?

"I won't get jailed for corrupting minors, will I?" he adds.

Oh wow! And I'm even promised to get corrupted.

"Nineteen," I reply.

"No way!" says the dark-haired guy. "Twenty-eight. Where can I find you?"

"You can find me at our halls." I give the address of our student halls. Don't give the dorm number, obviously.

"I'll be over there in an hour and a half," I lie. You can't just give out all your coordinates like that.

"Well, I'll be there earlier," he says, rubbing the back of his hand against the locket on my chest.

"Hm," I say, carefully tracking his movement.

I think: good thing I won't be there in an hour and a half. I turn around on my heels and head to Sasha, who has finished her chesty laughter with her shorter brunette. She is two steps away and has already pulled up a ride.

Former classmate Ruso turns out to be plump, nimble and fun. Upon meeting, he announces that we'd be ashamed of him, but that it'd be fun, feeding us chicken and watering us down with vodka so much that, afterwards, getting up from the table turns out to be very difficult. When I finally stand up... I realise I urgently need the toilet! The chicken and vodka have poured through me like a fountain.

In the living room, I rest on the sofa. Ruso plonks down onto the seat. Ruso won't leave. I am cheered up by his persistence, his snub nose and hanging belly. Even with all of this, he still feels completely flawless, confident in himself and continually chuckling, as if he is a running hedgehog and the grass is tickling his fancy.

The day of flawless men with bellies! For some reason I pat the pillow. An invitation to lie with me? How else would someone take that?

A frosty morning hangover. Ruso's friend drove us back to halls; I think his name was Nick. What Ruso did yesterday to my... (I am too embarrassed to say what). He sucked it all up like a peach. I had to simulate an orgasm straight away so that he wouldn't end up shoving something nasty up there, which would've been everything apart from his tongue. He said to come over today, that it'd be even better. Eugh, no...but sometimes I can be so... Actually, this is my forbidden fantasy from fourteen years of age. I blush deeply. Hopefully Sasha doesn't turn around. I imagine how my Sarcasm Slav, if he had been sitting next to Sasha instead of the driver, would have slightly turned his head, so that Sasha wouldn't see, and winked at me. I carry on smiling, as I lower my eyes and stop blushing.

The housekeeper with her crumpled face and low voice opens the door for us at six thirty and says: "Olga, somebody was expecting you here yesterday."

We walk in.

"I sent him to you twice," she adds.

"Who?" I ask, stepping further away from her, so that she won't smell the booze on me.

"Am I supposed to know that, or are you? Crop, Rap, or something, I don't remember. He said that he came to see Osha, supposedly Olga. And that he agreed to meet you here. By midnight he decided that you were probably sleeping and said that he'd come by today at seven. Really tall, dark. Like an Armenian or a Georgian. Sat there with his pager. It was beeping all the time. Probably a really busy person. Even left me a cake. I ate it."

We went to our rooms, puzzled.

"I don't know any Crops or Raps."

"Is that not the one who tugged on you last night at Moscovskaya square?" It dawned on Sasha on the staircase.

"Yes, Crep!" I stop.

"He didn't tug me, he gently stroked me," I correct her.

"Crop, Rap!" We laugh, as we climb higher.

297

CHAPTER TWO

Crep

In the evening he comes round with a cake and asks for some tea. With his eagle nose and Ukrainian surname. He comes over like this for a week. Then he disappears. I don't know the number of his pager, or his phone number, and decide either that he's married or that he no longer likes me.

A month later in a dark room in our halls, Vick and I are half dressed. Sasha comes running in, out of breath, shielding her eyes; she announces that she needs to talk in the corridor, urgently.

"Who?!" I shout down the whole corridor, doing up my zipper.

"Run, run, he's waiting downstairs," Sasha natters.

"Grab a jacket. It's frosty outside."

Seeing me in the halls' doorway, Crep climbs out of his car. His right hand is bandaged, his left holding red roses.

"So that's why you were gone for a whole month?" I say, walking up to him. "Growing roses? And scratched up your whole hand with those thorns?"

"Kitty, I'm sorry." He pecks me on the cheek. "Do you still remember me? Here, this is for you."

"Thank you," I reply.

"We were just driving, and we saw Sasha at the stop. Dropped her off. You busy?" he says quickly, but clearly. "Look, I'm going to drop somebody off and could stop in with some cake for tea after."

"I'll be waiting," I confidently say and even nod, instantly making up a plan to get rid of Vick.

As I pass the door of my room, I jump onto Vick with a bouquet of roses. The walls of the blue corridor gleam across his face. His face seems exhausted. I only now notice how much weight he's lost.

"Vick, you're skinny," I say, lowering the bouquet.

"And that's because," he says, leaning against the wall, "I eat little and shag lots."

"Yeah, this diet definitely works," I agree, all the while contemplating whether to let him down gently or straight up to his face. And my eyes are more or less jumping here and there.

He meets me halfway: "Yeah, I get that there won't be any sex at Moscovskaya square anymore, as chubby groom Crep is here now."

"You understand correctly, Comrade Novoseltsev." I smile. "Give a big hello to Vera. Now all of your sperm is in her hands."

"Vera is actually the case where it just melts in the mouth, and not the hands," he says, rubbing his neck with his thinning fingers.

"Eugh, awful. Go," I say.

And with his rude laugh I gently push him out of the room. Shutting the door, I hear him laughing for a few more seconds.

Thank God that Crep turned up, I think.

Vick? Vick emerged in halls the week after Crep's disappearance. With boredom upon his face and a bottle of vodka. After the drunken vodka and my frantic "How boring, Vick", he clambered over to kiss me.

I turned away, saying: "No slobbering faces. Just go for it."

That made me feel better. I like to give clear instructions, how, where, and with what. Him? I didn't ask. When it finished, he pulled up his trousers and said: "So, this is why I came over…"

I looked questioningly at him.

"To take, or not to take, Osha?"

"If they're giving – take it. Who?" I replied.

"Same one. Remember Vera?" He sparked up a cigarette.

"Ah, Vera. You still haven't? She's good. Take her," I answered, also sparking up. "I hope you don't think that, you know…" I pointed to the crumpled bed, "this is the beginning of something high and mighty."

"'Course not!" Vick giggled a little louder than the situation deemed necessary. And I saw exactly what he had been thinking.

Oh Vick, Vick. At least now there won't be any double meanings.

Vick has come round often. To smoke and talk on the crumpled bed about his all-understanding and all-forgiving boring Vera.

After the meetings I always feel empty.

I made first-year Misha fall for me, from the faculty of Turkish languages.

After hearing his confessions of love in Turkish and not understanding a damn thing, I escaped him with a blow job and now hide from him in the corridors.

"Thank God Crep got here," I conclude once again, grabbing the kettle as I walk to the kitchen.

CHAPTER THREE

A Real Date With an Unsurprising Conclusion

Crep drives to a cafe with black pearl tables, ultraviolet lighting, and paper umbrellas in cocktails. He waters me down with B52, mentioning that he broke his hand in a crash; that's why he'd stopped visiting.

He tells me a long story about his friend Ashot: that he doesn't do anything all day, he just climbs up onto the windowsill with his legs and shouts "Arrah! Ehh!" to every passing car. And if he likes the car, he shouts in a higher pitch; if he doesn't, then in a lower pitch. So, you end up getting this song: "Arrah! *Ehhh!*... Arrah! Ehhh!"

We get into a taxi, and he is still telling stories about Ashot, and I am still smiling. We'll definitely have to visit Ashot tomorrow, and he gives the taxi driver his address.

"You'll check my hut out." He winks. I smile. A naïve method to drag someone into bed! Thank you, now even the taxi driver knows – that at 10pm tonight I'll visit yours for the first time to check your hut out.

I am not impressed with the state of his hut. Although it is not a flat, but a detached house. Even though he shares it with his parents. But has his own entrance.

I stand in the middle of the horribly neglected room.

Old furniture, shabby wallpaper, a yellowing ceiling, a very old carpet hanging on the wall. An awful mess. Things lying around everywhere, wherever there is space and a flat surface. On the chair, the table, the bed, the armchair, the corner, the wardrobes there are entangled pieces of red, grey and blue underwear, socks, sleeves and trousers. The man is clearly suffering from delusions of filling surfaces with things. Only the TV and computer aren't filled up with things but they are both covered in a thick layer of dust. The presence of a computer calms me down a little. So, he isn't stupid. But he is single. Needs a woman's touch...

"Sit here for now," says Crep coolly, grabbing a bunch of clothes from the armchair with one hand and throwing them on the floor.

"I gotta quickly finish something. Sorry for the mess, Kitty, see, my hand doesn't work, and I don't have time to tidy up with just one."

"No, of course, I get it," I say, and calm down. He does only have one working hand after all.

"And anyway, I want to renovate this place. Tidy or not, everything's still old."

Hard not to agree, I think, but out loud, I change the subject: "What do you do on the computer?"

"People need orders," he says, leaning into the computer. Laconic. So, he's hiding his occupation. What could he even be doing? We'll figure it out with time. I love secrets to death. It's already eleven. I don't have much of a desire to sleep with him. But I don't have a lack of desire either. I move over to the bed and, surprising myself, fall asleep.

I wake up late in the morning, unclothed, under covers. A hairy, hot body is rubbing up against me with obscene overconfidence. Without much passion, downing half a bottle of water and chewing on an already bitten apple that had been there for at least a few days before, I feel for a condom in my bag, which is covered in bits of sunflower seed shells. Noticing his smile, with the second hand, I feel that he's already taken care of his side. I smile and in reply give myself to him.

This is what it means to have an experienced man. This is exactly what I want.

That morning I receive twenty hryvnas for the taxi and go to uni. The day doesn't start too badly.

After uni, he waits for me by the exit.

"What, you think I don't know where the Foreign Language Uni is?" he replies to my raised eyebrows. Nice. And it feels nice, because long-legged Ella has seen how I, too, am getting picked up in cars by hunks, just past that beige Volga, which is a Soviet classic car, according to Uncle Lyosha.

How he knows what time my lecture would finish I don't really care.

I no longer sleep in halls, just going over for some things every now and again. I tell everybody there that my new boyfriend doesn't drink, works from home and owns a pager.

The pager is a much-needed thing for Crep. It blows up every three to five minutes. In the evenings we drive to the right people and collect all sorts of papers with numbers – orders.

What do I care? I am in motion and riding in a car. Crep sits behind his computer till midnight, and a lot of the time, all night. What he does there, I don't think I need to know. We smoke weed during all of this time, and then I fall asleep. Yeah. We don't drink, but we smoke a hell of a lot of weed.

The whole of last year lined up like a straight and tidy mosaic; each day shaped just like that.

With Crep, everything is how it is supposed to be: after a month, he comes to Kholmysty to meet the parents. The parents like him. Tall, handsome, chatty, and a regular taxi user. He doesn't have his own car. But I don't use public transport nowadays.

Until that evening, when the fairy tale about Crep turns into one huge, rotten pumpkin.

Chapter Four

Beginning of the End of the Fairy Tale

I pour some pickled juice into my buckwheat soup. Sipping it with pleasure.

"Mm... Hot and sour..."

Crep pauses in the doorway. He leans against the sideboard, admiring me. I raise my eyes.

"No way, it can't be!" I say, startled.

"Oh yes it can," he replies triumphantly, cheekily raising his eyebrows.

I'm pregnant. Feeling both happy and scared. Happy about the new, scared to say goodbye to the past. Farewell to Ostap. My childhood. What if something's not right with the child? We smoked weed every day!

"Everything's gonna be fine, oi. Just don't smoke from the day when you start getting sick," says Ashot's wife.

"The embryo attaches to the wall two weeks after conception. Soon as it attaches – you'll start feeling sick! Whatever you smoked and drank in the first two weeks doesn't affect the child. That's what happened to me."

I look at five-year-old Gogik, their kid, and calm down. Hoping everything will be as smooth as Ashot's wife says it is.

Crep is proud. Attentive. His mum boils soft eggs every morning and warms up soup. Every morning she wraps up a sandwich for me to take to uni. Nobody in my life ever wrapped up sandwiches for me before.

Once, sitting at the table, Crep's mum says: "Of course, you've got to get married!"

"Of course, of course," Crep replies. And both of them wink at me.

My parents promise to take us to the market next to Odessa called The Seventh Kilometre. They sell cheap wedding outfits and bridal dresses there. And his parents have sold their car for these outfits and dresses.

Crep shoves a wad of notes into his chest pocket, putting on a serious look, admitting: "I feel like a different person."

And off we go to my parents. And it is here that I meet this different person.

"How can we get both your and our relatives together? Your parents are already quite old," says Mum. "Maybe we should celebrate twice, once in Kholmysty, the other in Kiev, and pay extra, if needs be?" She doesn't word her sentence very well at all.

I could never have imagined Crep that very second would take out the wad of notes from his chest pocket and slam it down with mighty rage onto the table. Right into the wide, flat plate of pilaf rice.

The money flaps onto the rice, and flies all around the well-placed forks, into the salads and onto the floor, like feathers from a shot-down swan.

This, of course, interrupts Dad's and my disputes in Mum's direction.

I open my mouth, and something inside just tenses up and stretches out. I want to scream. Crep jumps up from the table, running out of the room. He rushes back, grabs a twenty hryvnia note for the cab to Kiev. Then leaves the flat. Slamming the doors, shaking the windows.

The string inside of me snaps. I don't want to cry, nor scandalise.

"What did I say?" Mum says confusedly.

Dad coughs.

"What an idiot," I grumble.

The next day, on Saturday, instead of the trip to The Seventh Kilometre we fry sirniki and discuss whether it is possible to raise a child without a dad. Crep's money lies on top of the fridge in a tidy pile, covered in rice-fat stains.

On Monday Crep decides to meet me in Vydubychi with some tall roses, smiling guiltily, asking for my forgiveness, but pointing out that Mum had insulted him. I stare at him.

"She thinks that my parents are old, that they have no money and that there's no point in even knowing them…" he begins.

"Oh, come on, what are you on about, man?" I say. "She thought that your parents would find it difficult to get to Kholmysty and back, where we were planning to have the wedding. What does money have to do with it? And who has enough of it anyway?"

Crep cringes. This is the first time I've seen him like this.

"She has to apologise to me," he says.

I swallow a lump and say: "Making her apologise is too much, but we should sort out this misunderstanding."

In the evening, we dine as a whole family, happy and satisfied. Or so it seems.

For the first time during the pregnancy, I don't feel sick, and this creates an illusion of lightness in my mind. We decide to order the wedding dress from a tailor friend in Kiev.

CHAPTER FIVE

The End of the End of the Fairy Tale

"The embryo hasn't developed to eleven weeks, but just nine," the gynae-cologist states, with her watery haircut, two weeks later. With a clatter, she takes off one rubber glove, throws it in the bin, and grabs a pen.

"But it was counted as eleven," I say, dangling my legs from the gynaecologist's chair.

"I see that." She nods, noting something down on my card.

I get dressed, feeling surprised. It turns out that you can make a mistake by two whole weeks. Maybe that's normal. In which case that pot smoking didn't matter at all. And I even have time to go to the tailor's for the dress-fitting.

"Are you going to save the baby?" asks the gynaecologist blankly.

"Of course," I reply. Is she recommending that I have an abortion?

"Ring your husband; make sure he brings your pyjamas, toothbrush – what else: slippers, a dressing gown. I'll try to find you a ward now."

My heart squeezes together. "Why?"

"To save it, dear. Come on, grow up. And I'll have no crying in my office!" she barks, exiting.

Two hours later I'm still crying, this time not in the office, but in the corridor.

A sad Crep places a bag with gowns and pyjamas on the windowsill, hugging me, stroking my head.

"Kitty, everything's gonna be all right."

I'm crying, bitterly aware that the night when Crep threw the money on the table, it had been nine weeks...

The miscarriage happens the next morning. In the toilet. I look down at the blood-stained toilet. Sad. Bad. An ugly, abrupt ending to a life that hadn't yet begun. I should tell the doctor...

In the corridor opposite my ward, I observe the dusk outside. Just yesterday, the wedding loomed, along with the child, the dress-fitting.

Today, no child, no dress, blood in the toilet, uterus under anaesthesia, endometrectomy and other delights of hospital life.

Next Saturday I have to get married, but I'll be here for ten whole days, till Crep's birthday. I find it symbolic. I sniffle my nose, feeling sad and missing the little creature that for some reason stopped living. Stupid and foolish.

Poor Crep, he wanted a child so much and wanted marriage so much. Poor parents, who wanted a grandchild so much, and for me to get married. Poor me, I wanted to…

There, in the corridor of the hospital, opposite my ward, I look straight through the window, coated with snowflakes. The snow falls. Slush covers the narrow concrete roads. In the background of the sadness, with horror, I see the demonic sparks in my soul. Instead of Crep in the unwashed window, Ostap is there, his cunning eyes with the smile of a helpless child, the possibility of creating a family with him. The anticipation of the unknown makes my head spin. I look around. The blue walls of the empty evening corridor. It could still be, with him, there…and not here with the boring, nervy Crep.

"Shame on you," I tell myself. "A person loves you so much. So what if he doesn't understand your romantic letters? At least he calls you Kitty and brought you a jar of soup."

After ten days I'm discharged from the hospital, on Crep's birthday. Crep announces that he'll drink today. I'm happy. Finally, I'll see him drunk and won't be by myself as always, like a lonely white crow wanting a drink.

During the day, I'm with the girls. I've missed them so much. Mira is leaving to go to Nikolaev, and we drink beer at the train station. It is good fun.

We meet a soloist from the little-known band Ze Vio, ask him for his autograph, pick up Trubetzkoy's song "Ti bil v Kerchi", and sing it till Mira gets on her train.

On the way home I buy Trubetzkoy's tape. Crep will like it.

We celebrate Crep's birthday at Ashot's with champagne, cognac, chicken and pickled cucumbers. It is loud, fun and drunken. We ask each other about fifteen times, with the words from the Trubetzkoy song, "Have you been to Kerch?", instantaneously replying, "If you ain't been, shut it!", then erupting in hysterical laughter. I remember thinking that I should make

Crep drink more often, as he becomes a completely different person.

Happy, drunk, laughing, and smelling of the March breeze and cognac, Crep and I roll home at midnight.

"Let's do the song once more!" says Crep.

"OK, but more quietly. Your parents are asleep," I reply.

Tape in the player. Full volume. The walls begin to shake. I run over and turn the volume down.

"Damn it, your parents are asleep," I say to his wondering eyes.

He roughly pushes me out of the way and turns it back up. I puff up. Sitting at the table, I bury myself in the *Pravda* newspaper, last Monday's issue.

Crep walks into our room. I'm delighted. Maybe he'll fall asleep.

Soon, he comes back with my blue phone book. Dials a number.

"Who are you ringing this late?"

"Sasha," he replies dryly.

"Sasha's with her daughter this week. They're sleeping already. Crep, stop it."

I walk over to the player once again, turning down the volume, trying to take the book away from him.

The next second, I fly straight to the floor. His size-eleven boots shove me under the table, kicking me in the nose, from which blood instantly spurts. My cheek burns. I scream. Loud and ugly. His parents come in, brandishing a wet cloth.

And I think: they've probably been standing at the door this whole time, listening to the fuss and moistening the cloth with cold water. His dad helps me to climb out from under the table and sits me down. He grabs his heart. His mum puts the white cloth to my throbbing nose. Crep drums on the wide-open door, bellowing: "Dad, if something happens to you, tomorrow we'll have three corpses!"

Which three corpses, I don't really understand. Crep, his dad, and me? My parents and me? Mira, Ally and me, maybe?

Crep's mum takes me through to her room. I'm sobbing.

Till the morning, nobody apart from Crep sleeps. We listen to "Ti bil v Kerchi" on repeat. The walls judder. That night I find out from Crep's mum that Vanya (Crep's real name) has seizures when he drinks. Very valuable information. And the main thing is, just in time. Right after the miscarriage. The last seizure was a year and a half ago. He already had a bandaged hand then. Since then, he hasn't drunk. So that's why he disappeared for a whole month. Oh, how much better it would have been if Sasha had taken some other route.

And he also tied up his last girlfriend Luda and hit her.

Where did I take my shoes off last night?

I walk into our former room. Turn off the stale sound. Crep is snoring on the made bed, booted and fully clothed.

I take a pack of letters from the top shelf.

Pathetic romantic me. I roll my eyes. I look at his twisted mouth with disgust. I have got to leave. I don't belong to this soap opera. Small pieces of letters on the sleeping Crep, like white leaves.

"Who should I call? I'll ring 'em now!" Crep mumbles, waving away a white piece from his nose, as he turns on his side.

Next, I should flutter on out of the house, almost in flight, in my favourite boots and with a banged-up nose, but I can't find my second boot. Which completely leads me astray. Where's the other boot? I put on Crep's mum's galoshes and run around the block. Did he throw it out of the window during the night, so that I wouldn't leave? Well, it was in vain, because I'll just leave in Crep's mum's galoshes, even if she doesn't have anything to go to buy bread in.

I look in the fridge. Between the butter and the sausage, is my second boot. I suddenly want to become a psychologist and write a dissertation on the ingenuity of schizophrenics who've drunk a bit too much.

I ring Ally.

"I need to come to you. Right now. Wait for me?"

"Wow. It's almost six. Maybe I shouldn't go to work?" Ally's voice sounds sleepy, but alarmed.

"I'll make it before eight."

Chapter Six

Returning to the Person I Love

With a beaten nose, I go from Skovoroda's monument to Kharkivsky's massif in a cab. I decide to stay away from the metro. On the way, we pick up an old man going to Klovska. When the old man gets out, the driver says: "Grandpa's been on a massive one. Oh, the reek he's left."

I turn to the window, looking at the reflection of my beaten nose. Grandpa had nothing to do with the reek. It's me who's been on a massive one. I won't admit it and feel like a lousy, stinky kitten that's been grabbed and thrown out of Crep's life by an unknown force. Kicked out with size-eleven boots from the fairy tale about Crep.

I give in to the idea that there is a God in this world. For the first time, since the rape…

Just in case, I decide to stop discussing in halls the idea that God doesn't exist. Because things could have stayed the same: with no miscarriage, with the wedding and a child. It could have been a scary fate for the child. Oh, what that child could have seen. Dad kicking Mum around with his boots. Nightmare.

My beaten nose is now in Ally's rented flat. My beaten nose in the mirror of her dressing table, with a variety of perfume bottles. The scent of Hugo Boss and a beaten nose. I tell my parents that I'm staying in Kiev, in the hopes that my swelled nose will subside before next weekend.

Tired of seeing my tears and beaten nose, Ally takes me out to the circus.

The next weekend, the swelling has actually gone down, and I go home. Mum takes me to the zoo. Mira doesn't take me anywhere. She doesn't know anything about the beaten nose and is still in Nikolaev.

I tell my parents that I got into a minor car crash and fell out with Crep.

After the zoo, I begin to sob. Mum says: "My daughter. You need someone who'll bring you joy. You have that someone."

I tense up, preparing to hear Crep's name.

But Mum says: "You."

"Me?"

Mum continues: "Give yourself attention. Give yourself a haircut and start living. Start bringing yourself happiness."

I look away, say nothing and quietly agree with her.

I surprise myself the whole of the next week: I'm determined to bring myself happiness. Me?

To myself? Such strange words.

On Saturday I pop into the hairdresser's. I press the magazine to my chest, on the cover of which is a girl with a black-blue haircut.

I'm stunned, looking at myself. With a new haircut, exactly like the girl on the cover.

"Why didn't you have your hair like that before?" say Mira and Ally in one voice that evening.

In the evening, at a disco, I wave my hands around in different directions, and accidentally clip something lanky.

"You." The same soft face, the same smile of a helpless child.

"You." The same chill and tremble in my knees, the same elation of flying insects at the bottom of my stomach.

"Whatever you do to your hair, you always look amazing!" he shouts into my ear.

"Let's go to yours," I say simply.

"Five minutes. See you at the door," he replies, just as simply. As if we're negotiating the supply of milk on Thursdays and Saturdays.

"I need to go. Meet you tomorrow," I say to Mira, who's laughing with somebody. And not giving her a chance to express disagreement, as she's found someone to drink with, I hurriedly head towards the exit.

We walk quickly and silently.

"I hear you're getting married?" he says at last.

"You're listening to nonsense. You should listen to Radio ROKS instead," I reply.

He's silent. Just gripping my hand even more tightly. What pleasure do I get from reading these secret signals of his feelings? I'm tired. I don't want his feelings. I want him, and to wake up happy tomorrow. Not with a nagging feeling that he's beaten me once again, but with the happy feeling that I'm alive.

"What's with your nose?" He interrupts my flow of philosophical thoughts.

"Car crash." Our steps fall on the wet spring asphalt in the night, illuminated by the lamps.

"I was heading from Kiev three weeks ago. Just swerved along a road. Icy road it was."

"Driver fine?"

"Yeah, everything's fine. He just stopped abruptly...so we turned around, and then headed for an ambulance. Blood started pouring out of my nose."

Again, silence and steps. I bet he doesn't believe me. Though it is almost how it was. A similar accident happened to us about two months ago, when Crep and I decided to get married and went to Pirogov's Museum to book our marriage. Only my nose didn't suffer, and we didn't head for an ambulance, but just laughed about it: a sure sign to not celebrate our marriage in Pirogov's Museum.

Oh, Ostap. If only we hadn't rushed home to pull our pants and T-shirts off each other, but instead just sat on that bench among the oaks. It was still spring; our bums wouldn't have frozen. I would have asked, how are you able to make love to me as if I'm the navel of the earth and not ring me for a year and a half? You would have replied, like hammering a nail in, with the theory of the mechanical waves, that you're scared to live with a real girl. Your dad taught you to find and marry a cook whose legs are fused together, and to walk over live girls like me. And you're not scared because the live girl will stop being yours, but because of what other people may think in case she stops.

And what would people think, and why are living girls so scary?

Will it be the people who think, or will it be your dad? Who are you scared of the most?

We don't talk about any of this.

We silently, lightly and quickly step from the spring night right into your bed.

Love. Long and selfish. Your touches pour life into me. Here, look, my hands are alive. Here they are. And here is my neck, my face. My hair, it smells of the hairdresser's peach shampoo. How can this wonder be called "sleeping with your ex"?

And how is he an ex? He was never real. Tonight I'll do something to him that we have never done before. Will he judge me? Not ring me? Get scared that I have become completely perverse? So be it.

I come back from his alone, without a heavy feeling that he's used me once again. What's with this unfortunate flow of men? They hit me, use me or don't walk me home. If you don't count on a continuation, then only the main thing remains: enjoy the present.

A whole year and a half with Crep, and I never once flew how I did in this hour and a half. And I reached my orgasm, by the way. Like fireworks. So be it. Even once every year and a half. At least I'll have myself every day.

The next morning, I wake up and realise that I am alive.

I have myself.

I am the person I had been looking for.

And now everything really is going to be all right.

THE END

Epilogue Of The First Book

From the diary (for Pashya):

I enter the green room.

Crow, Alenushka and Slav turn around.

"You've got to the end of the story, found the problem, and because of that, we're going to London together," say I.

"Wait! This isn't the end of the story! We have to wait till we get the visa for England," says Alenushka.

"No point in dragging it out." Slav shrugs. "How did you give in to Crep's invitation to take you to the theatre a month later? Like you didn't know that you'd drink and would no longer care that he kicked you in the nose. You should have run home, and not let yourself be kissed near those oaks after the theatre. I'll have the remote..."

"The nightingale sang, and it was getting dark..." Alenushka admits.

"And I felt sorry for him. He was getting ready to change. He fasted for a week and was seeing a psychologist."

"He went to a woman with our photo. To the psychologist! By the way, she told him that he wasn't even close to us," Crow erupts.

"What does pity towards Crep and sex with Crep have to do with it? What does sex with Ostap have to do with it, if you've decided not to depend on him?" Slav says. "Sex is dependence. For us, anyway. We've reached this conclusion more than once. No sex – no dependence. If there is sex, there is dependence. You thought that if you slept with him, it'd end there? And it ended up being Crep's mum who came to us the next morning with open arms, crying: 'Olechka came back, Olechka!'"

I continue standing at the helm and smiling.

"You know what," Crow suddenly says. "Ostap isn't coming with us, so I don't need to protect you from anybody anymore."

She slips on her airy trench coat, perches her hood up, and pops her glasses on, as she walks out onto the balcony. "Tomorrow you're alone. Do what you want. Stand on your head if you like. The passengers will enjoy it." She shuts the doors quietly and firmly behind her.

Alenushka and Slav see the fright in each other's eyes.

"That's just great. We're going to London without responsibility," says Slav.

"Let's take the piss out of that Chocolate Denis tomorrow," says Alenushka.

"I'll let you take the helm only when I see fit." I nod.

"To hell with her. Go on, get out of here!" Slav is outraged.

"I'll disappear," say I. "But if you want me to come back, on my return I'll be the one taking the helm."

"No no no!" says Alenushka. "Please, get on out of here, sweet I. We're doing just fine without you."

I disappear. The bus crosses the border to Poland. England is a twenty-four-hour drive away.

2014

Acknowledgements

My special thanks to Mathew Borushko for the major help with translation and enrichment of the content with the slang and colloquial vocabulary, to Eilidh Thompson and Claire Reilly for editing the text and to the SilverWood team for all the support and assistance in making this book into the best shape and format.

www.ingramcontent.com/pod-product-compliance
Lightning Source LLC
Chambersburg PA
CBHW010824250626
47169CB00010B/2946